Weeds of War

Weeds of War

Those Who Bled at Dien Bien Phu

A Novel

Paul Kluge

Published by Phoenesse LLC
www.phoenesse.com

ISBN: 978-1-7366843-1-3

Photo of Paul Kluge by Patsy Dew.
Map artistry by Tyler Gardner; image retrieved online from
Library of Congress, Geography and Map Division.
Back cover image by Quang Nguyen Vinh from Pixabay.

Contents

Map of Area

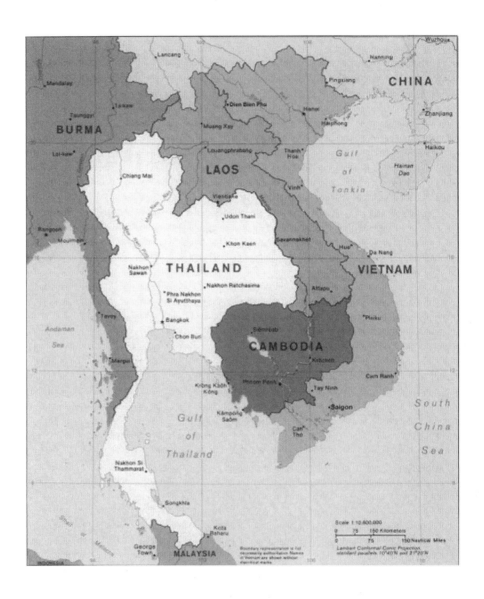

Glossary

Term or Acronym	Explanation (pronunciation)
AA	Anti-Aircraft
aó dài	Traditional Vietnamese dress (ow-zai)
bangalore torpedo	Explosive device in pole form
bush	Contested area outside perimeter of fortification
cadre	Military leaders
CHICOM	Chinese Communist (Chi-Com)
CIP	Communist International Party
CO	Commanding Officer
commissar	Political military post with party authority
CP	Command Post
DZ	Drop Zone
firefight	Shooting battle
grunt	Infantryman or rifleman
HE	High Explosive
Home Platoon	Rudimentary Vietminh Unit
ICP	Indochina Communist Party
kepi	Unique white hat awarded to Legionnaires
kit	Military gear, typically in rucksack form
LP	Listening Post
LT	Lieutenant
matériel	Military goods (ma-ter-ee-EL)
NCO	Non-Commissioned Officer – Corporals & Sergeants
Nguyen	Family name (win)
People's Army	Communist Army, a.k.a. Vietminh
Phu Doan	Village in Vietnam (foo zon)
quad-4	4-barrel .50 caliber machinegun
Red China	Communist China
RPG-6	Handheld anti-tank grenade
sapper	Interloper; expert in explosives
SNAFU	Situation Normal, All Fucked Up
The Party	Communist Party
The War	World War II
Thuy	Female name (two-ee)
wire	Perimeter; typically razor wire fencing

Introduction

Wars are not easy to explain and are impossible to understand. Any of them. All of them. Vietnam wars, even more so. Her conquerors over the centuries have inevitably foundered. Kowtowing and prostration to foreign masters somehow transforms the Vietnamese into selfless souls of courage and limitless sacrifice. Subjugate Vietnam at your own peril. Ask China. Ask France. Ask Japan. Ask America.

Political scrambles after World War II birthed communist brushfires around the globe. Eastern Europe was swallowed up. China went Red in 1949; the Americas were threatened, and Asia wallowed in turbulence. Communist insurgencies erupted in the Philippines, Indonesia, Malaysia, South Korea, Cambodia, Laos, and Vietnam.

The Allies might have hoped for political balance by offering a return of Indochina to Colonial France. The result was the French-Indochina War, 1946–1954. French resources were limited, but included the resolute Foreign Legion. Who else could withstand the consuming communist rival?

Weeds of War is a story of common soldiers, privates with no authority, but whose success is essential to the manufacture of victory. It is the young zealots of the communist Vietminh who do not hesitate to throw themselves into suicidal wave assaults. It is also those, such as a troubled and naive Irish teen, who enlist in a Foreign Legion teeming with Wehrmacht survivors— hard core, professional soldiers. An obscene maturity is promptly squeezed from the body and heart of youth on both sides. Young souls age quickly or are lost in the craggy fields of war. This is a world of strange bedfellows where patience and resilience prevail.

Three of French-Indochina War's great battles come into play in this telling. The despairing siege of Dien Bien Phu ends in an aftermath more toxic than the war itself. Insurgents win, perhaps, but victory is destined to fester into the next conflagration.

Chapter 1

Irish Eyes Not Smilin'

3 July 1943, Strabane, Northern Ireland

Northern Ireland is mostly Catholic, many of whom be the Republicans. They are the Irish Nationalists, who want an independent Ireland joined with the free Ireland to the south. It is the Unionists in Northern Ireland who find it proper to remain a part of the United Kingdom. They are mostly the Ulster Protestants. Resentment stirred the souls of many Irish natives wanting independence from the UK. Others were intent on preserving the birthright and civil liberties inherent in British law and practice.

The boy knew to keep clear of the loud voices. This kind of thing had upset him before. The words were angry, the voices shrill and insistent. Seamus Cavanaugh, the boy's father, was arguing with the two men, but not about dry cleaning. The boy's mother had left for market only minutes before. She could be gone for the better part of an hour, perhaps more if she gossiped. It occurred to the boy that the men came at this time because his mother was out. Patrick knew she would not be putting up with this.

It was only little Patrick there in the back room, quietly listening. Naturally bashful, the boy, who had just turned nine on Sunday, tended to remain in the workroom, where the dirt and stains of hard work and pleasure were treated equally. The glowering voices frightened the lad, yet he felt compelled to move up to the doorway and listen. A narrow space between doorjamb and curtain welcomed to him a more animated dimension of the broil. He watched.

"How the lovely Aideen puts up with a Protestant scum like you is a mystery for the ages," the older man sputtered. "But I am tellin' ya here and now, for the last time, stop agitatin' against the likes of us Nationalists, who have the good sense to see that Northern Ireland is being used—a victim of the English master!"

The younger of the two spoke up. "We Republicans, whether in Derry, Belfast, or Strabane, are as Irish as any. We need not be separated from Dublin and the free South. Together, we are the people of Ireland. We are not England. God meant for the Irish to be with Irish, and to be free from the tyranny of the grand colonizers of London. We Nationalists, we Republicans, are the hand of God to make it so." The words, hot and intense, flushed the man's face with distinction. "We must band together to be one Ireland and independent together! Or, Mr. Cavanaugh, we continue on as lapdogs of the king, licking the boots of foreign royalty. Unlike you, we do not relish the taste of bootblack."

The older picked it up again, this time with a deep undertone. "I would not like to be standin' in your shoes, Mr. Cavanaugh, after we Republicans next meet concerning your pigheadedness."

Instantly, Seamus shot back, "Would you be sayin' some ill should come to this house on account I consider your politics rubbish?"

Stony silence was returned in answer.

"Cat got yer tongue? How refreshing it is your intimidation now comes with intimated brownshirt tactics to make your point," Seamus continued. His practiced weapon of belittling words was sharp, and the blunt pinpricks continued. "If you Nationalist lunks knew how to deliver such intentions, I would not be askin' for clarification, now would I? Again, I ask, do I take your words to be a threat, sir? I trust even the likes of you two is capable of renderin' a common aye or nay." He continued his stare into the eyes of the younger man. The momentary quiet raised tensions even more. The squabble was not ended, and the hot words of Seamus were accepted as challenge.

Little Patrick did not understand much of it, but he was well aware the words spoken were trouble, more trouble even than the cursing of the longshoreman about. He had seen the older man before; somewhere he had seen them both. Afraid for himself, the one thing going through his mind over and over again: *If Mum was here, they would not be doin' this.*

The pause did not last. The eyes of the younger man bulged; his nostrils flared. He reached inside his jacket and from the lining pulled a length of tubing, a twelve-inch length of lead pipe, it appeared to Patrick. Flashing the iron up against the jaw of Seamus, he snarled, "One more such quip, Mister Smartarse, and you will be eatin' soup for a fortnight."

"You are not required to join the IRA, Miiiiister Cavanaugh," the older man added in a voice not at all cordial. "Keep yer trap shut around the other Nationalists hereabouts, or Mister Liam here will move that perky nose of yours a good bit to the right. If closing your mouth is left to us, it will be for good. Is that clear enough answer to your question?"

Seamus felt the beads of sweat appearing above his upper lip. They betrayed the courage of his hard stare. "What I understand," Seamus nevertheless fired back, "is that heavy-handed pricks like the two of you can kiss me royal ass! Fock you. Fock the both of you!"

It didn't take but an instant for the younger man to reach across the counter and latch onto a stiff collar. In one continuous motion, Seamus was pulled over the counter, scattering the clay birds Aideen had collected and painted over the years. In the mind of Patrick, one action was as bad and scary as the other—Papa being physically assaulted, and Mum's precious clay birds smashing to the hard floor. The anguish of the moment bore sharp into Patrick. He had always been small for his age and a bit of a loner; always the last to be picked on sports teams. He was picked first only when the neighborhood bullies needed a dupe for their entertainment.

In the moment, Patrick was enraged by the violence. Violence filled his head. *If I was big, I would burst through the curtain with Mum's rug beater and bash the man in the face—smash his nose and make him suffer. That devil should see what is coming at him and be scared as can be. The older bloke, he too must suffer—be left doubled up in pain and pleading for mercy.* Little Patrick could see it all. In the moment, nothing less would do.

Of course, none of that was possible.

Papa is big and strong, and he can do anything—anything in the world. Papa, stand up and beat them! Patrick's mind shouted.

Seamus was strong, perhaps, but he was not big. Papa did not beat the men, and rather than feel more pain, the boy withdrew, physically and emotionally. He tiptoed to the open back door and felt the warm sunshine on his face. He wanted to do something to help but knew he was at the mercy of those men if he showed himself. He would stay away.

But he couldn't. He had to know what was happening.

He returned to the curtain and saw the scenario escalate more. That was when he quietly swore revenge. Patrick could see that the older man had pinned back the sinewy arms of Seamus. It took a moment, but the struggling stopped. Seamus settled, needing then to regain his breath. Surprising to Patrick, his papa appeared to accept his loss of control. The men knew it too—had seen it before.

With his grip at the center of the pipe, the younger man, standing in front of Seamus, held it like a spear at his side. He shook it up and down just a little, getting ready for something. Eyes now flashed between the man and Papa. A second passed, maybe two or more; it seemed longer. Papa let out a growl deep from his gut; he understood the younger man's intention. The arm swung back as if about to throw a bowling ball. What swung forward was the lead pipe and 185 pounds of the man behind it. The blunt end found its mark, plowing into the gut of Seamus.

Breath gone, a weak squeal passed lips, eyes speaking fright in volume. Gasping but without air, the world of Seamus went dark. There would be no more Unionist speak—not from Seamus Cavanaugh. Not today, and not for many days.

The older man curled a smile, then released the dead weight. Seamus dropped like a final clay bird smashing to the floor. The image froze in Patrick's mind. He stared blankly, yet the image remained. There was nothing he wanted to see any longer, but there was nothing he could do to stop seeing it. The violence was in his head and would not leave. Somehow, the message to Patrick was that bad men could do unto others as they pleased. *What will it take for this moment to be removed? Dear God? Please take it back. Please?*

But there was no answer.

The worn bell over the shop door brought Patrick back. *Is it Mum? Praise and thanks to Mother Mary, it is her.*

"Patrick. Patrick Cavanaugh, where are you?" It was a startled Aideen. She was kneeling beside Seamus, a series of screeching questions in her throat. "Is that you, Patrick? What has happened, Patrick? Your papa is half-dead and you stand staring at the stove?" Her normally calm demeanor had abandoned her, leaving an unseemly gruffness. "What has happened here? Tell me!"

Patrick was dazed. That he couldn't think was true but obvious as well. He burst into tears as Aideen reached out to him and pulled him close. Almost immediately, she pushed him away again. "There is no time for tears, Patrick." Her voice was a beastly tone Patrick did not know. "You must run to Doctor Quinn's office and tell him Seamus is here on the floor half-dead; I don't know why."

"But, Mother, I was only—"

"Now, Patrick!" she shouted. "There is no time for babble." She grasped his shoulders. "Run all the way, or so help me, I will strap you myself." A wild look in her eye, she turned him down the street toward the doctor's office.

"Y—yes, Mum," the boy stammered. Patrick felt relieved in a way. His mother had just assured him that he was no longer required to think. He had only to do as told.

Aideen swatted his behind to get him moving. The slap wasn't intended to hurt, and it didn't, but sting it did.

"I said run! If the good doctor isn't here in ten minutes I will turn you out to live with rats in the dump. So help me, Patrick. Run!"

He turned and nearly smiled. His head was clearing, and he knew his mother didn't mean it—about the rats. She loved her family, and he realized her frightened threat was proof of that.

Although at a quick pace, it was fifteen minutes before Doc Quinn, with bag in hand, stepped onto the Cavanaugh front stoop. Head down, Patrick followed behind.

"This is most unusual for you folks," the Protestant doc piped to Aideen. "What seems to be the problem?"

The mission of Liam and his older partner had been successful. Whether it was damage to the gut that did it or the crack of his head on the floor, Seamus would never again be the same proselytizing Unionist. No more politics and not much talk at all from Seamus, which was truly strange. From then on, the talk from Seamus came out a bit childish, and not always appropriate.

Little Patrick became simply Patrick from that day on. His father was a good deal less help in the shop, and Patrick was needed to make up a good deal of the difference. Aideen was more than capable, but she needed help. The dry cleaning and mending continued as well as they could make it so. The greater involvement by Patrick molded a boy who would no longer regard himself as weak. In hardly more than a year, surely less than two, Patrick was practically doing the work of a full-grown man.

He was a good reader even before the incident, so it was natural in their situation that Aideen encouraged Patrick, after supper, to read for her and Seamus. Seamus seemed to enjoy listening while Aideen tended to her sewing and mending. Arithmetic was not so natural for Patrick, but Aideen, being the businesswoman she was, included slate time with Patrick for that as well. Grudgingly, he did learn the sums.

Since "the incident," as it was thereafter called, Sundays had become confusing to Seamus. He had never been a regular churchgoer, but when he had attended, it was with Patrick. Patrick was more comfortable in the Presbyterian church than in the cathedral, where Aideen attended. She was a regular. She and her situation were well known there. The priests were happy to take her confessions while offering needed encouragement.

Before the incident, she had gone early each morning to hear the word of God. There, she would ask for peace and forgiveness, and maybe a bit more business at the shop. After the incident, she went less often—due to time constraints, no doubt—but she became more intense and more selective about both what she heard and what she believed from "the Word." There were those who wondered, sometimes aloud, what Seamus had done to deserve such punishment. Those were prickly thoughts not appreciated by Aideen.

As Seamus grew more detached and more confused over time, there were some who whispered to her that she should put the poor dear out to charity while she was yet young enough to snare another, healthier man, as they put it. "At thirty-two, it takes more than good teeth and a straight spine to attract a good man, you know."

Patrick had grown cold with the church, both the Presbyterian and the Catholic. His father was not devout, and neither would he be. It did not matter which denomination he went with; they both left him feeling weak, inadequate, and unworthy. Yes, he was a sinner, but he was also strong enough and adequate enough to do a day's work with his hands and remain off the dole. *Could the priests and the bishop say the same—honestly?* he wondered. Still, as important as mass was to his mother, Patrick made it a point to go with her for the holiday service, be it Easter or Christmas. Doing so pleased her.

Patrick was fourteen when it became clear Seamus could no longer function in the shop. He had been less than helpful since the incident, but at least he had been cordial enough to customers. His recovery had turned a corner but then had begun going backwards. Both family and clientele experienced a growing, darker mood, which came to involve less appropriate behavior from Seamus.

In the beginning, customers had been pleasant and understanding enough—sympathetic, even. That all changed when Seamus began to act out his injured feelings. He remembered who was who most of the time, but not always. Some days were more confusing than others for him. When he began to stare at customers with cold suspicion, their sympathy and loyalty to the shop faltered. Seamus openly commented on the temperament of more than one household matron known to henpeck a husband. Grievous also were those occasions he took to blathering on regarding politics. The final red line he crossed was born of a memory quite personal to him.

It was a rainy, dreary Monday. "I remember you," he mumbled to Mrs. Finney, pointing a finger at her. His hand began to shake. Aideen tried to intercept him but was too late. "The high and mighty Mrs. Finney," he began. Aideen's fears were realized. "'Twas your man what dumped me on me head right here on this very floor."

Mrs. Finney was horrified. Her husband, the late public school principal, had passed to his eternal reward from consumption only a fortnight before. The widow was in mourning, and her husband was, in life, as genteel as a man could be, and certainly no ruffian—not the sort to be dumping people.

Patrick was sternly directed to assist Mr. Cavanaugh upstairs, where he could lie down and rest. Mrs. Cavanaugh would be up to check as soon as she could.

It wasn't until later that Aideen and Patrick determined the trigger of the outburst. But later did not resolve the issue. Because Seamus spent the better part of each day going over the Belfast Chronicle word for word, including redundant ads, there was little doubt he had seen Mr. Finney's picture in the obituary column the previous week. For whatever reason, that made a connection in his addled mind.

Bad enough that, but he had continued with his accusation: "Has the pope seen fit to absolve him for his actions, or has His Majesty reserved for him a chair near the Lord as reward for doing me in?"

The outburst cleared the shop of Catholics for some time. Mrs. Finney was helped out the door by Aideen, where the former could catch a breath of fresh air. It took a moment even there for her color to return. Aideen's profuse apologies could not make up for such behavior by Seamus, even in his present state. It had been coming for some time; the shop could no longer be run with Seamus in the front room.

As long as the daily paper arrived and he could read, Seamus was content to sit in the old rocker upstairs near the north window and do so. Aideen and Patrick were careful not to be loud or controversial, at least while working the business downstairs. There were two—or was it three?—occasions when something set the old boy off, and he came thundering down the stairs with fantastic alarm in his head. Those episodes became more and more difficult to deal with, if only because Seamus drifted farther and farther from reality.

That was why Aideen began to make it a point that either she or Patrick check on Seamus at the top of the hour throughout the day. It wasn't always convenient. Doing so became even more onerous when the ringing from the town's bell tower began to peeve the nerves of the poor man. If neither spouse nor son was there to calm and redirect his attention, Seamus was likely to realize his state of confusion, strange as that seemed, and become tearfully agitated.

Taking nourishment as he continued to do, strength, if not reason, remained with him. Seamus was a handful for both Aideen and Patrick on those occasions when the confusion could not be corralled. In the beginning, that was seldom the case, and it was usually Aideen who went upstairs to settle and assure him. Pointing to the paper and asking Seamus the prospect of a coming *fútbol* match was a fine maneuver for some time. Once his interest reverted to the paper, he was business as usual, reading every word. It was best to then hurry downstairs, apologizing all the way to customers.

His more frequent headaches were discouraging. At those times, Seamus could be found bent over in his rocker, head in hands, rocking in a slow rhythm. At times, the undulating shoulders gave way to quiet sobs. Aideen and Patrick could do nothing for him during those episodes. In the evenings, there were times when the pain of a caring wife would reveal itself in still more undulating shoulders. Patrick quietly despised it all.

Of course, business at the shop suffered. Those directly offended by Seamus found it best to take their business elsewhere. Others were simply influenced by rumors and the talk about town. Daily receipts thinned week after bloody week. Never flush with cash to begin with, the Cavanaughs' struggle included physical, emotional, and financial stress. Seamus was becoming an unreasonable handful, taking more and more time and energy while at the same time diminishing family resources.

Emotionally, Patrick remained apart and untouched. He was in a prison, he believed, not of his own making. He performed his duties, seldom complained, and responded to both his parents, albeit in different ways, of course. As he worked, he found release in fantasy, God forgive him. In his make-believe world, Patrick became a Charles Dickens character. From the depths of despair and poverty in his fantasy, Patrick would, in slow motion, evolve to valued status in a well-reasoned environment, where there were no dupes and all bullies soon thwarted. In such a fascinating state, Patrick's workdays ended swiftly.

Unless there was a problem in the shop. Then it was back to reality. There were more than enough problem days. *Someday,* Patrick promised himself, *justice will prevail, the sun will shine in the hearts of all, and Northern Ireland will be at peace.* Each day began, at least, with delightful fantasy.

Life continued on, much as change goes on. Reading became slower and more difficult for Seamus. Headaches remained oppressive, comprehension lessened, and, eventually, it was only disjointed memories that remained. Growing in his soul, however, was anger. When fits of rage joined with his strength, Aideen and Patrick felt themselves near danger. There was no reasoning with the man at such times. The result was bruises and fears of worse. Patrick only went deeper after those times, sidestepping the physical hurts while embracing the healing of fantasy.

Hope was all Doctor Quinn could offer: hope for a miracle, plus the suggestion that Father Coveney be called to deal with the matter sooner rather than later. Aideen knew what that meant. Patrick simply hoped something could be done. Father Coveney would have to accept Seamus for that something to be done. Most unlikely, since Seamus had been Protestant all his life. But if he were accepted, then he could go into a group setting where others like him were shepherded. Aideen well knew that said shepherding in those places did not include daily newspapers, rocking chairs, and north windows. But what choice did she have?

Father Coveney was quite well versed in the situation by the time he arrived the next day, unrequested by Aideen. Her daily mass attendance had been lacking for months, and, quite routinely, the Father had tried to comfort her when she did come. While not dismissive, Aideen had been defensive and scant with her explanations to him. Clearly, she felt shame and embarrassment.

Father Coveney's unexpected house call was a bit startling to her; she felt fortunate no one was in the shop when he arrived. Neither of them knew how she would respond to his presence there. The first thing she did, the instant she saw him on her stoop, was to break down. No stranger to tears, the Father invited himself in, removed some mending from a chair in order to sit, then, directly but gently, he prodded her.

Aideen plunked down on the other chair, not concerned with what was on it. She was trapped in her own shop. What could she do? She confessed, good Catholic that she was. Every detail that came to Aideen's mind was thrown in, to include even chamber-pot confusions in the night for Seamus and his painful admissions that his only relief would be to hang himself.

To his credit, Father Coveney only nodded, encouraging the purges until, finally, she sputtered her twisted confession to an end. Seamus had become so difficult. She could no longer handle the dear man, she had relayed, and yes, she desperately needed help. Could he do anything for Seamus other than admit him to the asylum? Could he do even the asylum for a lost Protestant? She wasn't certain what she was asking, and she had little idea what to expect. Aideen abhorred the idea of committing Seamus to the asylum, but there were few options. In truth, there were no honorable options.

"For heaven's sake, they think I should slit his throat and put him into the street? Several have suggested as much." Then, facetiously, she added, "And I could slit my own throat as well, but that would betray, good Father, the reward of the heavenly saints, now, wouldn't it?" Aideen was certain of very little other than the timeworn need to unburden herself, regardless of the consequence. When she finished, exhausted, her eyes dropped to the floor.

While this was going on, two customers came through the door, saw Father, the tears, and immediately left. They could have been Catholic or Protestant; instincts were the same—the devil in this house must now face the Christ! For once, Aideen was grateful for customers walking out.

Father Coveney took a breath. He sat for a moment, processing in his mind the likely future he saw for Aideen Cavanaugh, the humble and faithful believer. What he saw was darkness. A demented Seamus, being Protestant, would take her to an early grave. What could he, a Catholic priest, do with a sick and altogether damaged Protestant in an otherwise devout Catholic home, a home that served God and the community?

The Father quietly explained to her that she had already lost her best friend some time ago, when he was injured the way he was. Since then, she had remained true to her vows of marriage—"till death do us part." The question was, what could be done now to preserve decency and health? He was, of course, speaking of Aideen's health and salvation.

If only this Protestant were not so demented, Father Coveney kept thinking. Except for the weeping, all was quiet in the shop for some time. Patrick was in the workroom and possibly just beyond the curtain. There seemed to be no concern or thought regarding him. The Father's visit centered around Aideen. Apparently, nothing would change; many were on the dole, and what was two or three more? Everyone knew the dole was bare subsistence, if that, even if it could be had, and it was not unusual that politics betrayed a family's need. Being Protestant in a Catholic district was politics indeed.

Father Coveney knew the score. *The Cavanaughs have an active business here. They have customers. They have an income. The dole is for those without work and often without so much as a straw mat or a room to put one in. There would be a good deal of suffering to endure, and surely an eviction, before the county would step in to help. The hands of the church are tied, but only due to the faith consideration—Seamus being Protestant. His religion is the problem, and he is so damnably demented,* Father Coveney's mind muttered. *He should be sent across the River Foyle for the faithful Protestants to care for him,* he facetiously opined to himself.

Then it occurred to him, *Seamus is demented! He is a demented Protestant. He has never proclaimed himself a Catholic, much less a good Catholic, and, in this neighborhood, how can that be? Why would that be? Because he is demented, of course, and always has been! After all, he is married to a good Catholic, who minds her ps and qs and opens her heart to everyone. Why would he live in this Catholic neighborhood? He is the work of the devil—demented to the core and taking advantage of this dear woman! Therefore, if he were to rave in the asylum that he was beaten and kidnapped, then all the better. He's demented and an admitted Protestant! In the asylum of Lifford, on the Republic of Ireland side of the river, hardly more than a stone's throw from this spot, he would be normal. Not normal, you understand, but I'm certain you understand, Lord.*

The Father felt the spirit lift him off the rickety chair to stand before Aideen, his singular congregant of the day. He reached out to hold her hands and addressed her with practiced sincerity. "My dear woman, praise to the Almighty, for he is our rock, our sustenance, and our nourishment in times of trial and need. The night is darkest just before the sunrise as we struggle with the unknown in fear and tribulation. With your burden relieved by confession in the presence of His servant, I feel the hand of God upon me. With faith and a heavy heart, I leave your side to seek resolution and release for your prison of pain in this house. In good faith, I go forward to seek answers, and in that I feel a strength and purpose. Good day, madam." With that, Father Coveney turned and strode out the door.

Three days from then, late in the day, Father Coveney materialized upon the Cavanaugh stoop once again. "Good afternoon, Sister Aideen," he cheerily expressed. "Would you have a moment for me this day?"

Of course, Aideen had a moment and more for her priest. This time, she invited him in. He remained standing and did not look to find seating. The Father, with a decided twinkle in his eye, reached out with both hands and simultaneously patted both cheeks of a somewhat flustered Aideen. She could see he was in fine spirits. She couldn't help wondering if Father Coveney was in his cups this fine day before sundown. *Be that or not, his pleasantness must bode pleasant news,* she imagined.

Indeed, it was good news!

"Sister Aideen," he began, "I have this day arranged for brother Seamus to be treated at Lifford Asylum for the Faithful. He will be well cared for there; you can visit him and bring indulgences to him, if you wish, the first Sunday of each month. Glory be to the Almighty that Seamus may there recover and see the error of his ways at last. I shall return in the morning with two lads and a priest, who will assist me in walking with Seamus the two miles to Lifford. He needn't bring anything other than perhaps an additional pants and shirt, if he has them. The Holy Spirit will walk with us, and the host of Lifford shall care for his physical needs. There. You see? God answers prayer—thanks to Jesus and the Holy Mother."

"Why—I don't know what to say, Father," Aideen simply muttered.

"No questions? Very well, I will then see you and Seamus in the morning." With that, he was on his heels and back out the door.

Aideen was truly stunned. It may have been a full minute before the news touched her core. She broke into tears.

For God's sake, Lifford is across the River Foyle in Republic of Ireland! Aideen's mind could not accommodate the thought of a monthly tradition to such a place. *'Tis a Protestant asylum!* But she knew. She knew this was the only reprieve that could come to her, if not for Seamus as well. At last, he would be with his own kind. Many times, she had told herself, *With me, in a fine Catholic neighborhood, he will convert one day. And perhaps he shall,* she now added. *There, in the asylum, perhaps, he will see the errors of his ways, as Father Coveney said. Would not that be ironic?* She couldn't help but smile—briefly.

"Mother, what is it? From the yard, I saw Father Coveney leaving. Was it he who frightened you so?"

"Oh, Patrick, my big boy Patrick," she said, wiping away tears, "the news he brings is so rich I cannot think. The good Father has informed me that Papa Seamus will be accepted at the Lifford Asylum for the Faithful as of the early morning tomorrow. It is such good news. It is terrible news, I know. 'Tis a blessing, thanks be to God and Mother Mary. I cry only at the loss of your father, but if this is God's will . . ."

"Mother, do you mean Papa will be taken in the morning and gone from our lives?"

"No, my dear boy. We will go to him the first Sunday of each month. We will bring bread and salted fish. Our income will revive, you will see, and we can buy meat each week and even fruit at times."

"But, Mother, the asylum . . ."

"I know, I know, but this is truly best for us all. Does God want us to suffer and expire before our time?"

"Suffer, yes," Patrick quickly retorted. "But maybe God now has other plans for me? Do you think that could be?"

Aideen stiffened. "I think, Patrick, that God thinks about many things, but not so much the luxury of your life."

"Yes, Mum. I think God does not know my name."

Aideen, in this, her sanctified moment, did not ignore Patrick's insolent comment. But the joy in her heart would not allow for him to be slapped just now.

Morning came quickly despite the anxiety of so little sleep for Aideen. She awakened Seamus early and, despite his complaints, dressed him in the clean pants and shirt he owned. She quickly scrubbed out the dirty clothes and hung them to dry in the breeze outside. Then, it was porridge for just the two of them, but too early yet for the newspaper. Seamus had continued his struggle to read with little success and showed no sign of comprehension since last month.

Aideen told him he would be going out for a walk this day. Seamus had to think what that meant. He noticed the sunshine coming through the front room window and made mention. The prospect of feeling the sunshine cheered him. Then, no knock at the door, and Father Coveney was inside offering pleasantries to the Cavanaughs, particularly with Seamus in mind.

Aideen stepped in. "Time for your walk, Seamus, as was promised. Father Coveney will go with you." She raised her voice now. "He is our friend, Seamus. It will be a good walk in the sunshine." She quickly turned away to hide swelling tears.

Patrick, meanwhile, stood in the doorway of the back room. This time, the curtain was pulled back, but he said nothing. This wasn't right, he knew. But what was? He was not Catholic either; he was sure of it.

The front door opened. Sunlight flowed to the foot of Seamus, and down he looked. He smiled. It was a rare smile from the heart, although a vacant one, but even that was promising. Then he was out the door and gone.

Aideen did not turn back. She hadn't even kissed him goodbye. More tears.

Patrick stood quietly still for another moment. His mourning did not show. He appeared angry—frustrated, perhaps. What he began to feel was the embryo of a dream stirring inside him.

Their routine dashed as it was, Aideen and Patrick could have stumbled on clouds all the day long. They could not know it would be many days before balance and rhythm returned to their work.

Late afternoon of the day Seamus left, there was a sharp knock at the door. That was unusual. During the day, customers never knocked when bringing in their soiled woolens or mending needs. The Cavanaugh Cleaners shingle was out twenty-four hours a day, but folks respected their privacy near the supper hour and left them alone most evenings. A knock on the door at any time meant a joyful event, such as good friends or former neighbors calling, or it was something more earnest, such as the report of an illness or a death. This occasion would be no exception.

Patrick groaned slightly and arose from his half-eaten supper. He moved from the table and slowly pulled open the heavy oak door, not knowing what to expect. There before him stood Constable Coveney, all fit and proper in a well-worn uniform. Except the uniform was damp and dirty, which wasn't at all like Nolan to be looking shabby. Nolan Coveney was Father Coveney's younger brother. Already, he had been constable for a number of years. The Coveney family was not well-to-do, but they were decent and respected folk. Like his brother, Constable Coveney knew everyone and everyone knew him. Nolan was a prince of a man by most accounts.

"Patrick," he said, "is your mum home?"

"You can see she's right there, and we're eatin' supper," Patrick blurted. "What is it?"

Aideen was there at the door in a flash, thinking Patrick was disrespectful, be it suppertime or not. "Watch your mouth, Patrick. You may be wearin' full-growed pants, but sixteen hain't old enough to be jawin' a neighborly constable. That be right, Nolan?" she finished.

All was still for a moment, the constable ignoring the comments of both Aideen and Patrick. Then he looked briefly into Aideen's eyes. He was required to make an announcement, he said. Official-like, as though he'd been rehearsing, Nolan said, "I have news for you and Patrick, Mrs. Cavanaugh."

Patrick scowled as though still annoyed, but Aideen stiffened. The only possible news, much less official news, that would come to them from a constable would be an eviction notice or something about Seamus. On instinct, she mentally debated which she would prefer. There would be nothing to hear but bad news. Not soon enough, she cut the imaginings. "What is it, Nolan? For heaven's sake, tell me."

"Mrs. Cavanaugh and Patrick . . . ," he self-consciously mumbled. Going back to their school days, Nolan had then addressed Aideen by her nickname, Deenie. Once married, even to the Protestant, he ever after referred to her more properly as Aideen. Immediately, she closed her eyes, wishing she could will herself not to hear what was coming next.

"On the way to Lifford with your husband this morning, Mrs. Cavanaugh, we had a bit of a problem crossin' the Lifford Bridge."

"What do you mean, a bit of a problem, Constable?" Aideen responded a bit tightly.

"More than a bit of a problem it was. You see, your husband was pleasant and happy the whole way. Being out in the sunshine and all, he was laughin' and dancin'."

"Yes, so what happened at the Lifford Bridge?" By now, Aideen's voice was terse and sharp. "Would you be gettin' to the report, be it official or not, sir?"

"I must tell you this. Before we can think or even guess what he is doing, Seamus climbs up top the railing in the middle of the bridge. I swear, who would know he could even do such a thing as that?"

"Yes? And then, Nolan? What then?"

"Deenie," the constable confessed with tears now in his eyes, "the dear man looked up to the heavens, spread his arms, and leaped headfirst into the River Foyle."

"While the lot of ya is standing there with yer mouths hangin' open, no doubt. You didn't fish him out of the drink?"

"Good Lord, we wanted to! River Foyle is the quickest river in all of Europe, they say. You know well as me it runs wide past the bridge and then into the Irish Sea. We runned and tried to follow him from alongside. When we lost sight of him, we commandeered a boat and went out in it, but it was finding the needle, you know?"

"So, you are telling me Seamus Cavanaugh met his maker in the River Foyle this very day?" It wasn't a question but more of a statement, asking for a confirmation that wasn't necessary except to the widow. Somehow, Aideen seemed to calm, suddenly at peace. She asked, still with an edge, "You've been at this for the full day and just come to me now?"

"But we did not know hardly a thing until now. The body we found about a hour past. It was there in the Irish Sea where the current is nil at last. Nothing had got to him yet. You can do a funeral within a day or two, where folks can look and such."

"And where is he now?"

"On the Republic of Ireland side at Saint Gabriel Parish. The bishop asked if you would come see him at first daylight. The sooner the better for the funeral, he wants you to know."

It was a respectable funeral but not large. Likeable though Seamus was, it was complicated. A native from just west of the River Foyle, he then lived just east side of the River Foyle once married. His mixed marriage dampened his popularity on both sides of the river, and "the incident" only made things worse. There were those who well knew Seamus Cavanaugh but cared not enough to pay respects.

Still, now that he had passed, it was time for those offended by his abruptness at the shop to consider forgiving the man, and some even did. They attended the service with a degree of reverence and regret for what could have been. It helped that the women of Saint Gabriel set the example by serving a lunch for after the burial. Aideen preferred a wake, truth be told, but Constable Coveney advised against it due to the likely mixing. Neither side of the river was willing to tempt a mixture of politics, religion, and alcohol. Little doubt that would create the likelihood of trouble for the family of the deceased as well as others. Being constable, Nolan would be dealing with a good bit of it, which bore witness to his opinion on the matter.

Of course, it could have been a dry wake, no alcohol, but that would have been in name only. John Barleycorn cared not if he filled a flask or a punchbowl. There would be a drink or two for all, regardless the calling of it. With no wake, however, only those who truly cared about Seamus and the Cavanaughs would likely attend the funeral. Aideen believed that had the makings for a good demarcation of who was a legitimate friend of her and Seamus and who was not. That would not prove to be entirely true.

The standard milquetoast eulogy was supplied by the bishop. Likely because of that, Constable Coveney offered to say a few words in memory of his friend. They hadn't been close friends, but Nolan was everyone's friend, and Seamus had respected the constable. Nolan went to the lectern marching straight and tall as any grenadier. Direct as could be, he set the record straight concerning the nature of Seamus, that he was kind to children and animals, that he tended to mind his own business, for the most part, and that he was an enviable supporter of loyalty and justice.

It was all good and well, but most who were there heard what Nolan had meant by that last part. An avowed Unionist, Seamus had never tired until the incident of advocating for the Crown of England and loyalty to the King. It was meant by Nolan as a brief and honest comment, all things considered, but both the Unionists and the Nationalists, the Protestants and the Catholics, clearly heard the politics of it. The bishop let it pass, thank God.

Until the funeral, Patrick had endured the process by keeping to himself as much as he could. As the only son of the deceased, that was not easy to do. The shop had to remain open for customers to pick up their finished cleaning and such. Patrick was willing to work the shop during that time, but every last person he saw those two days mumbled and jumbled and professed undying support for Aideen. It was a goodly number of people stopped by to pay their respects. Not likely those would be crossing the river for the funeral. Aideen was not there, of course, and Patrick began to wonder if he was invisible—even to the people talking to him. People talked to the acting proprietor he was but not to him personally.

Remaining busy kept him from becoming morose, he reasoned. He seldom looked forward to dealing with people, but now, with the flood of people coming to the shop, there were no options, and time passed quickly. Because of it, Patrick maintained good spirits.

He knew nothing about funerals, and he was not consulted regarding the proceedings. Aideen mourned deeply and was pleased that Patrick had stepped up and took over the shop for those two days. The day of the funeral, the shop would be closed. For her, a good deal of those two days was spent with the Protestant bishop, who would be conducting the funeral, and Constable Coveney, who advised and comforted her throughout the process.

Being schoolmates, friends, and neighbors all their lives, Aideen and Nolan were comfortable with each other. Nolan had never married, although no one was quite certain why. As youngsters, it was well known that Nolan's hero was his older brother, the priest, and that he too wished to become a man of the cloth like Ryan. While that was true, others believed Nolan's heart had been broken early on by a Protestant girl across the river. During those adolescent years, it was true he had spent a good deal of time there. Heartbreak was a logical choice for his presumed celibacy. Still others did not presume.

In any case, when the time came, the service ended smoothly despite the turmoil of tangled souls and mixed theology. Then it was the normal parade of transporting the casket from meeting house to cemetery for the internment. The bishop led the way with the casket following and the family slowly behind. Nearly all others followed the family, although some did not, reserving with their bottoms a good seat for the lunch to follow at the meeting house. As the casket was placed atop the grave to be blessed before the prayerful lowering, the family moved behind it with the bishop. All others stopped solemnly in front.

As the bishop began his "ashes to ashes" speech, Patrick gazed out among the crowd, consciously looking for the various hypocrites he expected to see there. Seamus would like that. Identifying their presence for his father would validate the righteousness of the departed's soul. All his life, Patrick had heard the whispers on both sides of the river that Seamus was not a true believer. Whether he was raised in the wrong religion or married a woman with the wrong religion, others too often questioned the spiritual heart of his father.

In truth, Seamus was the rare man who spoke from the heart and not from a book of rules. The distrust and dislike so many people harbored over religious and status degrees of others were dishonest to both Seamus and Patrick. That people could be comfortable talking out of both sides of their mouths disgusted them both. Patrick suddenly realized he was proud to be that way. It wasn't easy to be different, but he was proud to be like his father and to have thought behind his beliefs.

As he scanned the crowd, Patrick caught something in the shadows that sent an intuitive shiver through him. The face was not clear, but the body form was distinctive and somehow familiar. He couldn't place the man. Then another figure stepped from behind a tree near the first man. He too seemed remotely familiar and instinctually repugnant to Patrick. Then one of them moved to stand alongside the other. That did it! Together they focused Patrick's mind. Their faces were clear enough.

Sure as the sun rose this mornin', it is the two bastards what killed me father! They couldn't stay away from the funeral, Patrick realized. *Incredible!* Emotions got the best of him, but only for a moment. He dropped his head and gruffly cleared his throat, his face reddened, and tears of emotion welled in his eyes.

The bishop stopped speaking and turned to see the source of the interruption. Patrick appeared to have been crying. The bishop smiled slightly. He was thankful the boy had finally broken down and could cry at the hour of his father's committal. *Such a blessing.* Had he actually been crying, it would have been the first since the original incident.

The bishop then reached out and placed in Patrick's hand a white hand-kerchief. It was elegantly monogrammed, Patrick noticed as he turned it over. Smartly stitched on one edge was "Saint Gabriel." What could have been there was the Archangel of Revelation and Patron of Diplomats, which Saint Gabriel was. Patrick knew his archangels. Such a blessing, indeed. Such irony. That Seamus was somehow connected with a diplomat for true faith and revelation was something that had not before occurred to him. He was heartened as he wiped his eyes and succeeded with a smile toward the bishop, which fully heartened the bishop.

Then Patrick remembered the two blokes in the rear. How could he forget? Still there. Not likely they would go into the meeting house for the lunch, and he was right—they didn't. Patrick was soon making excuses to Nolan, telling him he would try to make it back, but he needed to walk out his anxieties over the affair of Papa's internment. Not hungry, so forget him having lunch if he wasn't back in time.

The constable looked into Patrick's eyes and asked, "Are you sure about this?"

"Not a doubt in my mind," Patrick told him.

Nolan looked into Patrick's eyes again and slowly nodded his assent. But he didn't like it.

Patrick haltingly left the premises, stopping to look at grave markers here and there. He seemed as melancholy as any lad who had recently lost his papa. Once off the premises, however, he picked up the pace considerably. He was out of sight of the parishioners and barely within sight of the murderous pair, the older and the younger. That was where he needed to be.

Plenty of bushes and trees for him to duck behind should the need arise, Patrick kept pace with the pair ahead of him at such a distance until the two men reached the Green Pint Inn only a few blocks away and around the corner. It was on the Republic side, of course, which made sense to Patrick. He knew the place from traipsing around with Seamus well before the incident.

The incident! It all but made his blood boil thinking about it. This pub and its connection with Seamus upped Patrick's resolve. The Green Pint was a well-known black-market and fencing outlet, not that Seamus was ever involved in such things. Patrick smiled at the thought. To be sure, it was a collection of rough characters inside.

So as not to be spotted by them, Patrick walked around the block and checked out the back of the pub. He went to the side of the building, just around the corner from the back door. He didn't plan on going inside, and he didn't want to be too obvious. He noticed an egg crate under a filthy window.

That should do it. He turned the crate over and stepped up. Through a corner of the glass, he looked around at the scene inside. Only a handful of men there. That was good. There the two of them were, sitting at the bar, with a fresh pint before each of them, the younger at the very end of the bar. He had a clay pipe in his mouth that he fiddled with.

Quietly, Patrick stepped down and reviewed his surroundings. It was the back-alley usual: trash, burn barrel, clothesline, mostly flattened tins, and some full-sized utensils—a shovel or two and a hoe for who knew what garden. Not what he was looking for.

Then he spotted it. Not just a wire rug beater but an iron rug beater—the heavy kind. It was an industrial, heavy-duty beater, and it was just lying there on the ground. It was the kind of beater that dry cleaner shops should have but most couldn't afford. All the better.

Another smile.

The business end on it wasn't a waffle-looking affair, as were the cheaper ones. This was an iron coil, big as could be, bigger than a liter bottle. Patrick picked it up from the end of the handle and waggled it. Quite a bit longer than the one at home, and heavier, of course. He could adjust; no worries. Stepping back, Patrick held the beater straight out with arms outstretched. Then he moved back further, just to where the heavy end of the beater reached the end of the building. With the toe of his shoe, Patrick marked where he was standing. Yes, he already had something in mind.

Just then, he noticed what surely was a neighborhood regular turn from the street and into the alley. Patrick set down the beater and watched until the man turned again, this time to the back door of the pub. As he reached the stoop, Patrick softly called out to him in a near whisper.

"Friend. Come here. I need your help."

In most circumstances, such requests would raise a warning, but it translated into something more at the Green Pint. It registered one of two things: request for performance of an errand or action with the promise of reward, or it was the usual request to satisfy curiosity and be rolled for your interest.

The bloke was unshaven and dirty, grease under his fingernails. Clearly a man who worked for a living, at least sometimes. He looked at Patrick and saw a dapper boy who was no challenge whatsoever. No hesitation. He came close.

"Sir," Patrick began, "only by coincidence, you understand, I happened to overhear a bloke in the meetin' house today tell another gent about the very existence and location of a full case of new timepieces. He wished them to be in the hands of someone with connections in the London crowd. No doubt they could be sold at a considerable discount," Patrick added with a quick wink. "The other man was down on his chips, so them timepieces, sir, are no doubt yet available." Another wink. "For a gentleman with a good twist of the tongue, a bloke could make a tidy profit on Victoria Street with a full case of them. Would you be so kind as to go to the bar and inform the younger of two gents, the one with a workin' man's jacket at the end of the bar, that a bloke out back has such an offer? Likely he will have a pipe in his mouth. I happen to be of the understandin' that this gent is familiar with such business."

"Well, I don't know why I should. I am directly in need of a pint, you know."

That all but sealed it for Patrick. He reached into a pocket and quickly produced a large, round coin. For the drama of it, he glanced quickly around and pushed it into a dirty hand. "There be a quid for you, sir. That should whet your whistle and leave some for the morrow. And," he added for assurance, "should all go well this time, there is likely to be more business."

"Good and well, sir, but I have your coin now, do I not? What was it that you couldn't keep it in your own pocket and administer this bit of business yourself? If you don't mind me askin'," he added to sound proper.

Patrick cleared his throat quite intentionally. "Sir," he proceeded indignantly, "I may appear young to you, but I am no fool. Misunderstandings come along every day, and it's a known fact they have been known to go so far as a hangman's knot. I prefer not to be seen with the gentleman at the end of the bar. You see, if there was to be some trouble regarding what is proper and what is not—in a business sense, you understand—I should not want to be associated with nor accountable for his actions. Do I make myself clear?"

The grimy gent flipped over his coin, smiled a largely toothless grin, and headed directly for the back door.

Before the man reached the door, Patrick spoke up. "He must come alone. There will be no witnesses, lest there be no business a'tall."

The dayworker stopped and looked at Patrick. The smile continued to crease his face, but he gave no sign of assent or decline. He did, however, make it a point to lightly kiss the coin and bang the door shut behind him.

It wasn't long before Patrick heard the back door squeak very slowly open. The human behind this slow-motion propulsion was no doubt the younger. *He must be looking around with a degree of caution,* Patrick surmised to himself. He didn't mind that, although a quivering jaw said otherwise. Since the incident, Patrick had graphically imagined, over and over, a vision of vengeance he would put upon the younger man. It was the same vision he had seconds after he watched the lead pipe slam into Seamus. The vision was the smashed face of the younger man.

Now Patrick wanted to deliver a quivering jaw. He was self-conscious about quivering jaws; it happened to him sometimes, and he couldn't consciously make it stop. *Unless . . . unless, maybe, I can give it away?* From the very moment of the incident, it had plagued Patrick's mind that strength and power was achieved by overpowering others. In other words, *abuse profits the abuser.*

The younger stepped around the corner to see who was there. He recognized Patrick but could not believe it. He had seen him scarcely half an hour ago in the cemetery. That would explain why he froze for an instant. Maybe a hundred things rushed through his mind in that instant, but for certain there was no time to apply the tough-guy veneer. That was when, *bullseye!*, the industrial-strength rug beater smacked the right side of his face, jaw included. It likely would have landed at about his ear, moving upward, maybe doing enough damage to kill him outright, if he hadn't turned. Peripheral vision had warned him at the last possible instant, turning his head to see what was coming. He was hit flush on the jaw.

The blow did not kill him, and that was OK with Patrick. It did crush his face and knock him cold. It was a surprisingly quiet collision, iron instrument to head, considering the degree of damage. Patrick had watched as though it were slow motion—the head giving way to the impact, breaking and distorting. Then, grabbing feet, Patrick dragged his victim further around the corner so he could not be seen from the back door. He patted him down, looking for what—he didn't know. The lead pipe was still there. Patrick latched onto it with some satisfaction. By then blood had erupted from the younger's mouth. His nose, his ear, and right eye shed blood. But he was breathing. For now that was good. *If he ever wakes up he can see and maybe understand his circumstance.* Patrick wished for that, but it didn't matter a lot.

Since the younger wouldn't be returning to the pub, Patrick expected the older to be checking on his partner. He wasn't wrong. It was five minutes or so, but that gave Patrick time enough to calm himself and plan his next step. He had followed the men with no plan whatsoever other than revenge. *Isn't it ironic that my own father's funeral brought me to this opportunity?* he mused.

Physically Patrick was no match for the older, bigger man, but just as with the younger, Patrick had no intention of playing fair. He was as fair with these two as they had been with his father. *The bastards!* He decided to drag the younger further away from the wall. He would be more obvious that way, but not until the older turned the corner. There would likely be another frozen instant with time enough to strike again.

Finally he heard the squeak of the back door. Patrick was now flat against the wall, just around the corner of the back stoop. There was an assurance and confidence the way the door opened quickly and banged shut. Patrick heard the two steps down the wood stoop. Next, he heard the crunch of three more steps toward the corner of the building. It stopped. *He must be looking around.* Then three more steps and he was exposed, the partner there on the ground. As expected, he was within an arm's length of retaliation by Patrick, and he couldn't help but glare at his distorted partner on the bloodied ground hardly more than a yard in front of him.

With everything he had, Patrick swung the length of lead pipe directly into gut. *Almost funny,* Patrick thought. The older performed exactly as Seamus when struck—and from the very same instrument. With any luck at all, the bigger would suffer as Seamus had.

Something said no. Patrick looked around as the man fell. There was no hard floor for him to crash into. In a moment he and his head would be just fine lying there in the dirt. The older had grabbed for the pipe as it swung into him, but he was slightly late, not that he could have deflected it much anyway. His face displayed shock as he looked up, realizing now who had hit him. There would be internal injuries. Patrick didn't much care. He was more concerned there were no head injuries. With Seamus, the latter were the greater problem by far. Patrick felt justified to adjust the injury. With little effort, he drew back the pipe and belted the front side of the older's head. There was a crunching mush sound made by the blow as bone and cartilage gave way. It was louder this time, maybe because he was closer. The older remained conscious but wretched his fresh pint. The beer came out sideways. His jaw was distorted. It was several seconds before his head began to bleed.

As he stood there looking at the two heaps, Patrick realized the sight of these two goons in such a condition was not a proper calling card for the novice hoodlum responsible. He was almost sorry for what he had done. *Was it my mother's son what done this?* Patrick did not consider himself a hoodlum, and he wasn't interested in such a future. It was the revenge that had taken him.

He didn't panic, but he began to think of tomorrow now—and the day after. He began to wonder if he had done the right thing being so cruel. Then he passed it off, telling himself, *They are responsible for what they done to begin this, not me.*

The lead pipe was still in his hand, and he knew that any time now a half dozen more like these two would be out the back door and not happy with what they found. For some reason, Patrick tossed the pipe to the ground between the two. Then he reached down and briefly touched the rug beater. That was enough. On the double, he headed back toward the meeting house.

This business, this incident, hadn't taken long. Chances were good he could ease back in with the funeral crowd and assuage a growing appetite. There was then a feeling of surreal about him. It was a good surreal. For now. And he was hungry. Potato salad and smoked herring were better than expected.

The next day, Aideen was a bit more chipper now that the stress of decisions and people crowding her were over. She hadn't enough funds to completely pay for the funeral, but that was, by and large, normal in these parts. She would make it a point for an offering to the bishop on a regular basis. *Just because he is a Protestant bishop is no reason not to pay him what's proper,* she reasoned. *Business will pick up. Regular customers who left due to the behavior of Seamus will return. People in the neighborhood aware of the circumstance will take up with the cleaners again. Irish folks is good everywhere. They just need to understand how things is,* Aideen reasoned. *We must keep the cleaners going.*

At nearly seventeen, Patrick was key to that. He knew the business well by now and in the following days worked as long and hard as his mother. But throughout the days, his thoughts went elsewhere. He never heard the outcome of the blokes he had revenged on, but he could hardly get them off his mind. That, and he wanted to be elsewhere. There was more than one reason for that, but he kept quiet and did what he could to bring the business back.

Constable Coveney spent time around the shop now too. When not in uniform, he became plain old friend Nolan again. He enjoyed helping out, and soon enough he was spending off-time there. Patrick thought the world of him, and Aideen appreciated the support Nolan gave her. Often enough he stayed around for supper, but a fortnight after the funeral he did not.

Nevertheless, a report from across the River Foyle had come to Constable Coveney. He said nothing to Aideen and Patrick about it but went directly to and across the Lifford Bridge for details. He didn't show up at the shop at all that next day. The day after that he came early—in uniform. Aideen didn't seem to think too much about it. After all, the job of constable ebbed and flowed, much like the dry-cleaning business and most others.

While she stirred the porridge that morning, Nolan nodded to Patrick that he should go outside. Aideen looked up but said nothing as the two gents stepped out.

"Patrick, there's a report from Lifford proper that there be a witness to the beating two blokes took at the pub called Green Pint two weeks back. I believe the beatin' happened the day of your father's funeral, possibly about the time you stepped out for a settlin' walk."

Patrick's eyes widened, but Nolan continued in his intentional monotone.

"Not a witness exactly, I hear tell, but an old toothless dayworker claims to be known as a witness by the attacker—just one attacker, mind you, and the old gent is afraid for his life, they say. He talked to the man who surely done the business that day just before it all come about."

"I can explain," Patrick began to say.

"You will not be explainin' a thing," Nolan cut him off, sharply now. "You will not be explaining. I will not be askin', and we will understand each other. Am I makin' myself clear, Patrick Cavanaugh?"

It took a second or two, but then the message came into focus for Patrick. "Yes, sir, I take your meaning." His jaw began a slight quiver. "Nolan, do you know anything more about this—this incident?"

"I learned that the two blokes what got busted up good have what you could call 'business associates' who will be going out of their way to run down who done that. No constable is about to look hard into this, considering them two. But the kind of them two is already into it. They take care of their own—at least when they're not abusin' and bashin' each other. That's what else I know."

As casually as he could, Patrick wondered out loud what would become of the shop if his mother were alone there some day. He hoped he already knew the answer.

"Patrick, you have eyes, and I think you can see I have certain affection for your mother. Always have." Then he quickly added, "Now that she's a widow, you understand."

"She would need help, Nolan. She can't run the cleaners alone. With someone responsible—and I'm not saying anyone in particular—but if someone like you was there, it would work. But, Nolan, you already have a job."

"Along the way, that occurred to me as well, me boy. I know the people of this burg, and I know who's worth their salt and who to not bother with. Aideen could hire a good needin' soul who will match wages with work done. Your mum has settled considerably since the funeral, you know."

Despite looking a mite solemn, Patrick responded, "Might I say I am pleased and grateful to hear you say that, Nolan? After all this nasty business, I am also pleased to be old enough now to leave the nest and see what the world is about."

At that, Nolan gave Patrick a hard stare. He believed it would be best if the boy disappeared and maybe saved his mother more heartache.

"Let me remind you of something you already know, Patrick: Foyle Port isn't all that far away. Just off Victoria Road, almost every day, a ship or two from Lough Foyle steams into the Irish Sea and in no time is at a English port. Liverpool, they say, is where a good deal of honest work is there for the askin'."

Aideen called out, wondering where they were. Breakfast was getting cold.

"I was thinking that as well, Nolan." Then, only a mite louder, "Coming, Mum."

"The bloodsucking devils of the island are coming for the bloke what took down their own! Not likely they will quit a minute before they find the poor devil. Or devils. Constables are not waged to be smart, but little doubt that even *I* can come up with who done that business, an' he done it right smart, I hear. You think the hoodlums won't do the same?" Then Nolan trailed on, "And all the while your mum thinking she has somebody lookin' out for her—somebody who's spendin' each day thinkin' about what the world has in store for him."

Patrick felt his jaw tingle again. "If I was to look for sea or dock work, it would squeeze me. I have hardly a quid and some change. Good Lord, I cannot take money from the till and then duck out on Mum."

"Look, Patrick," and he dug in his pocket, "here's ten pounds. No, make that twelve quid. You can pay me back when you can. Go eat your breakfast, and if you decide to wander off, please give your mum a kiss and remind her of your love. I will see that she gets by."

Patrick was pale and wordless going inside for breakfast. The porridge was tasteless, the hardtack dry as dust in his throat. He swallowed hard. In such a state, he had only to look at Aideen. Without words she began to cry. They hugged; he kissed her hard on the cheek. He disappeared upstairs to collect clean clothes, wrapped them up in one of the shirts, and came back down.

Nolan had come in by then. He only nodded to Aideen. Patrick said nothing to his mum. As any mother would, she handed him a wax-paper package of hardtack and smoked herring. He took the package and looked at her one last time. "Mum, I'm so sorry." He was. He truly was. But not about the younger and the older. They deserved what they got. Not a word about the beating was said aloud. Aideen would know nothing. Nothing for certain, but she certainly knew. Then Patrick shook Nolan's hand, turned, and abruptly walked out the door, rushing down the street as though it were a race to beat the tears. As it was, he lost to the tears. But not for long. He would be finding drama and leaving more behind wherever he went.

Marching On, Uncle Ho, Marching On

Whispering softly, a new morning breeze,
Imploring God's focus while killers go free.
Indelicate truths the soldier knows well:
Typhoon and napalm; comrades now dead.

The hard side of nature, callous and crude,
Washed off a mountain, a 9-man squad.
Cut the loss, look away, and keep moving on.
Yesterday gives way to the cloud of what's past.

The brave, the wary, the foolhardy and stout
Face nature and truth – one beautiful, both not.
War so contrived, nature unsure;
Privates ordered to win where there is no score.

The Commissar blathers, preaching of soon,
When fires are safe, hot rice with nuoc mam.
Forced to push on, propaganda and gumption,
Harboring fantasies of love with hunks of pork fat.

–Paul Kluge

Chapter 2

Answer the Call: Part I

Spring 1951, After Four-plus Years of War

They were born the same month of the same year and only a few kilometers apart. You would not mistake them for brothers, and their backgrounds couldn't have been much different. What they had in common was *fútbol*. Both were good players, each on a better-than-decent home team. The neighborhood team of Pham Van Hieu almost always beat the village team of Nguyen Dac Pho, often by two or more goals. It was expected. Both boys opted not to be impressed by the other. Pham Van Hieu was quick to make a show of his skills; the Nguyen boy, on the other hand, was introverted, humble in every way. From a simple farming family, he didn't think much of the flamboyant Pham kid, but they were honest competitors. Both were gifted, but in different ways, other than *fútbol*. Neither of them would admit to giving the other much thought.

Pham Van Hieu grew up as a city boy on the edge of Haiphong in the north of Vietnam, not far from Hanoi. His family was of mandarin stock, his father an accountant, respected by neighbors and peers. As a busy port city, Haiphong had many accountants. Mr. Pham, like all the other Vietnamese accountants, was a commodity under the French system. There would be neither advancement nor much respect offered him by the French administrators. *Do your job, do not offer suggestions, and never complain,* was the unspoken code almost all indigents lived by. After all, there were many others happy to replace them.

At sixteen, the confident and ambitious Van Hieu surprised his family by joining a covert, irregular platoon of the communist Vietminh. Irregular platoons were part of a growing effort vowing to free the country from French colonialism. Not quite certain what communism was, Van Hieu reasoned it would surely be better than the demeaning culture the French imposed on them. Whatever it involved, life as an insurgent would be exciting. Adventure and opportunity for advancement within the Vietminh was assured. Smart and confident—some would say cocky—Van Hieu presented himself well and exhibited excellent posture to go along with piercing dark eyes. Handsome and popular, he was not afraid to look a pretty girl in the eye. Whatever could get him out of the dreary neighborhood and into the current of adventure was what he wanted. The Vietminh would gladly do that for Van Hieu.

The other boy, Dac Pho, grew up in a typical Red River delta village outside the city. His and all the village families were dirt-poor and dependent on two rice crops a year. Other than an unusually serious countenance, the plain-looking young man was hardly distinguishable from the other village boys. His complexion was somewhat ruddy, feet bare with splayed "rice pad-dy toes." His embarrassed smile and timid eyes indicated an almost painful shyness.

Both families, the Phams and the Nguyens, observed French law for the most part, read whatever was available to read, and listened to propaganda on the street. Both families paid taxes, one with money, the other with rice. Both families struggled a fair bit to get on with life.

The Vietminh had made inroads, but it was the French who controlled the Tonkin region where they lived. Still, if the tide turned just a bit, and if a convincing Vietminh team came through the village or into the neighbor-hood, there could be another set of rules and more taxes to pay. Nobody was happy about such arrangements, but living at the bottom of the food chain, the village farmers and the oppressed city folk could grumble only to them-selves. They were the ones left watching as sons and sometimes daughters went off to one of the competing armies, either the Vietminh of the commu-nist People's Army or the National Army complementing the colonial French Force.

Over the years and decades, the French presence had devastated Vietnam culture. The proud and ancient mandarin system was largely undone by mod-ernization and French contempt. Over time, the disrespect shown Mr. Pham soured any allegiance the family had to their self-professed protectors. Van Hieu suspected but never knew for certain that his father was a member of a secret society striving for independence. There were many secret societ-ies and clandestine political parties among the indigenous. The French were sensitive and punitive regarding what they viewed as potential insurrection. There had been demonstrations and several revolutions over the years. All were crushed with a heavy hand.

Nguyen Dac Pho, the farmer's son, was recruited by a Vietminh team—told that the people, the People's Army, needed his assistance in the Viet Bac region. Not one to resist given direction, and his family too timid to oppose, he left home to become a civilian laborer, a coolie. Had he not agreed, the team would have been more insistent. Like most, the boy pliantly accepted what life served him, knowing better than to offend.

Little could the Nguyen and Pham boys appreciate in 1951 that their days of *fútbol* were over. They were suddenly on divergent life paths that would eventually channel them back together into the nucleus of a world that would affect millions everywhere.

1950, Thanks to China

In Vietnam, the People's Army grew and strengthened with time, as did Ho Chi Minh's communist Indo-China Party. In France, a strong segment of her citizens, including politicos, were opposed to the Indochina War. Always more money and matériel were needed for the French to maintain control in Vietnam. But then came another blow. In 1949 the People's Liberation Army across the Vietnamese border in China defeated the American-supported Chinese Nationalists. Large stocks of American war matériel were abandoned on the Chinese mainland by the Nationalists. Those of the defeated who could, escaped to the island of Formosa, which would be renamed Taiwan. Through that victory, China's Mao Zedong and his Red Army were in a position to significantly upgrade the Vietminh war effort against the French.

A formal agreement was signed committing China to support Ho Chi Minh in establishing a communist government throughout Vietnam. The war was expanded. Experienced Chinese cadre trained Vietminh troops and formed them into conventional units with modern arms and proven tactics. The cost of the French-Indochina War escalated significantly with the Chinese infusion of support.

The one robust free nation in the world at that time was the United States. Not wishing to condone colonialism but deathly fearful of rampant communism, hard decisions were forced. Rather than allow Indochina to go communist, the US extended increased support to the French effort. There remained the ebb and flow of contesting belligerents at war, but costing more for all concerned: Vietnam, China, Russia, and the US. For the French to gain control anywhere outside the city centers was slow going and often not at all. Going after Vietminh sanctuaries and training centers in China was ruled out. There was no appetite to provoke a Chinese military response, especially not after the Chinese crossed the border into Korea so recently and so heartily.

Meanwhile, training and sanctuary continued in China for Vietminh troops who freely crossed the border. The Viet Bac region of far northwest

Vietnam, virtually inaccessible to the French Force, began to fill with large stocks of matériel and well-trained Vietminh troops. The French were well aware of the centralized stores and activity there but struggled to counter it. Penetrating the Viet Bac in force had never been done. That would change.

Nguyen the Coolie

His thoughts drifted back two years to where he began as a civilian laborer on a roadwork crew. The first days and weeks had been difficult and painful. It was a mental as well as physical challenge, and more than enough of both. In time, however, his work hardening replaced angst with feelings of accomplishment. For the first time in his life, other than in *fútbol*, the introvert Nguyen began to feel connected with those around him.

To be a coolie meant not only to work hard but to always be hungry. Growing up in the village, there was never too much food, meals being simple and nominal but adequate. Obesity was not known except for the very rich, and the very rich did not live in the village. Everyone worked hard, few calories were stored, none wasted.

In the coolie work crews, living and working together, sharing all and dealing with the challenges of each day as a team was the norm. Some days the teams mourned a lost comrade or a failure of some kind. The washout of yesterday's work was pitiful. But there was also camaraderie, and each day the team contributed methodically and patiently. Propaganda helped too. With only one side to the propaganda coin, there was little to question. It was dedication and effort that would overcome and build a new society free of French tyranny.

Exhausted and even dazed at times by the effort, Nguyen Dac Pho performed as best he could. Then a reputation began to build around him in a strange way. He hadn't realized it, but at math he was a crackerjack—downright gifted. To him, numbers were common sense. Consequently he began sharing simple calculations within his work crew, offering generally accurate estimates of labor hours for given projects. Encouraged by a competent team leader and aided by experience, his estimates improved while his confidence grew. His calculations provided a better balance of labor, making the crew more efficient. Although it was often engineering that calculated material needs for projects, the hands-on Nguyen could better detail the orderly need for them. When the right materials were available, the project continued without hitting work delays and unnecessary frustrations. Greater efficiency improved morale and even diminished accidents.

It wasn't long before his crew's quotas were being consistently met, often despite common, unanticipated problems. Sometimes it was weather-related issues, and other times it was sickness or injury slowing a project. Soil density, water, and rock formations also created slowdowns. Yet Nguyen's crew consistently matched or exceeded the production of the other crews. Quiet and shy though he was, coolie Nguyen became popular and respected. The success of the work crew was noticed. Unannounced, an inspector showed up one day to inspect and account for their superior productivity. His two-word report to The Party: "Coolie efficiency."

August 1952, Nguyen Dac Pho

After successful assaults, General Giap's three new divisions were suddenly up to their armpits in the frantic effort to get refitted and resupplied. They had overrun a series of small French forts in the High Region but were suddenly ordered some hundred kilometers south. The opportunity to catch a large and vulnerable French Force was available to them.

The fallback position for the French Force survivors of the recently vanquished forts was to collect at the valley of Na-San, where a well-positioned French post would be fortified to defend them all. One problem: the Na-San valley was many kilometers from supply depots. But there was an airstrip. It was strengthened and lengthened so air transport could be the supply line. General Giap, with his new Vietminh divisions, was well aware of the Na-San limitations. He knew he must strike before fortifications in the valley were complete. But first things first.

The organization and resources necessary to support such a Vietminh operation were challenging. With little experience in moving an army of division size and greater, it was necessary to mark time—several weeks, in fact, before beginning the march to Na-San. Russian motorized vehicles were coming online—they needed fuel and the troops needed rations. Not enough porters; they were hard to come by in the sparsely populated hills. Guns and rifles were low on ammunition from the recent French fort attacks. With General Giap's first opportunity to cut down a combined French Force, everything that could go wrong pretty much went that way.

Ready to move out or not, no division force would get far without a traversable surface for wheeled and motorized vehicles. Coolie work crews had been tasked to provide that surface, time was of the essence, and Nguyen Dac Pho's crew was assigned the lead.

By then, Nguyen was working with the team leader and even the engineers. Nguyen was able to provide realistic estimates of labor and time necessary to drive pilings for bridges, for example, and the number of coolies needed to clear foliage and stay ahead of digging crews as trails were widened and solidified. Often, in the past, the process had been held up unnecessarily when a clear understanding of what was needed would have made all the difference. Something as simple as the number of shovels and cubic meters of filler soil needed to span a swamp could make a great difference.

Nguyen, dull and reserved as he had seemed, matured with his gift and provided a good deal of common sense. The engineers came to know what was helpful for the work crew to know, and the coolies began volunteering helpful information through the team leader. Working smarter was the theme.

15 October 1953, 57th Regiment, People's Army

Guerilla fighters categorically despised formations, especially when the troops were required to stand at attention or parade rest for extended periods of time. The 57th was a regiment of three infantry battalions and an artillery battalion. From their guerilla band origin, they had evolved into a conventional unit of some distinction. However, the core soldiers resented the impersonal formality to which their army had come. Formations and close-order drills became requirements: right face, forward march, and all that.

But it was a beautiful morning! The birds sang with excitement while the soldiers stood in formation, waiting for the commander to arrive. It wasn't unusual to wait. This was an army, an army of many moving parts after all.

The air temperature was warm but not enough to break a sweat, especially while standing immobile in formation. The result was a nauseous feeling for some. The troops were dehydrated, yes, or maybe last month's touch of malaria was the nausea catalyst. Like it mattered—it didn't.

The regimental staff people were the lucky ones. They had shade from the stand of cinnamon trees on the east side of the clearing. Mature trees— looked to be twenty meters from ground to tip. Napalm canisters had barely missed enflaming them the year before. French napalm accounted for much of the clearing in which the troops now stood. The tree shade was welcome, the air was humid, and the stationary troops remained stifled.

Such a regimental formation was just what the French Force dreamt of coming up against. An entire regiment in close quarters could be slaughtered utterly. That would not be the problem of the day. And should a maverick plane fly over them, the regiment would rely on camouflage for protection. Their camouflage skills had been proven over and over. Within seconds, Colonel Ky's full regiment would become to the aerial onlooker a verdant field. Each soldier was responsible to provide fresh flora to the soldier ahead of him or her, which had already been done. Everyone lying quietly on the ground created a bucolic effect. It would be only the security details not present and in formation.

There was no enemy known to be in the area, but regiments were precious tools of the Vietminh requiring ongoing security. Give or take, there were fifteen hundred troops at that time in the regiment, including staff. Technically shorthanded, the numbers were always a give-and-take proposition, with new troops coming in and others lost for whatever reasons. The 57th Regiment was a carryover from before the Chinese program of building conventional units. Guerilla units were yet effective and useful, but it was the new conventional army that could turn the tide and potentially win the war.

Jungle, however, was still the natural element of the 57th, not parade ground formalities. Being called to regimental formation likely meant a mission that encompassed the entire regiment. That was a big deal. Simply gathering as a regiment was a big deal. There was always the potential for airstrikes or artillery fire put upon them if the French could pinpoint their location. There were, after all, French artillery batteries within fifteen or twenty kilometers, and French airpower was always worthy of respect. It seemed the colonel would be making an important point or passing on a general order whenever he decided to make his appearance.

The command group did break from the colonel's shelter, which was a tattered yet functional GP-Medium tent left over from World War II. The deputy commander performed first. "Reg-i-ment!" The command was gruffly repeated down-level to battalion to company to platoon level. "Ten-hut!" and three thousand feet snapped together as hands slapped thighs.

Many of the troops did not care for such displays of colonialism as they saw it. It was mostly the ranking officers and especially the turncoats of whatever rank who appreciated the resonating sound of *thwack!* the way they had been trained. For the former Nationalists, the formation drills were a familiar sense of security and cohesion. For them it was a collective strength and pride in the sound of all things clicking in unison. Beyond that, officers of all stripes sensed control in the unison movements, control being the salve of confidence. "Pa-rade rest!" and fifteen hundred feet stomped the earth in unison. Admitted or not, there was energy in those collective sounds.

The anxiety of being addressed by the regimental commander and the joint execution of commands, plus the bump of another degree in temperature, broke the spell. Like yesterday and many yesterdays before that, body pores at that certain point magically opened in their unique sync. It was like hearing a musical's overture for the first or the hundredth time—expected or not, an uplifting experience. As beads of perspiration appeared, tensions lessened. All in all, there was the breath of fresh calm settling the troops into a new day.

Then he appeared. With the assistance of an aide's firm shoulder, the slender, slight-framed man stepped up and onto the makeshift dais. As usual, neither the commander's scowling countenance nor his rigid posture was compromised by the assistance given him. The colonel had been in it even before the war had been proclaimed in November of '46. He was not a kid and certainly no fool. At the prime military age of thirty-five, the colonel did not suffer fools lightly.

His eyes casually swept the sea of rigid subordinates before him. Then his mind's eye glazed over for several seconds. To the regiment it seemed longer than seconds. His mind sifted through faces no longer there. An image of the hamlets and villages those faces came from pressed his mind. He saw the frail fathers of fallen patriots, the still-squabbling mothers, squatting comfortably in a circle chewing the betel nut, teeth black and rotted. Mama-san wasn't pregnant again and not likely to be—too old now. Briefly, their pain touched him. It seemed to the knowledgeable Colonel Ky that the war would continue until either the French lost the support of America or until Ho Chi Minh could produce no more patriots. How those aspects of the war were going he did not know. *The fallen have died with purpose,* he assured himself.

At that point he paused his mind and collected himself. There was a slight breeze from the south. No whine of aircraft, no dogs barking, the message could begin.

The impromptu dais was an ancient anthill. Colonel Ky was able to identify the hero by the red crescent sewn on his breast pocket, a mark of distinguished valor. He also recognized that the replacement platoon appeared nervous and anxious. *This is good. This will go well,* he told himself. Other than that, the young private was indistinguishable from the other replacements, some not quite mature enough for whiskers. *Ninety-one new privates for the month. Not enough, but ninety-one helps,* Ky reasoned.

The colonel would give his message once—all personnel at one time. There was to be no misunderstanding. Details were vital to the success of the colonel and to the regiment.

The colonel began his speech by directing it to the replacement platoon. He had heard plenty about this Nguyen Dac Pho. The colonel was ready for him, this so-called hero.

"My personal welcome to replacement troops," he boomed. But he did not smile. "A number of you have been here for some weeks, but this is my first opportunity to greet you personally. Welcome." He then paused, scanning the new troops again, this time for effect. Finally he pointed at Private Nguyen. All new soldiers seemed to look alike, but the colonel knew his man. "Private Nguyen Dac Pho, is it not?"

Nguyen's wide, innocent eyes carried an anxious but hopeful expression. The boy was a classic village Vietnamese. If nothing else, his bare feet sold him as a peasant boy, and he likely had not volunteered for service. It pleased the new soldier that soon he would be sporting tire sandals suitable for marching now that he was a real Vietminh. There had been no basic training for him, but he had picked up Vietminh vernacular while recovering, and as a coolie he had seen plenty of military protocol. Despite the disadvantage, Nguyen Dac Pho was now Private Nguyen Dac Pho, conscripted and assigned to the 57th Regiment. He was still humble but less naïve and aware of the vulnerability of being a private.

As in all armies in all wars, the saying remains common and is often true: ignorance is bliss. The innocence of young warriors is the bread of life to the military, as is their courage the wine to wash it down. Whatever Private Nguyen was or could have been elsewhere, he was then and there in the French-Indochina War for the duration. There were no three- or four-year enlistments; no two-year draftees, and no twelve- or thirteen-month tours in the war zone. Whether conscript or volunteer, like everyone else, Private Nguyen was to be engaged as long as he had the capacity to do so or until the war ended. He had not volunteered.

It was about a year after saving the howitzer that Nguyen was healed up enough to be inducted. Detached from the coolie program, he was assigned to Colonel Ky's 57th Regiment. He was startled to be personally addressed by an officer, much less a colonel, his regimental commander. The entire regiment was instantly alert. They knew the name Nguyen Dac Pho, and a noticeable surge of energy rippled through the ranks. The veterans who comprised the bulk of the regiment, however, knew the colonel did not call out a soldier without reason. Some of the troops, especially the newer ones, felt a giddiness of pride to now be serving with a celebrity. For the veterans it was a cautious curiosity, knowing well the colonel's disposition.

It began casually enough. "With others here, Private Nguyen, you are a welcome replacement with the 57th Regiment. We depend on you and all comrades with your great courage." He bowed ever so slightly and then intoned less casually, "You are what—famous, I think it is fair to say?"

Already standing at parade rest, Private Nguyen involuntarily stiffened, embarrassed but also proud. He understood the question to be rhetorical.

Colonel Ky continued, "We do not know you. We know *of* you, but I do not know you. Please help me to understand." There came then a certain clamminess to his tone. "You are a hero of all who love and revere our Great Leader, Uncle Ho Chi Minh. All these soldiers," he waved his arms across the field, "are true Vietnam patriots, a tribute to our Great Leader."

The colonel paused just long enough for the Ho Chi Minh reference to be appropriately absorbed and honored. Being a man of some ambition and learned of political bearing and theatre, the colonel played his part well. With facial gesturing coming up barely shy of a cruel smile, he began again. This time it was with drawn-out words that seemed to whine from his mouth. "Youuuu aaaare fleshhhh, are you not, Private?"

"Uh, sir—I am flesh, sir?" Private Nguyen was confused by the question. Had he heard wrong? He was aware he must be on his toes with officers and especially with commanders and political commissars, but he didn't expect to be called out at his first formation. He did not know where this was going, but if the colonel meant to be intimidating, he was.

"Please tell how it is our countrymen hail you as martyr while you yet stand in formation before me. How can you be a martyr when you are quite living? By all appearance you are alive, is that not so?" The colonel was pleased by the highly unusual snickering coming from the ranks. Others felt the anxiousness of the private's circumstance. The colonel had anticipated and counted on the former. Then the commander's voice colored brightly with sarcasm. "Of course—*that* is why you are a martyr. Of all people in Vietnam, in Indochina, Nguyen Dac Pho is the one coolie to make the ultimate sacrifice. You have thrown your own body under the wheel of a howitzer to stop it from crashing off a mountain. Your body saved the five-thousand-pound cannon. Is that not so, Private Nguyen?"

"Uh. Yes, sir."

"Please speak loudly, Private Nguyen. The whole of the regiment must know of your heroism."

Self-conscious and feeling defenseless, the frightened village boy knew he must show deference to the commander. *I am not ambitious if that is what the colonel thinks,* he told himself. *I simply want to perform my duty, to perform faithfully and without issue until the war is behind us.* His greatest wish was to return to his village and begin a family. That would please the ancestors and his parents.

Clearing his throat, Nguyen spoke as graciously as he could in a surprisingly loud voice. The words came out raspy, surprising only himself. "I am told that, sir. I have no memory after the gun began to roll and the earth gave way."

The colonel's voice raised. He had hoped this one to be so perplexed by the question he would respond with babble. *At least I have humiliated him.*

Now I will make the hero dig deep. "You say that was you, but you do not remember? If you do not remember, perhaps it was someone else." *This hero will not slide off the hook so easily,* the commander promised himself. The insults took on a hard and searing quality. "You are more deserving than your comrades here? These comrades who have faced fire by such howitzers as you say you saved? Our ranks of comrades who have felt the never-ending burn of white phosphorous and the insufferable heat of napalm delivered by devils from the sky? These comrades who turn and then spit in the face of the cowardly French Force—and ultimately will defeat them? More deserving of honors are you than the devoted commander who delivers such heroes as these?"

Those last words squealed like a tin clarion inside Nguyen's head. *"Commander who delivers such heroes as these?"* Stabbing at Nguyen or not, the words cracked open the door to understanding what was happening. *I am a threat? I am only a replacement with a reputation I never asked for. The commander assumes credit for his troops' actions and rightly so, but how does my presence steal his gallantry?* It was confusing, but Nguyen knew that Ho Chi Minh had, again and again the past year, proclaimed the saving of the cannon a noble act performed by a true patriot, a patriot all citizens should aspire to. Being new to soldiery, and immediately rebuked by his commander, made for Private Nguyen an ill-omened first day.

Feign ignorance is what I must do. Be humble and contrite while praising the colonel and my comrades. Within a minute after that the private felt his mind glaze over. His eyes remained focused, but he was tired, his back ached, but at least he appeared composed. In his year of recovery, he had seen officers compete in their less-than-manly gamesmanship, touting where and how they served and with whom, and the praises of their latest review. An embarrassment to overhearing privates, it was also dangerous for a private to know of such things. Nguyen Dac Pho had volunteered for none of it.

Colonel Ky took a breath and silently reviewed his theory as the regiment waited at parade rest. *Why is this private in my regiment?* he could ask only himself. *Does the Great Leader believe patriotic fervor can be heightened with a hero in my regiment? The comrades here will envy him and be jealous of him. Morale will suffer. Is it possible he was placed in my regiment because his presence will poison me?* It had been declared and he had assumed the coolie was killed by the howitzer. *Of course he would be killed if that actually happened. This village fool has been touted as a martyr for the past year. If it is announced that he survived and is here, I will become a dupe fostering the dead hero who lives. I can easily imagine the slights and jokes at my expense. "The commander of the 57th Regiment is a fool," they will say. But,* he decided, *I would gladly accept the honors bestowed upon a dead martyr. Alive he makes me a fool, but dead the martyr paints me with the shimmer and gloss of his presumed heroics.* A dark cloud hanging over Ky suddenly brightened. *This hero stands at parade rest to my front! He is all mine.*

Colonel Ky did not see himself as a callous man, but there was no question that losing troops on the battlefield flared rather than diminished his aggressiveness. Some could interpret that as defensiveness, but oh well. Today was different. It was the pressures, the circumstances, the beautiful morning—something about the day had allowed him to think of the casualties and those killed in action. *That was a slip. No more. My job, my duty, is to send young men and women into harm's way for the cause of ultimate victory, and that is all.*

Recently the colonel had begun to think in terms of promotion. *Why not? My regiment is well trained and more capable than ever. I have studied Chinese tactics. Through my regiment the People's Army now chooses battles to win, not simply to harass. We will no longer rely on taking punishment from the enemy only to weaken him, but, rather, I now deliver the punishment, and that punishment will be recognized. As commander I am resolute and aggressive. No longer do I hold back in the face of opportunity. My regiment is to be in action, in the news, and its commander the acknowledged hero. All the more reason no snot-nose coolie or private will be allowed to belittle my regiment and me. I, a true Vietminh hero who has scrapped, fought, and contrived myself past any number of captains, majors, and lieutenant colonels. I have endured, and I have earned this position of distinction. Colonel Ky is a man of action and distinction. That will not change! I will not change! I will attack as never before on all fronts!*

During the internal rant, Private Nguyen remained silent and ramrod straight, eyes fixed ahead, all the while feeling the rage coming from the dais. He could only hope Colonel Ky would soon realize that his emotional state and shrill words were neither reasonable nor productive. *Or do all colonels behave in this manner?* Nguyen wished he were not a hero and surely not a private in the 57th Regiment.

The colonel's voice lowered but only briefly. Not giving it up he then punched out question after question: "Was it you? Maybe all a lie—propaganda? Who was crushed under the wheel? Anyone? Did it happen at all?"

Nguyen dared not react. *The commander's knowledge of the matter is lacking. He must not be further antagonized.* Such was Nguyen's good sense.

In his home village as in the military, it was proper to be contrite when conversing with an elder or any authority. Nguyen focused his attention on a small stone in front of his feet. Only his gaze differed from the rigid pa-rade-rest position being maintained by the entire regiment. There was no eye contact.

Colonel Ky accepted the deference shown by the private's slightly bowed head. Seconds passed.

At last it seemed to the private a respectable hesitation. Nguyen nodded his head almost imperceptibly and raised as kindly a gaze as he could toward Colonel Ky. "Sir," he began, "such a thing did indeed occur. Perhaps I can explain in a more comfortable setting."

A logical suggestion it was, but quite horrifying to the commander. His stiffening face added a distinct wariness feature to the colonel's already hag-gard appearance.

This private is presuming I am to follow his instruction? Ky's mind raged. Such a piercing statement could come from a general officer, perhaps, or a highly placed diplomat or politician, but not from a private. *Do the village sons and daughters here recognize the insult given by this replacement?* the colonel asked himself. The boy had presumed what the commander should do! While on the surface it may have seemed harmless, its lack of protocol was insulting and demeaning to say the least. Fortunately, anyone who rec-ognized the insult would not dare to comment. Surely it would be as though it had never happened. One thing certain: it was paramount that the colonel maintain control. To lose face would be nearly as bad as losing his command. There was no question he would act in a manner showing a strong hand.

Everyone knew that to be Vietnamese was to read between the lines all that was spoken and a good deal that was left entirely unsaid. Much could be conveyed in ways most subtle. Colonel Ky could be sure that many of his officers and non-commissioned officers interpreted the private's statement for what it was: passive effrontery.

On the other hand, no one could say for certain what was behind the comment, and the troops may have accepted it as respecting the command-er's position, that this was a matter best discussed between commander and hero. Perhaps that was reasonable for the troops. If so, they must learn differently.

Can there be more to this than an imbecile boy making trouble for him-self? Not likely, the Colonel decided. His next thought was the former polit-ical commissar. *Could that have anything to do with this?* he wondered. *Is not every soldier in the regiment subservient to the commander? Every last soldier must know absolutely that his or her place is to respond to the com-mander, not the other way around. Likely this Private Nguyen is a truly igno-rant waif from some isolated and insignificant village. Resolution is simple:*

I will simply have him dispatched. Snuffed like a candle. A wonderful tool, the summary execution. The imbeciles of the regiment must internalize the need to honor the rules of courtesy and command. Private Nguyen can have martyrdom—at least for those who wish to believe in such things. He will be a martyr who can no longer offend me nor make a fool of me.

The colonel raised a shaky finger toward Private Nguyen. Just then, and uncharacteristically, Deputy Commander Major Vuong interrupted the commander with a muffled cough.

"Please to excuse, Colonel. I too must add a voice of honor. Today is a great occasion in the presence of the new comrade known for bravery and extreme sacrifice. He is now one of the family, a member of the 57th Regiment. Private Nguyen's courage and sacrifice add to the colonel and the regiment's distinction and resolve to quash the tyrannical French Force. We shall soon evict all capitalists and colony masters from this land."

Colonel Ky took a short breath. *What is this? The major's remarks are clearly political.* It then occurred to him that the major was now the acting commissar. The former regimental commissar had gone down more than a week ago. Ky had made a report to The Party, and soon after, orders designating the major as acting commissar had arrived. It seemed odd that The Party would try to operate this way—a field-grade officer acting as commissar. *I certainly prefer not to have a commissar, but since we must, it is fine that Major Vuong be it—as long as he doesn't go extreme. This interruption of his is not a good beginning.*

Ky resisted his typical scowl. He offered instead a thinly patronizing smile, realizing it didn't matter why such a brazen remark had been thrown at his feet by a green private. *Soon enough I will take care of him. Private Nguyen is a total disruption to the regiment. The Russian and Chinese press will likely want to interview him. But if the boy has become a true martyr, the foreign press will find a much better interview with the regimental commander.*

There then appeared an authentic smile.

Colonel Ky orated to himself while Major Vuong orated to the troops a dandy speech of courage and glory. All the while, Ky remained on the dais, nodding and smiling, the wheels of his mind whirring and rambling. *Perhaps, rather than summary execution, it may be best if this private becomes a simple training accident. The name Colonel Ky must come forward as the true hero of the people. Or would that be General Ky?* Perhaps it was a better day than he had anticipated.

August 1952, Private Pham Van Hieu

The replacement platoon stood at attention before him. The entire regiment was formed behind the replacements. Commander, 141st Regiment, Colonel Dau began, as was common, with the replacements. His address to them was their first. It was important for the commander to pick out a new soldier to make an example of—get them all off on the right foot. Within seconds he found what he was looking for. He began. "Excuse me, please. Mr. Pham? Pham is your family name?" The hand-scrawled name presented itself on a dirty shirt. The boy-soldier was disheveled, clothes and body lacking hygiene.

"Yes, sir. Private Pham Van Hieu." The voice was strong but tired.

"So, Private Pham Van Hieu, what have you to say for yourself?"

"Sir, I was not sleeping," but the voice rang defensive. "My eyes have been open since you began talking. I walked most of the night to be here. Sir." He rested his case, hoping that would be the end of it.

The People's Army and Pham Van Hieu had melded well in the beginning, but that was more than a year ago. The young private was pleasant and surprisingly confident. His was a city background centering on neighborhood gangs and roughhousing, neither of which appealed to him. At the tender age of sixteen, he had been identified by an embedded Vietminh agent as a potential asset to the effort. The French controlled the city of Haiphong, but still The Party was able to recruit there. It helped that the boy was promised academic advancement and a great future by the agent.

After only a few weeks of indoctrination with the local underground irregular platoon, he was sent to the Communist International Academy, known simply as Comintern. It was a year-long program for gifted recruits and potential leaders in the growing communist system. A battery of tests and interviews suggested Pham Van Hieu's aptitudes and people skills could lead to a future in administration, military, or even governance. He performed well in the year-long academy and was assigned to the 141st Regiment, a separate regional unit. His work was to be covert, a political officer or commissar unknown to the regiment. He would go undercover as a private. It would be his trial by fire, a true test. If there was something suspicious within the command, Private Pham was to find it and report it to The Party. Standing there in formation, it seemed to the young private there was already suspicion regarding the commander.

Years before, Ho Chi Minh himself had been trained at the original Comintern Academy in Moscow. At least as far back as 1920, Ho's dream was to form and lead a Communist Party in Vietnam. With support from Russia and within China's borders, he believed he could help convert all of Indochina's sects and clandestine politics to communism. Ho successfully catered to both competing powers in China, the Nationalists of Chiang Kai Shek, and the Reds of Mao Zedung. At that time he was a thirty-year-old and not leader of anything. Nevertheless, he was on the move, having been a founding member of the French Communist Party in 1920.

As a youth, Ho had left Vietnam in 1911 and did not return for thirty years. He traveled the world, furthered his education in France and Moscow, and spent most of those years investing in communism, often in China, and under assumed names everywhere. Before settling on the name Ho Chi Minh when he returned to Vietnam near the end of World War II, he had used at least fifty assumed names and perhaps as many as two hundred aliases. The stately and historic Parker House Hotel in Boston, Massachusetts laid claim to employing Ho Chi Minh as a pastry chef in 1912. Ho sailed the world for a number of those years, working as a shipboard cook.

The Soviet Union was the first to support Ho's military and political ambitions. Moscow replicated the local Comintern Academy in Vietnam after Ho proved he could consolidate power there. Up until then, a few hand-picked Vietnamese were sent to Moscow each year for training. As expected, the local program proved more effective than the distractions, challenges, and temptations of a foreign culture and big city. In no time the school was humming with activity and churning out graduates. It was sure to cushion the distinct need for proper-thinking leaders and skilled administrators in a liberated Indochina. Joe Stalin and his Soviet Union willingly invested in communist domination over the West.

The academy was placed in the snug Viet Bac region where it would be safe near the Chinese border. A topography of no roads, trails only, and a heavily forested range of hills with natural caves kept the Viet Bac safe from outsiders. Access was tenuous and the rugged terrain hostile to all but the sometimes-inglorious revolutionaries over the ages.

Pham was a good student. He was intellectually hungry and smart enough to keep a lid on the growing ambitions inside him. He had grown up weary of the mandarin self-image. At the academy, it did not take long for Private Pham to see a bright future for himself. After the war, with the benefit of military experience, he could fully advance himself. Studying law in Paris or Hanoi would be a solid beginning and perhaps lead to politics.

Upon graduation from Comintern, he had anticipated the equivalent of a Vietminh officer's commission. Being given instead a clandestine position as a private was taken as a rebuke. Then he wised up. His gifts of intellect and guile were ideal to secretly review leadership at the regimental level. It was a rare but dangerous opportunity, he was told. The Party did have concerns with certain regiments, and Pham Van Hieu was to quietly investigate, incognito. Presently the 141st Regional Regiment had no political commissar, although Private Pham was about to change that without anyone knowing. He was given a cover story and told not to disclose his mission to anyone under any circumstance. It would be dangerous if he were found out. Too many commissars were being lost, some perhaps mysteriously. His orders were to report only to The Party. Any suspicious activity that was counter to Ho Chi Minh ideals and The Party was to be documented and reported. Private Pham could not help but smile at the prospect of assumed authority. The posting would lead to even greater opportunities, although what could be greater than clandestine authority at the regimental level? Now he would be where adventure lived and thrived. That was for certain.

"Open, perhaps," the questioning from the dais continued, "but vacant. If you do not respect your comrades, you do not respect your commander, Private Pham. If you do not respect me, you do not respect the People's Army, and you do not respect the Great Leader. You bring shame to the Vietminh family. Is that not true, Private Pham?"

"Sir." Private Pham paused, then softly muttered, "If you say, it must be true, sir." Softer yet, "I was thinking of family—thinking fondly of Mother." It was the first thing he could come up with.

"Of course you were. This is normal."

Private Pham heard reprieve if not clemency in the remark.

Colonel Dau's voice softened to something of a paternal tone. "This is your first time away from family and village?" He did not wait for an answer. "Adjustment can be tiresome. This will pass quickly for a soldier of character and discipline." The hardened tone then returned. "Are not soldiers—good soldiers—are they not people of character and discipline?" Again the commander did not wait for an answer. "Did you not celebrate the funeral your village provided for you?" It was an honor to be given a funeral before leaving the village for war. Yes, the colonel had assumed. "Were you not honored, then, and the woman who gave birth to you—did she not weep with other women as you went off to serve the people? After all, you are no longer a child, Private Pham. As with all soldiers of this regiment—of this People's Army—you have the responsibility to serve faithfully and proudly. Soldiers as one, together with all others, will achieve destiny and defeat the French tyrants. Or perhaps your commander is wrong and does not sufficiently understand?"

Private Pham certainly looked the part of village bumpkin, and that is what he would be from then on.

"No, sir; no, sir. I apologize to you and all soldiers." Smiling on the inside, Pham enjoyed performing phony prostration. "I allowed distraction by my weak thoughts. This will not happen again, sir. Your words benefit me greatly. Comrades, my new brothers and sisters, please help me in this transition to the regional force."

The air then became still, the silence thick. Seconds ticked by slowly and loudly in Private Pham's mind. A rattled thought struck him. *The colonel expects more? My kowtowing was good, I thought.* Pham's self-assured mind seldom let him down. He scrambled to think of what must be done. Finally, "I—I thank you for adjusting my thoughts and actions, sir. I wish to be a soldier of character and discipline, to offer strength and deliver action to benefit the people. Thank you, sir." He bowed low and humbly. Again he bowed.

Colonel Dau very nearly smiled. The exchange demonstrated an element of what had been taught at Comintern. There would be others. Colonel Dau could see he had a good one with Private Pham. He didn't know this good one was a commissar.

A recent contact with the French Force had ravaged a company of the 141st caught in the open. Ambush had been the Vietminh forte, but they were not immune to ambush themselves. It is also true that any attack invites casualty and death, especially when artillery or aircraft becomes involved. On that recent occasion, the successful ambush of a French patrol ended with the overhead arrival of two F8F-1 Bearcats dropping cylinders of napalm on the Vietminh. In the engagement, six of the 141st troops had been incinerated, another four left painfully alive, and the remainder of the company forever scarred by the memory. It was those four canisters of napalm that brought Pham Van Hieu and three conscripts to the 141st Vietminh Regiment as replacements.

Ghastly was a fair description of casualty by napalm. The result of contact was the stench of burning flesh and flora mixed with the foulness of chemicals, gasoline, and god-awful screams. The flash and waves of incinerating heat in the mixture's bouncing center prompted, in that incident, a wave of dread that passed on to the balance of the regiment. Although the bulk of the troops were not involved, reports by the survivors were searing and emotionally invasive. The stories became something of a joint relief at not being subjected to the napalm but tinged by being related to those who were. It was a solemn joy only they could share.

Hard-core troops survived in many ways. Passed on to rookies was the intentioned bullet myth—or truth it was if you were a survivor. "The bullet with your name on it will find you. It will turn corners to do you. Seriously. Want to survive? Accept the grunt way." Shared victimhood became a kinship and fatalism another reprieve.

As for the severely wounded? Survival for them hinged on resistance to infection. The regiment moved on and the victims' futures lost to history but presumed dead. Somewhere mothers waited. Military actions continued. More casualties. More replacements.

Replacements were seldom enough and hardly ever were they even a short-term answer. Drawing from irregular platoons, the replacements were largely blank slates. Watchdog work, intelligence, and mild subterfuge against the enemy was the typical extent of their experience. Often enough the irregular platoon soldiers were accustomed to stress and familiar enough with sleep deprivation due to the nighttime ploys. Burying a mine or two in the road was hard work in compacted soil. Setting a tripwire mine or booby trap on a trail was easier and the saboteur not as likely to be caught. Generally it was training with the regional units that made for combat-hardened soldiers. Many boy-soldiers looked forward to being just that.

One caution: If there were mass casualties in an irregular platoon's backyard, it was they who cleaned up the mess. Why? The regionals would be tactically involved with the enemy, and the regulars whose mission the original attack was were long gone. There was little envy of cleanup work, especially when bodies were burned, disemboweled, or dismembered.

It was the forced smiles of Pham and other recruits that betrayed them. Otherwise they were just green recruits reporting to the regiment that first day in formation. The pretense of happiness and smiling was strong evidence of ignorance. It wasn't talked about, but there was a natural distancing between the old and the new. Replacements were poor excuses for the burned alive or torn-open and dismembered comrades. Replacement was only a word; rookies could not replace the lost. Replacements were forever a burden, a burden until proven otherwise. It was natural and even logical to resent them until they were no longer replacements. If a new soldier did not survive the transition, a likely prospect, then the veterans' distancing was worthwhile and no emotion wasted.

"You did not have a colonel or a commissar in your irregular platoon, Private Pham. Today you have both. This is Deputy Commander Major Tran, your commissar." By then Major Tran was also on the dais, and Colonel Dau seemed satisfied with the pound of flesh he had taken. Private Pham had been a good choice as victim. The regiment now felt aptly chastised and alert.

Major Tran began speaking to the formation. He was slick. "You have me, your acting commissar, Major Tran, to hear you—to support you. I listen to concerns when you suffer, I offer suggestions for you to do well here. If you have a problem, I have a problem." And on he went with his lecture.

Private Pham wondered why the major was acting as commissar. *Does The Party know? First opportunity I will report this.*

The Party believed itself to be all-knowing while at the same time afraid it may not be all-knowing. The commissar was the insurance policy. Theirs was absolute political authority of every unit and all personnel within each unit. The commissar held no rank and reported directly to The Party. The Party oversaw the actions of the military. Period. As for responsibilities, the commissar held the upper hand for party values, ethics, morale, cooperation, and sacrifice—even certain training. A good deal of attitude adjustment was performed by the commissars. They lectured, learned, and reported—intimidation for all. Sometimes the commissar was the problem. And sometimes the commissar wasn't the commissar.

"Bullshit. Total bullshit."

The hushed but gruff words came from someone close, but Private Pham dared not turn his head to see who it was. The words unnerved him more than he already was. "What?" Private Pham whispered, trying not to betray himself. "What?" he repeated.

Although undertoned, the voice was discernable. "All lies. He will sell you out. Do not believe him." Too loudly the voice finished, "I know it is bullshit."

Others heard talking in formation. That included Colonel Dau and the major. The ranks began to stir. The major stopped talking; the commander's body language said he was taking over. Tensions rose as the colonel slowly swept a visual over the regiment. The obvious was in front of him. "Private Pham."

Oh shit.

"I did not realize you had something further. What did you say?"

"Nothing, sir. That was not me." He wanted to believe the colonel was being facetious with his casual-sounding question. Pham's answer contained a degree of confidence. Then it occurred to him, *I am not the voice in question, but seconds ago, I did respond to it in my own voice. Did I just lie to my commander?*

"You are certain you said nothing, Private Pham?" Dau squinted. His eyes carried a wildness Private Pham had not yet seen. Now it was personal—again. "It is not good to begin service in 141st Regiment with lies." Then, staring directly into Pham's eyes, he slowly growled, "Not good at aaaall."

That got to him. Pham stammered, "S—sir, I said one thing, quietly, but I did not talk."

"One thing? It is proper to speak one thing in formation before spoken to, Private Pham? Where in hell you from, Private?"

"Only one word. Sir." He managed not to stutter that time.

"Ah, so it is proper to speak in formation if only one word. I see."

Now what could he say? "Sir, I can only tell you what I did. I now realize that was not proper. I apologize—will not happen again."

"I am certain, Private Pham. Now, you tell me—who was speaking if not you?"

A dozen or more thoughts went through Pham's mind. Finally, the barest of truths. "I do not know, sir. I fail to know the names of people in my regiment. I came here in the dark. Very late. Last night."

Colonel Dau chuckled for all the regiment to see. For some, the commander's chuckle lessened the tension. For Private Pham it did not. "As a green recruit you are most resourceful, Private Pham. I take it you do not know the name of soldier who spoke in formation." The voice became terse again. "Point out, please, the person who interrupted the regiment." With drawn-out, but strong emphasis he added, *"Now!"*

Even more intimidated, Pham had to risk alienating his new comrade. Out squeaked, "Sir, I did not see the speaker, but he is to my right."

Colonel Dau slowly nodded his head, taking his time about it. "Was it the gentleman next to you, Private?"

The private swallowed hard. "It may be, sir."

"*May* be?" That stare again. Colonel Dau let it hang there in the fashion of a simmering glare, directly at the young, supposedly naïve Private Pham.

Pham caved completely. "Yes, sir, I believe that is so." *Is there any way I can be more humiliated?* he internally cried. Feeling a flush of hotness course through his body, it occurred to him that he needed to consciously hold his water. Wetting himself would be counterproductive.

By now the commander had come off the dais, without assistance, and approached the replacement platoon. Looking into the eyes of Private Pham from a position of no more than a meter, his radiating, practiced glare was nothing short of inspirational. Colonel Dau's gaze then slowly turned to the man on Pham's right. Then, still slowly, back again at Pham. "What," he wanted to know, "did this soldier say, Private Pham?"

The emphasis on the word "soldier"—*what did that mean?* Private Pham felt it somehow significant.

Still intimidated, Private Pham needed to come clean. He didn't need or want friction with the commander. He did need to be the major's ally, and this would be the time to show he could muster up. Pham cleared his throat. "He say 'bullshit,' sir. 'It is all lies,' and we are not to believe what the commissar tells us. Sir."

Colonel Dau did not react to the words. He took his time again reviewing the young man to the right of Private Pham, slowly down the length of his body and back up, as the regiment held a collective breath. He leaned into the private, studied his nametag, then looked into his eyes for a full ten seconds or more. It lasted forever. The commander then nodded slightly and stood erect.

At that point, the subject of the commander's interest felt a bead of perspiration inch down his sternum, slowly at first, and then a cold, fast run to the belt. He dared not flinch.

"Is that so, Private Thom?" the commander asked the soldier to the right of Pham. "One week or two weeks ago you came to me with a problem, Private Thom? Is that right?"

"No, sir," the soldier stiffened. "I did not have a problem. It was three weeks."

The commander smiled. The regiment breathed. "I see. What problem did you *not* have three weeks ago, Private?"

"I hardly recall, sir. I maybe was accused of minor larceny. If so, it was not proven, sir. Perhaps that is what you speak of. Sir."

Private Pham was amazed his neighbor could speak with such gritty strength.

"Yes, I now recall. Thank you. Three weeks ago you were new here. Three weeks ago. Hmm. You responded to the accusation that you had stolen the fifty-piaster note found in your pocket. You brought it from the village, you said."

"That is true, sir. You then warned me; one more report will be serious trouble. I am certain there has not been one more report. Sir."

The commander lightly but deliberately squeezed his chin—slowly, of course. "No proof, the accusation was not proven, I believe was how that went. The accuser suggested you knew of the note when traveling here with you. He said you pilfered his pocket in the night. But," the colonel threw up his hands, "no proof."

"That is correct, sir. I was innocent. No proof."

"Nothing proved three weeks ago. Nothing proved now. Today is only the word of Private Pham. Please come with me, Private Thom. The regiment must see that no injustice comes to you."

The regiment was standing at a rigid parade rest the entire time, stiff legs by then complaining. This interaction, however, seemed to the regiment worth the mild distress. It was obvious something unusual and fascinating was about to happen.

"Of course, sir." Private Thom gave Pham a quick "fish eye," then broke ranks to follow Colonel Dau. The dais was large enough for them both, as Major Tran was now off to the side. The colonel motioned the private to step up first, then the colonel followed, without assistance this time, and stood behind the recruit.

Back in the ranks, Pham silently breathed relief into the universe. His first formation experience was almost over. It didn't please him to have alienated Private Thom, a new comrade. What was worse, he had been on the hot seat with Colonel Dau over nothing. Choosing an enemy between the colonel and Thom, however, Thom would be the loser every time. Still Pham was concerned. Would Thom be at all gracious toward him after this? He wondered, but not for long.

"Please speak to the regiment, Private Thom, of your innocence," commanded Dau. "Everyone can see and hear you."

For a village boy, Private Thom was unusually bold, as already witnessed. He was prominent now on the dais. Directly behind him stood Colonel Dau. This was Thom's opportunity to speak out and be known. He threw out his chest and spoke for all to hear.

"I was accused. Two times I was accused. But there was no proof. I was wronged. Comrades, be wary of lies, of false testament." He paused, choosing his next words carefully, mouth partly open.

Watching intently, Pham sensed something was off but not certain what. Was it that a lowly private was on the dais speaking to the regiment? Or was it because, in front of his regiment, the colonel was behind the private? Pham felt hyperawareness replacing fatigue.

It was at first overwhelming to come alone into a new unit. Everyone was a stranger, and his interaction with the commander nothing short of stunning. He could not allow himself to be crossed up with the commander, and his acceptance by the regiment was a priority. *If only they knew I was the commissar—the real commissar. Things would be different then. I have the authority and the responsibility to report such matters as this. Or do I?*

In the next instant, the actions on the dais melded into a surreal, slow-motion scene. A spurt of something from Private Thom's mouth was closely followed by an abrupt gurgle. In nearly the same instant Thom's penetrating eyes went blank as the background issued a muffled *pop*. It did not register with Private Pham. There was no sense to it. Then Private Thom began to shrink. He did not fall forward. He shrank to the sod floor, life escaping him like air from a punctured balloon. His body crumpled on the front edge of the dais. There was a sudden and distinct splatter of blood and gray matter on Thom's face. How had this come to be? The answer was revealed in Colonel Dau, standing there for all the world to see. In his hand a pistol. Not unlike the wake-up smell of coffee in the morning . . . the light morning breeze spread the burnt cordite smell.

Private Pham's slow conjecture only then crystallized as a weary expression of annoyed disgust colored the colonel. His face, too, was lightly speckled with red and gray matter, which was what seemed to explain his annoyance. A glance, a cursory look, completed the commander's review of the warm cadaver. A firm foot roll cleared it from the top of the dais, rolling down the anthill and into the dirt at the head of the replacement platoon. It stopped, frozen in a dead stare.

"Oh my God," Pham muttered. In those few seconds, a bucket of innocence was lost as ants began marking their territory.

As one, the formation of troops leaned ever so slightly forward, stiffly craning to see what they knew was there. Seconds passed. Then, pistol holstered, Colonel Dau moved to a parade- rest position himself—feet shoulder-width apart, hands together behind his back, standing tall. The troops edged back to their full position of parade rest.

"Do you see, my friends?" the colonel drawled. "Proven or not proven, this is the prize waiting for thieves, liars, and malcontents." He went on. "Come what may, the 141st Regiment will survive war with honor. I trust you; you trust me. That is so." Holding their attention tightly, the commander went on. "It is likely that few original members of the regiment will survive this war. That is as it should be. This is war. While there are many dozens more regiments, only *we* fight, only *we* die as People's Army, 141st Regiment. It is good to die—to die means the ultimate gain of honor. All who die sacrifice for the honor of all others. Our service for the greater good is the earthly trial we suffer—Buddhist and Catholic the same. Long life is not common; the aged ones are blessed. We are blessed, but not as they. Our blessing is the privilege of duty with honor, provided we live our honor. And we shall!" His voice suddenly went shrill. "We are sons of bitches. We are 141st Regiment!"

With that, any pretense of standing at attention or parade rest was gone. The colonel stopped talking as energy shot through the regiment, tensions released. There came then a small cheer followed by whoops and yells from entire platoons. The yelling proclaimed their new namesake, "Sons of bitches," filled the air.

Colonel Dau raised a hand. All went still and quiet. "The Western world sees us as having a callous disregard for life. That is not so. What we have is acceptance of natural mortality. All die. Do others not see how mothers wail and openly mourn our deaths? As Vietnam citizens, we mourn loudly and righteously. Then it is over; we move on. There is no absence of life in Vietnam. We are many people. We many people live—then we move on. Under Ho Chi Minh and communism, we have service. Service is our life, a life filled with purpose and fortitude. Life is death. Death is living on. The 141st moves on now, together as one, determined to expel the filthy enemy. Long live sons of bitches!"

As Colonel Dau stepped off the dais, the cheers rose. "Sons of bitches, sons of bitches, SONS OF BITCHES!" Louder still as the deputy commander stepped back up. When his hand went up, they quieted. His message was short. He calmly ordered the troops to pack their gear and be ready to march within the hour. They knew, then, they would soon be in it. The replacement platoon already was.

There were few personal effects to pack. The unspoken priority was eating within the hour. It would be their last meal for some time to come, they knew. The mood had quickly turned ominous. There was little talking, no laughing, only a lasting hush punctuated by coarse, loud whispers and clicking chopsticks. The former Private Thom lay unburied, literally left in the dust.

Going into the unknown mission, the Private Thom incident integrated itself nicely into the 141st. Typically the regiment would face the unknown and follow orders blindly, without hesitation, then falling back to safety. Almost always it would fall back. Now their war would include stand-and-fight battles despite obvious and distinct handicaps—handicaps such as limited artillery, little or no anti-aircraft weaponry, and zero air support.

The French wasted troops and resources to rescue beleaguered units, almost regardless of circumstance. Rescue had come to be the forte of the Airborne Legion units. Rather than write off a company of colonial Vietnamese or Thais who were fast running out of ammunition and hope, a Legionnaire Battalion was as likely as not to swoop in, flank the assaulting Vietminh, and retrieve the survivors. Not so with the People's Army, the Vietminh. If a unit was cut off and foundering, it was guilty of not following one or more basic Vietminh tenets: 1) It had allowed itself to be attacked, or 2) it had attacked without assurance of victory. In either case, additional resources would not be jeopardized to salvage the actions and poor judgment of subpar performers. They were simple tenets. They were followed closely.

Private Pham, like any rational soldier, feared he may not be brave and strong in the face of the enemy. Fear, he suspected, was the creeping shadow of cowardice. Could he face danger or imminent death and not dishonor his comrades and family? The fear of fear was a pain also kept to oneself. Few shared with others this grief of fear. Pham was no exception.

Anything could be calamitous for the grunt, and too often was. Fortunately, the commissars had adages for all occasions and circumstances. "Stand as one for victory"; "the greater good to prevail"; "independence is all" were just some of the lecture titles preached at every opportunity, whether on the march or not. Private Pham had had enough of the adage business at Comintern Academy, but now they distracted him with some purpose—anything to give him the strength to keep moving. *Useless thoughts. I am too tired to waste energy punishing myself with hyperbolic quips,* he silently complained. And, finally, the daily grind smothered useless thoughts. *I will live or die—be crippled or not, captured or not. I have had it with suffering.* The mantras still resonated in his head, but his gut remained skeptical. Being a private was taxing and challenging, *but at least I am a commissar, and I have a good memory for what I see and learn.* He continued to wonder when he would be notified to report his findings. *Being a private is hard, it is stressful, and it isn't at all like fútbol.*

Chapter 3

Answer the Call: Part II

The French Force troops often did business with villagers; they traded goods, ate Vietnamese food, drank local beer, some bought or traded for pot and opium, and many negotiated for "short-time" girls. Often, those connections produced a collegial, good-time environment. Everyone could be happy; the townspeople prospered and the soldiers relaxed. Even so, the French could and eventually would stumble onto contraband or become suspicious of too many questions, whether looking for trouble or not. Searches were likely to follow, interrogations conducted, and trust shattered. When that happened, the good-time French Force troops had a bone to chew on. They had been deceived and duped by the local population, they felt. That never ended well. French Force troops could not be fools and would not stand being treated as fools!

General disrespect was the first dish served to the locals in response. Actively demeaning the villagers who were already intimidated by both the French Force and the Vietminh did not promote anything genuine. After that, the locals produced little more than overzealous smiles and speciously nodding heads. The kowtowing worked for many of the soldiers. They observed it from the perspective of their superior status. Others of them felt patronized and were insulted. Either way added to the disrespect of the people. Sullied friendships and violated trust brought out the worst among those who were superior. Especially when they were not.

The High Region

No French Force armor-supported operation ever traveled surreptitiously. By the clank and clatter of smelly machines and equipment, they announced themselves. Tanks and big guns always had the advantage. However, when it came to the Viet Bac area of the High Region, the playing field was more than level for the home team, that being the Vietminh. The

57

wilderness of high hills and rugged terrain had always been an effective deterrent to outsiders. While it was true that French Force paratroopers could drop from the sky, even that had limitations. Paratroopers could parachute into trees, bogs, and hillsides, but not without unsustainable loss. Not to be underappreciated, the Viet dogs fussed at the sound of airplanes as well as the smell of Europeans—two good reasons for dogs not to be supper.

Sometime after 1951 the Vietminh had begun working on improving the Viet Bac trails. Building roadbed for their own purposes became a priority even though the movement of heavy units by either side was virtually impossible during the monsoon season.

The High Region is a good chunk of the tribal area flowing southwest from China and northwest Vietnam into much of Laos. It is also the ancestral home of fierce tribes whose heritage and actions resist outsiders. Those tribes include the Nung, Tho, Khmu, Meo, Yao, Muong, and Lolo; also the Black, the White, and the Red Thai, each named for their women's color of dress. There were the Nung people, who found it in their best interests to work with the French. Only later would the Vietminh develop allies among the tribes as well.

The High Region could be used as a shortcut from China and northern Vietnam to the government-controlled portion of Laos to the south. However, forays through the tribal areas by either French Forces or Vietminh was typically an exercise in vulnerability. Passing through meant having no supply line but plenty of resistance from the tribes. It was also generally pointless. The topography of the High Region was steep and rugged, the few trails quickly overgrown. Wary of ambush and dealing with rugged terrain, the French Force had little choice but to move slowly when breaking into the High Region.

It was little different for the Vietminh. The indigenous tribes were wholly adapted and literally at home there, and especially eager to resist the Vietnamese lowlanders. Historically having been brutally treated and considered savages by them, the tribes returned the favor of brutality whenever offered the opportunity.

On the other hand, well-armed, small, native cells began to appear, supported by a French officer or NCO. Amenable tribesmen already adept in free-ranging warfare were trained, armed, and paid a monthly stipend, often in salt, by the French. Their purpose was to seal off the High Region from the Vietminh. With modern weapons, they loosely followed the French leaders' orders. These small units relished throwing harm at any Vietminh unit in their space.

It was not unusual for the French officer or NCO to "go local," remaining in the bush for years, learning from the tribesmen, aggravating the enemy, and even raising families with local women. One such French officer reported a sticky circumstance involving a tribal enemy force assaulting a village and kidnapping the mother of one of the officer's guerrilla team members. The assault provoked a team council that did not include the officer. Their explanation for then turning in their modern arms was that they could not risk losing French property in the pursuit of a personal issue. The team left in the night and returned several days later. With them was a prize piece of tarpaulin they had acquired. Opened, it displayed five severed heads. Vengeance was theirs.

The High Region was alive with death. Whether by ambush, hit-and-run attacks, or procuring intelligence critical to the French Force effort, the tribal guerrillas performed exceptionally well. Many would say their finest hour was in the fall of 1952. In a coordinated effort, they effectively screened the tattered evacuation of the small-fort survivors desperate to reach the relative safety of Na-San. An entire communist division in hot pursuit was hit and diverted, again and again, by their savage guerrilla attacks.

It was from over the border in China that Ho Chi Minh launched the Indochina Communist Party (ICP) in 1930. His timing was exceptional; the rice harvest failed that year, and world recession, the Great Depression, led to near starvation for many. Hungry, frustrated, and resentful of the status quo, the people were eager for the promise of solutions. The ICP was that. In April 1931 the Soviet Union fully recognized the ICP and supported Ho. Later, China and the Soviet Union came to formal terms with Ho Chi Minh, intending to continue their shared doctrine of communism throughout Southeast Asia. France was in nominal control of Indochina, but there were scads of local, political, and quasi-military sects and societies, especially in Vietnam, all chafing against their colonial status.

Of course they could not resist the invitation of the charismatic Ho Chi Minh to cordially gather and share ideology. Perhaps they could coordinate efforts and push forward their overall objective. Hungry for relief and independence, the bulk of the sect and political party leadership in Vietnam crossed the northern border to meet with Ho Chi Minh. Safe from French eyes, the assembled leadership met with high hopes. If the various societies could negotiate a unifying coalition, their combined strength would be an undeniable voice for independence shouted to the world. As planned, with the help of Moscow and China's Mao, Ho managed control of the conference and worked his magic, gaining dominance over the various groups. One by one, the sect and party leaders were either won over by intellect or propaganda and, if not that, by strongarm. Particularly stubborn or insistent sect leaders who failed to comport were simply eliminated. When a leader was unable to think as one with the ICP, he was regarded as working against the people, a traitor. A short trial and execution were sure to dampen further dissension. It was something of a clean sweep. Communism would be the way forward.

Soon after, the numbers of communist sympathizers ballooned and conventional army units were born, outfitted, and trained. The public support by Red China of the Vietminh from 1949 on served to ramp up Soviet support as well. It was the Russians, after all, who initiated the Communist International Party, advocating and working toward world domination. Vietnam, Laos, and Cambodia, which comprised Indochina, were plum candidates for domination. Even without Indochina, communism ruled one-third of the planet by 1965.

September 1952: Opportunity Knocks

By then, General Giap was maneuvering 10,000-man divisions, each soldier armed and trained by China. Giap's conventional force began the sweep across the High Region, crushing the string of French forts meant to protect the expanse. That began the rush of fort survivors abandoning their posts with the thought of living to fight another day. The plan was to gather for a defensive stand at the remote Na-San Valley garrison, well south of the forts. It was a minimum sixty-kilometer trek through the hills for the closest survivors, and much longer for others. From ground level, it was up and down steep hills, hostile to the hilt. The trek was precarious for the survivors as well-trained Vietminh troops did their best to hunt them down. Predictably, many of the fort survivors failed to reach Na-San, although the screen provided by the Thai cells under French direction helped considerably.

When General Giap learned the French collection point was Na-San, he knew he had them where he wanted. The only available resupply for the French at Na-San would have to come by way of the minimal airstrip there. The gathering French Forces, so far from their supply depots, were extremely vulnerable. Giap knew his heavy weapons and new divisions could, much like a tsunami, overwhelm Na-San and demolish it whole. Getting the divisions and matériel to Na-San quickly was the key. They would have to arrive before the French could collect, organize, and properly fortify the garrison.

Giap, however, was forced to deal with conventional-army issues. The problem of inadequate infrastructure to move the whole of his army was tackled by hundreds of civilian laborer work crews such as that of Nguyen Dac Pho's coolie team. Meager trails were to be broadened, bridges built, and a much-increased supply chain assembled. It would be an ongoing process for some time to come. Rudimentary manhandling was necessary to move Giap's heavy war machinery.

Legions of coolies along with the soldiers themselves began the process, pushing the stubborn wheel of progress. Opportunity for the Vietminh: howitzers, the heavy artillery guns, would be most effective if they could be placed high in the hills where their crews could see their targets and shoot down at them with direct fire. The complicated practice of shooting over hills and beyond the sight of targets was, for the novice Vietminh gunners, most unlikely. It was Chinese benevolence that had provided the howitzers, and it was Chinese advisors who taught the basics of their use. Heavy artillery was new to the People's Army, and simplicity was key.

Consequently, a few big guns were hand-maneuvered and placed in positions relatively close to the Na-San stronghold. Transporting howitzers through the hills involved significant challenges. The constant concern was losing the five-thousand-pound chunks of steel over the side of a mountain. Rocks, weather, mud, and grades of ascent and descent were the obvious and variable factors in the process. The guns were to be protected at all costs. It was considered far worse to lose such a weapon than the crushing of a few horrified coolies or privates by a runaway gun. Hundred-person teams worked in shifts around the clock for a full week to place a single gun in the hills. Oxen, rope, and block-and-tackle were used to muscle each cannon up, over, through the terrain, and into position.

Tens of thousands of coolies were laboring to support General Giap's opportunity, and there were even more porters than coolies. One Vietminh division without motorized vehicles required fifty thousand porters for resupply. Giap had three full divisions headed for Na-San, more elsewhere, and still more training in China. The math was simple. Thousands of camouflaged troops and scores of carts, a multitude of pack bicycles, and legions of porters began snaking their way through the hills and valleys of northern Vietnam. Fronting it all was Nguyen Dac Pho's work crew. They were an experienced and dependable team given a specialty mission.

Nguyen was eighteen now. His team was assigned to move one of the 105mm howitzers to Na-San and from there into a protected hillside casement of their own construction. The 105 became the premier artillery piece of the People's Army before any of them fired even a single shell.

For the Vietminh to move such a beast as the 105 howitzers through the

High Region was borderline impossible as seen by Western military minds. It had been discussed. Trails were not roads. Any number of rivers required bridges. The ground was muddy and soft from daily rains, and the mountain ascents and descents were treacherous. Western minds, however, were wrong.

More than a few times as they were transported, the carriage of a gun jerked to one side or the other, especially on mountain inclines. There was a pitch to the right or left, depending on which wheel turned, while the other wheel was stopped by a hidden rock or the red, sucking mud. The handling teams were constantly on edge, and the higher they ascended for placement, the more volatile the operation. To halt the process for meals and rest breaks required the wheels of the gun to be well chocked and the carriage tied down with multiple lines.

At mid-shift one fine day, Nguyen's exhausted team, hungry and anxious, carefully secured their transport as usual. The volatility issue was openly discussed as chopsticks appeared. Food was passed around, followed closely by the pungent nuoc-mam fish sauce, the all-purpose brightener of Asian victuals. Affirmative comments were made, marking the day as having made decent progress so far. A certain pulling rhythm among the rope handlers had been moving the gun well.

The break over, Nguyen took his place behind the left wheel which was adjacent to the drop-off side of the mountain. He had learned to feel the tension of the wheel. More than once he had been able to warn the rope handlers that the gun was about to slip, and which way. The team could then compensate right or left with the ropes and maintain the integrity of the gun. With everyone in position, the carriage tie-down ropes were released and the wood wheel chocks removed. Everything was normal. Ropes tight, the handlers groaned in unison on the first pull. The gun inched forward, then stopped abruptly, apparently having hit something solid but unseen. The rope handlers released tension for another lunge forward precisely as the gun lurched backward. From there began the legend.

"Yes, sir," Private Nguyen finally responded to the colonel. "The howitzer involved many dozen coolies pulling on lines, hour after hour, to inch the gun up the final mountain. Late in the shift, we were tired and weakening. I was behind the gun, pushing the left wheel. We stopped to catch our breath, I think. On a hard count, the people on the lines pulled while I pushed. Suddenly the wheel came back at me and the ground collapsed. The trail was most rugged—no wider than the wheels of the gun. We were high up and on the steepest part of the mountain. As the ground gave way, I saw in my mind that we had failed the Great Leader. A valuable gun would be smashed in the valley far below because we did not follow orders."

"What orders did you not follow?" Colonel Ky asked.

"We were instructed not to allow the howitzer to slip back and fall off the mountain. The officer was most explicit."

"Yes," the commander responded quickly. "Yes, yes, I see." A very slight smile pursed his lips.

"Then a miracle happened," Private Nguyen flatly stated.

The smile remained. "Exactly what happened? Every detail, please."

"Yes, sir. I was behind the wheel that gave way. At my feet was a wheel chock—to keep the gun stationary. I kicked it in place, they tell me, but too late. Earth—"

"The earth gave way. The gun continued to roll," the colonel quickly stated.

"True, Colonel. But I tried. The chock was behind the wheel, but the earth continued to cave. The valley was many hundred meters below, and the gun was about to slide off the mountain. All I had was me—my body."

"So you threw your body behind the howitzer's wheel?" The colonel believed he was seeing the lie coming out. His mind voiced the play-by-play: *The so-called hero is standing here, alive, saying that he sacrificed himself. That cannot be. The howitzer continued rolling back and crushed the coolie like a June bug. There is no question. You are now exposed, Private Nguyen.*

But Nguyen was not finished. "As I say, the earth was soft. It gave way under the wheel. The wood chock slowed but did not stop the gun. Then it happened. The Buddha, I think, placed me there, but I remember nothing after that."

Colonel Ky spoke up loudly then. "Despite your connection to the Buddha, a howitzer would have crushed you instantly." He stated it matter-of-factly. There was a certain cynicism of finality in his voice.

"Not exactly, sir. The chock slowed the carriage but did not stop it. I was struck by the wheel but maybe slowed the carriage more."

"The five-thousand-pound howitzer did not kill you?" the colonel asked incredulously. "That is impossible!"

"The ground opened. I do not have memory of it, but comrades on ropes were quick to tie off the gun on trees and rocks ahead. I was buried with the wheel over me, they say. Between two logs I was buried. The wood chocks protected me. I was unconscious and buried in the earth under the left wheel.

Everyone saw me as dead. I was dead. Comrades used poles as levers to raise the wheel. Quickly they dug out me. That is the story. I was dead from stopping the cannon."

A wilted tone came from the commander. "Comrades dug you out. You came back to life." It wasn't a question. He could see the writing on the wall, and it had the ring of truth to it. He was not pleased.

"Yes, sir. They say I was dead for some time. Now I am here."

"Of that I am well aware, Private." He dragged out the word "private" to convince himself of the status difference between he and thee. "No more talk of hero," he commanded. "In the 57th Regiment, all soldiers are heroes. Do you understand?"

"Oh yes, Colonel Ky. There will be no talk of saving a cannon—only of serving Colonel Ky and the 57th Regiment."

Ky knew he would hear plenty about his hero from others—including those who outranked him, and over which he had no control. *Because the Great Leader speaks of the hero, much will be made of the hero.* While most commanders may welcome such a soldier into their charge, this one could see only competition and loss of respect for himself. The privates of the 57th Regiment looked up to the hero, and that, he believed, reduced his stature. Ky did not care for acknowledged heroes in his regiment when they were someone other than himself. He would be the one to shine, not, as he would put it, piss-poor village privates. *Peasants and privates are born to serve,* he assured himself. *To serve and be expendable is a great honor.* He may have believed the story of Private Nguyen Dac Pho, but he could not accept it. He was obsessed.

5 November 1952

Lucky for Private Pham Van Hieu, he already had three months of training with the regiment under his belt. During the training he did not see it as any kind of luck—not of the good variety anyway. After the mostly academic work at the academy, it was difficult for him to align his mental focus and dedicate his physical energies. It was nothing but short-order drills and practicing tactics. Everything was done in rote; never explained. Particularly aggravating was that the tactics and rehearsals had little to do with Pham's real duty. His new comrades were patient but generally annoyed with him. The thing was, the 141st hadn't been in combat since his arrival. Despite over two years in service, Private Pham's actual military experience was hardly more than those three months. Scant days at remote villages for covert training in the irregular platoon amounted to little. Almost immediately after that he had been sent to the academy, which the 141st did not know. Being a dutiful private in the eyes of the regiment until he could report to The Party was taxing and not assured.

The regional force training was intense and, like it or not, he needed the exposure of it to learn. He knew he could find himself in combat one day, and he would need to know that stuff. Then came General Giap's order. It changed everything. Everyone in the regiment would be deeply affected. Immediate action was demanded.

One day, for the sake of his sanity, Private Pham asked comrades what day of the week it was. It seemed a good thing to know, not that he tried to keep track. Consensus: "today." No one was concerned about niggling matters such as days of the week, although the position of which moon they were in was clear in everyone's head. As for the daily grind, every day was the same. Until it wasn't.

For the record, it was midday when Colonel Dau called the battalions together for another of his rare, full-regimental formations. Causing no small stir, the commander announced that the regiment would be moving out at first daylight. That was it. He had already briefed the battalion commanders who, by then, had met with their company commanders and executive officers. Company commanders were expected to brief platoon leaders and NCOs.

Immediately after the announcement, Colonel Dau hustled back to his shelter, presumably to close up shop. Following the commander on the dais was Major Tran, the deputy commander. Major Tran colored the colonel's order with significant context and a fair bit of inspiration.

"Soldiers of the regiment," he began, "word has come that, while three of our regular army divisions are away, marching southwest on enemy puppets in Laos, many enemy battalions are advancing on the Viet Bac from different directions. Intelligence understands the enemy to come together and attack at Phu Doan." It was well known that Phu Doan was the major supply depot of the Vietminh, which, up to the present, was considered too remote and protected for the French Force to attack. "The enemy intends to destroy critical stores of rice and war matériel there. Such an attempt is most foolish. For us, soldiers of the 141st Regiment, it is the opportunity to display our successful training. It is a great honor to be one of the regional forces to block the oppressor, to destroy his convoy, his equipment, and his soldiers. This enemy comes from some distance; comes to Phu Doan with many trucks and big guns—tanks also!" He emphasized the word "tank." The advent of tanks in the Viet Bac region was new. "We are to answer, comrades, with cunning surprise. We will strike! We will cover the enemy advance as ants cover the day-old carcass. The many tanks and trucks are heavy with war matériel. They move slowly on winding trail and ancient path, stopping many times to make water crossings. They stop again and again to clear, to fortify, and to build. Together, comrades, we will quick-march to Phu Doan where we will crush them. We, the 141st Regiment, not only will harass and ambush the enemy, but we will also face them head-on, careful to dodge the full power of the clumsy enemy. At Phu Doan, comrades, the enemy will be farthest from home bases and resupply. They are most weak there. That is why we confront them at the crest of Phu Doan. We will thrash this beast of Indochina who dares enter the Viet Bac. We bring to battle, comrades!"

He stopped talking at that point and stared into the assembled battalions. Slowly his hard gaze turned, right to left and back again. He had their attention. They understood Phu Doan would be a critical battle, that they would be fighting outside their region, and they would be vastly outnumbered. They did not know how vast.

The French Force operation was the culmination of months of preparation and coordination by the French. Not just a complicated and mechanized convoy, the operation was huge. It included an airborne group, four motorized groups, two armored groups, and two riverine groups. In total, 30,000 French Force troops and personnel were involved. It was the greatest single effort the French Forces had put together up to that time.

With gusto and emotion, Major Tran began again. "Not one soldier will hesitate—not one! We are the future of a socialist republic of Vietnam where all citizens are equal and free." At that point, the major kicked up the emotion even more, speaking faster and louder, intensity building as he spoke. "The crest of Phu Doan is where we stop the French dog. We will do the work of the regular army. *We do so now!* The Great Leader will blush with pride when he is told of the 141st Regiment's action against the French vermin. Will we succeed, comrades? I ASK, WILL WE SUCCEED?"

"YES, COMRADE! WE WILL SUCCEED!" It was a freakin' chorus, and a loud freakin' chorus at that. The regiment had accepted the challenge.

It was the regulars, not regionals like the 141st, who traveled great distances and often attacked where least expected. The regulars hit hard and moved fast. Before being outflanked or boxed in, their forte was to disperse as best they could and disappear, only to regroup later. It was a great accomplishment to swoop in and create an angry hornets' nest for the French. It was a great victory to leave the French damaged and frustrated with nothing but ghosts to fight with their airpower and artillery. But this fight—this fight at Phu Doan would belong to the regional regiments, not the regulars. The 141st would be the A-Team for once and committed to stopping the French

Force desecration of the Viet Bac stores.

As regionals, their area of operation (AO) was defined and specific. Each regiment was familiar and comfortable with its own AO; they worked it, they used its features, and they faced the music that came to it. It was the regionals who remained after an attack by the regulars. It was often the regionals who took the heat of the frustrated French forces. Much like the wily ring fighter, the regionals were adept at jabbing—feinting and weaving, generally keeping away from the bigger opponent's hook and uppercut. The war effort and General Giap depended on them to step up. They would do their best.

The Viet Bac was not in the AO of the 141st, but it had been a training ground for them. There was familiarity for them, and it would not be easily conceded to the enemy. What the 141st and the other regional regiments joining the fight couldn't know was the dimension of what they were getting into.

The makeup of the attacking French Force included battalions from the rich Tonkin delta region. That meant the defenses of the French Force home base of Tonkin were spread thin in the delta. There was a borrowing of French Force battalions here, there, and everywhere for the Phu Doan mission. French knowledge of the three Vietminh divisions marching on Laos seemed to mitigate the risk of thin defenses in Tonkin. The gamble of thinning Tonkin defenses seemed worth the risk. The French counted on General Giap turning back his three divisions to defend Phu Doan, thereby making them concentrated targets for airstrikes and French artillery. In place at Phu Doan, the French would be on the high ground, anxious to engage the returning divisions of General Giap. The Vietminh would be smothered.

Battle of Phu Doan

The 141st Regiment moved out, humping fast to reach Phu Doan before the French Force could get there. While on the march, Private Pham and his comrades became aware of single platoons being dropped off along the way. Seeing the regiment watered down, even a platoon here and there made no sense to them. There were some things—no, many things—Pham and his comrades did not know, didn't realize, and couldn't appreciate about the People's Army. What they *did* know was that it was best to keep their mouths shut about things questionable.

It occurred to Pham that the 141st may be intended as cannon fodder. Their odds of stopping a mechanized French Force were minuscule, he realized. Resigning himself to circumstance, he couldn't help but smile. Irony on such a scale toyed with his mind. It had been some time since smiles were part of his day, he realized. *If we are sacrificed, my year at Comintern Academy was wasted. But my funeral was not,* he swiftly added, continuing with an even bigger smile. That made things better. Sure it did.

That was the point where the business of warfare lost its hallucinatory quality. Not so many thoughts of glory anymore for Private Pham. Fantasy was replaced by the creeping sense of reality. He said nothing but had begun paying attention to what was going on around him rather than feeling above it all. With a canvas tube filled with rice across his chest, a Soviet rifle on his shoulder, and ammunition, water, and salt pouch dangling from a web belt, Pham trudged onward to destiny.

All things considered, the understrength regiment moved quickly, more quickly than the bloated French convoy or a Vietminh division, for that matter. They reached Phu Doan ahead of the French Force and ahead of the other regional regiments. They arrived at the crest of the final hill with Phu Doan to their front.

An overdue rest was called. It had been many hours on the march, covering nearly two full days and much of the night between. The troops had barely been able to fortify themselves on the way, although they had water. Small fires had been permitted in the night; rice was cooked all up and down the line. Thankful for the blessing of reaching Phu Doan ahead of the French, they could again eat, and again it would be cooked rice with a little fat. The Vietminh stores, the armories, were there at Phu Doan and beyond.

The 141st Regiment would make its stand exactly there, just over the crest. The regiments not yet arrived would set up farther down the line behind them, probably on the other side of the village. Together commanders surveyed the area on foot and worked out a battle plan. Nothing could be accomplished without a plan, and the Vietminh practiced what they preached. The choreography of their attack was mapped out in detail with escape routes and instructions down to the squad and three-person team level.

Meanwhile, the French columns had combined from different directions and had begun moving as one, which slowed them further. That was fortunate for Colonel Dau's platoons, those that had been peeled off on the march. They had time to prepare quality ambush sites. The French Force column had no choice but to move only one way: loudly. Their location and rate of advance was no secret. Internal combustion engines, machetes, axes, hammers, and working shovels, as well as occasional gaggles of gunshots— mostly at ghosts—highlighted their advance.

For the better part of two days on the trail, there was one well-placed Vietminh ambush after another. The French had a good deal more firepower, but their avenue of approach was predictable, and they were inviting targets through the winding trails. Every bend in the trail was a likely ambush site, and there were plenty of both. The simple fact that the force was ascending more than descending made their advance treacherous. With the Vietminh advantage of high ground ahead of the convoy, there was little chance for the French Force to preempt many of the strikes, at least in the traditional sense.

Protecting convoys in heavy bush country was nearly impossible. Normally outrigger troops were put to the sides of the trail to clear the way. Off-trail flankers trying to cover that large convoy were vulnerable and all but walking sacrifices. Mostly, however, the ambushers faded into the background until the flankers had passed and then moved in for the chaos, stopping the convoy by hitting a truck or two before disappearing again. Ammunition trucks made for the greatest spectacles, but any destroyed vehicle added limitation to the French effort.

Call it salvation, if you will, and it was close to that in the minds of many. The French Force column sported the M-2, a .50-caliber machine gun on every tank, and many of the personnel carriers. The ambushes continued, but the M-2 minimized several ambushes, swept some away, and generally kept the convoy moving. The sound and sight of the M-2's red tracers nurtured morale all up and down the line. Six-and-a-half-centimeter chunks of copper-jacketed lead ripped through bush and trees with unparalleled impact. Any flesh and bone encountered on the way were brutally torn and smashed with no exceptions.

So effective was the .50-caliber that, going into the second day on the combined trail, the decision was made to "recon by fire," as they called it. It was using the intimidation of the M-2s to blindly perform a kind of reconnaissance or clearing of the enemy. Firing the mounted crew weapons indiscriminately into the bush at likely ambush sites lowered any head with reason in it, thereby keeping the convoy moving. Attacks continued but were softened by the threat of that one weapon.

While the Vietminh ambushes damaged or destroyed vehicles, caused casualties, and created setbacks, they were, in the end, little more than minor slowdowns of an advancing tsunami. For the French generals in Hanoi, the ambushes were nothing more than an annoyance trying their patience. The generals wanted a set-piece battle at Phu Doan without delay.

Colonel Dau's 141st Regiment was fluent in camouflage, that was certain, but this major engagement also required a different savvy not yet possessed by them. If they were going to be effective against the colossal strike force coming their way, they would need savvy beyond camouflage and courage. Fighting in place was an untested skill set for them. The colonel had to wonder what would be left of his regiment when this was over.

The preparations came together quickly. It was all hands on deck, adrenaline flowing. Precise trenches were dug in optimum locations, bunkers fashioned just off the trail at the edge of the bush. Machine guns were set low for grazing cross fire. Camouflage was perfect. Each fighting position was supplied with appropriate armaments; most positions were occupied by seasoned troops. The armories there supplied hardware and volumes of munitions, munitions often relished or requisitioned but never before delivered to regionals. There was access to rocket-propelled grenades, those armor killers they had only ever heard about. The permanent cadre at Phu Doan was experienced and quick to provide direction and support. The regionals were a stout force, no question. In comparison to what was nearly upon them, however, they were truly a small force. They would put up a fight, but what then?

There were the coolies and porters. They would play a significant role in the defense of Phu Doan. Their mission was to move and displace the rice and munition stores out of the immediate area. Everyone toiled. When time allowed, the troops too were moving supplies and munitions.

Not so for Privates Pham, Ninh, and Cho. They were the first to be put to work on the Phu Doan side of the hill's crest. With a borrowed field hoe, they worked to break up the soil's hardpan and began fashioning a narrow trench. The three knew each other from their first days in the regiment. Together they were a fire team. The three had come to the regiment at the same time and, of course, were the more naïve and inexperienced. They were also the most expendable. Ever since Colonel Dau had made an example of Pham in front of the regiment, Ninh and Cho felt a kinship with him in their shared timidity. What Ninh and Cho hadn't yet realized was that Pham Van Hieu, as well as Colonel Dau, could be calculating.

As they worked, the dirt from their digging was piled on the crest side of the trench and tamped down, making a thin parapet. The trench was in the open, perpendicular to and just off the trail on the Phu Doan side of the crest. They were number one—the first defensive position to face the enemy.

"Deeper. Dig deeper."

Surprised, the three privates looked up to stare blankly at the colonel.

"The opening salvo of battle begins here!" Their blank looks gave them away. "You did not know this?" Silence. "No?" Solemnly, the privates half shook and half nodded their acknowledgment to the colonel's message. It was the first they had heard, but now it was obvious.

"We are to fire the first shots?" Private Pham asked incredulously.

Each of them now had an issued rifle, but their experience with them was nil, save for a few training shots, no experience, and most of those were dry-fire—no bullets. It was news to the three of them that this short, narrow trench or fighting hole would take the first shot. They would essentially be the baton to initiate the overture. For his new fire team, the colonel's news was the kiss of death. The three of them against thousands.

The colonel was moving on down the line by the time Pham had mumbled his response. Realizing he'd not been heard, Pham turned back to Ninh and Cho and, in a listless tone, half whispered, "I did not think we would die so soon." They would be the very first to announce themselves targets. If anything in the world could save them, it would be a deep trench, superb camouflage, and uncanny, God-given luck.

Being exceptional in its use, camouflage was normally the gift of confidence for the Vietminh. The three privates were now challenged to test the limits of camouflage. As for fighting, impeccable Vietminh discipline often went a long way towards achieving turmoil or even chaos within a French Force unit.

Scant minutes after the colonel left, which was well before the three virgins had regained their wits, they were visited by their company commander, Captain Ngai. They knew him only by name and reputation—had never before addressed him or been addressed by him. Under more normal circumstances they would have been intimidated by his position and reputation. Not so much now, knowing their true circumstance and, by then, the sound of enemy gunfire in the background.

Privates Pham, Ninh, and Cho were filthy dirty from the recent forty-eight hours and bone tired from exertion and limited sleep. Each felt a kind of hollowness, or was it the sense of their surreal circumstance? The feeling could have been from the recent news provided by Colonel Dau, but most likely it was a combination of everything. Making peace with mortal reality was upon them, and echoes of the French column filled their ears. If it was an honor to be the first target of the overwhelming enemy, they had not yet discovered the pride involved.

There was no question they were willing to follow orders. It was expected. Putting their thoughts in order was the greater challenge. Although they had been well indoctrinated, their few months in the regiment wasn't adequate preparation for this. Ninh and Cho were naïve peasants stressed and prodded into a degree of military readiness, but only a degree. They took some comfort in being with their discerning new friend who could be assertive, and he seemed to understand how the world worked. Private Pham saw himself as the diminished city boy sitting in a hole with dolts he didn't particularly care to die with. Imminent doom before them, their thoughts were jumbled, swirling in a sea of angst. They continued to dig, and they dug earnestly.

Of the three, Ninh was the true believer. He had been convinced along the way that subservience to master Communism was the answer to justice and universal harmony. In his eyes, it was all for one and one for all. Pham, on the other hand, saw communism as a simplistic and suspicious way to motivate the peasantry. As for Cho, he never complained and was one of many who never questioned and performed as directed by authority—any authority. He would smile if asked while doing so.

The commander and commissar speeches were forever gallant and delivered with enthusiasm. Communism seemed a filmy enchantment to Private Pham. With counterarguments forbidden, it was logical to him that whatever ideology was brought forward, it was expected to be received as light and truth for all. Privately that was most irritating to him. Declared and demonstrated dedication would be rewarded, they were told. Private Ninh was good at believing. Private Cho was good at doing, and Private Pham was good at asking critical questions—but only to himself.

Captain Ngai came out of nowhere wearing his all-time serious face. The French juggernaut, he explained, was close and should be there in a short hour. He was so proud, he suggested, that his company was given the honor of being the first line of defense. The trio looked blankly at him and said nothing. Internally, only Private Ninh did not question the captain's veracity. Kneeling in front of the privates' trench, the captain was reminded it was manned by three green recruits who had yet to see an enemy combatant alive or dead or hear the buzz of a blistering bullet passing close by. *The three of them,* the captain's mind surmised, *could be no more effective than scarecrows. But distracting the enemy for even a moment may be helpful.*

To cover his anxious thoughts the captain yelled, "This trench is to disable the first French vehicle! You know that is so. Why did you not dig deep? I see only rifles. Who in the name of Buddha put you three in number one trench?"

Private Ninh was the brave one. "Sir, we were told only to dig a three-man fighting hole exactly here. To make it narrow. We do not know how we are to disable the enemy."

The tirade had only begun. "Mosin-Nagant rifles? They do not pierce armor. Fools! You are to stop a tank, not infantry! Now we lose three rifles—and three privates?" Seconds passed with the trio silently dazed. Finally the captain shook his head slightly and grumbled, "You sit there with scraps of cold rice—a total waste of resource." Instinctively the remaining bits of rice were whisked into dry mouths. Disgusted, the captain spat.

At that moment a nameless and breathless coolie came running, her arms cradling several heavy cylinders. "I was told to bring to you, sir." The girl carefully set them on the ground and faced Captain Ngai. It was three substantial metal tubes, each about thirty centimeters long, maybe ten centimeters in diameter.

"Finally," the captain said. "That is it? No more?"

"Coolies took others elsewhere, sir. It was a major who handed them out."

The captain shook his head, then looked down at his three soldiers in the trench. The coolie took that as her chance to get lost. She had already noticed Pham Van Hieu. He recognized her as a sprightly girl about his age from one of the villages. He didn't recall which one or her name. She was a girl that he and his pubescent hormones had noticed while training with the irregular platoon in one of the villages. There was one quickly raised eyebrow to him and then she was gone.

"Three grenades are more than enough," the captain sputtered out loud. He wasn't convincing. "Do you know how to pitch pineapples—the cull pineapples?"

"Yes, sir," Private Ninh spoke up. "We are from villages outside the delta. All village boys throw pineapple culls."

Thuy is her name, Pham announced to himself. *I would have liked to taste that.*

"I throw pineapples farther than anyone in the village," Private Cho bragged.

Still thinking of Thuy, Pham said nothing.

"There is no excuse. This will work," Captain Ngai insisted. He went on to explain in no-nonsense terms what he expected them to do when the time came. He ended his orders where he had begun them. "Now do what I say. Make that trench deep! Do it now!"

As narrow and deep as their trench already was, only one person at a time had room to swing a hoe and chip away at the hard soil. It was mostly red clay, and it was dry. But it was what they had to work with, and work with it they did. At least Private Cho did, happy to do as told. With the sounds of the French Force coming closer, the other two did not need further encouragement. They went directly to the bush and retrieved fresh greenery for camouflage. Barely off the trail, the trench would have to be completely covered with flora. It would appear to be a growth of bushes.

Before applying the vegetation, however, the three of them got down into it side by side. They practiced throwing with clumps of clay as the captain had instructed. Cramped as it was, only one at a time could throw. The trench was then so deep and narrow it was impossible to completely rotate the throwing arm back and forward as needed for a strong pitch. Their practice throws were short and weak.

It was Pham who came up with the answer. "One of us goes down on hands and knees. The one who throws will stand on his back. Higher up, our elbows can reach back and clear the trench." The three of them worked it out with practice. The system seemed to work, although one of them had to manipulate the camouflage each time.

Handheld anti-tank grenades were not something they could understand, but if believing in them suspended thoughts of imminent demise, they believed in them.

A regimental headquarters had been set up well behind them, down from the crest and on the other side of the village. It was a simple affair, a central location where command staffs could meet, food could be cooked and disseminated, and central control maintained unless or until the French Force broke through. The HQ was temporary. Word was passed that one trooper could receive and take food back for him or herself and two others. The idea was that most of the soldiers remain at their posts. Private Cho was first out of the trench, saying he would be back shortly with supper. He did return quickly enough, balancing a palm leaf with three rations of rice. Best of all, the rice had bits of meat in it. Food being a big deal, by now the new privates of the People's Army had learned to resist wolfing down rations. *Relax, eat slowly, and feel human again.* The rice was still warm. When they closed their eyes, it smelled of home. Slowly they chewed, eyes shut tightly in sad delight.

Still it was impossible to keep out thoughts of the French force soon breaking through to the crest. Eyes then open, they were yet in the narrow trench with instructions to destroy tanks using short lengths of heavy pipe. Private Pham smiled as this new irony washed over him. Three boys stuck in a hole, waiting for thousands to attack them with tanks—and, no doubt, artillery and airstrikes close behind. Playing war as kids back in the village was never like this. Then they were heroes, not cannon fodder used as dung on the enemy shoe to slow him down a half step. *But what a nice funeral I was given,* Pham remembered. He was half serious. Another wry smile crossed his face. The look was more than a little cynical. Only so much irony was a good thing.

It was then he did think of his mother. It brought to Pham a tender, more genuine smile. Their mothers loved them, but they had to accept the reality of loss—even the presumed deaths of their sons. All three were Buddhists with a prayer and a mantra intended to deal with such things. Except for a far-off rifle shot, probably a sniper, silence surrounded them for a moment.

Pham took the quiet as a sign. With slight tremors in his voice, he spoke: "I invoke the Green Tara, mother of liberation, to bring deliverance from suffering and delusion, paving the way for compassion and enlightenment." The common mantra had never before meant as much to them. All three stood quietly. They blessed themselves and each other. They would die as naïve boys trying to be soldiers, and that was OK. Doing so would encourage enlightenment in the next life.

Before the rice was gone, the shooting became louder and more insistent. A rifle shot, then another. Short bursts of heavy machine-gun fire stood out. One main gun fired, probably the 75mm. The echo of splintering wood screeched over them, and then faint shouting, perhaps. It was hard to tell.

Within the hour the creak and squeal of tracked vehicles became distinct and constant. Between the metallic squeals came the swish of swinging machetes and the bite of an ax or two. They were that close. The sound of the tracked vehicles was more intimidating than the intermittent firing, which had become almost casual. Enemy tanks and trucks had made it through the congested trails and washouts. Confrontation was now beyond imminent. Only the lie of emotions said it couldn't be.

Private Pham felt a lightheadedness as the coming staccato of insolent noise, and austere circumstance trumped the warm rice in his belly. Cho stared blankly. But Private Ninh—it was important to Private Ninh that he be the bravest. Regardless, rubber legs betrayed him; he leaned back against the trench wall. Talking turned to whispers among the young privates, then there was nothing to say. Rice with pork bits congealed in place. Uncomfortable as it was, they noticed but were not distracted.

"Hey! You know what you do?" It was Captain Ngai leaning over, peering into the trench again. This time his appearance was a relief to the privates, their solemn moment broken.

Private Ninh, on tiptoe, his forehead nearly touching Ngai's chin, felt compelled to answer. "Sir, we practiced as you say. We will do best as we can."

"Today you do more than best. Be patient, then strike with great force. Understood? Force! Throw hard! Use all three grenades. Use them all! Is that clear?"

In unison of three, "Yes, sir." Then he was gone, and none too soon. The creaking treads were louder still. Anxiety persisted as they waited, each boy alone with his thoughts. Pham strangely remembered then how anxiety had a way of activating his kidneys. *Would that be a problem?* he wondered. It took about a second for him to realize that was possibly his oddest thought ever, considering the circumstance. *I am living and I am present. This dying business isn't easy,* he further processed.

The first sight of the convoy was exhaust fumes. Then, peering through the camouflage, they next saw the long barrel of the main gun. After that came the sight of the clanking, squealing treads, and after that the heavy M-2 machine gun atop the turret. Finally it was the tank commander, standing tall in the open hatch, both hands positioning the .50-caliber gun right, then left, about thirty degrees each way. He looked without finding a reason to open up. He paid no attention to the tuft of brush just to the left of the trail. Had he noticed the fresh dirt around it he would have looked closer.

At this point the camouflage was well within the arc of his gun. No infantry walking ahead or alongside. That was fortunate for the fire team. The snipers must have done their job well. As expected, the lead in the convoy was a tank, and with two just like it following behind. Spirits sank in the number-one fighting hole, but the waiting was over and the resolve or the lack of it would now materialize.

The big machine creaked and groaned its way almost to full view. Slowly it liberated the ascent by tipping forward, then continuing the crawl toward village and objective. Too late, Pham only then realized their trench, dug perpendicular to the trail, was a poor position from which to strike the tank when closest to them. Throwing a full pitch into the side of the tank would require removal of their deepest camouflage, that being toward the trail. There was no interest in making their position obvious to whatever followed the first tank.

Pham spoke up. "We wait. The tank will pass. Then we strike the rear plate."

Cho and Ninh's agreement was immediate. The rear was a smaller, more challenging target, and the tank would be farther away, but there was another problem: the angle. Even a perfectly thrown grenade would strike the rear panel at an angle. Would it glance off without penetrating? As they understood it from Captain Ngai, their state-of-the-art RPG-6 armor grenades would, upon striking the target, discharge a jet of hot metal penetrating the plating of the tank. An instant later the TNT flowing from the head of the grenade would ignite inside the tank. With any luck at all, the munitions inside would also ignite.

Cho then shouted the obvious: "This is why three grenades only. We will be lucky to launch two!" They would be dead by then was the inference. There was no need for an explanation. Cho and Pham were on the same page while Ninh remained flush with determined courage.

"Look," Ninh pleaded, "this is duty. Our families will be proud that we saved rice and munitions for the People's Army. The Party is trusting us—now is our time."

Cho looked to Pham, seeking absolution perhaps. Pham saw Cho's pain and felt his own. As their last moments on earth, the trio used them to make peace with the universe and, except for Ninh, not so much with the People's Army. "Good, bad—right, wrong—we join the ancestors with love and greater understanding." The courage of acceptance swept over them. They were as ready as they could be.

The tank was four or five steps away as it chugged along. Ninh was deadpan serious and grim. "This is our duty—our calling. Wisdom of the Buddha comes with challenge and reflection."

Pham and Cho glanced at each other again. Had there been time, they would have been distracted by Ninh's insight. Duty, however, was precedence. They understood each other if not themselves. That was enough for one lifetime.

The tank by then was past. As if the gravity of the circumstance itself weren't enough, the warring noises fired adrenaline to new heights. At the moment it was helpful. Three green privates required to act boldly and on cue. They looked at each other. "I will," Private Ninh called.

Pham dropped down to become Ninh's platform. Cho pushed back a corner of the vegetation to clear a throwing path. Ninh placed his feet, one over Pham's shoulders, the other over his hips. The private then blessed himself, "God willing," and rotated his arm back then forward with all the push he could generate. The tank was close enough, but the target was small and at an angle, not directly in front of them. The odds were not good, but it had to work. If the left track of the tank hadn't been shielding much of the rear because of the angle, or if the tank hadn't shifted, it would have ended differently.

The grenade skimmed off the edge of the rear plate and struck the inside of the right tread. The explosion wasn't instantaneous, but it came when it did with showering impact. Metal shards, parts, and pieces of track flew in all directions. The trio hadn't anticipated the backlash. Reacting to the flash, Cho dropped to his belly on the bottom of the trench. Pham was already there, elbows in the dirt and hands over ears. Although losing his platform, Ninh was lucky. A ten-centimeter chunk of steel plowed into the earth alongside him near the top of the trench. A small piece of shrapnel did Ninh a favor by grazing him just above his right ear. It breezed by, barely touching flesh. It was plenty enough, however, for a knockdown, providing him a degree of safety. The camouflage canopy was roughed up but not blown free.

The tank was wounded but not out of the fight. Only the right track was destroyed. Everything else, including the .50-caliber machine gun, the 75mm cannon, and a human crew of five were in good shape and desperate for a target. Gunning the engine, the driver tried to hustle the rig forward, but the only movement was the pull on the left side tread which swiveled the rear of the iron lunk around and placed the unadorned right side of the tank directly in front of the trench.

"That's it!" Pham screamed. "Stay there, Cho." Dead in the water, the repositioned tank was now fully exposed. Pham grabbed another grenade and none too gingerly stepped onto Cho's back.

The tank commander desperately searched to orient himself and to see where the attack had come from. The turret began traversing, racing to accommodate a full 180-degree sweep of the caliber .50 from where it was. Finally, target located, a single set of brown eyes stared back at him.

The tanker's eyes widened when he recognized the RPG. The turret rotation was hardly late at all. It was a quick scramble as Pham reached back his throwing arm, grenade in hand. A desperate burst began tearing clumps of sod in a stitching swing directly at the trench. Pham's grenade struck the side plate squarely, just below and ahead of the turret. Pham then registered .50-caliber rounds striking the back wall of the trench.

A slow-motion instant later, a chain reaction lit up the inside of the Chaffee and spilled over. The grenade's TNT and the tank munitions generated one extended explosion. The 75mm and .50-caliber, and also .30-caliber and some .45s—virtually all the ammunition inside the tank—went up in one ominous firestorm. Like a tin can over a firecracker, the solid steel turret lifted off the body of the Chaffee and came to rest five meters away, upside down. The commander simply disappeared, his heavy .50 flying ten meters or more portside. The three privates hugged the bottom of the trench on top of each other.

Clambering upright seconds later, they first caught the feel of the vibrations and then heard more .50-caliber rounds plowing into the ground just beyond the end of their trench. They didn't know yet that the machine gun on the original target was toast. These rounds were coming from the second Chaffee tank now adjacent to the trench, off to their right and on the trail. It was a couple meters or so from the trench if that. That tank commander had seen them and was targeting them. Unfortunately for the commander, he was too close. He could not drop the barrel of his gun low enough to reach the interior of the trench.

Barely soon enough, Pham and Cho recognized the opportunity. They did not think but reacted only. The rounds hit just over the trench as the tank chugged forward. Another five meters farther away, this tank's .50-caliber would be eating up the slender trench. Already it was hitting the far end and inching toward them. Pham dropped to hands and knees; Cho grabbed the last grenade and jumped on Pham's back. From the end closest to the tank, Cho pushed away what was left of the greenery and chucked the grenade with madman gusto. Everything he had went into a javelin-like pitch.

The release of the grenade matched the tank trying to grind into a faster gear. The commander was yelling, and the driver was doing his best to get more distance between tank and trench. The Cadillac engines gained RPMs. The driver, desperate to shift into second gear and gain distance, was quick on the clutch. Too quick. Transmission gears clashed with steel-crunching sounds. The tank rocked back and forth, then stopped, stalled out, engine dead. Regardless, the caliber .50 opened up again. Cho's grenade cleared the treads and bogie wheels to smack cleanly onto the side armor. TNT briefly percolated. The commander may have gotten a few rounds into the trench, but by then the three privates were taking up little of its open space. They were again a flat, compact unit on the hard earth.

It was all over when the charge ignited. Five tankers were killed instantly, fortunately for them. Cho had little interest in watching the harvest of his work, and the bottom of the trench was quite comfortable. The heat from the blast filled the lair quickly if only temporarily. Again the turret was blown, also to the side, making for congestion both on and off the trail. The engine and chassis blazed fire. The young privates' ears were temporarily fogged from the blasts, but they imagined what was happening above. That image was short-lived, however.

The third tank hesitated, then crested the rise. When it did, its advance on the trail was blocked by the two iron sisters in flames. It pulled off to the left and stopped, creating a hard shadow over the tight quarters of the fire team.

There was little appetite for the third Chaffee to crash into the brush where there would be little field of vision and zero protection. For now, it would be vigilant and wait for the walking infantry that should have been there to begin with. Meanwhile, blistering sounds came from two tanks crackling in flames and the rough idle of the third tank's engine serving accompaniment. It had stopped directly over the narrow fighting hole. There was distraction enough by the calamity to not notice the then-naked trench. The privates knew instinctively what had just happened. It was a continuing situation but a new circumstance. In a sense, they were protected, but they were also trapped. The enemy was above them, and more would soon be around them. The privates were bewildered but alive. Adrenaline and fate, so far, were good to the fire team.

The convoy was stopped. A dozen French Force grunts cautiously cleared the rise, rifles at the ready, knowing to expect bad stuff. A young French lieutenant, excited and angry, yelled for them to cover the tank. In their bent and laden infantry gait, the men circled the live tank, unable to ignore the smoking dead lemmings nearby. The area had to be secured before anything else could happen or be decided. Eyes darted back and forth, trying to watch both sides of the trail for aggressors. The same eyes were further distracted as loose shells in the destroyed tanks began cooking off. The grunts second-guessed their source and fired bursts into the bush. There was no response. The third tank continued running but remained still, seeming to be gasping for plan and direction. None was forthcoming.

If an actual target in the bush could be identified, blazing French guns would be in order. But there was no target—only the fear of one. Or more than one. The lieutenant got the shooting to stop. The resulting quiet was alluring but not calming. The heaving, live tank was yet spreading noxious exhaust fumes. Laboring eyes watered and stung as the breeze shifted.

The spell was finally broken when the grunt lieutenant declared the site secure. The convoy must get moving again, always a priority. The off-trail surface seemed firm enough for light tanks. The M-24 Chaffee was a light tank. The lieutenant yelled for his troops to form parallel security lines alongside the live tank so it could safely move forward around the two dead tanks and their clutter. The commander in the third Chaffee wanted infantry ahead of him and alongside him, and, by now, he wasn't crazy about being the lead vehicle of the convoy. He yelled a question at the lieutenant, the lieutenant who had little idea what they were up against. Based on his experience and the damage done, it was a fair bet that, although the Vietminh force was heavily armed, it had pulled up stakes and withdrawn. That would have been a losing bet.

The tank commander turned from his gun again to yell at the lieutenant. As he did, a sheet of small-arms fire poured out from the low hidden bunkers lining the bush. The first to go down was the commander, his chest riddled. The tank engine revved, jerking into action, pawing the Chaffee in place, right and left, looking for an optional travel lane. Yet unseen, the squad of Vietminh crouching in their trench line of fresh bunkers were only a meter or two away. The driver's head projecting through the front hatch was the second-choice target. A cascade of bullets rattled the front of the tank. The engine jerked, chugged, and stopped, the driver's face a dripping block of swiss cheese.

The French lieutenant remained standing, dumbfounded, as groundfire buzzed past him, some splashing dirt at his feet. He looked one way and then another, realizing the absence of options. The infantrymen other than the lieutenant were already on the ground but had no real cover. From where they were they could blindly fire into the bush and hope for the best while it lasted or hug the ground and try crawling back to and over the rise. Three of them lay still, pooling blood on the ground, three others were bleeding but moving.

At that point the lieutenant's mind snapped. Still standing, seeing his men fall and the tank commander riddled, he drew his .45 and stared into the heart of the now-obvious ambush. Firing blindly, he charged his enemy. The brave and insane action drew the attention of most aggressors. In two or three steps the lieutenant was hit several times but did not go down; his eyes only bulged, and his body jerked with each hit. He stumbled toward the bunkers, one step, then another, soon triggering an empty pistol. On the third step, a rising Vietminh lieutenant leveled a Luger pistol to his counterpart's head and calmly tagged the lieutenant's forehead with two 9mm slugs.

The lieutenant's dramatic interlude offered opportunity for the French Force grunts on the ground. There was a moment, maybe a few seconds, left for the undead. Instinctively they crawled like frightened vipers, back to the rise and then over. One of them was dragged from the collar by another on his back. Heels digging into the ground and pushing, the lesser wounded was able to move them both, a valiant action. Remaining on the ground were the dead and their weapons. The small clearing was the kill zone of every infantryman's dream. What was left was a crackling burn accenting the solemnity.

A long minute passed. The halted tank showed no sign of hostile action from the crew inside. Presumably they had personal weapons, but the main gun could not drop low enough to be helpful to them, and deadly exposure awaited anyone trying to use the .50-caliber. Aware of the status of their sister tanks and expecting their own to be victim of the same, the survivors were quick to surrender, hands high. Almost eagerly, the three of them clambered out the hatch, arms remaining in the air. They did not, however, survive the surrender.

That left the third tank being loosely spooned underneath by three green privates. Still green they were, but considerably less so than minutes earlier. Eardrums ringing, the trio sat stunned at the bottom of their trench, all in all not displeased to be alive. What next? They could hardly question.

A bit wide-eyed, the surviving French Force grunts reaching the far side of the rise breathed deeply and signed crosses of thanks across their chests as they were able. With immediate assistance, the woundeds' bleeding was stanched for the most part. No sucking chest wounds, they were littered and moved back to be attended by a senior medical staff. The convoy below the rise was in turmoil, which seemed to surprise none of the enlisted. Security troops were already in the bush on either side of the remaining convoy, the M-2s now silent but haunting. A major and a lieutenant colonel came up the line and quickly debriefed the surviving infantry. Had the infantry been up and walking with the tanks, it was likely no RPGs would have been pitched, and maybe fifteen tankers would yet be living. As it was, the machete and ax work had worn them down, they had fallen behind, and the brutish tanks had plowed ahead, hardly fearful of their ignorance.

Knowing by now that the village of Phu Doan was just ahead, mortar fire was called in by the colonel. It was directed to drop on either side of the ambush site but not too close. It was important to recover the surviving tank. The major got on his radio and directed a company commander, despite the looming darkness, to send a platoon into the bush on either side of the clearing. If the Vietminh were still there, they would make themselves known. The ambush site would have to wait for tomorrow's first light to reconnoiter and clean up.

Private Ninh, meanwhile, had regained most of his senses. The fire team didn't know what all had happened above them, but they generally understood their situation, and there wasn't much they could do about anything. Just enough room in the trench allowed for three frightened young men to squat at the bottom on the ground. They clenched rifles they barely knew how to load. Private Pham wondered to himself how an abstract artist would portray their sorry circumstance. That thought was good for a smile as the mortar bombs hissed and burst on either side of the clearing. Alive but trapped, with a Hercules of sorts having them pinned. Or was Hercules protecting them? Quietly, in the closing twilight, Pham idly expressed their common thought: "We have to get the fuck out of here."

It was obvious they were safer where they were at the moment than out in the clearing. There, it was mortar bombs and dead men. On the other hand, morning light would bring a French column and disaster. At present, as far as they knew, the tank above them was complete with armaments and ammunition. If all else failed and the home team didn't blast it, the owners would reclaim their property and move it, revealing them. Either way the fire team was duck soup. The three privates would be shot on the spot, or they could be roughly interrogated before being murdered. *You say interrogation; I say torture.* That's what they knew would happen when captured. It was simple logic. This was war, and the three of them were responsible for death, destruction, fear, and inconvenience. There had always been plenty of talk about the kinds of torture the enemy enjoyed with prisoners. None of them cared to think about it, but stopping the visions was another thing entirely.

"I have one hand grenade," Cho volunteered. "When they come I will blow us up ."

There was no discussion and no disagreement.

Then it was Pham, again with an idea. "We have the hoe. We can dig. When all is dark we can scratch a channel out. Then all we do is crawl out. If lucky, we can escape to Phu Doan in the dark."

"We are surrounded," Ninh flatly stated. "It does not matter by whom. They are watching, and when movement is seen we will be shot many times." If that wasn't enough, his open hand sliced the air for emphasis.

"The battle must continue," Cho grunted, whatever that meant.

A strained minute later it was Pham who spoke up, this time with his calming voice. "Patience, comrades. We cannot direct circumstance. We will remain calm and wait for circumstance to direct us."

Ever so slowly, Cho first, and then a nod from Ninh. They wished not to be negative or suicidal, but there was so little positive to be seen.

"Comrades," Pham began again, "we are alive. The Buddha guides us."

Ninh and Cho knew he was right. That was pretty much the formal acceptance of Pham as the team leader. It was Ninh who said, "Brave soldiers have strong leaders—we are brave—we have a leader." That sealed it. A surge of pride came to them as they considered what they had managed to accomplish. It felt strange to be alive somehow. Now they would wait. Patience was good. The hurry-up was done for the time being. They could wait. All armies were alike that way. And the rice in their guts began to digest.

Meanwhile, Back in France: Post-World War II

The homeland citizenry was hurt, angry, and suffering from bitterness. World War II had ravaged them only a few years before. Much was made of the continuing divisiveness among the politicians and the people. There was no political equilibrium. There were the Vichy Government supporters and the Free French factions. They blamed each other, and the socialists blamed the communists, and the communists blamed the socialists. The right and the left were always at each other's throats. True patriots rose and fell by the variance of definition. Agreement on any matter was difficult and often unmanageable. Weak governments, one after another, faltered and failed.

Despite such downsides, regaining the plum of a colonial Indochina was too great an incentive for whoever was in power. Largely in agreement by French citizens, however, was the disgust of the waste and the unnecessary debacle of it all. As it was, maintaining occupation forces in the recently established French sector of Europe was a strain on France. The North Atlantic

Treaty Organization was a blessing, but it was also a responsibility and a challenge to French resources. Conscription of French citizens was necessary for home security and NATO, but conscription was unpopular and the quotas difficult to fill. There was a great deal of rebuilding yet to do on the home front. The Indochina War was not essential. Its cost was an abomination. Lean coffers were depriving citizens of essentials, and sacrificing more young Frenchmen was seen as no bargain.

Of course, then, there was the self-image and dignity of France. The country striving to rebuild and reposition itself back into the world order after The War. The French Expeditionary Force in Vietnam consisted of colonial, Indochinese, and Foreign Legion battalions, all needing and using French officers necessary to maintain control and cohesion. Year after year, the bulk of the French Military Academy graduates, the new lieutenants, were siphoned off for the Indochina War.

Meanwhile, the French Parliament was responding to the anti-war sentiment. Law passed prohibiting Indochina combatants from the benefit of French blood drives. Blood would not be available for the wounded; not French blood, in any case. Since the Communist Party was legal and active in France, which included Members of Parliament, it too had a hand in the tumult. Organized resistance was in place and active, attempting to shut down the war. There was also the issue of the seven or eight failed governments in succession, each clinging to a vision of France returning to world power status. Reclaiming Indochina—regaining its resources and cheap labor—would be a significant boost toward French restoration to the elite world order.

And so the French-Indochina War continued.

Chapter 4

First Jump

L ined up on the hard jump seats they sat, waiting for the door to open and their moment of truth. Beads of sweat pooled on Recruit Aiden Conner's forehead. Even at five hundred meters, the Dakota C-47's deck wasn't all that warm. Because the jump door wasn't open yet, communication was only difficult, not impossible.

"I met the standard, Master Sergeant," he said for the second time. The first time it had come out even more feeble.

The master sergeant glanced at the recruit, then pursed his lips and looked away.

Sweat beads began pooling on the strawberry-blonde eyebrows. They looked about to break through and make the short run for green eyes. Just in time, the recruit wiped them away with the back of a hand. There was something else now. The young man's morning ablution was letting him down. Must have been the anxiety. He caught a whiff of himself when he raised his arm to wipe the sweat. It wasn't bad, but it was there. "You know I did, Master Sergeant." More of the whine, but at least it was loud enough to hear. He wasn't earning points with the master sergeant, but he had cornered his attention.

Sergeant Phillips turned to the recruit again, this time making eye contact. *This is as good a time as any,* Phillips told himself, and with that he began. "I've been watching you, Conner. How you made it this far in boot camp is a friggin' miracle. Why the lieutenant saw fit to put you aboard today is beyond me. As fresh off mother's milk as you are, a Boy Scout camp is where you belong. From all manner of boys and men I have turned into Legionnaires, desperados included, there are no mama's boys. I don't see you breaking that spell. But, young man, if you refuse your jump this morning, I simply take you off the training manifest. That ends it. We are done with each other. You would be saved a good deal of misery, and you can then stowaway back across the Channel. Or I can wait for you to buckle under. It will be a pleasure to boot your ass out the front gate. Just give me one chance to get rid of you, recruit, and I won't pass on it. I promise to the saints I will not."

"But I met the standard, Master Sergeant. You know that." He was getting stronger and even more insistent.

"Listen, recruit, bones can be strong and muscles meet the standard, but inside is where it counts—counts most—precisely where you are soft. The lieutenant can't see it, not like me. Your comrades here, they know it. You cloud the air with that pansy-ass comportment of yours. A handful of years ago, half these men were either marching on Berlin or parading goosesteps for the Fuhrer. It was bad times in The War. If you weren't butchering, you were getting butchered. Most of these blokes lost everything there was to lose. Now here they are, doing what they're good at because of that fucking war. For them it's a chance at a new start. I don't see you with the iron in your gut to survive the bush—even if you do meet the standard. You excel in one thing: getting by."

At that he stopped, not taking his eyes off Conner. Then he matched a single nod of his head with a nasal exhale. He as well as laughed at the kid. Then he started in again. "Maybe you convinced yourself that boot camp is so much bullshit, something to endure and then move on from. You may very well be moving on, Mr. Conner. It's not likely a drill instructor, a limey bastard like me, can relate to a sensitive and bright carrot top like you. Isn't that right? Getting by isn't the answer in this man's Legion. Think you can survive five years and get the perks? French citizenship after five, and your name here isn't legal until then. After *that*, the world is yours, trainee. Meanwhile, you get to listen to me until you are done here or one of us is dead or worse." It was pretty much a fact that all drill instructors had the gift of provocation. "You will work your heinie off, Recruit. That thin-skinned baby face isn't as special as you think, and I don't care what you are running away from. Just don't think you're so clever that getting by will get you by. Cowardice is a contagion that spreads faster than melancholy and is more dangerous times ten. It begins in recruits like you who are given a pass in boot camp. Getting by does not materialize here. If you are awarded the kepi, you will have earned it. And not until then are you a Legionnaire."

Private Conner no longer heard the pitched drone of the two radial engines. He no longer felt the aluminum deck cracking his backside in the turbulence. *How could I have thought it would work—that the Legion would be better and safer than staying home and facing the music?* he asked himself. That was where his emotion machine spilled over. *The honor and glory of the French Foreign Legion is bullshit! It's nothing but misery, and taunting misery at that.*

With nothing to lose now, he began to say his piece out loud. "Sir, I am a full seventeen—going on eighteen. I am no boy. And my hair is not red, not like others." He hesitated. "Not that I'm trying to correct you, Master Sergeant." He heard what he was saying and had second thoughts, toning it down. But he was committed; he could not go home. "I can and will do whatever is required, Master Sergeant. I am just younger than the others is all."

Phillips nodded ever so slightly. He responded calmly but then stepped it up more quickly than he meant to. "It isn't your age. Or even your stubborn mick blood. You see, I am the sage who sees into the future." At that, he stopped to smile. "You bog-hoppers should understand that," he provoked.

There he took a breath and pushed himself to continue, not certain where he would end or how. "I have more life experience than any bloke here cares to think about. 'Tis true the stripes on my sleeves provide just a bit of privilege and authority. Do you understand why you show respect and treat me with reverence? 'Tis because I control your destiny is why! I have insight regarding the likes of all my recruits. And I see you swallowed up by these mates of yours the minute I push you out from under my wing. Yes, you are under my wing, Recruit, whether you see that or not. Should I shelter you until we go to field, it will be the Vietminh what swallow you up. You hear me? This first jump is a gut test, and presently, you are at the Rubicon. Do you test yourself and cross or do you recognize your limits? Either way, you are a damn fool. Think about it."

Time passed. Then he began again. "I have a wish for you, Conner. Assuming you find some resolve and carry on with us to war, what then? You would likely meet up with a Soviet machinegun at some Vietnam trailhead. There, you will have the opportunity to learn a good deal about your relationship with time, which now you so abuse. In that instant, there is for you no time. There is no enemy, no mates, no world, even. Only you and the hot gun barrel spitting green tracers at you." The sergeant paused to let that sink in. "With no time, there can be no thinking. It is when every cell in your body shuts down, good as lifeless. Or your body responds to the drill and instruction provided by your bloody drill sergeant in boot camp. With no time, Conner, there be no choices. You either do it or you do not. The grand party we know as time will resume for one of you—either you or the gunner behind the machine gun, not both. Your chance at life is how you use this opportunity, this boot camp. Is it bullshit or is it for real?"

The recruit wanted to babble, wanted to cry, but instead the truth came out. "This is all new to me, Sergeant. It is fast—it comes so quickly. Sometimes I'm overwhelmed, but I can catch up if you give me a chance. And these mates—why are they against me? They have background and experience, but I have background as well, only different. What of *Honneur et Fidélité*, the honor and fidelity of the Legion? Does that not include the young and innocent? Surely you were innocent once, Master Sergeant?"

Sergeant Phillips left it there for the time being. He turned and made a production of filling his pipe. Aiden Conner was angry, but maybe more hurt than angry. The man who could see the future was too often pained by what he saw. Twice, Phillips had been a recruit himself. He had made mistakes. But he was honorable.

A few draws on the pipe and he began again. "Honor, my boy, is the difference between watching your patrol bleed to death, one by one, or counterattacking against all odds. Look at you. You are not special. Yes, you can learn like everyone else. You are not special, but as a Legionnaire you can be special." The master sergeant went silent again. Two more draws on the pipe. "Being prepared and responding to the attack—that is where the battle begins. Facing the devil is the easy part. Your job is to push the bastard even as he jumps in your face, and he will hurt you in ways you could not before imagine. You do your job even if you cannot save your mates, even if you cannot save yourself. Your job is to scratch at the eyes of doom for the honor and glory of the Legion. Your salvation is the Legion. Wearing the kepi? My boy, I do not today see a Legionnaire in you.

"Whatever it is that brought you here from Mama's bosom is proof that life will never again be as it was. You know that, but in your head, you pretend it is not so. No more is there Mama's tea and crumpets. There is only the Legion. Where in you is there a real soldier? I see a near-soldier, and near-soldiers are cannon fodder disposed to whither. Maybe they survive for a time—who knows? Some may even make it through. But they are not soldiers, not in this service. When the final day comes, there are those who wither and those who face the reaper. Those who whither can do nothing but go to their grave as a mewling cow—a hollow, limpid creature dragging along a putrid list of getting by. You tell me if their maker will be impressed. I think not. Or, Recruit Aiden Conner, you can step up, do your sworn duty, and add to the honor and glory of the Legion for all time. Your drill instructor's job is to abet recruits—for them to discern which way is theirs. Do you die as a mewling cow or as a man, a Legionnaire? You choose."

Eyes open, fellow recruits, both seasoned soldiers and new, had tuned in to the master sergeant's lecture. No need for Phillips to look around, he knew. Sensing further opportunity, he continued the rant directed at Conner.

"Now, if you choose my side of the street, there comes with it the Vietminh mortar bombs. They come from the heavens, straight down on you. You likely hear the *crump* of the firing tube, so you know it is coming. Then comes the bloody shriek as it falls all the way to target. You know the target is you. You cannot make yourself small enough or get deep enough into the ground to be safe. You can only wait. Before it finally hits, you feel as if it has grabbed your very spine and twisted. In the beginning you may piss your drawers. Good for you. Doing so can be a warm and comforting distraction. You hope and pray to hear the blast. You know if you do not hear it you are either dead or in exceedingly deep shit. After the first one or two, the mortar bomb begins to walk: the next one is either away from you or closing on you. Odds are good they do not stray far. It is chaos in your mind, and your only defense is to make peace with the hand of fate.

"For you with no heart, Conner, you see yourself doomed. There is no thought of duty and honor. The crux of the matter is your fear, and that is a magnet drawing bombs and bullets to you. Unusual it is for an Irish boy to sprout with neither heart nor balls. If you continue to 'meet the standard,' as you say today, and are awarded the kepi, hooray for you. You are the number-one candidate to jump full up at first ambush. Do you know why? Only to take a few rounds, and that to end the anguish within. But no, you were not born a coward. You allowed yourself to believe in one. Worse yet, you refuse to become a Legionnaire of heart."

The master sergeant continued playing to the crowd through the private. "Now listen to me, boy. I'll not have it, I tell you—I simply will not have it! If you are going to break down, then do it here and now so I can justly throw you off this bloody aeroplane. Later, I will not waste time and energy when I have both men and mission to see after. Look at me, Conner. I see in your quivering eye and jaw the temptation of the jump door. Yes, 'tis an option for the mewling cow—be it your idea or mine. And the air is fine this morning, albeit a bit thin for free-falling. Know this: there is not one bloke present, no legionnaire anywhere, to comfort you in weakness. Do you hear me, lad? Legionnaires will comfort you out of strength alone, and you display none at all! I say, do you hear me?"

Ashen-faced, Private Conner stared blankly at the sky well beyond the opening jump door. A moment passed. Then another. Sergeant Phillips knew he had beaten to a pulp another thin-skinned recruit. Maybe enough to make him think. As sincere as the kid seemed to be, maybe he would engage himself and hang on. Phillips saw Conner as a fifty-fifty chance at best.

Just as the sergeant had described, time and space had been suspended for Conner when he stalked the culprits and revenged the attack on his father. That had got him where he was now. Despite the likelihood of personal peril, he had taken chances. He had challenged circumstance, and he had survived. The acknowledgment gave him a degree of hope. *Might there be a dawning, a future overcoming fear, if I can make myself allow it? The world is brutal, yet I am capable of pushing through. I know because I have done so.* It was as if a fog had lifted from the past and the present itself refocused. As always, the future would take care of itself.

Master Sergeant Phillips leaned back against the bulkhead and struck a match, now to one of his foul Turkish cigarettes. He had said his piece; due diligence performed; however awkward, an opportunity for the private.

Aiden Conner inhaled a lungful of secondhand smoke. The same blue haze of the smoking habit infected every environment that involved military men, given the means and opportunity. It was the times. At least the recruit had acclimated to the wide range of smokes, smells, and stinks of military life. Most were only slightly distasteful to him now. *Still, this world is not Northern Ireland,* he told himself for the thousandth time. *And not for the better.*

The belly of the Dakota was stuffed with twenty-two other recruits, mostly war veterans, but a number of them also tasting today their first jump. Each of them dragged along his own bleak thoughts from a life story looking for rehab.

Conner slowly shifted his gaze to the face of the drill instructor. He saw an ever-so-slight and drawn-out smile.

The master sergeant knew he had given one of his better speeches, and it pleased him. Eyes closed, he surprised himself with a silent prayer of thanks to the Almighty. Just maybe he had gotten through to the recruit. That, or he had broken whatever spirit was in him. *If that is all it takes to defeat the lad, then he should be pitched off this bloody perch.* The boy's soul had been reached and touched. As a near-soldier, could he survive long enough to become a Legionnaire? Like all things and all matters, it rested at future's feet.

The yellow light flashed. "Hook up!" he bellowed. "Clip in those static lines, lads! Check the man in front of you."

Chapter 5

Le Thuy Prevails

"Van Hieu," she whispered.

No response.

"Van Hieu," but louder. Finally, "Pham Van Hieu, are you alive? Please, anyone alive?" Her voice cracked through the impractically loud stage whisper.

"Whaaaat?" He heard his name, but it made no sense to his fatigued brain. All three had fallen into a hard sleep. They had no idea what time it was; it was dark within the tank-covered trench. Slowly they came to life, remembering where they were and their circumstance. It was eerie and silent now, no shooting. There was only the distant boom of faraway artillery.

"Shhhhh." From deep in the trench Private Ninh whispered in Pham's ear. "It must be a trick. They are baiting us. We come out, they kill us."

As close as she was, she couldn't help but hear the counter whispers. As softly and calmly as possible, she spoke again, this time in her own voice. "Pham Van Hieu, this is Le Thuy. You remember, from yesterday? Le family from the village?"

Now it began to make some kind of sense. *But how could she or her voice be so near?* Private Pham wondered. *Is this her spirit voice? Was she killed in the battle yesterday, and now comes to us? Why? To warn us? To bury us? Such an appearance could be helpful,* he knew, *but spirits are full of tricks, and we are three privates already in a grave.* A quickening heartbeat helped to clear Private Pham's head, but not entirely. Without raising his voice, he finally asked, "Who are you, really, and what do you want?" He said it as authoritatively yet as quietly as he could.

"Van Hieu, you are alive." She seemed happy about that. "You saw me yesterday, you remember? No one knows if you three are alive or dead. You know, don't you, that you are not in a good place when daylight comes?"

There was no response. Pham did not recognize her unnatural voice. A disquieting tension continued building.

Thuy, on the other hand, was becoming angry. "You do not believe it is me? You think I am a ghost? Look to the front, the front of the tank. Yes, look over the top of the trench, ignorant boys. What do you see?"

One at a time, all three stood and pulled themselves high enough to get their noses over the top. There she seemed to be, but it was dark. Despite their fully dilated pupils, however, they could not swear it was the girl who brought the grenades. Fortunately for them, their desperate circumstance was quite convincing.

"How did you get here?" Pham demanded in a coarse but hushed voice. It was said as though he were her commanding officer.

"No time for that," she tersely responded. "If you are not dead, maybe leaving this trench would be a good plan now?"

The three privates either missed the sarcasm in her voice or chose to ignore it. But they did agree about the good plan thing. It wasn't like they could pop up and roll out. Their trench was deep, and the tank above offered them little head room. The fire team did not know their status but rightly assumed remaining there was short-term.

"Of course you are right," Pham responded. He felt around until he found the hoe. He began chopping a channel in the side of their trench toward Thuy to make a short, inclined escape channel. Pulling the broken soil into the trench helped by raising the floor for easier egress. Pham had spoken of doing such digging yesterday, but with neither hope nor plan, there was no action. Within minutes he had honest sweat dripping from his chin and a rough channel to the surface.

"What direction is safe?" Ninh wanted to know.

"No direction is safe," Thuy fired back. "French Force is all around. They do not know you are here, I think, but they keep watch on this tank."

"Then we have no chance," an exasperated Private Cho responded.

"Listen to me. On signal, my signal, Vietminh friends will make a diversion in the bush. When the French react to the diversion, we go that way quickly. If we are lucky, French soldiers busy with the diversion will not see us."

"Go toward the French shooting?" Cho asked too loudly. "No! We must go away from diversion or be killed for sure!"

"As you please, but I will go to where soldiers are looking the other way." She had a way about her.

By then, all of them were flat on their bellies under the front half of the tank, breathing in anxious gulps. Just then, a parachute flare went up in the near distance. "Close your eyes! Do not look at the light," Pham hoarsely whispered. "We must maintain night vision."

"Very good," Thuy calmly responded with closed eyes. "The enemy looks, and night vision is lost to them only. When the flare burns out, we throw this American hand grenade toward the village. That is our signal. My friends will then shoot two mortar rounds into the bush close to here. The French cover their heads from the falling mortar bombs. We then run like hell."

"You are out of your mind, woman! We must crawl slowly and use camouflage. Then we go opposite way from mortar explosion." It was Private Ninh, the brave one.

From there, Private Pham took over, not unlike a drill sergeant. "Hush. Thuy is right. While enemy heads are down, we run. There won't be much time, so we must run. Going the other way is to run into the French Force who will by then be looking this way. Toward the mortars we go; the other side is mostly blocked from view by the tanks." That seemed to settle things, so Private Pham went on. "Cho, you are strong and you can throw far. Thuy, Cho is close to you. Find and put the grenade in his hand, please, before the flare goes out. Cho, you crawl out from under the tank so you can throw. When the flare goes out, you pull the pin and throw the grenade as far as you can toward the village."

Cho grunted his acceptance of Pham's orders. The privates were green but good at responding to the voice of command. Firm orders relieved the feeling of helplessness. Eyes remaining closed, the grenade was transferred. Cho edged up to what he could feel was the front of the tank. They soon recognized the flare's final flickers. Private Cho rubbed his throwing arm and shoulder as a warm-up, and his mind visualized the throw. The flare light sputtered its last as Cho rose to one knee and reached his arm back to throw.

"Pull the pin!"

Eyes wide open by then, the others shared their advice in a chorus of frantic whispers. He had forgotten the part about the pin but stopped and quickly pulled it out. Rattled, he then incidentally released the spoon, activating the chemical that would ignite the grenade in short seconds. They all heard the snap of the released spoon and knew what he had done.

It would make sense to release the spoon before throwing, intending it to explode as it reached the target, or even in the air over the target—if one had the guts. For Private Cho, it was not about guts, it was about being flustered. But it worked out. Probably because the sudden realization of what he had done gave his system an extra shot of adrenaline. He threw hard, he threw high, and he threw long.

Private Ninh was pretty sure he heard it bounce once and then roll, although all their eardrums had taken a beating a few hours before. Since that's what they wanted to hear, the other two agreed with Ninh's whispered assessment. Regardless of what kind of throw it was, the grenade did not explode, and that was a problem. Being an American grenade made it more disappointing, since they were more reliable than the Chicom variety.

"I have one more," Thuy hissed. She stuffed it into Private Cho's hand and slid back under the tank. "I pray my soldier friends understand this takes a long time and they still do as I ask."

She needn't have worried. This time Cho pulled the pin without coaching, and the spoon released only as it left his hand. The grenade definitely bounced, and bounced another time or two, before rolling down toward the village. It seemed to take forever, but then, as they all began to be concerned, it finished with a splendid little blast, drawing a good deal of attention. The enemy was surely looking toward the grenade's explosion when the *crump* of a mortar round leaving its tube far to their right was clearly heard.

"That is my friends," Thuy let them know. Then another *crump* just as the overhead whistle of the first round began its descent. "Follow me," she told them as she scrambled onto her feet and began running.

She may have saved them, but Private Pham was just a little irritated. Thuy acted like the boss, telling them what to do. She wasn't even in the People's Army—she was a coolie!

That was when he tripped. It was one of the two bodies on the direct path between the tank and the bush. His night vision was good enough to see them, but his head wasn't where it should have been. He hoped she wouldn't know, both that he had tripped and that she was in his head.

Private Cho had no such thoughts. He was in Thuy's shadow, had there been a shadow, and was keeping pace with her on their short sprint to the bush.

Private Ninh was yet reluctant to go towards the known enemy. It was when he realized it was either go with them or be on his own, possibly toward enemy looking his way, that he kicked in the afterburner and followed.

The first mortar hit while they were yet a few steps from the bush. The second mortar seemed to be screaming directly down on them, if anybody cared. Certainly, the neighborhood enemy cared, and their heads were down. Had their path to the bush been slightly different, the foursome could have been cut down by one or the other of the mortars, they were that close. But they were not cut down, and they were thankful the mortars were close, keeping enemy heads buried. The quartet had not jumped directly into an enemy position, but they were close. It would not be long before they realized how close.

Further out, a couple wild shots from a nervous French rifle and then a machine gun initiated a firefight against shadows in the direction of the active mortar tube. It was normal to anticipate an attack after mortar incoming, so it was typical for troops to imagine all kinds of things and then rip off shots into the bush, just to be safe. The team was surprised that a machine gun, shooting away from them, opened up to their immediate right, maybe twenty paces away. Not good, but now they knew what it was and where it was, and it was not friendly.

In a low voice, as the spotty firing continued, Thuy assured the others she knew where the 141st Regiment was. Could she now get them there was the question.

The firing died out. Everyone, friend and foe, was now alert and on edge. No chance to move, nor could they so much as make a sound while the machinegun crew was close by. They lay flat on their stomachs the rest of the night, conscious not to make a sound or sleep.

At the first hint of daylight, the action picked up again in a big way. A soldier from the machine-gun position stood up and began walking toward the fire team. Just before reaching them, he stopped and unbuttoned his trousers, apparently to relieve himself. He was unarmed, and there was no sign he had seen them. As he began to pee, he relaxed and looked up to his front. He blinked as if in disbelief. The Algerian looked into a very wide-open pair of Asian eyes. It was Private Cho, who clutched his rifle but did nothing more than gape. The pee stopped. The Algerian soldier turned his head toward the machine gun. He had the beginnings of an open mouth just as Private Ninh rammed a bayonet into his chest. Only a small grunt left the trooper's mouth. The bayonet had missed the sternum, glanced off the edge of a rib, and struck the heart cleanly. He dropped like a rock, quietly bleeding out.

Bad luck or good, who knew what it was? A corpse would not be returning to the gun crew, so the gunner would be missed. Without question they had to move immediately.

"Here, put on his helmet, Ninh, and stand up like you're him doing his business," Pham instructed. "I will try to get behind their position."

The team didn't know how many others there were at that point. Without a word, Private Ninh plopped the steel pot on his head and stood up with his back toward the gun nest, trying to look big. Private Pham was already low-crawling with his rifle toward the gun position.

Halfway there, one other of the Algerian-French hissed at his distanced buddy, asking what was taking him so long. There was just enough light to see images, but not clearly. The hissing soldier stood to get a better look. He was unarmed and no doubt dealing with the priority of relieving his own bladder as soon as his buddy returned. Then, something didn't look right to him. He took a few steps forward. With that, he was certain, and with some urgency in his eyes turned to the third man at the position who was still on the ground, half-asleep.

Pham rose from a crouch, holding his rifle in bayonet stance. The trooper turned toward him and watched in disbelief as Pham closed in three steps. Swinging his hips around propelled the bottom edge of Pham's rifle stock at his target's bare head. The leading edge of hardwood landed flush on the soldier's left temple, a crushing blow dropping him, probably lifeless, on the spot.

Then it was the matter of the recently sleeping enemy who witnessed the attack and immediately reached for the pistol in his belt. Before Pham could orient himself to deal with the new imminent danger, the 1911 Colt was raised and the trigger pulled. Only a metal *clack* resulted.

Both combatants realized the firing chamber was empty, an intentional and common safety precaution with pistols. The third gunner hesitated, realizing the mistake. The receiver slide was pulled halfway back to chamber a round when it clattered forward, and the gunner's head dropped. He seemed to be watching the blood roll down his chest. Private Pham hadn't touched him—he had no bayonet.

It was Thuy. At the sound of the crushed head, she had picked up Cho's bayoneted rifle and charged. It was the sudden and surreal drama with Pham that had captured the focus of the third gunner. He never knew another was closing on him. Thuy had recognized the circumstance. She saw the gunner was trying to correct his pistol problem. From a distance of three meters, and much like an underhand softball throw, she thrust Cho's rifle at him, trying to strike before he could chamber the round and shoot. Her thrust missed his chest completely. What it did find was tissue, bone, and a critical neck vein. That was ground zero. Without so much as a shot fired, three French Force machine gunners lay dead, leaving the Vietminh fire team and their coolie helper free to advance, hoping to find their unit and relative safety. It would not be all that easy.

In short order they were up and past the enemy machine-gun position. Every second of increased daylight threatened them more. Despite having escaped the tomb of the trench, they felt little safer. They hopscotched short distances through the bush, jumping from one brush thicket to the next.

A hundred yards out from the bodies, they stopped to consider their plight. Being captured now would not go well. It would be obvious they had something to do with the destruction of two tanks and the death of nearby troops exposed and lying about. If captured now, it would not be for long. The French would surely add them to their belligerents' body count. Names would not be involved, of course, only the number of bodies. That was one reason why the Vietminh made it a priority to drag away dead comrades and hide the bodies, often in unmarked mass graves. It was important that the French Force not know the extent of damage inflicted.

But the escapees had to keep moving. The French Force behind them was real and it was massive. Except for that business at the clearing yesterday, there would already have been sweeps by them through the countryside.

Not knowing the size of the French unit they were among kept them from moving fast. Probably no more than a platoon alongside the clearing, tasked with protecting and keeping an eye on the stalled French tank in the clearing. Whatever size unit it was, they were also guarding against a Vietminh attack from the other way. That could make it a company- or even battalion-size force for the fire team to maneuver through.

As Thuy and Pham quietly debated how to continue their escape, Privates Cho and Ninh—both now helmeted as a form of camouflage—kept watch on their surroundings. By then it was full daylight; they were surprised there was so little activity. From where they were, they could still see when someone approached to check on the machine-gun crew. No one had yet. About all that would be found was the machine gun and bodies. Cho and Ninh had carefully rifled the bodies, searching for food. There was little of that, so they appropriated what they could: water bottles and ammunition—a good haul at that. The machine gun itself was a prize, but traveling light meant traveling fast. A machine gun was too much considering their circumstances. Their priority was survival.

When it came, it didn't come quietly. From below the familiar rise in front of the village, they heard what must have been the approach of a large vehicle. It could have been a truck but sounded more like a tank. Noisy action in the clearing would be a good distraction for a successful escape. They watched from the tall weeds and waited. First came soldiers. Over the rise, a half dozen troopers trudged, rifles more or less at the ready. Then came the belching machine. It was a tracked vehicle, but not a tank—rather a large bulldozer with two uncomfortable passengers crouching behind the driver's seat. They were holding on for dear life. Just over the rise on the Phu Doan side, the behemoth stopped. Cautiously, the grunts began to investigate the carnage. The bodies had signs of bloat already; the two demolished tank hulks were thoroughly burned out but still warm.

The grunts carefully surveyed all parts, both mechanical and human. Slowly they moved among it, inspecting where they must, using rifle barrels as probing tools. A young French lieutenant on the other side of the clearing stepped out of the bush. "Should be all right. Nobody's been out there."

Private Pham and the others heard him. It was a good sign. The lieutenant's comment lessened tensions for the grunts. Little did any of them know.

"Vietminh mines and booby traps are a big part of the war," Master Sergeant Phillips had stressed many times to his recruits, "whether buried in the ground, wrapped among twisted, burned-out pieces of metal, or hidden in dead bodies." The investigation moved along but remained cautious. The stalled tank was inspected inside and out. Nothing suspicious was found and nothing blew up.

A corporal, the one with two stripes on his sleeve, pointed at the dozer and shouted over the throbbing engine, "Ist good. You come fix." The uncomfortable travelers cautiously climbed down from the dozer, muscling a couple of oversized toolboxes from a compartment behind the engine. Once lugged to the tank, oversized wrenches were liberated, and the mechanics cautiously went to work. They were not happy mechanics today. Working on the front line was part of the deal, but not their forte—especially not with day-old body parts scattered about.

Meanwhile, the infantry troops dragged the human remains off to one side and then policed up the armaments and kits scattered about. When that was accomplished, the dozer operator was ready to begin his end of the cleanup. He revved the big diesel. It bellowed black smoke for several seconds. The resulting dark cloud hung in the air, slowly spreading a field of vile fumes. Both Pham and Thuy recognized opportunity in the distraction. With a simple but urgent nod of her head, Privates Pham, Ninh and Cho followed Thuy. They were like ducklings behind their mama.

It was working. Bent low, they moved quietly and quickly, but no running. They stopped often, looking for signs of enemy. Most of all, they hoped they were heading toward the security of the regiment. After about fifteen minutes of start and stop, Thuy stood up straight and breathed a loud sigh. They all stood up straight then, a relief to their aching backs. They reasonably believed they were out of the hostile zone. Heavier and more uncomfortable than they had expected, the helmets Ninh and Cho wore during their march through the weeds were unceremoniously dropped and left where they fell.

"The regiment was here last night," Thuy authoritatively stated. That did not appear to be the case. Looking closely, however, they spotted thin trails of fresh dirt in a pattern indicating slit trenches very recently closed.

From a near tree limb, and adding to the party, an armed Viet dropped to the ground behind them. His landing was soft but, to the escapees, no less alarming than a cannon blast behind them.

"Why are you here?" the armed stranger demanded. "If it wasn't for the

Vietminh scarf this one is wearing, I would have shot you all. Only the enemy is behind me now," which was exactly from where they came. His tone radiated anger, but his open hand trembled. "The 141st pulled back in the night. I was left as the solitary lookout." Of course, he was scared.

With a full measure of pride, Ninh touched his scarf. The others made it a point not to notice.

It was Pham who spoke up. "We were trapped in place at the village overnight. Just now we escaped. We are privates in the 141st Regiment. Where are they? Captain Ngai probably thinks we are dead."

"Captain Ngai? You took part in the tank destruction at the crest of Phu Doan?"

Four heads nodded vigorously.

The armed stranger seemed impressed. Finally he could relax. "Now I see. You will find the trail, maybe thirty meters north from here. Follow it to find 141st. They will be happy to see you."

"Not me," Thuy spoke up. "I am coolie. Where are the coolie teams?"

"Not know, sister. Maybe farther north of the trail to hide munitions. That is what they do now."

There were no more questions, and the sentinel was anxious to get back into his tree. Privates Cho and Ninh immediately struck out to find the trail. Pham followed, then stopped. He came back to within arm's length of Thuy.

"You were good help to us." He paused. That was the extent of his "thank you." But then he continued on another level. "Maybe you will be Vietminh soon?"

Thuy jerked slightly, looking at him as if he had offended her. A new thought, a surprise that someone would suggest she could one day be a soldier. It was a pleasant thought, however. She said nothing.

Pham broke eye contact and reached out. He casually cupped her left breast with his hand. She was not startled, only puzzled.

"Small but adequate," he stated. "Enough for babies when the war is done. You ask to be private in 141st Regiment. I will help. We will be together." With that, he turned and walked off toward the trail.

Accustomed to shy village sons, Thuy was certain she did not understand the ways of city boys like Private Pham. *Yes, he is beautiful and confident, but is he wise as he thinks?* She would consider his invitation. *Babies? At least it would be after the war*, she reasoned. *Being a soldier would offer the dignity I do not have as a coolie.* In that moment, she decided. *It is good to be wanted.* She turned and headed north, quite briskly, an innocent smile on her face.

She crossed the trail and continued north through the bush with much now on her mind. So much that she became careless. She did not notice stepping over a booted footprint. Then it was the snap of a twig behind her she did not notice. When she recognized the rush of footsteps behind her, it was too late. Strong limbs were suddenly around her, trapping both arms. She would not scream, but she dug her heels into the ground and pushed as hard as she could with her legs, tumbling herself and her attacker back and onto the ground where the hold might be broken. It was. She thrashed back an elbow, finding a hard jaw and causing a muffled curse. She then threw the other elbow back, but not far enough. It was blocked by an arm. Then she was rolled over and smothered by a body much heavier than her own. She hadn't yet seen her attacker but visualized a European male, a Frenchman if she was lucky, a Legionnaire if she was not.

Her torso and head were pressed into the soft earth, pinned by the hard body now on top of her. In an instant there was no choice; she must capitulate. She did so with the grunt of a person whose lungs were suddenly voided. Realizing then it was not so much a choice but something that happened on its own, she felt a small ray of peace. *Perhaps a forced capitulation is not dishonorable,* she told herself. *I can die and be raped, or raped and then killed, but I am forced.* Her thoughts were somewhat assuring, and her body went limp.

It was a heavily accented voice that spoke in French, "You are plucky girl. My mother is plucky. But she is not small and weak like you." Quiet and not fighting him, he soon turned her over. "Much anger in you, but pretty face. You think I must kill you now?"

She hotly responded in French and with great wrath. "I would think a brave and strong soldier like you would want to fuck me first," she taunted. She cautiously raised a knee to his crotch as if to rub.

The soldier blocked her leg with his arm.

"But only if you are man and not the boy I see straddling me now," Thuy continued. "What of your cock? There is nothing hard where you should be man. You have never been with a woman," she accused. "I can tell by your look—you are nothing but a fucking virgin! A virgin looking for a young girl to violate. A girl with no experience who cannot judge your performance. Go ahead, I dare you. After that you can kill me."

The soldier blushed furiously. Realizing his sudden and unexpected embarrassment, he backhanded the girl, his nostrils flaring. Her head jolted, but she only glared at him, challenging him to again defend his masculinity. She refused to give quarter.

"Girl," he barked with fury, raising his hand to again strike. There he caught himself. He took two long breaths through his nose, consciously calming himself. Finally, his hand lowered. He withdrew his right leg to kneel on the ground beside yet over her.

Thuy was lucky, but not so lucky as she had hoped. She was still alive, but the soldier was a Legionnaire. So far, he had not killed her; not even raped her. He was young and naïve, she already knew. It gave her hope. She spoke again. "What do you want from me? I am not Vietminh. I am a simple coolie, lost in bush. That is the truth. You must help me." *Is that pushing it? Probably,* but she didn't know.

The young soldier too was lost, temporarily at least, both geographically and psychologically. He didn't know where he was, and he had been confused and humiliated by this girl, this waif, this bitch cat beside him. "What is your name?" he flatly asked, not knowing what else to say.

She hesitated. Again, her words came sharp and in attack. "My name is Thuy. My coolie team is north of here. Let me go to them. They are worried for me. Why did you attack me, and what is your name?" *I ask his name to be pleasant,* she rationalized to herself. Then she redirected her defense. *I must talk and be his friend.* Her words softened. "I am a village girl. Where are you from?" Her tone was yet stilted, but it was the best she could do for the moment.

"Thuy, you say. That is maybe nice name. You do not talk like nice girl. How can you be that—how can you be nice girl?"

Her answer was simple and true. "I am what I must be," she softly announced.

"I see," was all the Legionnaire answered, but he seemed to understand. It did resonate with him. A brief silence later, his eyes smiled. "Your talk is like hair on back of frightened dog—raised and angry. You are that dog, I think. You try to scare tiger with angry voice. I am cautious for you. But not afraid," he insisted, remembering his recent embarrassment. Several seconds passed. Finally, "I am from Northern Ireland. Not Republic of Ireland, but Northern Ireland. My name is Conner. Aiden Conner."

The internal winds calmed. Thuy's breath came easier. Aiden Conner's breath came easier as well.

"Aiden Conner from Northern Ireland. How do you do?"

They both sat quietly after that until she looked around. There was no sign that Aiden Conner was about to lead any parade. At the risk of upsetting the figurative apple cart that seemed to have balanced itself, Thuy's spirit decided to take charge. She stood up.

"Your Legionnaire comrades are behind you to the south. Believe me, I know that to be true. You go that way, and I will surely find my comrades to the north." She looked at the single stripe on his sleeve. "Pleased to meet you, Private Aiden Conner."

They were both standing by then and facing each other.

Taken aback by her assured firmness, it simply happened. She had told him where he needed to go. That was good. He believed her, and that was better. She could have reached for his hand to shake, but, rather, she stood on outstretched toes and kissed him on the cheek. The left cheek. It was a pleasant kiss. It was a kind kiss.

The softness and the tenderness of it warmed him. When he opened his eyes, she was thirty meters off to the north. What could he do? He turned and walked south—reluctantly.

Chapter 6

Battle for Na-San

Fall 1952

" A hundred miles from civilization, that particular valley in the High Region was nothing more than a dozen brush-covered hills with a dirt landing strip in the middle. But it was the best chance to defend against an otherwise overwhelming force. Survivors of the purge north came to us every day like stray cats creeping into the granary. All felt violated their entire way there.

"General Giap thought his new army could annihilate us. We buckled down to stand the test. My unit included two officers and 108 dedicated men. We were the 11th Company, III Battalion of 5th Foreign Legion Regiment. For three solid days, we worked to reconfigure one broad hill in the Na-San Valley. Hardly more than three hectares in size, it was declared Strongpoint PA-8, at half a mile north of Central Camp. There was a dozen or so other hilltop strongpoints surrounding the airstrip and Central.

"Our company commander was Captain Letestu, who was ideal to the task. Throughout the valley, men dug into the highest hillsides to build independent defensive fortifications. Each was surrounded by parallel fences of razor and barbed wire. Letestu went well beyond the norm. He was a veteran of the Maginot Line from The War; his aptitude, experience, and insistence on a well-laid-out and exceptionally stout fortification served us well. A volume of hardwood beams was brought in. Hundreds and hundreds of sandbags were filled and moved on the backs of soldiers as well as a good number of prisoners. Those we could trust we brought along and put to work. Sandbag blockhouses we built at the corners of the strongpoints to give us an expansive field of overlapping fire. An abundance of machine guns seeded both the perimeter and the elevated interior positions. Each weapon was required to have cached with it, or nearby, the amount of ammunition that would be expected to meet the needs of thirty-six hours fighting; also, water and three days rations were stocked at each post."

Sergeant Phillips stopped and closed his eyes, reviewing the memory before he continued. "All Legionnaires detest the mole work. But, if you are man enough to operate a rifle in the bush with the Legion, you will learn the working end of the shovel as well in this service. Men of the Legion believe themselves to be special, and we are. We are, by God! We are operatives in the bush, on the plain, and in the desert; we hunt down the enemy when others shy away. We confront the ambush. We bleed and, too often, we die; too often we die cold and alone. But we are proud of the distinction, proud to be significant if only in how we stand—how we fight and die. We pride ourselves on accepting the challenge where others falter. We are thrown into the breach or dropped from the sky whenever and wherever it most matters. We prefer duty outside the wire. To fight the oppressor toe to toe, in the wilderness, our wit and wiles open to option—that is our connection to Spirit.

"We are special in another way, Private. Not loved and worried over as other soldiers are. It is not often a Legionnaire has family or loved ones to return to. We are expendable, you see. Most of us have walked away from some trouble or danger in our life. That is why we are here—to be with others like ourselves. The Legion gives us a name and character, the opportunity to make a difference. While we are not loved like others, it is our drive and perseverance that has value; it is our dignity. We are respected by those who command us and those who raise arms against us. We do not like the mole work, the digging, but we do so when ordered and we fight wherever we are needed. We do so as long as it takes, Private Conner. It is at the end we can rest. 'God willing,' as the Muslims say.

"It was our third day at Na-San. At supper, we believed we could rest, thinking the enemy was yet many kilometers away. We somehow felt our mole work would protect us. It was the Creator who humbled us that day.

"Not a minute. Not a second. There was no warning whatsoever. It was approaching twenty hundred hours—8:00 p.m.—and every man in the company bone tired. Corporal Fischer had put together a fine supper. The captain acknowledged our motivation and hard work by doubling the wine ration. The Legion is good that way—good food; excellent food, if at all possible, and a daily wine ration. At times, of course, the commodity wine is supplemented with liquor or beer or a better-quality wine. It is appreciated. Know that benefits coming to us are earned. With a good captain, we earn respect and know we are appreciated.

"The airstrip in the Central Camp was by then covered with PSP, the pierced-steel plating linked together into a hard surface. It handles even the Dakota and the Flying Boxcar or 'Banjo,' as we call the C-119. Fortifications were not yet complete; getting the artillery flown in was the greatest need. To complete the fortification, there would be more jeeps, trucks, timber, barbed wire, ponies, and mules to run supply trains out from Central Camp. Weather wasn't helpful; the valley was fogged in daily until around eleven. Six hours a day was the maximum window of any air supply. Everything depended on air supply. Loaded cargo planes came in like clockwork that whole time every day."

"That is incredible, Master Sergeant! The Legion is most organized."

"It wasn't the Legion, Private." Phillips' voice had become one of absurd annoyance. "The finest of the French military reside in Hanoi, and some of them are sober enough now and again to earn their pay. They did us no favors at Na-San. They performed their duty."

That was a cheeky comment, was it not? The private wasn't certain. He simply nodded and silently considered the sergeant's heritage. It was the scant smile and the softening of the master sergeant's eyes that won over the private. The well-guarded secret of English military humanity was suddenly exposed, and the private absorbed it eagerly.

"It seems odd now that there was so little tension at the end of those three days," the sergeant went on as if nothing had changed. "We ate, drank, began to relax after supper. We were basically ready. We were also wrong. Knowing the Vietminh divisions had been marauding the northern frontier and routing the Red River outposts, we had all along expected to be part of the response to that. Often, we jumped in ahead or behind the enemy and closed on them. Sometimes we were ambushed doing that, but to be expected.

"The rout of those Vietminh devils continued against a similar string of outposts along the Black River, fifty or so kilometers south of where they had begun, but closer to our valley. After that, there was nothing to stop them from hitting Laos. They could go all the way to Luang Prabang or Vientiane where they could resupply and find booty. With their three full divisions of trained and fit troops, it couldn't have been more serious.

"We were thrown into Na-San with orders to stop the Vietminh advance and to protect the incoming survivors from the forts. The defenders had scattered like pigeons on the parade ground at reveille. As sanctuary for them, Na-San had been prearranged. 'Scatter if you must, then escape to Na-San,' was the word to the outposts.

"Word of the assemblage at Na-San brought out challenge in the Viets. We would seem vulnerable, which was what our commanders wanted. For us, it would be the opportunity to confront an assembled division or more. We would devastate them with our machine guns, our artillery, and air strikes. After all, our garrison was impregnable. They took the bait. Our isolation was enough, it turned out, for a confident enemy to give us the assault we wanted. Or was it we who took their bait?"

"But you *did* beat them, Sergeant. I know you did. Why did you say it like that?"

The master sergeant became a bit distant at that point. He gave Private Conner a hollow stare. It took him a moment to soften. "Be a good private and listen, Conner. Vo Nguyen Giap, the Vietminh commanding general, saw Na-San as his opportunity to do real damage—to expose the vulnerability of the French after six years of war. To exploit and defeat a significant French force such as Na-San had become and would show the world, especially America, the dominance of the People's Army and the futility of supporting France. After all, why would money and human life be squandered when France is yet in tatters from World War II?

"Such is the opinion of many French citizens. French governments continue to fail, one after the other, maybe a dozen by then, but still the Indochina War has gone on and on, and every day that a Frenchman picks up a newspaper, citizens hurt and soldiers bleed—all a little more."

He wasn't yet done. From there, the master sergeant amused himself by going into a squeaky and hyperbolic speech, speaking as Ho Chi Minh himself. "'The world must take note once the mighty French master is humbled in a fight of his own making—a set-piece battle. Guerrilla warfare by my Vietminh has greatly damaged the French, but it is the grand, set-piece battle that consolidates and qualifies as victory. Our Vietminh are no longer orphans. With the assistance of Moscow and the Red Chinese, the Vietminh are an unremitting force. General Giap delivers with a limitless field of soldiers—tens of thousands of privates with the birthright to battle tyranny unto death's door. To perform such a feat, to crush a French force of a dozen or more battalions, General Giap moves against the French contamination in the valley of Na-San.'" Sergeant Phillips paused to catch his breath.

"'Get to them before French defenses are complete; get to them while they are yet awkward with little defensive plan; get to them before they can expect to be hit. Yes, I understand there will be loss, but that is secondary. The French will suffer more. Victory will invigorate the people. Yes, victory will more than replace any loss we may suffer. The French will lose face with the world, and America will reconsider its support of the illegitimate authority we suffer under.'"

Sergeant Phillips stopped talking, took a breath, then tried to relight his pipe. The long-dead coals failed to respond, setting in motion the well-paced routine of knocking away dead ash and a thorough stem cleaning combined with quiet focus. Upon opening his tobacco pouch and refilling the bowl by feel, the sometimes-jaded veteran began again, this time speaking as himself. The Na-San battle of nearly a year ago filled his head.

"The company was inside the wire, safe enough; most troopers in their trenches, weapons nearby. All SOP. Same with the blockhouse machine-gun crews and mortar teams. Nothing unusual to be seen or heard. Only the small jangle of a tin can or two in the wire, likely the cause of a slight breeze. That is common as takin' a breath, you will see. The cans are simple warning but sometimes better than the mines. Warm as it was, any breeze was welcome, and along with the breeze comes the scent of the moldering jungle. To the sensitive among us, the scent changes from day to day. That day, I recall, it seemed a particular heavy and musky scent. I could have seen it as a sign, a warning, but I did not.

"It was an attack that should not have happened. When the initial charges in the wire detonated, my brain could not immediately comprehend. How could a master sergeant with years of combat under his belt be surprised by such a thing? It was for that reason, I believe, that all action came to me in slow motion—my brain jolted into a high rate of speed for several seconds. It was as a vision before me: men screaming their instincts in drawn-out, surreal actions. As I came out of the cloud, disgust at myself engaged the fight. Private, you must not be dumbfounded by the enemy."

The comment was confusing to Private Conner. *Am I again faulted as a soldier?*

Sergeant Phillips recognized the difficulty. "It happens," he continued. "It can happen, but you will do your job as a Legionnaire with pride."

Conner's heart quickened, feeling a charge of confidence. *Does Sergeant Phillips believe in me after all? Perhaps.*

"It took some seconds before we could see through the haze of dust from the blasts. Peering into the wire was a ruddy sight. The bangalores and likely some satchel charges had done damage. No bugles, no shouts and orders, just the crushing explosions. Fortunate for us, chunks of wire was clipped clean, making strands and curls of the biting barbs everywhere in the devils' charging lanes. No perfectly clear alleys for them to charge through at first. Some of the first Viets were snagged by the loose ends and then fell or were even pulled back into the wire as it ran taut. Some of the attackers charging from behind the snared troops were tripped up by the bodies of their comrades, slowing access to the trenches. Our troopers hardly realized, it happened so fast; the guns in their hands were barking without aim and still finding flesh and bone.

"The bite of the attack was intense. Astonishment mattered little as men dropped in the fire storm. It is good to know that pulling the trigger on a target brings a calmness to the well-trained soldier. Fighting back offers a sense of control, small though it may be. There were targets—many charging through opening assault lanes. I could see the ripping of tracer rounds into the barbed wire, onto the bare earth, and into the dark of night from our machine guns. Something I find strange—the noise of the guns somehow gets tuned out. What I hear in the moment and long after is the cries of the wounded, both us and the enemy. That and the shouts of command, although they come in jumbled spurts. They overlap each other through the spastic gunfire. The words cannot be heard clearly, but their meaning is clear. If the men have been in combat before, and most here has been, then they are assured by words of command. The men need to see leadership and know what is expected of them. They know full well their world depends on meeting that expectation.

"It was the first seconds what emptied the trenchers' first magazine. The Viets were on our men in the front trenches before magazines could be exchanged. The men stood their ground, but it was rifle butt against bayonet, and entrenching tools fighting stick grenades and full clips. The first line of trenches was gone.

"Hardly five bloody minutes into it, Captain Letestu was rounding up whomever he could to counterattack the enemy in the overrun trenches. Left there, they would pick us off in no time, which was already happening. One of the first to go down was Lieutenant Durand. His demise was quick and painless—a rifle round to the head. At the time, I didn't know where the lieutenant was or if something had happened to him. As next senior man, I then had the responsibility for directing the blockhouses and the mortar crew. One way or another, I was then certain it would take a good deal of slaughter on both sides for the matter to be resolved."

Private Conner drew in a long breath and remained quiet.

"It lasted until nine-thirty, when the firing let up. Captain Letestu had prevailed in the counterattack by then. His tired survivors quickly busied themselves by throwing the dead Vietminh out of the trenches. Quiet though it was, everyone knew the battle had only begun. Already, fifteen Legionnaires lay dead, and another thirty or so were bad wounded, reducing our effectives to less than sixty percent. A C-47 Dakota by then was circling our strongpoint and dropping flares. They did so until morning, thank God. You've seen flare light, I'm sure—a blazing glare while at the same time is filled with shadows . . . and ambivalence, I should say. That's the way it was for us all that night.

"We had stowed enough ammo for the time being, but there was only sixty-three of us effectives by then; our perimeter was shattered and minefield gone. Yet we felt strong with the wee parachutes dropping light from the sky. Vietminh bodies no longer stirred in the wire, dozens more bodies lay crumpled in front of the trenches, riddled with automatic gunfire and peppered with shrapnel. Outside the wire, more bodies lay in contorted shapes before the assault lanes. Some of their bodies was dragged away by the enemy, but far from all. When bodies are left for us, we know we badly hurt them."

The private perked up at that, oddly enough. "You beat them, Master Sergeant."

Again, Sergeant Phillips offered a pitiful glance. "The carnage was far from done. There is more to a battle or firefight than shooting back and forth. The Viet doesn't know he's done until he no longer exists. The action at the front trenches that night was critical from the start. When I saw the captain collecting men for the early counterattack, I did the best I could to make a quick round of the blockhouses. Each blockhouse at the corners was manned by three or more Legionnaires, every gun positioned to lay down bursts in a low-to-the-ground field of fire. At the same time, those men had to watch for enemy who had breached the wire and were coming at them from the rear. They came with grenades and satchel charges.

"Corporal Patron was team leader in the blockhouse directly facing the assault. That position was the most critical and, therefore, the most prominent target for the Viet. From Patron's position, his machineguns swept the entire 210-degree approach. Hand grenades were popping at its walls from the start, and soon the recoilless rifle tubes opened up on them from the bush.

"The blasts were coming close when I got there. Two of their recoilless rounds got smothered by the sandbag and timber walls. As they hit, the blockhouse groaned and shook; a storm of dust both inside and out kicked up. Well-built, the integrity of the blockhouse remained.

"As you know, the blast from the recoilless tube and the bazooka is seen before it is heard. It takes a quick eye to catch the firing point. When you do, that is when you want to put a machinegun burst on it—when you know where the tube is, and that is while the round is coming in. Of course, if it's headed your way, it's not the easiest thing to do. Shooting with accuracy while your head is behind sandbags does not work, so you have to stare down the devil with your hot lead. It's a real soldier can face the recoilless head on.

"Patron and his men had caught on that their guns had to keep hosing down every area that sported flash points—both the recoilless and the machine guns out there. I had to peel off two of his men to attend to Vietminh inside the wire bringing satchel charges and grenades. With rifles and their own grenades, Patron's men did well.

"Still, it was a bloody business. Rifle and machinegun rounds more than occasionally happened through a blockhouse porthole. The gunners inside was the most vulnerable. Patron took a round, and that a skimming shot what creased his helmet without piercing it. He was stunned enough that the assistant gunner moved up to maintain the rate of fire.

"After I moved on to the next blockhouse, one of Patron's outside men loosed a grenade when, straightaway, a rifle bullet smashed a rib on the right side of his chest. It missed his heart but hit a artery. One of the privates moved up to take his place, but there was no hand available to stop the bleeding. A man down is only that. He simply adds to the responsibilities of the survivors, and bullet on bone is neither pleasant nor painless. He died quickly—his last wish. Unfortunate he passed before the assault was stayed. It would have pleased him to know the assault that killed him was repelled.

"The Viet withdrew again. Soon enough, it was heavy mortars dropping on us. They stir the blood for some of us. It meant we were about to receive another assault. Oh, one thing more: we had mortars, but still thin on artillery, which I may have told you. The Legion heavy mortar company at Central Camp had no fire plans drawn up yet. Captain Letestu was able, finally, to connect via radio with them. After their first long shots, he talked them in by radio. In no time we had ten mortars dropping high-explosive bombs, one after the other, into the approach gullies. A Dakota kept dropping illumination flares at a steady pace. But still, the bloody Viet did not stop.

"Before that assault began, a company of the 3rd Parachute Battalion was brought up a half mile from the Central Camp to reinforce our near-depleted company. Their 23:00-hour arrival made all the difference. They were hardly inside the wire when the next assault came at us. The additional guns and muscle could not keep the enemy out, but it did keep them from overtaking the compound. Their second officer, a lieutenant, had a bit of bad luck right off. He was directing a platoon to fortify the trenches when a lucky bullet struck him in the neck. A stream of blood spurted two or three feet before the good lad dropped.

"Captain Letestu had no problem displaying mettle and leadership to the reinforcements. Right off, their captain had radioed Central Camp and told them he had arrived 'to retake the strongpoint.' I am telling you, we may have been overrun, but we had not lost the strongpoint! In the very moment, Captain Letestu demanded the reinforcing captain to radio Central and correct the record. It was done.

"There was a third wave assault, this at about 00:30. It too was narrowly repulsed. The bloody Viet was stopped by one of their own, a prisoner. We trusted and used him to convey ammunition. The 60mm mortar team was hit.

The tube was still good while the mortarmen were out of it. This Vietminh kid, with no help or orders from any authority, took over and, on his own, loaded, aimed, and fired the tube until he destroyed the Viet machine gun that was wracking us. Good show it was. Shortly after that, it was over. The dust settled. Then a starkness filled the vacuum. The acrid smell of cordite slowly began its drift out the valley. The stench of death, however, remained.

"That is the kind of upside-down war this is, Conner. With no more sense than that, if the Vietminh kid was on the other side that night, he could well be one of those hanging in the wire and, 'bout as likely, I'd be dead from that machinegun he would not then have destroyed. That was the first battle at Na-San. It was one of the few times I saw the Viets not retrieve all their dead and wounded. It was near daylight when they backed off. As the sun rose, a patrol went out to assess the damage we put to the enemy. The count was sixty-four fresh bodies and five live ones left behind by the Viet. There was no more fighting that day. Colonel de Castries, the base commander, came out and told us personally that our two Legion companies and Captain Letestu had saved Na-San."

"You were a hero!" Private Conner spouted. "You beat them."

"We beat them back, each man performing as trained is what got us by. As survivor I was lucky, not a hero. There was no hero business, only Legionnaire business. I point out that was the first go-round only. General Giap had hustled two or three light battalions to Na-San because he thought he could take advantage of us before we would be ready for them. When that didn't work, he more properly prepared and waited for the rest of his force with heavy artillery to arrive. After a week he attacked again. This time it was a western hilltop strongpoint. It was so ferocious that the Thai company defending it gave way in twenty minutes, falling back to the airstrip. The strongpoint was vital. It was high enough to observe both the airstrip and the Central Camp mortar pits and artillery. With an advantage such as that, the enemy would be master of all the camp in no time. Without artillery and the airstrip, we would soon be choked. The fortress commander, bless his frog heart, called for saturation bombing of the lost strongpoint. Heavy mortar was fired on it from 03:30 until 06:00. Under the parachute flares we could see the bodies being thrown about as the salvos came in. A Legion company counterattacked at first daylight and repossessed the hill with little resistance.

"The northwestern strongpoint was the next to be hit. Defended by a company each of Thai and Moroccan infantry, they were supported by heavy mortar. The full complement of artillery had been flown in by then. Still, on the third human wave assault the strongpoint was overrun. That was at about 03:00. At first daylight again, a counterattack was launched. The Vietminh resisted fiercely. They had dug in on the hill's backside to us. They were the devil to drive out. It was a ten-hour battle complete with artillery and bombing runs from the air. Documents found later on a dead Vietminh officer explained the priority General Giap had placed on the strongpoint. Having taken it, antiaircraft and 120mm mortars were intended to be installed. The heavy French mortars and the airstrip were observable from there as well.

"The next night was similar, only on PA-21, the farthest southwest corner of the perimeter. It was Lieutenant Bonnet's 10th Company of Legionnaires, a hundred men building their second strongpoint for the defense of Na-San. It, too, was built on a steep hill overlooking the Headquarters Camp and airstrip. Hearing sounds of approach, the lieutenant called in artillery before an enemy rush. As in the previous attacks, the first wave assault began with sappers blowing lanes in the wire igniting a long, close battle. Lieutenant Bonnet was killed trying to return an enemy grenade from his trench. Lieutenant Bachelier took over. He was wounded but continued to direct his men from the open. He was shot in the neck and killed. Two gunners moved a machinegun from their blockhouse for a greater field of fire out in the open. The men were magnificent on their own. Finally, about 04:00 the attack halted. The 9th Legion Company came up in support at daylight. Patrols went out to survey the damage. This time, it was 350 enemy dead and about 50 wounded lying about. We wore them down.

"To the east, another strongpoint was hit that same night. A battalion of Legionnaires this time withstood the best efforts of four Vietminh wave assaults. Two blockhouses were knocked out but the Legionnaires prevailed nonetheless. Friendly patrols next morning counted 260 Vietminh bodies left on that battle site. It was the final chapter of General Giap's effort to overwhelm a major French force at Na-San. His Vietminh suffered at least three thousand casualties in the effort. I would like to have witnessed the self-criticism following that defeat. But make no mistake, there was much to be learned in that loss."

Not knowing quite what Phillips meant, Private Conner asked, "For who, Sergeant Phillips? For who to learn?"

Phillips eyed the private, then almost grudgingly spelled it out. "Both sides, Private Conner. The French commanders, yes; but in defeat, it was surely General Giap who learned the most."

Reliving the battle in the cold manner he had described may have been therapeutic for Sergeant Phillips but emotionally depleting as well. Private Conner didn't take it personally when the sergeant barked, "More questions?" It was a closing comment, not a question.

Conner had the good sense to be silent when addressed with such solemnity. As they interacted in the coming days, however, the private did find himself having more questions. After rehearsing a particular question several times, Conner once again spoke up, despite knowing he may be squashed. His words came out squeaky, but out they came. "I don't understand, Master Sergeant. Why do the Vietminh want to kill us? There are many other Vietnamese who do not. Are not the Vietminh like others here? France wants to make it like it was before The War, isn't that right? The Japanese are gone now, so France is here to administer things and make it safe again. Isn't that right?" It was fortunate the young private was tentative in his questioning.

The master sergeant slowly, almost imperceptibly, shook his head back and forth, then took in a principally large chestful of air. He released most of it before replying. "My dear boy. To begin with, it's as you yourself have intimated. We cannot judge what we do not understand. You'll be learning a thing or two in these next weeks and months, provided you pay attention and don't get yourself killed. Here's the thing: don't ever think you understand the ways of government and the war department! Since this war began, the French government has been in flux. Whoever was in charge of France last week, or will be next week or next year, has and will likely continue the vision of a robust Indochina colony. For your information, the Michelin Rubber Company from France has some millions of rubber trees growing and doing well here. Commercial pineapple plantations are in place here, and fisheries too. This country has minerals, industry, but most of all, cheap labor. With abundant, cheap labor, there is profit for all concerned. As simple as that."

"For the peasants too?" Private Conner heard himself ask.

"For God's sake, no. But that's why it's profitable, don't you see? Simply deprive the peasant of his rice paddy by taxation or decree and you have a man and his family available to work for cheap."

"Really?" Conner was stunned. "What of the rice paddy, then? What happens to it?"

The master sergeant chuckled. "Politics, dear boy. A friend and partner of the government, new or old, is always available to improve confiscated property and real estate—at a profit."

"Cannot the peasants develop a trade or do something other than work for low wages?"

"At one time, my innocent friend, peasants were illiterate, and mandarins were the capable and literate administrators. Now, Ho Chi Minh sees fit to teach the countryside peasants while the French treat the mandarins as domestics. Oh, by the way, most here were honest at one time as well. Peasants were respected, if you can believe that."

"How would you know all that?" Conner bravely questioned.

"On the authority of an old mandarin I knew some time ago. At one time, the peasants grew their own crops and worked within a supply system that was ancient and slow but efficient enough to be sustainable. The Red River Delta in the north and the Mekong Delta in the south are ideal for crops, especially rice, a valuable commodity throughout the world. Fish are in the ocean for the taking and water buffalo available to pull the plow. Life was hard, but life was honest here at one time; dignity and honor important. Industry was far away, largely unknown, and unnecessary for such life. That was before the civilized world spread gospel and invested in colonies.

"That, my young private, is when the benevolent French arrived and insisted on protecting Indochina. From what, no one knew. Yes, there once was a system and a way of life here quite sustainable. Then came French masters with gunboats and battalions of armed men. They came to protect the French missionaries who came before them, but the captains became captains of industry, remaining here to benefit themselves and France. Their control widened—they took over the government and declared the three-state region a colony. What they had to protect was the new profitable system. The mandarins were replaced with French technicians. It was progress, and everything changes with progress. Political connections became necessary for land to remain in the ownership of the farmer. Debts were incurred, hungry mouths went unfed, and unpaid taxes defaulted the land, turning farmers into cheap labor units. Everything progressed, even language. In Vietnamese, 'dignity' and 'respect' became hollow."

"And the enriched became rich," Private Conner butted in.

"Now you're catching on, Private. That is the purpose of the colony—to profit the patron by controlling the people and stealing the resources, be they natural, cultivated, or human."

"But," countered Conner, now feeling brave, "some Vietnamese are educated in France, are they not?"

"Yes, of course. Everyone can feel good about doing such things for the selected few. But where does it advance the people, or even those who were educated? They are fortunate to have assistant and secretary jobs with no chance for advancement. You will have opportunity here to look around and see what advantage there is for such men. Truly, I would like to know—is it opportunity or is it bitterness that follows a Parisian education?"

Chapter 7

End of the Line

For any chance of success, the 141st Regiment had to get to Phu Doan ahead of the French Force. They made it, and with just enough time to set up an initial defense at the crest as well as to plan and organize a continuing attack. That it was three rookie privates who bested French Legionnaires at the crest was inspirational. The loss of two enemy tanks and three tank crews at a premier bottleneck had stopped the enemy for twelve hours. That was enough time to move tons of munitions and rice beyond Phu Doan. From there, the ongoing French operation required the 141st Vietminh Regional Regiment to dance the old soft shoe. For several days, the battle was all punch and duck. Realistically, it could hardly have gone better for the Vietminh. Glass half full or half empty—perspective is all.

Breaking through at Phu Doan, the tide of the French Force swept across thousands of hectares in a wide swath. Sweeps in all directions destroyed Vietminh matériel as far as thirty kilometers away. Still, a good bit of it remained well hidden. And, there was more safely beyond the thirty-kilometer reach of the raiders.

In one sense, the regional regiments were a comfortable match for the French Force. They quickly resorted to what they knew best. It was strike and withdraw, over and over. While the tactic did not overwhelm the French Force, it never failed to stop them long enough to ensure their defense and reassess the next step forward. For the Vietminh, that was affect enough. The fits and jerks gave the porters, coolies, villagers, and soldiers more time to salvage a fair volume of munitions and stores. Goods were moved and scattered over that wide area, literally in one-meter-cubed bundles, well camouflaged. A fair volume did survive to serve the People's Army. As for the divisions in Laos, General Giap did something far more sinister than turn back his divisions from there.

Within three days of reaching their objective, the French Force had little choice but to withdraw. They had ranged and destroyed, but they had also exhausted their own resources of time and distance. They had no supply line. Fuel was the big reason, but also ammunition and ration levels dictated they turn for home. Withdrawal meant returning the way they came. That was a problem.

General Giap released two regiments only to engage the French withdrawal from Phu Doan. Return to home turf for the French Force was dramatic, slow, and casualty-strewn; more so than the battle getting to Phu Doan. The French Force took casualties nearly the entire way. The People's Army was not destroyed, Vietminh stores were replaced by China, and the French took a beating. Besides that, the war carried on.

She was made an honorary private of the 141st Regiment. With some reluctance, Captain Ngai accepted the oral petition of Private Pham to induct or at least accept Le Thuy into his company. The captain could hardly reject the person responsible for safely extracting his troops from their self-made tomb, especially after their absolute success. The fire-team trio owed their lives to Thuy. Capture or death had been imminent for the fire team; then along came Le Thuy in the dark of night, resurrecting them from under the very nose of the enemy. Whether the privates survived their circumstance due to cleverness or heartfelt affection even Thuy was uncertain.

Captain Ngai would not diminish the notoriety of his company's heroic stand at the crest of Phu Doan, but his silence did diminish Thuy's contribution. He tooted no horns extolling her resourcefulness or even her follow-through. In the end it didn't matter. The Vietminh had no heroes, only those revered and admired. The captain could claim no preparation or action to safeguard or retrieve the team. Le Thuy was king of the hill but didn't know it. Her informal acceptance into the 141st did not include, by the way, sharing with anyone her dramatic brush with a sandy-haired enemy private. It was her concern for others, combined with strength of character, that saved three privates at the crest of Phu Doan. Her own survival at the hands of a Legionnaire was surely due to those same qualities.

After her tender kiss upon the cheek of the enemy, Le Thuy headed north to find her coolie team. Ever after, she professed not to have found them, which would explain her turning up at the 141st Regiment. Yet it was surely her interest in the handsome Private Pham that motivated her to orchestrate and conduct the incredibly dangerous escape plan. The attraction would also account for her surprising appearance at the regiment's camp.

With the tacit approval of Captain Ngai, Thuy attached herself to the three-person fire team she had saved. Capable, smart, and tough, Thuy did not diminish the team in any way. Her presence brought out a certain maturity in the boys. Respecting her as they did, and themselves having been a part of the slaughter at the crest of Phu Doan, life was taking on a more somber tone for them.

Except, that is, for Private Pham. While Cho and Ninh became more reserved and serious than they had been, Pham was different. He began displaying a skeptical side, something that played as though he was above the others and had more authority. Complaints were not acceptable in the Vietminh system, but carefully crafted joking took its place. Pham Van Hieu was plenty smart enough to be crafty. By now, he was quite disappointed not to have received any further direction from The Party concerning his commissar work. Being ignored began to heighten a developing trust issue for him. He had heard nothing from The Party since he left the academy.

It had begun with the French back in his Haiphong neighborhood. Responding to his disgust of them had ultimately placed him in the 141st Regiment as a private, which was no joy whatsoever. By all appearances he was just another private being misused and treated as cannon fodder. What Pham Van Hieu had, however, was the smarts to recognize his circumstance and react.

Despite what he had done and gone through, Private Pham was not looked upon as special. He was not appreciated as he thought due him. His natural charisma and confidence had made him leader of the fire team, but more and more, he was distracted and sarcastic. Thuy kept him honest by laughing and calling out his attitude. Cho and Ninh put up with it, not saying much, but they lived with it too. For the time being, they all put up with each other while the gravity of recent life events pooled around them.

Since Phu Doan, there was no more talk of babies or life after the war. Still, Thuy saw Private Pham as worth fighting for, realizing he was a man of ambition and would be a strong partner. Being called out by her did not please him even if it did improve his behavior. They felt they were being tested, and military life was an uneasy transition for them both. The near-death incidents had planted uncomfortable pits inside them.

Survival was one thing, but outright killing was different. Yes, the filthy enemy must be exterminated. Hate of the enemy was always encouraged, and new soldiers readily swallowed and used it. For some, however, the actual killing left a lump going down. For all their good luck and bravado, no one had mutilated bodies at Phu Doan. Pham wondered if they should have. Maybe that would make them feel better about it. Adrenaline ruled the day in combat. Leadership lacking, revenge on enemy bodies could seem logical and appropriate; or, leadership present could encourage such action. The judging of others in combat typically ran quiet and often came much later. Pham knew only to repeat to himself, *It is the fruits of war. Shit happened but I'm alive.*

Only a few days after Phu Doan came a new challenge. It was again highlighted as an opportunity. Of course. For Private Pham, it raised a warning flag. The others wondered if he was right. Sure enough, soon they were all on the march again, this time headed for Na-San, a valley rather than a hilltop. Word had it that resourceful coolies were trying to transport wheeled 105mm howitzers the many kilometers to the valley.

Pham decried the notion to his team. "Ridiculous! Heavy guns cannot traverse the deeply rutted and narrow trails to get there. And Na-San has an airstrip. The French can fly their heavy artillery in and bomb from the air anything a few coolies could possibly manhandle there."

At the time, everyone knew the Vietminh artillery consisted of bazookas, recoilless rifles, mortars, and some 75mm field guns, all light and portable. If there were heavy guns coming from China, there was no way to traverse them through the hills and narrow trails of the High Region.

General Giap assumed the French Force was demoralized after Phu Doan. It would take time for them to construct proper fortifications at Na-San, which was true. An immediate attack was sure to achieve victory for the Vietminh, since the French had no conventional supply line.

Again the 141st troops were the jackrabbits. They were in position to get there first, the greater opportunity. It was true the French Force was not expecting a Vietminh assault any time soon. General Giap's divisions were two or more weeks from Na-San. The sooner the light 141st Regiment could get there, the greater the chances for success. They had not been demolished as some had anticipated at Phu Doan. They were, in fact, highly confident after Phu Doan. They were proven fast movers on the trail and greater the glory.

Their arrival was unheralded. The French Force was preoccupied, working on hillock strongpoints around the Central Camp and airstrip. The French heavy artillery had not yet been flown in. Intelligence from Hanoi assured them no Vietminh division could be there before a week, probably more.

After Phu Doan, Colonel Dau passed word that the 141st had earned the lucky charm moniker of the People's Army. The commander reported to General Giap the minute his regiment breathlessly arrived at Na-San. His wireless message stated, "The enemy does not know we are here. Their troops can be seen relaxing and drinking as the sun sets behind the mountains. Our troops chew on cold supper: sticky rice and dried water buffalo strips, a treat. As the sun dips, we ready ourselves to strike." The complete message was coded and sent as nearly all messages were, via continuous wave—Morse code.

Sappers with their satchel charges and bangalore torpedoes inched their way to the French Force perimeter. The barbed wire fencing completely circled the hilltop objective several times over. There were, at minimum, three, and in some areas five, parallel fences surrounding the two-hectare compound. Ever so slowly, on the strongpoint's north side, the sappers evaded French mines and crept to the perimeter without notice. It was a remarkable performance.

Sometime later, Colonel Dau described the initial human wave assault to a Vietminh regular army colonel.

"At 20:00 hours we struck. The enemy soldiers were mostly in position, but they were not expecting attack. Nearly in unison, our bangalores blew jagged assault lanes in the wire. Assault troops and sappers were up and charging even before the blasts cleared. The sappers went down first, none able to reach the blockhouses. Most were shot, some tangled in the wire and killed. Hung up in the wire, some satchels exploded there, which both hurt and helped. The shortest distance to go: the near trenches. Many made it to the front trenches and battled a stunned enemy. Others were shot on the way, and still others became tangled in loose wire.

"The enemy in the trenches was soon overcome. They stood their ground, which served little purpose. They battled bravely with rifle butts, knives, and entrenching tools. But, with bayonets, grenades, and full magazines, our soldiers overtook them. To our advantage, the French mortars were slow in opening up. It was some time before they were a problem. Our light artillery targeted the blockhouses immediately. Their several hits were absorbed by sandbags.

"Our troops, now in French trenches, began picking off more enemy. A French officer managed to initiate counterattack. That battle lasted for some time. Meanwhile, their blockhouse machineguns struck down many of our assault troops. We were unable to silence them. Control of the compound, however, hinged on control of the trenches. In the end, the enemy counterattack overwhelmed us. Those who could pulled back about 21:30 hours. We prepared for a second assault."

The reprieve was temporary. Private Pham and his fire team took part in the second assault, that of the 2nd Battalion. Honorary Private Le Thuy had been held back but was eager afterwards to understand what had happened. It was sometime later before Pham was able and willing to describe his experience to her.

"At 23:00 hours we stood and rushed the hilltop just as our mortar barrage stopped," the damaged private began. "We were many, as you know, almost all the battalion. The hill was steep, and many 1st Battalion bodies and loose wire slowed our assault. Once snagged in wire, it was difficult not to panic. I was one caught. As I pulled away from it, the wire curled and wrapped tighter. Privates Cho and Ninh went on ahead in the assault.

"At first, enemy grenades were tossed down the hill. They exploded while rolling, hurting and distracting us. I forced myself to stop the struggle and began to pick the barbs out of trousers and legs, one at a time. I folded the wire so it would not snarl again. Finally free, I took up my rifle and rushed to the top. There were many bodies from both sides. Several comrades—I did not count—were hanging in the wire, most lifeless. Mortar bombs were screaming and exploding; I did not know who they were intended for, us or the enemy. It did not matter.

"Remaining low at the crest of the hill seemed prudent. I was afraid but also eager to kill. This was the opportunity to prove myself. I realized my position was good for sniping. The enemy paid no attention to me among the bodies, even as near as I was. I waited for a proper target. Soon I saw a young lieutenant standing in the open, issuing orders to his men in trenches. He was an officer, so I knew he was French.

"I despise French. They are devils. They disrespect the people and they steal our land and our livelihood with unjust taxes.

"The lieutenant was no more than forty meters from me. It was a good chance. My rifle sights followed him walking back and forth, waiting for him to be still. At last, he not only stopped, he turned. Truly, he looked into the perimeter where I waited to end his life. The French lieutenant did not move. Rather, he stood and waited for my bullet. I remained calm. I pulled the trigger slowly, and my rifle barked. I was pleased by the accommodation of the lieutenant, but I did not strike his chest where I aimed. His body did not jerk from impact and he did not fall. I could only think I missed completely. Then, he and I saw results at the same time, I think. Blood spouted from his neck. Each beat of his heart expressed a red stream. The delicious irony came to me that we were now taking lifeblood back from the French, and I smiled.

"When the lieutenant realized what had happened, he did a strange thing. He looked up to see his killer—me. His eyes screamed, 'Do you not know I am so soon from officer academy? My beautiful fiancée will be desolate.' That is what I heard. But I did not care. Then his eyes became quiet; he faltered; he fell. An image of his mother came to me, I swear. I must despise her too, so I then turned and dismissed her image from my mind by shooting all my bullets into the wall of the nearby blockhouse. Is it hate or is it love that I do that? Hate is good, I think. It makes me strong.

"Mortars continued coming in. I saw the enemy mortar position furiously loading and firing, and then, suddenly, the mortar tube went quiet. An unchallenged machinegun had silenced it and was doing great damage against the French. Then I saw a Vietnamese boy, a prisoner, at the French mortar tube. Alone, he loaded, aimed, and fired. I could do nothing just then as my rifle was empty. That one boy destroyed our machinegun on his second or third round. *Why would a Viet do such a thing?* I wondered. Then two French Force troops came from the near blockhouse with a recoilless tube, close enough to see me behind the crest of the hill. Their bazooka round exploded somewhere to my front. I think I was blinded, and the blast threw me down the hill. My body was singed. The Buddha has since taught me much about patience and acceptance.

"Others tell me they saw the blast and watched me fall. How long I laid at the bottom of the hill I do not know. Thuy, you were with me when I woke. I knew your voice but nothing else. My head was not right. You helped me to safety.

"Word came that we overran the strongpoint. Everyone cheered, I remember. More were then sent into the strongpoint to defend against the counterattack that would be coming. That did not go well, I was told. Insistent firepower of the French Force wore down our troops as our ammunition was depleted. Casualties were gravely high, but the French Force was weakened, and we yet had 3rd Battalion to fight."

After a short breather, a worked-up Private Pham continued. "At 00:30 hours the 3rd Battalion made the third assault on PA-8. I asked about Cho and Ninh, but Thuy, you say that is not known. So many comrades were down. Again it was a desperate battle. Again our troops stormed the strongpoint and fought the enemy to standstill. Enemy artillery from the French

Central Camp was by then eating us up in the bush and in the approach gullies. Inside or outside the compound, we were mostly in the open while the enemy fought from bunkers, blockhouses, and trenches. There was no end to the French ammunition, and finally we were vanquished. The bodies of many comrades were left where they fell. We could not save them all and ourselves as well."

Exhausted, Private Pham rested. There was not a mark on his body from the blast other than the singed hair and healing burns. Yet, on and off for days, dastardly headaches brought tears to his eyes. He had no appetite and refused most food. It was difficult for Thuy to keep him hydrated, although she managed. He weakened steadily for three days.

Finally, Privates Ninh and Cho turned up, in a manner of speaking. Cho had been found among the wounded; someone from the Third Battalion had dragged him to safety but didn't know where he belonged. He had taken several bullets that stitched across his torso, missing vital organs. A sucking chest wound nearly took his life and, but for an experienced Hanoi nurse in the regiment, it would have.

When reconnected, both Cho and Pham reclaimed a will to heal. There was little in the way of chit-chat for them. It was a full day before they could talk to each other. There was still significant pain, physical and otherwise, for both to work through.

At last, Pham was able to ask about Ninh, the fearless one. Private Ninh's absence had been a mystery, like many others, but eventually his story was shared by a survivor who knew him. The primary blockhouse of PA-8 had been hit with recoilless rockets several times, all without collapsing. In large part it was the machineguns inside and the bazooka on top that had kept the assaulters at bay. The blockhouse had been built properly; it would take a satchel charge tossed inside to clear it. At least three sappers had come close but took bullets or hand grenade blasts before they could deploy their ordnance.

Privates Cho and Ninh were trying to provide cover for the sappers. The two had fought their way to the front of the pandemonium. Both were wounded, yet, with Ninh inspiring Cho, they continued on, providing cover until the last sapper went down. Seeing that, Ninh ran forward, scooped up a dropped satchel, and sprinted toward the nearest porthole of the blockhouse. Arming the satchel as he ran, Ninh tossed the charge through the portal and turned. Up top the blockhouse, a French recoilless tube had also been discharging round after round against the assault. Ninh was a dozen or so long steps from the blockhouse when the 57mm shell from above ravaged him, a direct hit. His body shattered. He died as he had wished. Private Ninh joined the ancestors as a patriot doing his honorable best against the fiercest of foes. What he would never know, thankfully, was that his satchel charge was a dud.

What was left of the regiment was ordered to dig in on a reverse slope in the hills north of Na-San. There they would keep an eye on the French position while recouping and waiting for General Giap's divisions to arrive. The numbers of the proud 141st were substantially reduced. Understrength before, they were now at less than half strength, with hundreds having been killed and seriously wounded in the three human wave attacks. The wounded they could retrieve had been brought with them to the temporary camp. Others went missing, which meant they may have been captured or their dead bodies not retrieved. There was little left of the 141st with which to be an effective fighting force. General Giap concurred with Colonel Dau's recommendation that the 141st Regiment presently cease and desist against Na-San.

A week later, the general's forces had consolidated in the hills around Na-San, and assault plans formed. Four different French Force strongpoints were ultimately attacked by Giap's divisions. The 141st was held in reserve. Unceasing damage inflicted by the conventional divisions resulted in all four French strongpoints being overrun. In each case, however, counterattacks somehow prevailed. The "somehow" included heavy artillery bombardment and airstrikes.

The final night of human wave assaults took place on the southwest side, Strongpoint PA-21. That was the final rejection, the rebuff that broke the back of General Giap's strategic effort. They had come so far, had come so close, but had lost so much. The French artillery was devastating to them. Once on the attack or even while forming to attack, there was nowhere for the Vietminh troops to find cover. The human waves were vicious but also harbingers of mass casualties. Machineguns and 105mm artillery salvos, along with heavy mortar bombs, served broad swaths of obliteration among tight Vietminh ranks.

It was at about 20:30 hours the evening of 1 December 1953 that Lieutenant Bonnet called in the first artillery barrage after hearing signs of an approaching enemy force. It was a single Legion company, in that case only a hundred men defending the strongpoint. The Legionnaires would be outnumbered by at least ten to one that night. Despite the artillery barrage, surviving enemy continued their creep forward as was acknowledged by the occasional tripped mine. The explosions gave the Legion mortar crews a general target area, which they then lit up with the heavy mortar fire. The assault relented, but only temporarily.

Not until 01:30 hours did the actual wave assault come. It began with Vietminh mortar and 75mm recoilless rifle fire from the bush. Assault lanes were blown, and the comrades poured into them. The Legion machineguns and rifles countered, both sides taking casualties. Lieutenant Bonnet, directing his men from a trench, was forced to dance with an incoming Chicom grenade, then tried to return it. Not quick enough, it killed him. Lieutenant Bachelier took over the company. He was soon killed, taking equally lethal wounds in the chest and neck. As a fighting unit, however, the Vietminh suffered more, unable to duck the continuing support barrages from Central Camp's howitzers and heavy mortars. Again and then again the two forces clashed, each time the attackers thrown back.

The desperate Vietminh commander directed the remnants of the 141st Regiment to join the next assault, hoping to tilt the scale of fate. It would in fact be the final assault of the 141st. They fought until there was nothing left. The assaults ended about 04:00 hours. It wasn't until first light that the devastation could be assessed. The carnage rebuked civility. One blockhouse had taken eight direct blasts but still stood. Bodies, weapons, and debris were scattered everywhere, all coated with the smoky dust of battle. A reinforcing Legion company was sent from Central Camp. It swept the enemy assault avenues with minimal resistance—only meager shooting from the bush. The Viets had left 350 dead comrades on the field as well as 50 wounded. Hundreds of weapons left scattered were proof of a smashed enemy. The Vietminh had withdrawn, a small but effective rear guard protecting them.

It was a milestone as well as a great victory for the French Force. News of a win at Na-San circled the globe. The victory professed the distinct sense of progress in an otherwise strangled war. The French ruled the delta with virtual impunity, while the Vietminh did the same inland, controlling the hills, the mountains, and jungles. With the now-proven method of "airbridge" fighting, the French Force had at last identified the magic key. Even deep in the wilderness, and without traditional supply lines, the French Force was victorious against everything General Giap could throw at them, guerilla or conventional. To defeat the Vietminh hordes, all that was needed by the French was an airstrip and reliable air transport. A reinforced airstrip would deliver the matériel and even move troops in and out as needed.

A well-circulated analogy after the Na-San battle aligned itself with French culture: by squinting just a little from even the farthest balcony, the

French could visualize the victory waiting for them at center stage. History notes that, within a year, the French bastion at Na-San was vacated. Whether marauding or substantial, all Vietminh forces entering the region made a point of bypassing the fortress.

Na-San was clear defeat of the Vietminh. It was sorrowful news, especially for comrades and units that had otherwise done so well. The 141st Regional Regiment would be no more. Any survivors, almost all of them wounded, were assimilated into the 57 Regular Army Regiment of the 304th Infantry Division. From regional to regular army was a promotion, at least of honor, but the few survivors were diminished of the pride and distinction they had accrued with the 141st. The guerilla regiment could have been rebuilt, but it was not.

Colonel Dau and his deputy commander, Major Tran, had both survived the battle, their greatest sin. Remaining in shelter while the regiment not only lost the battle but was purged to disintegration could not be atoned. That they were removed was all that was known. Perhaps they went on to serve in another capacity. Then again, perhaps not. It was, after all, Ho Chi Minh's communist system. No mercy made for good examples and good business.

Private Pham, Private Cho, Honorary Private Le Thuy, and a few dozen others in similar shape and condition became neglected "new guys" all over again in a despondent set of circumstances.

The Party still had not contacted Private Pham about his commissar business. He continued to wait. He continued to wonder. He continued to smolder.

Chapter 8

Boy Meets Real

"Twentieth of November, '53, was the big day. It got screwed up right away. Oh, it could have been worse, but we met the primary objective." That was Sergeant Phillips' comment on the full brigade's combat jump. What he meant was that it went about as well as could be expected. Combat jumps never went as planned. First off, the valley of Dien Bien Phu was far from vacant that day as their two flights of Dakotas, of them, dropped off the 2nd Airborne Brigade from 2,500 feet.

Intelligence analysis from Hanoi, which included aerial photography, reported nothing more than a random regimental headquarters in the valley. That was it. Oh, and a carpet of green grass to land on. Unfortunately, things had changed by the time they got there; the intelligence was not fresh or not fresh enough. The airborne veterans had the good sense to assume nothing. None of them was shocked when the operation unraveled even before boots touched ground. The game plan had included the likelihood of capturing the Vietminh headquarters staff with documents, which would have been a solid intelligence coup, whoever they were. That didn't happen.

As it turned out, a Vietminh heavy weapons company was conducting a training exercise on the old airstrip. Mortar tubes had been set up and were operational. Recoilless guns and a number of infantry companies were taking part in a live-fire exercise. Vietminh troops with ammunition were pretty much everywhere. As for the ground canopy, much of the "green grass" was, in fact, two-meter-tall elephant grass. Visibility for many of the troops, once on the ground, was a distance of a meter in any direction. Collecting troopers into cohesive units was a challenge at best.

Private Conner was loaded up for the jump. Among other things, he carried C-rations, rifle, extra ammunition, entrenching tool, two canteens of water, hand grenades, medical kit, plus two mortar shells. Skinny as he was, like everyone else, Private Conner was one heavy dude on jump day. He dropped his kit just before landing and still hit hard thanks to an inadequate

1940s-style parachute. The landing jolted him, but that was the least of it. Almost as soon as he cleared the Dakota, his chute had jerked him stiff, but at the time he was comforted it had opened fully.

The greater part of his concern quickly became conditions below. He saw that the supposedly undefended landing was anything but undefended. There were enemy troops down there, and they were not running away. In fact, they were running toward the ballooning dots of air-filled silk. They also did not wait for the paratroopers to land; they were shooting into the air at them! Clipping along through the air as they were, the troopers were challenging targets at best. Tragic it was then, that the trooper who had jumped just ahead of Conner was struck squarely under the chin by a Vietminh bullet. It was the trooper who sat next to him on the Dakota. "Stay close to me, kid," was the last thing the Legionnaire had said.

Total luck, Private Conner told himself, as if this were a game he could dismiss. It was the first military death he had seen, and he was close enough to see blood and brains splattering the still air as the dead paratrooper's head flopped listlessly to one side.

Hearing screams, Conner looked back and caught the sight well behind him of a trooper's chutes, both the main and reserve, well tangled, driving the terrified trooper to a speedy death. Private Conner had anticipated a wakeup, but he had not expected to see his own people die; not like this. It was fully clear to him by then that airborne jumps in combat were dangerous and included fatalities.

Not all the Dakotas were able to release their human cargo as intended. The morning fog had cleared for the day, but low, drifting clouds kept several of the Dakotas from getting under the overcast on the first lift. The pilots who didn't get a decent view of the drop zone had to come around again to deliver their product. Some drops ended up happening well off the mark. Some units landed three kilometers up the valley. The prescribed battle order had become a hash.

The private had no idea where he was in the valley when he rolled onto Mother Earth. He was alone, and he wasn't certain of his directions. Many troopers carried a compass. He did not. From the air, paratroopers could identify their own unit by the color of the smoke canister their leaders, first to jump, had popped. Once on the ground, head for your color of smoke and get organized. However, wouldn't you know it, some of the colored smoke canisters had been mismarked, creating a significant unforced error and a good deal of confusion. Conditions added up to general disorder, which surprised only the officers.

Although amazed by the invasion, the enemy accepted the challenge, regrouped on the fly, and engaged with gusto. It was an ad hoc battle on both sides. The paratroopers had no chance to flank, much less cordon off and capture the enemy headquarters.

It was a hard landing for Private Conner, but the fun didn't stop there. Other than a couple wind-dragged chutes in the distance, there was no sign of friendly forces. Shooting, yes; comrades, no. The grass was mostly taller than Conner. No compass, and he was directionally challenged. After stowing his parachute, the private collected several deep and slow breaths to settle himself. Gunfire was farther away but increasing, which made sense because more friendlies were now on the ground and engaging. He tried but couldn't help flinching at the buzz of rifle bullets passing overhead. The distinctly deep *crump* of mortars lifting off in the distance did anything but clear his head. The mortars could be friend or foe, although the blast pattern seemed to be coming closer. *Close but not that close—enemy.* Whether from instinct or training, Private Conner did not hesitate to move toward the sound of battle. He was determined to be a stellar soldier and a good Legionnaire.

He had to get his bearings. Looking around for physical features, he popped up above the grass and spotted a landmark. It was the upper part of a brick colonial building. *Must be a two-story.* From his knees Conner closed his eyes and grappled with his recollection of the map and pictures they had been lectured on some hours before. Guessing it was probably the one substantial building in the valley, he considered himself fortunate to have landed where he did, despite the elephant grass. From there he deduced that other Legionnaires in similar circumstance were identifying the structure and also moving toward it. His relief to finally be acting on a plan was short-lived, however.

Moving cautiously but steadily below the crest of the grass, it wasn't many minutes before he sensed movement ahead, followed by the unmistakable crunch of footsteps. He froze. Another step, and then another. Kneeling on the ground, the private rotated his rifle barrel upward, stock on the ground. He reminded himself not to shoot blindly; only at identified targets. His thumb released the safety, hoping it would be quiet. It was. *Most likely it is a comrade, a Legionnaire,* he told himself. *I'm probably overreacting. But then why would a friendly be coming this way when the battle is in the other direction?*

With that thought, Private Conner tensed into a freeze and instantly found himself short of breath. His breathes became deliberate and as quiet as he could make them. He would not shoot until he knew it was enemy. But he wanted to. He had to be the one to shoot first. *I don't want to die!* His finger on the trigger; his thoughts on survival. Training won out. He waited. The moving grass and the slow-motion crunching continued directly toward him. *Friend or foe, he is probably lost and scared. Oh God; that means* he *is ready to shoot first and think later.*

Private Conner was alone, for which he was not prepared. He felt weak and hollow. If it were an enemy closing on him, could he stand and fight? *Just wait.* He was cold. Sweating, and so cold. Odd. It was all odd. *In the hothouse of Vietnam, wouldn't it be funny if my last sensation on earth was that of a frigid sweat?* There was no one to laugh, of course, even if it had been funny. At least the thought diverted some of the tension. Then another, longer crunch on the valley floor, this one louder, more personal than the others. Without turning his head, Conner refined his view down and to the left, toward the sound. There it was in front of him.

A homemade tire sandal rested on the thick sod no more than thirty centimeters in front of his left knee. His mind reeled as he visualized rather than saw a seasoned Vietminh standing over him, rifle barrel pointed inches from his skull.

The end, was his only thought. He had let everyone down; he was hurt and regretful. *Not a soldier—I only pretend.* What he missed was that warriors sometimes stumbled into the void between play soldier and dead soldier. Occasionally they woke up in time, and sometimes they just got lucky. All other times, they died. In defeat and self-pity, Conner felt ashamed. The shame was accentuated by the lowly tire sandal. He simply closed his eyes and waited. Thoughts turned to family. *I killed no one, Mum.* Perhaps she would be proud? But if he did kill, would that release the shame? Private Conner did not yet understand war, and now it was too late.

The fatal shot wouldn't come, the seconds resisting the time they were made of, stretching and dragging, finding pleasure in sadism. *Is he waiting for me to look up and see him?* He sensed motion but he couldn't make himself look up. Eyes slightly opened, the private again saw the thick sandal. It was still there, but now arched upward. *He is stretching to see over the grass. He must be alone and hasn't seen me.*

A prick of hope surprised Conner, and that was when he saw it. Scratched into the edge of the sandal's sole was the iconic image of "Kilroy Was Here," the bald head with fingers and large nose flopped over the outline of a wall. If he weren't about to die so green, Private Conner would have laughed at the irony of a cartoon just then.

Then the heel came down, the sandal lifted, and forward it stepped, barely missing the private's knee. Another cautious step of the sandal, and with the third step Conner breathed a quiet sigh of relief, supposing he might possibly remain among the living after all.

Strangely, it occurred to Conner his job was to kill those who wore tire sandals. His head lifted, but only a little. He rotated his upper body as much as he could and pointed his rifle. A real soldier would turn the tables on this nightmare. *A real soldier would kill this godless communist. No need to aim at this distance. A hit anywhere in the back will put him down. Then I can slit his throat if need be.*

He had suddenly become quite brave. On the fourth—or maybe it was the fifth—drifting step, Private Conner mentally crossed himself. Then he physically crossed himself and glanced at the heavens. Rifle stock yet on the ground, Conner centered the barrel at the middle of the shadowy target and not so gingerly squeezed the trigger. As the rookie he was, Conner jerked from the anticipation of a recoil. There was no recoil, only a *click*. Just the sound of firing pin slapping steel.

Oh my God, save me from this, he quickly and silently prayed. He ducked down and waited—another awkward freeze. But the enemy did not shoot or even turn around, at least not as far as Conner could tell through the grass. Mind spinning, it took a moment for him to realize the chamber of his rifle was empty. *I am not a solider,* he berated himself. *I tried to shoot without a bullet.* Again he felt shamed. Be that as it may, Private Conner had survived. *Why did the enemy not turn and kill me? He must have heard. Why didn't he see me?*

After two or three minutes of serious contemplation, the young private found a better perspective. He managed to convince himself that he would have regretted shooting a man in the back. Well, it was something. He breathed deeply, crossed himself, literally again, and thanked God for his life such as it was. His behavior was that of a man of faith, which surprised him.

But the Kilroy had escaped. *At least no one was here to see what happened. I froze, numb with fear. I couldn't think. Forgive me, Father, for I have sinned—I failed to kill.* Conner was careful not to add, "Amen."

"A dozen French Force radios were damaged and made inoperable by hard landings," the after-action report would state. Under the circumstance, it was difficult putting random soldiers together to make a cohesive assault. Eventually it all worked, the report also pointed out. A dozen radios had been wrecked by the hard landing, but finally a lieutenant saved the day by coming up with one that was serviceable. The LT was able to relay the ground situation to the command-and-control aircraft circling overhead, where the big decisions were made. Looking for all the world like a vulture up there, the commander was furious that so much had gone so wrong so quickly. After all, this was the start of an operation intended to harken defeat to the enemy and bring victory and honor to France and colony.

By then, the sixty-five delivering Dakotas were on their way, three hundred kilometers back to Hanoi, for the second lift of paratroops. With communication established between ground and command, and the air by then crystal clear, tactical air support could be called in. High explosive bombs and napalm were sure to dampen the spirit of even an insistent enemy.

Private Conner held with his plan to head for the two-story brick colonial. He would retrace the tracks made by the enemy soldier until they no longer pointed that way. The bent and broken grass was just distinct enough to follow. Conner's thoughts were then coming from everywhere, and he could not stop them. The encounter with the sandaled Kilroy man and the brains and blood he had witnessed jounced loudly in his mind along with the image of the trooper screaming to his death in tangled cord and silk. It all looped in his brain, over and over again.

I will think of home, he decided. *No, I must be focused. Focused on what?* Then came the ghost image of meeting another enemy in the tall grass. He tightened the grip on his rifle. *I need to remain focused,* he scolded himself. Instead of that, however, the private's mind diverted to an unanswered question he had posed long ago. *Survival for the warrior is chance, is it not? Or is it preordained by a higher power?* Private Conner was experiencing the stress of war and he hadn't yet fired a shot.

It was his assumed-death incident with Kilroy that got to him. Strength and bravery had suddenly become hollow words. Chance and dumb luck now stood large and naked before him. *Training and leadership give me a better chance, but we get killed anyway. Half of what the Legion does is suicidal, and that doesn't seem so sexy anymore.* No longer was the life of Legionnaires cool. And he was still alone. The private scrambled for something he could hold onto, to see him through this. *Just do the right thing! Sergeant Phillips says so.*

It occurred to him that Mum always had too. *But everything is chance. Anything can happen at any time.* That seemed obvious, but living it as an axiom was scary. *Enough thinking,* as he mentally stamped his feet. *Just don't be a stooge. Whatever this business is, it is different than I ever knew.* He could now acknowledge that going into combat as a green private was hell. *As much hell as you care to make it,* he quickly added.

He had always admired honor and glory. Also, they came with a chest full of medals. There had been many thoughts of victory and returning home a giant of a man, respected by all. But, at the moment, his emotions were engaged in all things being either immaterial or chance happenings. Actions right or actions wrong were no longer so clear. The new reality quickly staked out a claim in his head and moved around some stagnant things up there. Buying into the rote lectures of patriotism wasn't the answer for Private Conner—not today. Boot camp had insisted on imagining the legion of souls on the other side of life's curtain all chiming, *"Legio Patria Nostra!"* Just now, that seemed a bit farfetched.

Moving forward in the elephant grass was ploddingly slow for Conner. His gear hung heavy on him, and although still intact, it was bulky and cumbersome. He was sure he was way more bulky than the lithe Vietminh who had evaded him. He could only hope the swaths of grass he now disturbed weren't obvious to more of the bad guys. *How did the Kilroy man not see my trail through the grass?* He couldn't think about that. Leaving a trail was a given. One short, calculated step at a time could but minimize the grass disturbance. Progress was slow; maintaining heightened senses was most critical. When his mind returned to the present, he asked himself, *Did I? Yes, I did ram a bullet into the chamber. I'm sure of it.*

The trail continued toward the brick building, and Private Conner continued muttering to himself. *Still headed there. That's good. Did the Vietminh come from there? The grass is shorter here.* He considered popping up for just a second to see if anything else was out there. *No, not yet. It's the movement that attracts attention,* he remembered.

After half a minute of five-second intervals between steps, an open field displayed itself between thinning blades of grass. That left the private with a serious decision. Leaving the tall grass would put him entirely in the open and totally vulnerable to an enemy anywhere to his front. *On the other hand, little chance of finding comrades if I remain where I am.* For the first time since the initial formation in boot camp, Aiden Conner longed for an officer or an NCO to tell him what to do. Having that would relieve him from the hard decisions. Crazy funny, but he wanted someone to blame if his decisions went south. *Heck, at this point, even a corporal will do.*

On both knees now, the private took a breath and reached back for a canteen on his web belt. He had been hard on that canteen. He stiffened his back and tipped it almost vertical to catch every last drop.

Zing! It was like a weird kind of insect zipping past his ear. A buzz like a bee, but not a bee—an air beam streaming past at speed of light. In the instant it happened, he couldn't understand. Then came the source. It wasn't a pop or a bang, it was a sharp *crack!* That clarified the matter.

The instinct of self-preservation somehow contorted his body backwards, completely over the kit on his back. One shoulder strap of the rucksack had come off during the somersault, and the other had slipped down to his elbow. Intentional or not, the kit provided some concealment and even cover, as dense as it was. Private Conner was left flat on his face in the grassy sod. *Was it just one shot?* He wasn't sure. *Where did it come from? Again, not sure, but likely it came from the brick colonial, now two hundred meters away, well within rifle range. From a second-floor window or, better yet, on the roof would be the catbird seat for snipers.*

What to do? There knelt Private Conner, a green private surrounded by battle, and no one to tell him what to do. The two-story colonial seemed to be the crux of the matter. If he knew who controlled it, he could figure out what to do. His body remained stationary, but he did realize he was more vulnerable now, this close to the clearing.

It then occurred to him that he had already been seen. He lay still, but he couldn't just lie there and wait for any supporting enemy to round him up or simply shoot him. Very slowly, the private tilted his head upward, finding a slot between blades of grass that gave him a partial view of the colonial. Scanning the roof as best he could, it didn't take long to spot something at the near corner that was not roof-like. It was something out of place. Its shape was familiar, almost round like a helmet but not quite.

Wait—that's it! It is a helmet—an American helmet. Now that he thought of it that way, it was plain to see even from two hundred meters. It was moving slightly, not right or left, up or down, but as if on a swivel—or on the head of a trooper scanning the horizon.

"Vietminh do not wear American helmets; we do," Conner said, out loud this time and with authority. *Assuming that's true and it is a French Force comrade up there, how do I communicate to him that I am not enemy?* That kind of thing was covered in boot camp, but when one was stressed, bone tired, thirsty and hungry, who could remember all that lecture crap?

Humbly, and under his breath, the private answered his own question: "Talk French, for starters." Still far less than fluent in French, he felt clumsy trying to communicate in complete sentences. He was clumsy. Mostly he was afraid of not being understood or not being credible. Or getting shot—he was concerned about that too.

Moreover, he realized, if he could see the enemy sniper—if that's what it was up there on the roof—then the shooter could see him. The gear on the private's web belt and the overstuffed rucksack did not seem like good things to be handicapping movement. The web belt was still loaded up despite the loss of one canteen. "I should have brought three," he muttered to himself in English.

In the next instant, he unhooked the belt and stuttered backwards on his knees into deeper grass. None too soon. His brain didn't register any *zing* or even the *crack*, but he saw the muffled puff of dirt exactly where his midsection had been hardly a moment before. He scampered farther, still backwards on all fours, remaining low as he could. It was a scramble to safety before the next shot came in. And come in it did—two or three more. His rifle, he saw, was still held tightly in his left hand. It had been slapping ground with each hand-step of his retreat.

Frustrated with himself, Conner grabbed the rucksack with both hands and rolled it another few meters back up the trail, then he quickly lay flat. This time, he heard the cracks. Before the grass settled, the shooter emptied his magazine on the area where the pack had stopped rolling. Then all went quiet—for maybe half a minute.

That's when it came to Conner that the crack of the gun was familiar to him. *Of course, it's an M-1 Garand—our rifle!* That was a strong clue it was French Forces up on the roof. Conner didn't know what he could do other than stand up and announce himself. Lying there all day didn't seem a good option. "Screw it." He shouted in French, "For God's sake, stop shooting! I am not Vietminh. I am French Force." He spit his message out plainly.

Another accented voice answered, "Then stand so I can see you."

"How do I know you will not shoot me if I stand?"

"You do not know. If you are French Force, you will not be afraid. Your voice tells me where you are. Stand up or be shot dead!"

"But I do not know what you are. What are you?"

After some silence came, *"Legio Patria Nostra."*

It was proof enough. It was a fellow Legionnaire—a soldier who shared "The Legion is Our Fatherland." That would mean a comrade, a soldier to be trusted. And a marksman.

Still not eager to do so, Conner slowly rose, as did the helmet on the roof corner. The *zing* went over his head, followed by the sound of the shot. He stood his ground and moved not a muscle.

"Oy vey! So, you are soldier of the Legion—you trust me. Not all do, you know. Come quickly here. I will cover for you."

Without answering, Conner replaced the steel pot, retrieved his violated rucksack, his rifle, hooked the web belt back up, and began lumbering through the tall grass directly to the colonial. Once through the grass moved him along faster.

"Use door at end of building. Come to roof," he was told.

Without looking right, left, up, or down, Private Conner headed directly for the set of doors at the end of the building. Once inside, it was as if a huge weight had been lifted from his shoulders. Literally, that was true, and he smiled at one more irony. Dropping the pack, and after two or three deep breaths, he hit the steps two at a time, up the two flights of stairs with rifle in hand. Already it was ingrained in him that the rifle was a part of him. *Never leave your rifle.* Reaching the roof, he slumped down, winded and tired, grateful to be safe, even knowing it was temporary.

"Why you take so long? Where is gear? You are not tourist, you know. Need rucksack and gear. Go to them and bring back."

He had just been through a lot, and this was bullshit. He didn't need to be jerked around—and for what? By what? He looked up and immediately understood. He should have known the voice: Corporal Mundt, of course! Conner looked around, ignoring Mundt's attitude and the order to retrieve his gear. "Where is everybody?"

"Is only me. And good thing for you. I save you."

"After you tried to kill me! You couldn't see who I was? Why were you shooting?"

"I see Viet near where you are when I first here. By time I have ready, he is gone. I think you are then him. My shooting *sehr gut*?"

"My kit thinks so. You killed it."

Neither of them laughed. The comment had a bitter edge to it.

"Where is the company?" Private Conner wanted to know. "I didn't see anybody once I hit the ground. A few open chutes—and they disappeared."

"We scatter everywhere in that focking elephant grass. How you get here I do not know. Mother Mary bless you, I think. Did Vietminh I see kiss you on cheek and point for you to come this way?" he asked.

As a Legionnaire the private was insulted. Whenever no one else was around, the corporal discounted and talked down to privates, especially this one. Having recently completed the unrivalled basic training, and in a foreign language too, Private Conner had every right to feel good about himself. Corporal Mundt was good at turning those feelings around. He tried too hard to keep new privates in their place, it seemed to Conner.

"We wait here for others to come. When we have officer, then we join fight."

Surprised it would take the presence of an officer for a Legionnaire to join the fight, the private looked out and scanned the horizon. From now on, he would stay away from the corporal as much as he could.

It wasn't long before another trooper came cautiously out of the long grass. Corporal Mundt stood and ran a sweep of his arms from side to side, then signed a cross indicating friendly force collection point. A simple high sign was returned, and soon, other troops materialized. Up and down the edge of the elephant grass, others broke through. Private Conner wasn't nearly as alone as he had thought. Within minutes it was nearly a platoon-sized collection of troopers.

The first to come out was Master Sergeant Phillips. He posted two troopers at the doors as security. The rest he directed to come with him into the colonial. No doubt they would come to the roof. They did.

"How did you find us?" Private Conner could only begin to ask.

"I heard the local shooting about five minutes ago, and I'm certain it's the same for these blokes. We headed for it," Sergeant Phillips announced. "How did you have enough sense to come here, Private? Or did you land here?" Not enriching comments, but offense wasn't taken.

"Where I did land, Master Sergeant, the only thing I could see was the top of this building, and it seemed obvious that others would be thinking like me and head for it too."

"That's it? Then what in hell was the shooting I heard?"

"Well, Corporal Mundt was already up here, and—"

But that was as far as he got. Mundt jumped in.

"Der vas Viet in tall grass—headed back to where he come from, I think. I shoot. Too bad private there too—almost in same spot. I not see him or I do not shoot."

The master sergeant's eyes followed Private Conner's look down at the shot-up kit one of the men had hauled upstairs. "That yours, Private?"

"Yes, sir." That was it. Private Conner wouldn't challenge the corporal's story, but he wasn't going to back it up. He knew being green was a sin, and he wasn't stupid enough to contradict a corporal or anybody else who outranked him. Not at that point, anyway. From now on, when Corporal Mundt berated him, he would simply ignore the bastard. It was a good feeling having made the decision.

"You see the Vietminh down there? Just one?"

Again, "Yes, sir. He almost stepped on me."

"But you are OK. What about him, the enemy?"

"That ist the thing, Sarge," Corporal Mundt again interrupted. "Green little fock do nothing. You check rifle. Not shoot! He hides in long grass. He see me, then come here to be safe."

"That right, Private?" The master sergeant reached for Connor's rifle. He opened the breech and a fresh round popped out. The sergeant then bent down and sniffed. He said nothing.

Conner was flummoxed. *What is happening?* "Uhhh, after he passed me, I tried to shoot then."

"But you didn't." It was a statement, not a question.

Conner felt betrayed. And humiliated. Already pale complexion turned crimson. Not a funny clown-red crimson—more of a not-funny, guilty-as-hell crimson.

"I pulled the trigger, Master Sergeant," came out pretty much defensive-like.

"And . . . ?"

"I hadn't chambered a round."

Corporal Mundt let out a squawk. "Ha! The boy never means to fight! And I save his sorry arse."

The lowly private wanted to be lower, much lower. He wanted to disappear. He and the corporal had never clicked, but Mundt was an NCO—someone to be respected or at least obeyed. Now, being accused of cowardice by him was over the line. Stunned, Connor didn't know what he dared say, or what not to say. As he hesitated, Mundt's words flashed through his mind, and he knew it appeared he was too scared to fight. *Mundt just made me out a coward, and there can be no such thing in the Legion!*

The corporal knew what he was doing. Of course, he demeaned Conner to make himself look good to the platoon sergeant. That was the answer, but not the end of it. Without intending to, it came hot out of Private Conner's mouth. *"Hell no."* Neither scream nor cry, it came from deep within, the low growl of a sound intense and sincere. It brought acute attention all around.

Sergeant Phillips cut him off. "That will be enough, Private. The battle plan today has no clause for debate. We'll not deal with this matter now, but thank you for coming forward, Corporal. Take these men downstairs and form them up so we can see what we have. I expect the colonel would like to see us join the battle."

"Whatever you say, Sarge." The men present heard it all and automatically headed down the stairs. Many were from Sergeant Phillips's platoon, others not. After a quick formation, they spread out and headed toward the sound of the fray. Ahead of them, mortar bombs were still falling and machine guns spitting in regular bursts.

"Stay spread out and eyes open. As we get into it, we will calculate options. Keep them moving, Corporal."

Heads nodded. Feet moved. They were close to the action, and the sergeant was in his natural habitat.

There was something about Corporal Mundt that Sergeant Phillips couldn't quite put his finger on. What it wasn't was the German versus English thing—they had gotten past that. There was something about this Private Conner, too, but the master sergeant knew what that was.

As soon as the enemy was suppressed, the next order of business in the valley would be to get going on the upgrade of the old airstrip. To receive heavy-load aircraft, the strip would have to be lengthened and generally reinforced. As it was, the dirt surface of potholes and mud was useless.

Next day, a bulldozer was flown in to jumpstart the modification. Pushed out the back of a C-119 Flying Boxcar, or Packet, as the French called it, the sendoff wasn't good. The delivery bobbled hard in what quickly became a tangle of parachutes. It came down two or three times faster than intended—so fast it didn't want to stop when it met the ground. It did not bury itself, but it was a good start, and it was junk. Another dozer was located and brought in the next day—successfully. True to form for the Legionnaires, the crashed dozer stuck around as a bad joke. It became less of a joke as time went on. The airstrip was their lifeline.

Chapter 9

A Pistol Shot

It was early December 1953, near Dien Bien Phu, Vietnam, that he opened his eyes and saw nothing but open spaces. He blinked. No troops. The regiment was gone. The words "Colonel Ky" seemed to float through the air and somehow land on him. *Someone calling me?* Twice more, his name. He turned. It was Major Vuong.

"Colonel, we go now. It has been a long march. You are most proud of the regiment. The staff has delivered regimental documents and the commander's personal effects to our temporary headquarters. Reconnaissance teams report much enemy activity in the valley. We can now plan compliance with the general's order."

It was a bit hazy, but he then remembered hearing his own voice announcing to the regiment. *Ah yes—that is why I am standing on the dais.* He hesitated, then considered his deputy commander. *Or is this a trick by Major Vuong?* There was so much confusion. The stress had been pounding him every day. *I know I am being watched—observed and judged by others who do not know and cannot understand. Can they not see General Giap's orders are impossible?* The colonel was bone tired, and the arduous march had compounded the effects of accumulating stress.

Colonel Ky was not a commander who overlooked being second-guessed, particularly when he discovered it being done behind his back. More to the point, he had come to view any opinion different than his own as second-guessing. Consequently, all differing opinions and second-guessing were done behind his back. Of course he sensed they were keeping things from him. In a similar category were those he had no control over.

I so despise that everything is subject to judgment by these spies they call commissars. They are not soldiers. They report nothing more than opinion to the final authority, The Party.

It was true. The enlisted, and sometimes officers, lost rank, authority, and even their lives because a commissar presumed some action or inaction to be out of line. More than once, Colonel Ky had vented to Major Vuong that "the commissars are typically incapable of understanding battlefield circumstance and necessary actions." Afterwards, he had worried because of the outburst, but the major had always been loyal to him. *Political officers have greater power than even commanders such as myself. It isn't the commissar but I who carry the responsibility of the regiment.* There was nothing he could do about the system; it was intended to keep everyone focused and loyal. The colonel worked with the commissars, which usually offered some sense of control, but never enough for him to feel unhindered. Recent events came to mind. *The last commissar was incredibly ignorant, thinking he could suspend my authority on his say-so. How unfortunate an assassin pierced his heart and cut out his voice box. The Party wished to interrogate the traitor, but he was killed in battle and his body ravaged by pigs. A most unfortunate series of events,* Colonel Ky had reported. Then he smiled broadly with his thoughts.

As gracious and helpful as the major had tried to be, Colonel Ky eventually saw pretense in his helpfulness and ambition in his assertiveness. *An eagerness for a command of his own is his goal, Ky mused.* The colonel had turned the corner on trust and found distrust. No longer did he entirely believe the deputy commander. Ironically, it was Major Vuong's helpfulness that made obvious the increasing neediness of Colonel Ky. The major, it seemed to Ky, always seemed to be meddling in the colonel's affairs, both military and personal. *I have to be careful not to be vulnerable to ambitious fools. I will be strong,* the colonel promised himself.

Then he looked down. The document was still in his hand. It was the updated order from the People's Army, High Command. The regiment was being tasked to provide the layout of the French fortifications in the valley and also the French armaments there, their precise locations, the quantity and quality of the defenders, and the traffic patterns within the fortress. On and on it went. Precise and accurate information was critical to the planning of any Vietminh attack, but this one especially. It seemed unlikely to Ky that an assault on the developing fortress could be successful. He well recalled the battle for Na-San a year ago. Yes, this valley, too, is remote to French resupply, and in that sense it is vulnerable. *But,* he cautioned himself silently, *Dien Bien Phu is wilderness for us as well, and we have no airforce.* Nevertheless, it was up to Ky to set the stage for the grand battle, the battle that would likely determine the outcome of the war. *If we are to lose this battle, it will come back on me,* he understood. And that was likely.

The world was watching. The order also forbade the colonel to allow French Force patrols of any size to explore the hills around the valley. The

French must be denied the precise local topography and the extent of fortifications being placed in the hills. The Vietminh divisions were on the way, but for the time being, the 57th Regiment alone must make preparations and deal with all DBP matters. The colonel was to make maps of enemy fortifications to pinpoint headquarters bunkers and gun positions. They were also to note activities. Since he could trust no one, the colonel was forced to delegate responsibility of the requirements with great anguish. It was an impossible mission for him. He felt at the mercy of others.

Why must I work with backbiting fools? he lamented to himself. Colonels in the People's Army could, like Ky, be skeptical and even neurotic, but always at the risk of annoying a commissar and being reported to The Party. What Ky understood was that preparation for an assured Vietminh victory would require more than supreme intelligence or even good luck—factors he could only imagine would be necessary. Primarily, the suppression of French air traffic. Only by seriously inhibiting the flow of resupply could the French Force be hobbled. Doing so was a pipe dream, and Ky was stuck with the dreams of others.

General Giap was depending on Colonel Ky and his 57th Regiment for what seemed like an assurance of victory. But, engaged once again, the colonel rolled up the orders and stuffed them into a cargo pocket. He would take matters into his own hands. The conventional Vietminh divisions were yet well north of them. They were slow, loaded down with tons of equipment and ordnance. No longer was General Giap stashing a tube of rice and a handful of bullets on each soldier and sending them out to ambush French patrols with hit-and-run tactics. A great deal of replenishment would be necessary to feed the dozens of artillery pieces, rifles, and machine guns to be used in sustained attack by his full divisions. Although the same was true for the defenders, the French had a plan for resupply. Colonel Ky couldn't yet know that General Giap had a plan, a very different plan, to keep the wheels turning and grinding down the enemy. Only one plan would weather the storm.

Within twenty-four hours of paratroopers hitting the ground, the Dien Bien Phu airstrip was getting a retrofit: a much longer and wider surface. "Airbridge" was what the French called it. All the equipment, supplies, and troops they needed would simply be flown in. Materials for building revetments were brought in to house a fleet of F-8 and F-6 fighter planes, and also spotter planes to be immediately responsive as needed. With spotter planes, active Vietminh artillery would be located and then roasted with artillery or the fighter-bombers. Artillery missions directed by airborne forward observers were almost always textbook: linger a spotter plane in the area to pinpoint the active enemy, report the location to artillery control, then adjust the friendly battery shots until the kill was complete.

The French knew the People's Army had few roads substantial enough to move heavy ordnance. The French believed that few if any big guns could be brought in over the hills and that, if howitzers did come in, they could not be supplied with a stock of shells consequential enough to harm the fortress.

To his staff Colonel Ky announced, "The 57th Regiment is tasked with this great honor. We will provide General Giap with the intelligence necessary to map out a failsafe plan to overwhelm the French Force in place." His voice pushed for effect, but the vocal cords were raspy, inspiration suspect.

Ky did not know that a Geneva Conference was scheduled for May. It would consist of USSR, USA, France, and Britain delegations meeting in Geneva to chiefly consider the Korean and Indochina situations. The shooting had stopped in Korea, but the armistice was not complete. Forces there remained facing each other at the 38th parallel.

To world leaders, a political solution to the Indochina issue seemed the likely resolution after nearly eight years of discord and expanding bloodshed in Vietnam. Both the current French president and Ho Chi Minh had privately suggested as much by then. The Geneva Conference would likely determine where the war would end and how the politics would settle. The military positioning of the two forces by 8 May 1954, would weigh heavily on the outcome. The conference of the world powers would begin in earnest on that date. The outcome at Dien Bien Phu was of significant consequence.

The tone of the written order Colonel Ky was given suggested attack was a foregone conclusion. It was time to roll the dice, whether the players knew why or even how. As the dedicated commander he was, the colonel would follow his orders as precisely as possible, but he was filled with reservation. *Must we fight the French as they wish us to fight them? Must we attack them from the open expanse of the valley and against their stout fortifications and limitless firepower? We fight well from the jungle and the hills. The sky is their jungle. They will fill it with blazing death when it pleases them. It is insane to fight them in this manner. Yet the general wishes it to be so; I cannot miscarry my orders. I fear for my regiment.*

Ten days ago, the orders were received. The colonel had thought of little else since. "To Colonel Ky, Commander: In all haste the 57th Regiment is to separate from the 304th Division and march to the hills north of Dien Bien

Phu. The outcome of the war depends on your urgent arrival and performance of duty once there. Depart immediately. Signed, General of the Army, People's Army, Vo Nguyen Giap."

Three hundred kilometers through the High Region in ten days under rudimentary trail conditions was a feat to be proud of. It was also the feat expected by the commanding general and his general staff. Traveling light, the regiment complied and arrived intact, but they arrived exhausted. Vulnerable the whole way, moving as fast as they did, a trail was pioneered for all others of the People's Army to follow. Yet the colonel was disturbed. Beyond intelligence gathering, he was responsible to stop any and all French Force probes or sweeps beyond the valley floor. "At all costs, the enemy must not access the hills of Dien Bien Phu," read the orders. The enemy must not go beyond the valley. I have an exhausted, understrength regiment with light arms only, while the enemy is rich with men and armaments. They will soon be sweeping the hills if we cannot stop them.

Major Vuong had already reported to him that a cargo plane was landing every ten minutes with French Force matériel. Munitions, supplies, and equipment—even disassembled tanks, otherwise too large for the cargo planes—had arrived. With them, it was believed mechanics arrived to reconstitute and maintain them. The feverish tempo of construction would likely continue for some time, and the pressure bore directly down on Colonel Ky.

"We conduct the staff meeting in perhaps . . . two hours, colonel?"

The commander continued staring at the paper in his hand; no response.

The major nodded to the staff. The message went out: regimental staff meeting at 14:00 hours.

The battalion commanders with their staff people arrived well before the two hours. There was light chatter only. It was grim times with grim faces, knowing what they did and surmising what they did not. At last, Colonel Ky seemed to have it together. To no one in particular the commander stated, "We will advance small teams of scouts near the valley floor. They will warn of enemy patrols or enemy advances toward the hills. With a ready reaction force we will attack at once, as hammer on anvil. No mercy! We will restrict our enemy to the valley floor by whatever means necessary. This is final!" His intensity was cold, and not a word or question came forward.

The meeting continued with the major dictating specifics of the colonel's plan, specifics he had to come up with on his own. Details Ky chose to think of as Major Vuong's responsibility.

Meanwhile, Ky's thoughts turned to Private Nguyen, the presumed hero. Somehow that coolie-private is involved in all this. It must be The Party that spies on me. All the more reason to eliminate him. The colonel was quite serious and, perhaps, quite unwell.

The staff recorded the colonel's directive as a regimental order to be provided to each battalion and company-level commander. After reading it, the colonel scribbled a signature on each copy. That completed, the staff looked to Major Vuong again, who glanced at the colonel before continuing with the business at hand. The major went over the details of the General Order. The stark orders bore no questions. Major Vuong nodded slightly. They would be carried out to the last soldier, if necessary. There were zero smiles and no chatter. Everyone understood.

As for the colonel, he could think more clearly when he was moving or otherwise active. Back and forth, after the meeting, he paced inside the tent. He recalled the recent formation. His communication to the troops had been generally to the point but with something less than his normal intensity. As always, his pretense was well camouflaged, but that occasion had not been his best effort. Next time I will do better, he promised himself. He reviewed the earlier formation in his mind. Doing so did not calm him.

"What is it, Colonel? You seem agitated. Can I help?"

"Of course not, Major—I am fit and well. Do not concern yourself with me. My duty and responsibilities you cannot share. I will alert you for necessary assistance."

"Yes, sir." It was a "yes, sir" moment. "Come sit; camp stool here, Colonel. The orderly will bring hot rice with nuoc mam and monkey meat. Greens too. You will be pleased. We can speak of the staff meeting then if you like." It was his job, and the major did it well. Much like the privates and colonel, Major Vuong too was talented in the business of camouflage and hidden pretense.

Colonel Ky did feel better after eating and resting. His mind seemed to settle. Major Vuong read back the minutes of the meeting for the colonel. Together the battalion commanders had discussed the required intelligence gathering and how it would be documented. They were somber yet amicable, well aware of the colonel's demeanor. The greater discussions were centered on the organization necessary for stopping French forays into the hills. The battalion commanders understood the priority of the order—that it came directly from General Giap. Failure was not acceptable, nor would it be tolerated by Colonel Ky.

It was decided that small teams would be used to observe specific segments of the valley. Much of the regiment consisted now of troops original to home platoons. Training there was limited, but most were experienced in observable intelligence. Nearly to a person they excelled at it, in part because it was often competitive among the young recruits. Eliciting information from

French Force troops was gratifying. The youth, in seeming innocence, often witnessed or accessed information that, when combined with other information, could be quite significant and helpful to the cause.

Every day from then on, the observers recorded French Force activity. Specifically the teams noted manpower, equipment, weapons, stockpiles of matériel, and positioning. The number of steps taken by a soldier going from point A to point B offered accurate distances, which would be important to Vietminh infantry and artillery alike. Maps of each team's assigned area were drawn to scale. At regimental headquarters, the maps were merged to compile an accurate representation of the valley defenses, although not all areas were visible. No detail was likely to be overlooked. Changes and adjustments were noted daily.

It began the next morning, the day after the regiment's arrival at Dien Bien Phu. The two-person intel teams were sent out at predawn. While the bulk of the regiment set up camp, provided security, and dug in, the intel teams were oriented as to the process and degree of their intelligence duties. Literacy was a requirement for all intel team members. The specific details were to be recorded and quantified in a jargon of uniformity. Any activity by French patrols outside the circle of strongpoints was to prompt an alert, initiating immediate attack.

As a private, Nguyen Dac Pho remained his normal soft-spoken self, but he was quite literate. The people's hero was matched with a Corporal Nai and assigned to recon the strongpoint far from Central Camp to the northeast. Vietminh radio intercepts identified it as Strongpoint Beatrice. Being distant from Central Camp, Beatrice was an obvious first choice for attack but also a natural choice from which to make French Force sorties into the hills. Strongpoint Beatrice was favored by both sides.

Seven other French strongpoints were scattered, but jointly they surrounded Central Camp and the airstrip. All eight were given female French names. It was commonly suggested they were named for the mistresses of fortress commander de Castries. Each strongpoint was fashioned from rising hillocks and surrounded by multiple rows of barbed or razor wire fences parallel to each other. At a minimum, each strongpoint featured a command bunker, trenchwork, blockhouses at the corners, and machineguns, mortar and recoilless artillery tubes. Some were defended by only a company or two, but each was a pointedly defensible position. A significant feature was that each was positioned to support another two or even three strongpoints with firepower and potentially with reinforcing troops.

Colonel Ky remained anxious, Major Vuong observed. That was to be expected, considering the circumstances. Yet, as he could, the major shadowed Ky's movements their first full day at Dien Bien Phu. As deputy commander, Vuong was responsible for Ky. He knew reporting the colonel's irregular actions of late would be seen by the colonel as betrayal, making their working relationship untenable. The major chose to keep an eye on Colonel Ky and cover for him where necessary. That would continue unless or until the colonel's behavior deteriorated significantly further. If the behavior continued to degrade, the major would be forced at some point to draw the line and report to division and General Giap. There was no manual on how that worked. It wasn't good business, and no matter what could happen, the outcome would be nasty for someone, and likely more than one. Vuong knew he needed to have clear and just cause and be able to prove whatever such a report claimed before moving forward with such action.

The colonel was not up the next morning until after the intel teams had left camp. No one knew if that was intentional or not. He had not left orders to be awakened. After a bland meal of plain white rice and a cup of black tea, the colonel made it known he would personally review the intel teams. He would inspect their positions and activity after completing the daily situation report to division. He steadfastly kept to his reporting routine.

About midmorning, Colonel Ky collected an extra canteen and a machete, saying he needed only a single attendant and would return when he was satisfied that his instructions were being followed. With his operations staff sergeant, to whom he handed the machete, he headed for the farthest intel post on that end of the valley. Coming from the south, the wind pushed to them the clattering of machines and men, at least occasionally mixed with cursing in several languages. Major Vuong was reluctant to see the colonel go out basically alone but didn't want to appear obvious in his watchfulness.

Four hours later, the staff sergeant returned with news that all was well and the commander had sent him back. After a solo stop at the last intel team, the colonel would be returning to camp.

Meanwhile, at that last intel post, Private Nguyen and Corporal Nai were working out a common voice for their observation and documentation. They hadn't known each other previously and struggled much of the day to work out a homogenous communication process. The introvert, Nguyen, was having difficulty being specific and consistent in his oral communication. He was new to many of the required terms and wasn't practiced at declaring specific military observations. To his credit, the corporal pressed the need for clear communication and proper terms to provide accurate and consistent reporting. They were good at taking turns. While one of them verbalized what was observed, the other noted in script. Each verbal report resulted in an entry that was discussed and sometimes adjusted.

Well into the afternoon and busy with their observations and adjustments, neither was aware of the officer behind them in the bush, quietly observing. Eventually the officer moved up, coming close to being obvious.

At that point, the two enlisted men were both facing the valley. Private Nguyen was concentrating on spitting out in proper vernacular a Strongpoint Beatrice observation. The officer was mere feet behind Corporal Nai before announcing his presence. The corporal spun around, only to absorb the explosion of a bullet into his face. The bullet struck just to the side of his nose and into his throat an instant before plowing through skull bone. Great and ugly damage was done, but nothing vital had been struck. On the ground now, the corporal screamed at an incredibly high pitch, shocked at what was happening. The officer's boot came down on the corporal's neck a second before another pistol shot rang out, this one slamming into the victim's left temple, killing him instantly and dispelling gurgled screams.

Having also turned, Nguyen stared down at the dead corporal, then up at the officer with spattered blood on his face. Nguyen was quite frozen in time and space, allowing the officer to again raise his pistol, now to the private's face. The shot rang out. The jarring effect was enough to prod the pistol from the officer's hand. Nearly as quickly, the new victim fell forward. Released suddenly by instinct, the private jumped back. The officer slumped forward at his feet. Nguyen was beyond astonished to witness a small round hole in the back of Colonel Ky's head. Major Vuong then lowered his pistol and stared hard into the future of Nguyen Dac Pho and the private's new regimental commander.

Chapter 10

Eye for an Eye

Colonel Ky was not a large man. Compared to the Western model, neither was Private Nguyen. Nguyen first tried to drag Ky's body, then employed the fireman's carry to move the colonel a few steps at a time. After half an hour's exertion he had gotten the body as far as the regiment's security ring. From there, two nervous privates carried the deceased the rest of the way while others went forward to retrieve the corporal's body.

A dead regimental commander was big news. Troops of all ranks appeared and followed the body back to the rear at regimental headquarters. Others not on specific duty soon heard the news and gathered to see for themselves. A special supper was already being served in recognition of the regiment's swift travel and safe arrival at the valley. With chopsticks and bowls of pho, their favorite, a couple hundred troops loosely congregated in front of the headquarters shelter to gawk at the body. Although muted, there was much speculation and an array of rumors. Others waited for relief at their posts with the prospect of seeing the dead commander themselves.

Colonel Ky had been a severe commander. Not everyone was personally saddened by his demise, but certainly everyone was shocked. The colonel was the last person they expected to see shot through the head. At first there was little notice of the blood-spattered and mud-smeared Private Nguyen who trailed the body. That would change.

The normally quiet Nguyen was exhausted from the initial carry and still dazed from the shock of it all. He began sputtering explanations as soon as he reached the headquarters. It didn't matter. No one seemed to notice him much less listen to him. The troops were, instead, fascinated by their commander's lifeless body on the ground in front of them. Left to their own, they crowded around the spectacle and needlessly questioned each other as to what had happened.

The rough appearance of the body did not faze them. Virtually all were accustomed to seeing such things. Handling torn bodies was common, even normal. This one was still fresh. Most of the observers were the privates whose job it was to cope with torn heads, ripped-open torsos, and random body parts, decomposed or not. Each grade had its own cross to bear. It was the officers who coped with illogical orders from above and urgent paperwork that served little purpose. At least that was how it often seemed to them. The noncommissioned officers kept the system honest by developing the privates and tempering the officers. There were degrees of resistance all around, but it was a system that generally worked.

The rampant and speculative comments continued. The troops were needing an explanation, some kind of accounting. There was none. Onlookers began turning to the new guy who accompanied the body into camp. By then Nguyen was reluctant to speak; he didn't know what to say, although he knew what not to say.

The body of the popular Corporal Nai arrived. Attention shifted. The turmoil and noise ramped back up. Timing called for Major Vuong to appear, and he did. Brushing aside a tent flap, he stepped out of the HQ tent. The atmosphere changed instantly. The major appeared stern but calm. The crowd settled but remained anxious. He had no problem with the prevailing anxiety. It served to keep the troops sharp.

Attention reverted from the major back to the bodies. That was disappointing. He had hoped to hear a general calling for him as commander. *Too sudden and too soon,* he reasoned, but he wouldn't soon forget the unintended insult. Military manner was absent; the regimental commander dead; clamor again rose in the ranks, a sense of surreal. Officers and non-coms stepped up with weak reprimands, themselves part of the fog. The troops were excited; the rumble continued, regardless, and even grew.

Looking around with some concern, Major Vuong then displayed his style of leadership. Drawing his pistol, he fired three rounds into the air. Military bearing reinstated instantly. Everyone turned to look. The troops backed away from the bodies as the major came forward. With a grim expression, he holstered the pistol and scanned the crowd, which backed them further. He briefly viewed the bodies, offereing no change of expression until he noticed the disheveled and dirty Private Nguyen. The major may have softened somewhat then.

"Soldiers of 57th Regiment," he began, "this is not the time to abandon discipline and duty. In good time now you will be called to formation. You will know then what I know and what I am about to learn. As you finish our fine supper this evening, please return promptly to your duty posts. Inform your comrades of this tragedy. We have a great challenge before us—much more than at any other time. Please encourage others to continue performing their duty well as you do yours. It is what Colonel Ky would expect and what I do expect. All are to mourn the death of the honorable commander, Colonel Ky. Remain alert. We do not know yet what the French Force devils are up to. We must stop them and stop them here. Listening posts will be doubled and moved closer to the valley tonight. Carry on. That is all."

Private Nguyen began shivering as soon as the major motioned him to the headquarters tent. As directed, he sat on a stool before the major. He could not stop shaking. Being a good village boy and scared to death, he stared at the dirt floor. When addressed, the young private in him attempted eye contact with the major but for hardly more than a second. Almost immediately, his self-conscious stare resorted to the floor. Half a dozen of the regimental staff was in the shelter, all unsure suddenly of their own status. For nearly a minute the major contemplated the soiled and forlorn hero-boy. The major looked around and saw nothing but anxious officers. He sighed.

"Leave us," he spoke sharply.

The officers left briskly, asking no questions. The last to go, a nervous lieutenant orderly, was called back. Major Vuong politely asked him to claim two bowls of pho and a half-filled wash bowl. Half an hour later, the private's bearing and outlook had changed. The shivering had stopped while the major and he slurped the hot soup. Clean face and hands, good food; pressure in the shelter had lessened considerably.

"Private, I know you do not understand," the major cautiously began. Then he flirted with a question, this one rather bold: "It is certain we trust each other. That true, Private?" There was no response. Then he gently added, "You are a hero and favorite of the people. Perhaps I am regimental commander and soon to be colonel. You are a new private wishing to do well."

Nguyen observed a gentle manner and heard the message within. As a private, the bottom of all ranks, his very life was contingent on the grace of the commander. Both he and the major knew that the circumstance of Colonel Ky's death could never be divulged. *Can it be the major feels he can trust me? Never mind that I am a green private answerable to anyone in the People's Army.* Then came a surprise more fascinating than frightening to him.

"You are also my confidant, Private Nguyen. I respect you. All things change. You know that. All things happen in good time." At that he stopped and intentionally waited. After several seconds, the response was eye contact and a simple nod of the private's head. The message was clear. He would be loyal to Vuong above all else. The major could go on.

"After much pressure of command," he spoke directly, "Colonel Ky had become paranoid and suspicious of everyone, even those who labored to assist and protect him. The end became clear when he feared you. He believed you to be a false hero, sent here to bring him down. He did not trust you, and he believed he had to diminish or kill you. The colonel could trust only himself to do so. You do know that, don't you? There could be no witnesses."

"Which is why he killed Corporal Nai," Nguyen volunteered. His cheeks warmed from the comment, whether with fear or anger he did not know.

Vuong went on. "Colonel Ky could trust no one to do it—no one other than himself," he repeated. "While my duty was to protect the integrity of the colonel and assist him, my dilemma came to be choosing one or the other—him or you. It could not be both. I chose you." The major again stopped and waited.

Stunned, Nguyen could not understand. "Why me? I am only a private."

"Private, yes, but you are rich with humanity. You are valuable as the people's hero. Colonel Ky did not understand that. As with all privates in the People's Army, you have no authority. Yet you live the example of the people's authority through your courage and dedication. That is why you were inducted. From coolie to private you reveal your notoriety to all who serve the People's Army. The colonels and the generals have each other to please. Your rank and your humanity reflect back on the people and especially the privates. You are a hero, as are all privates. You and they are the heroes, you and they are that authority. You understand each other. You love each other, and, therefore, the People's Army understands its needs. It depends on you and on all privates." The major was pleased to have said it well.

"Now think about the future through the past, Private Nguyen. If Colonel Ky had successfully carried out his plan, would he have been saved because you died for him? No! You are not Jesus. His paranoia would continue, grow worse, and soon it would destroy the regiment and perhaps more. I could not allow that to happen."

Realization swept over Nguyen like a wave. Over time he would have to process all that his new commander had told him. Presently he managed a shallow breath and the obvious question: "What will become of us now, sir? Can The Party and General Giap be so understanding they will believe what happened here today?"

"For a village boy, you are bright," the major mused.

Nguyen welcomed the assurance of the comment but was not certain it was a compliment.

"This truth is most preposterous," the major flatly stated, "as you well know. Of course they cannot believe this truth. That is why you must understand. Do you?" It was awkward and haunting yet seemed to be reassurance. There was nothing Private Nguyen could say. Major Vuong cleared his throat, irritated by what seemed the private's hesitation. "At your intel position near the valley, Private, tell me what happened today." The major had become stern again.

That their wellbeing had become entwined was obvious to Nguyen, but it was still confusing. He was at a loss to tell the major what happened. *What an odd thing for him to ask. The major knows what happened better than I. I cannot possibly answer that properly.*

The major remained silent and still, calmly focusing on a small stone on the ground to his front.

The pressure stuck. The only thing Nguyen could think to do was review in his mind what the major had said since they entered the headquarters shelter. It was a full minute later when bright eyes flashed open, settling on the major's face. As enlightenment, it was encouraging to both men. "Sir, I now remember recording Corporal Nai's observation. I was looking down at my notebook. Colonel Ky was with us at the time to observe our manner of intelligence collection. One second, Corporal Nai was detailing his observation, and the next second, his head shattered. He had been standing in front of me. I reached out to him. We both fell to ground. Just as we began falling, *bang!* I heard the report of the rifle. I knew then it was a sniper had shot him from a distance. Only a second later I heard another rifle report. I wanted to help Corporal Nai but, hearing the second shot, I turned to the commander. He was already falling to the ground. That is what happened, Major," he finished with some authority.

Not until the final word of the private's report did Major Vuong raise his eyes. "Fine report, Private." He hesitated. "Was there no third shot?"

Nguyen thought for a moment before it came to him. "Oh yes. The first and second shots were close together. I heard them both. I am sure one of those bullets was meant for me, but both hit Corporal Nai. That is what happened, Major."

"Yes, I think that is exactly correct—that is what happened, Private. It is best to remind yourself of all details. There will be many questions. Precise answers are always good to assure investigators."

Next morning, the regiment's communications cell received a message from division. Immediately decoded, it was hand-carried to Major Vuong.

"To Major Vuong, Acting Commander, 57th Regiment, 304th Division. Balance of division in transit at this time. ETA, 7 days. Existing orders remain valid and of greatest importance. We trust Private Nguyen is well? Signed, Commander 304th Division."

Those few words spoke a great deal to Major Vuong. Likely the powers-that-be were satisfied with his written report concerning Ky's death. Being referred to as the Acting Commander of the 57th Regiment put to rest any question on that front. Division brass would normally investigate the death of a regimental commander, but these were not normal times. The major was confident these two casualties at Dien Bien Phu were only the beginning. There were far greater matters at hand than needless investigations. Surprisingly, Private Nguyen, the people's hero, was included in the communiqué. Some staff officers of the 57th were of the opinion there was more concern for Private Nguyen than for the deceased colonel or perhaps even the regiment.

There was little time for anyone to mourn the colonel. The show must go on, and go on it did. The next day, a well-armed French Force patrol eased out of Strongpoint Beatrice and with some intensity trooped northeast toward the hills. From his intel post, Nguyen signaled the urgent need of a reaction squad to confront the intruders. They were capable of making a fuss, whatever the enemy's size or action. Their duty was to defeat or stall whatever was approaching. A larger reaction force would be reinforcing them as time and distance permitted. The French Force patrol was not a feint; it continued on a path directly to the hills. Without fail, the security eight-person squad must stop them. Scurrying, they positioned themselves behind the crest of the first hill. They chose a location based on topography that would likely draw the enemy to their immediate front.

Unlike former days when weapons were limited, every member of the 57th Regiment was then armed. The reaction squad members were armed with the Soviet Mosin-Nagant Model 1891, the most produced bolt-action rifle in history. A bit long and heavy, some would say, but the results it produced were inarguable: domination of Eastern Europe and, so far, a huge chunk of Asia. The Chicom stick grenades in each of their belts were effective as well, although duds among them were fairly common.

All eight of the responding reaction squad members were experienced in ambush technique and discipline. They were anxious, of course, but confident of inflicting damage and holding off a French patrol not all that much larger than themselves. The intel team had counted eleven in the French patrol.

It was a significant advantage to fight from behind the berm of the hill. The enemy had the disadvantage of trying to advance while exposed and travelling uphill. There was no time to place mines and, due to the terrain, the preferred L-shape ambush would not be in play. Still, the small reaction squad was confident and well suited.

The French Force patrol, meanwhile, plotted a slow and cautious advance. They were aware of activity in the hills.

Ten days before, when the Dakotas swooped in with a brigade of Legionnaire paratroopers, there were nearly a hundred hamlets and small villages in the valley. In the beginning most remained, retaining their homes and continuing to work the fields and rice paddies. Historically, they had been able to *coexist* with whomever controlled the valley, and both sides had. The T'ai indigents, as they were known, did their best to be neutral, although both the French and the Vietminh worked to recruit and use them. The tribal dwellers simply wanted to farm and live peacefully—maybe kill a few opposing tribal folks, but that was it. Few had yet left. That would change.

The backup reaction force, a full platoon, was hustling to the confrontation site and would be there in minutes. Meanwhile, decision time had closed in on the reaction squad leader. Corporal Diep had joined the Vietminh more than three years before. At twenty-two, he was a model soldier, his leadership role well earned. The promotion to corporal and being given his own squad was recent, so recent that he was yet searching for a sense of authority in directing them. As for independent decisions: no experience.

This was the first time for Corporal Diep to trigger an ambush himself. That would be a critical decision—the triggering. It was an eleven-man enemy patrol, and they must not reach the crest of the hill they were ascending. With no one to consult with or be directed by, it was left to Corporal Diep to flip the switch, make the call, do the right thing. There could be no mistake.

As he watched the enemy advance unwittingly toward his squad's position, a rush of anxiety enveloped the corporal. It had come out of nowhere. One moment he was proud and confident, the next he was unsure and internally shaken. Above all, he wanted to appear strong and decisive to his squad. Good plan, but he needn't have been concerned. They knew he was scared! They were too. For him, it was only beginner's jitters—he was otherwise well prepared. His mind went through a series of questions. *Why does the enemy come here? What support must they have? The squad is watching me. Have I missed something? I am responsible for stopping them! Where is the reaction platoon?* Through it all, Corporal Diep knew he must shake indecision. He then raised his chin in faux confidence, telling himself, *I must be stronger than I am.*

One deep inhale—and he made the call: "FIRE!"

The corporal and his men opened with rifle fire, quickly jacking in new rounds and shooting again and again, as fast as they could. After the patrol below them had all gone to ground, it was grenades. Corporal Diep directed his squad to toss grenades down the hill. *The reaction platoon will be here soon with an officer and machine guns,* he reasoned. Flat on their bellies, the Legion patrol returned fire, seeming to suppress the rifle fire. No instinct in the world could willingly raise a soldier's head to look and aim while the sound and feel of enemy bullets was passing through his or her personal space. That was especially true when the source was semi-automatic or automatic gunfire. The French Force patrol was using both. By comparison, the Vietminh bolt-action rifles were slow and clumsy.

Corporal Diep had appropriately switched to grenades. His people could pitch grenades downhill all day long with minimal exposure. Of course, they had only about three grenades each. Also, they needed to know what was going on down there—what the enemy was doing. Intermittently, heads popped up to direct a grenade or squeeze off a hurried round toward the Legionnaires. They were doing well and they knew it. Multiple screams below had become distinct. They had hurt at least a couple of them, probably more. Corporal Diep and his squad were holding their own while maintaining low exposure. The corporal was now proud of his people. As for the French Force patrol, several were hurt, two of them badly.

The Chicom grenades were sparking and doing their job. The good thing about any grenade was that it did not explode until its travel time had expired. They were most effective, of course, when their detonation occurred in the near environs of the enemy. The bad thing about any grenade was that the travel time could be too long. Striking a target or bouncing off a hard surface did not cause detonation. The expiration of a specific few seconds set it off. Therefore, if an intended target, a soldier, had the time to throw it back before blastoff, that could be a personal problem for others if it exploded near them.

Shortly after the opening shots and everybody hunkering down, Corporal Diep's sense of duty called him to move laterally behind the crest of the hill. Away from the ambush he was able to stand and fully observe. Not the safest thing in the world, but it seemed unlikely he would be noticed by the enemy in their present circumstance. His positioning gave him a bigger picture of what was happening. He could feel good about directing his people as needed.

Then it happened. Diep̃ was suddenly observing horror. A thrown Chicom stick grenade was caught in the air by a Legionnaire and, in one motion, lobbed back at the crest of the hill. It was not a dud. While yet in the air, it exploded, showering the center of the Vietminh squad with a sharp blast of hot shrapnel.

Seeing it detonate over the area where he had been only a minute or two before, Corporal Diep's weapon dropped to the ground. Of the two women in his squad, one was killed outright, it appeared, and the other was badly hurt. Two others took shrapnel, were robbed of their hearing, but would recover if they survived the firefight. The squad members on either end of the ambush were injured superficially but otherwise only dazed.

Immediately at the blast, however, the NCO of the French patrol got his Legionnaires up and moving. They did not retreat back down the hill. Master Sergeant Phillips had presumed serious damage done to the ambush when he saw where the grenade had burst. Scarcely a moment before, the French Force patrol could not move in any direction without exposing themselves more. Advancing into the fire of the ambush would have been suicide, and there was almost no chance to flank the ambushers without extreme exposure. Then, out of nowhere, one grenade, one enemy grenade, essentially shut the ambush down on itself.

Except for the yelps of the injured, all went still, but not for long. The seven Legionnaires yet operative had jumped up and charged the twelve or fifteen meters to the top with hardly a shot fired at them. Gaining the crest, they riddled the Vietminh squad, killing them all. At the same time an out of breath Vietminh reaction platoon crested the ridge above the ambush squad. Recognizing the chaos and mix of bodies, both enemy and friendly troops below, they stopped to assess the scene and their surroundings.

The French Force patrol was seasoned and led well enough to understand the action required of them. From there, Sergeant Phillips with four of the Legionnaires blunted any meaningful response from the reaction platoon by placing and maintaining semi and automatic fire on them. The Legionnaires alternated in locking fresh magazines into their weapons and controlling their fire as they walked backwards down the hill. Two of the wounded Legionnaires hobbled as best they could while the two slightly wounded were able to carry the badly wounded to the valley floor.

The French Force mortar tubes began to pour it on even before Phillips and his men reached flat ground. Strongpoint Beatrice boasted a trio of mortar tubes; all three resounded repeatedly. The first mortar bombs came down behind the reaction platoon and to the right. Two rounds later they had found both range and target. The mortarmen loaded fast and rhythmically. It was *crump, crump, crump*—one after another as each shell lifted off. The whistling bombs shrieked down and began striking between the lower and upper ridges—just where the reaction platoon had pulled up short and were basically exposed. Some hunkered down, hard to do on the front of a sharp hillside. Most scattered, or tried to, while half a dozen paid the ultimate price for being exposed.

What was lost on everyone was Corporal Diep. He was left idly straddling the ambush crest thirty meters from his squad. They were dead. All of them. He was not. It was his squad. It had been his first independent ambush. They were gone, his dirty rifle was jammed, and he was not among the dead. He wished he were. He had watched them die. He saw the reaction platoon arrive—just late enough to be slaughtered. He had helplessly witnessed the carnage of both units.

After it finished, the corporal remained listless on the sidelines. Nothing had touched him; nothing physically. His fate was to live. But the French Force patrol had not breached the crest. Corporal Diep had succeeded, and he could hardly bear it.

Chapter 11

Sergeant in Time Saves Nine

Including himself, Master Sergeant Phillips had saved nine from the ambush of the first reconnaissance probe into the hills north of the valley. There had been eleven of them, but the two badly wounded did not make it. The incident didn't slam the door shut on outside probes for the French Force, but it left an obvious dent. They put it out there again and again, trying to gauge the resources of the enemy. Each time they were stiffly rejected and incurred unsustainable loss. By the middle of December 1953, they were ready to try something else.

It was a crafty plan to be sure. Daring it was, but ingenious and foolproof it was not. The attempted probes into the hills had become desperate scrambles. General Giap played his hand well and stopped cold all forays. The French were unable to determine what they were up against. They could project confidence in stout fortifications and resupply by air. Beyond that, it was believed a breakout operation would prove to the world that the French Force was not bottled up and under siege. The world was watching—watching and waiting to see if communism would take over more countries. This was seen as the pitched battle to stem communism or not. In the end, what the mission did display to the world was the depth of denial France was able to create.

The plan was to move a select military column thirty miles west to Sop Nao, where they would link up with a marching column of three battalions coming north from southern Laos. For both columns it would be a rugged slog through rough terrain and a determined enemy.

The hills north and east of Dien Bien Phu remained locked up by Major Vuong's 57th Regiment. Vietminh divisional units had filtered in along with thousands of coolies and porters with tons of supplies, munitions, artillery, and even anti-aircraft guns unknown to the French. The AA guns would be used to shocking effect.

Major Vuong learned that meager High Region trails had been broken open. It was finally possible to access vehicular traffic as far as Dien Bien Phu, which meant the arrival of trucks, heavy-wheeled artillery, and hundreds of tons more war matériel and troops.

To the west and south of the valley, the security ring was much less robust. Only more wilderness to endure there. Arriving Vietminh had only begun to shore up the entire perimeter of the valley. The northeast trail out of the valley was the traditional route back to civilization, and it was then inaccessible to the French Force.

On 21 December 1953, the column of Legionnaires made their move. With surprise on their side as well as artillery and tactical air support, if necessary, the French column broke clear of the Vietminh perimeter and moved quickly into the rugged landscape west of Dien Bien Phu.

Elements of the 304th Vietminh Division had just begun arriving. A smaller Vietminh column was assembled to follow, harass, and destroy, if possible, the fast-moving French Force column. Major Vuong's staff was able to uncomfortably peel off three capable platoons for that purpose.

The abruptness of the mission resulted in a several hours' head start for the French column. They were aware of and respected the heavy mortar capability of the Vietminh. The plan was to reach the five-kilometer mark at a double-time march before slowing to catch their collective breath. They would still be in range of enemy mortars at that point, but only if the Viet had the Soviet 122mm available, which it was believed they did not. If they *did* have the 122mm, how willing would they be to expend a limited and valuable inventory of shells on an unseen long shot? Artillery at that range without a forward observer would be a total shot in the dark and very unlikely. The French Force column expected to be safe from Vietminh artillery after five kilometers.

The Regiment's artillery commander was immediately advised of the breakout. No firing plan had been worked out for the area west of the valley, of course, but General Giap had sent one of the long-range 122mm guns with the 57th. With it came a small inventory of high-explosive (HE) bombs. The captain went to his maps and, with the help of his executive officer, came up with the likely areas and times the Legionnaire column would inhabit them, assuming they remained on the trail and moved at a speculated pace. It was sketchy to say the least, and any number of authorizations had to be given before firing off the scarce bombs.

They decided on a limit of six ranging shots. The French column had almost an hour into their march by the time maps could be found and studied by the artillery captain of the 57th. A quick study indicated a wide area of the trail nearly five kilometers out that the big shells should be able to saturate if they could catch the French column in that space. Not only was it a long shot, it was also the only shot by then. Pausing half a minute between each firing, the heavy rounds fired off. The idea was that the French column would not know in those thirty-second intervals if they should remain in whatever cover they had found or if they should move to get themselves out of range. They could be vulnerable either way.

Both lucky and well calculated, the sixth HE round dropped literally in the middle of the column. Master Sergeant Phillips' platoon was hit. The column was well discipled and had been spread out to minimize potential casualties, but the sixth mortar stopped them cold.

Diving for cover at the sound of the incoming did not save them. There was no cover in the open area of the trail. The best the troops could do was hug ground and hope for the best. Two were killed; more were wounded, hit with hot shrapnel. The bomb hit only a dozen feet from Private Conner. Amazingly he was not struck by shrapnel, but the concussion caught him square. He was knocked unconscious, blood trickling from both ears.

The two privates killed were thirty feet away, one on his knees as though praying, and the other as he stood flat-footed, undecided which way to turn. He was split open and left thrashing until a medic got an ampule of morphine into him. He would pass within the hour and was left behind. While not hurt badly, Master Sergeant Phillips had taken a dozen or more small fragments, most peppering his legs. He was left barely ambulatory.

After taking the hit, the officers and NCOs quickly assessed their remaining level of effectiveness. The decision was to carry on with the mission while leaving the wounded and KIA behind. Phillips expected Vietminh to show up behind them but believed he could go into the bush with the casualties and possibly make it back to the valley. Any Vietminh encountering the blast area, he suggested, would be tasked with running down the French Force column and probably not spend much time looking for wounded. He could only hope he was right. It was true that the element of surprise had caught the People's Army flat-footed. If they meant to catch the French Force column, they could not stop anywhere for long.

Phillips believed he could get himself and the wounded back, provided his legs and most of the others could endure. To that end he quickly triaged the casualties, stopped the bleeding, and dressed the wounds. For the trooper killed outright it was a cursory confirmation. The staring eyes had made his condition obvious. Phillips spent a precious moment with the trooper who was split open, assuring him he would come back with more dope as soon as he could. When he got to Private Conner, he felt no pulse, he could detect no breathing, and could only assume he had passed. Corporal Mundt was lying there also. He had a minor gash across his backside but had lost little blood. The shrapnel hadn't entered his body, and it was not a deep cut. Phillips dressed the wound and then directed the corporal to move out and catch up with the column since he wasn't badly hurt. That brought a bit of scorn from the corporal who, by then, had calculated his best option for survival was a return to the valley.

"But I am wounded. You expect me to march and fight like full-strength trooper?"

"Yes," Phillips replied, "and the longer you draw this out, the more vulnerable you will be catching up with the column."

In deliberate fashion, Mundt strapped on his kit and picked up his rifle, not saying another word. Down the trail he went, limping all the way, until he was out of sight.

The sergeant's next priority was to get the wounded off the trail, somewhere they could regroup, rest, and not be discovered by likely approaching Vietminh. Getting the four wounded hidden in the bush took some time and strength. There wasn't an abundance of either. As for the dead, Phillips was not able to move them. The scattered kits and weapons he pushed off the trail to at least hide them. He then literally crawled into the bush with the wounded, where they all pointed themselves east toward the valley.

About two hours later, the Vietminh did approach, moving smartly with little kit other than weapons and water. They were three understrength platoons, not even a full company, that could be spared from the perimeter duties at Dien Bien Phu. Their focus was to catch and damage the French Force column. Seeing the gore of the killed, they only smiled and kept moving, happy for their comrades' good luck with artillery.

A confident Private Pham was in the third hustling platoon. He too felt an air of satisfaction when he saw the enemy and inhaled the fumes of their death. Knowing there were no other Vietminh troops behind them to follow up, he smiled and looked to his fire team partners, Thuy and Cho.

"Thuy, you stay behind and search the dead for valuables and whatever we can use. Work quickly. Then catch back up."

Indignant, Thuy retorted, "Why must you boss me so? Because I am female? Like me, you are a private—not even a squad leader," she scolded. But she was taken with him. *He is so strong of mind and pretty,* she knew. *He tells me he is important.*

She did not understand, and she stood stoop-shouldered for a moment before the enemy dead. She would rather have eviscerated a water buffalo than contend with the effects of three dead soldiers, even if they were enemy. It was too personal. Soldiers carried pictures—always pictures when there was a significant other. Often, too, a picture with family. *When a person is killed like this, there is something that is wrong about handling and looking at the pictures. Whose responsibility is the picture if I have it in my hand and I do not even know the dead soldier? It would be better if such things were left with the body to rot and be part of the transitioning spirit.*

Nevertheless, Thuy straightened up and went about the necessary business. The gutted soldier had made a mess over everything, and it wasn't only blood. His intestines had splattered and spilled feces beyond his own body, making everything less comfortable to explore. She looked around before digging in and saw intact kits of the French Force scattered in the nearby brush. They were valuable, but she knew she wouldn't be able to carry several kits and also catch up to the hustling platoons. As near as she yet was to the valley, she decided she would take the booty back to her company.

She knelt and rolled the fouled dead soldier over onto his stomach, or what was left of a stomach. That helped to some degree. She straightened up and moved to the other side of the bodies and began digging into pockets. She dug into one of the front trouser pockets and pulled out what proved to be crackers wrapped in wax paper. They were still crisp, two of them, and she could see salt on them. Without hesitation Thuy delighted in the snap and the fresh, delicate taste. She took small bites and chewed long on each until there was little left to swallow. Well before she was sated, they were gone.

What other delights may be in pockets? she wondered. Stuffing her hand back in, Thuy groped at the broad bottom of one deep pocket until she did find something more. It took a minute to get hold of it for some reason, but even then, it wouldn't come out. Manipulation was required. At that point Thuy could believe she had discovered a sausage. It was exciting!

A sausage it was, a very personal sausage belonging to a dead man. Briefly, Thuy was confused when her sausage seemed to flourish. When her mind snapped to, she could hardly believe what she was thinking. She looked back at the pocket's resident, the face of the cadaver. What she saw stunned her. *This*, she breathed, *is the sandy-haired private I kissed on the cheek at Phu Doan! I have his penis in my hand, and it is alive!* It was true. The sausage was growing. *Does that mean what I think it does?* She wasn't certain.

She discovered her unintended fondling had created or at least was presently connected with a now-evident heartbeat. She could only assume her fondling had saved the man's life. Eyelids began to flutter. Suddenly his lungs gulped and then continued with the rise and fall of nourishing air. Thuy quickly retrieved her hand from the pocket and opened a canteen. She wetted the private's forehead and cheeks. No response. What seemed proper at that point was to put the canteen to his lips and provide the source of life. She may have miscalculated. Beyond refreshing, the water hit his throat, forcing his body to half-swallow and half-choke. He sputtered, slowly at first, but in seconds it was a lofty sputter and coughing. *He is alive,* Thuy smiled, assuring herself.

When the coughing subsided somewhat, the groggy private was able to open his eyes, but only a slit. His head pounded and thinking produced more fog. He struggled to work the puzzle. This wouldn't be heaven—and he hoped he had not died. *What is going on? Where am I? Who am I?* Sketchy awareness returned slowly. Then he became cognizant of the body hovering over him. Eyelids fluttered again, trying to distinguish more. It was a female, but not the Virgin Mary. She seemed vaguely familiar, but he couldn't make sense of who she was or any connection with her.

"You were dead!" she said loudly in French. "Now you are alive. You have a big sausage," and she softly patted the bottom of his pocket. It wasn't a joke—that is what came to her that brought him back to life, Westerner that he was.

The voice helped bring her identity into focus for him. He opened his eyes more fully, and as much as he could he stared for a moment to be sure. Unable to raise his voice while still coughing, what came out in stammering English was, "Bloody hell! It is you!" He should have been happy, and perhaps he was, but neither he nor his throat were pleased, and everything hurt to the very quick.

Thuy did not need a translator to understand the essence of his sputtering. She continued in French, telling him to rest while rolling him on his side and pounding his back.

He was confused and hurt to the point that he chose to believe her. When the coughing ceased, he began to relax. His addled mind needed rest; his injured body needed sleep. He drifted off quickly and breathed a sense of contentment in doing so.

Meanwhile, Thuy continued her search. In one of the kits she found more crackers and dried fish. She ate none of it, intending to share with her patient when he awoke. Whatever she found in pockets she stuffed into one of the kits. Then she waited for the private to awaken.

Two hours later he did. She had looked him over very well, watched him, and wondered, and pondered. She decided what she was going to do about him—with him, if possible.

He carefully took water then and was able to eat both fish and crackers with her. Far from perfect, he felt remarkably better. They were pleased to share with each other despite the strangeness of breaking bread with the enemy. For both of them, there were few thoughts of the past and none of the future. The future was abstract and not available for comment. Life was treasured in the present.

"Do you remember when I kissed your cheek?" she eventually asked, crackers and fish gone.

He did not answer right away. Instead, he looked into her eyes to see how she meant such a question. When satisfied, he answered, "I think of it every day. You did not lie to me then. I found my unit." Then, looking at her Vietminh scarf, he added, "But I see now you do lie."

"Now I am Vietminh, yes. But like you I am human, and does it matter what I am and what you are? We both have humanity, do we not? Do you understand what I say?"

He hesitated. Good or bad was how Private Conner understood life. That was his world. Still, it would be difficult to argue her point. He did not wish to argue. It was true, they both had humanity, and that felt quite good to him.

She was gazing into his eyes when he finally looked up. She brushed his cheek with the back of her hand and smiled at him. He admired her, the dark eyes and direct, honest character. He responded by cautiously stroking her long, black hair, ending with the wisp of a touch on her bronze shoulder. She did anything but flinch. No words were spoken. No words were needed. His pain melted.

He reached for her. She slowly ran her hand down his bare chest. So smooth, so firm, so quietly exciting. She nuzzled herself up against him. He gently wrapped his arms around her and felt skin on skin. It was heaven. Then his lips found her neck. Hands in her hair, gently squeezing her skull, he ran kisses from the middle of her throat to the back of her neck. The petite Thuy melted into him and moaned softly. Once again, she became aware of his hardness, and she was not afraid.

Slowly they joined. He was her first. She was his first. The momentary pain was not delightful, but in a way it was pleasurable for them both. He shared her sensitivity. He was delicate, not forcing, not dominating, but with strength craving every bit of her. He had never before realized how badly he needed tenderness and the kindness of touching and sharing. So, very slowly, they ground into each other, sharing the arrival of each new sensation. Together they blended needs and personal sensations. So much so that in moments they completed the cycle of joy. Eyes then glistening, they held tightly to each other.

There, among the dead, the bitterness, and the cultural confusions and contrasting ideology, they slept together in peace. Then up with the new day's sun, they rearranged themselves and tried to adjust their thoughts back to the reality of the valley and the world. They carried with them the valuable kits and, also now, a set of new emotions only slightly used.

Sergeant Phillips was off the trail with his fellow wounded, slowly making for the valley. They had little water and even less food. Three of the four complained of not having a radio. With benefit of a radio, the camp would probably send out a reinforced patrol to bring them in. The dissenting man, the sergeant, believed he knew better. The standard PRC-25 RF radio would be an additional forty pounds to drag with them, and using it would alert the intercept gods of the Vietminh. If there was a radio, it would be used, and if used, their transmissions would be intercepted, and when intercepted the search would be on. They would be run down and then violated in any manner the enemy chose. Slow as their progress was, it would be even slower with a radio, and likely the battery would expire before they were in a position to make arrangements with friendly forces in the valley.

By helping each other, they could travel, but not far at any one time, and not fast. Conditions were less than sanitary, medical supplies limited. All of them carried iron in their bodies from the shelling, and some of the trapped bits and pieces moved when they moved while struggling to gain another hundred meters. That was how they traveled: a hundred meters at a time—when they could. Their batting average was lousy. Seldom did they make it the full hundred before having to stop. Before their first day ended, their goal became fifty meters at a time. The junkyard in their innards and limbs occasionally struck a nerve, which involved an involuntary yelp or worse. That was a problem. Phillips didn't say anything then, but he hoped the troopers would be desensitized to pain before they reached the valley. Reentry of the valley he didn't want to think about.

They hadn't gone too far when Phillips realized the kits abandoned back on the trail would be useful or even essential in their return. Private Skluzacek was the obvious choice to retrieve them. He was the most mobile of the wounded bunch. Besides two or three shards of shrapnel in his body, his upper left arm had been smashed. His arm was useless, but he could walk, think, and communicate.

The sun was low by the time the private found his way back to the site of the mortar strike. Good soldiers were cautious and skeptical, and doubly so when alone. Slowly entering the area, Skluzacek saw no sign of enemy. He spotted kits off the trail. Two KIA were there as well, lying in an insect-infested heap. His peripheral vision caught movement to his left, behind vegetation. He froze. After nothing appeared to change, he slowly repositioned himself to get a better look. It took some maneuvering until he realized what he was looking at.

The kid, Private Conner, was on the ground being ridden, cowgirl style, by a young Viet woman. Skluzacek's head rocked back and forth. He needed to make sure it was working. The scene reminded him of Slovakia at the end of The War. That kind of thing was a common sight, except it would be a Russian soldier on top, riding a local girl. *Is Private Conner being raped? Are there others in the area?* All was quiet except for the slowly thrashing couple, and Connor seemed to be holding up a little too well for a dead man.

Emboldened by the distracted pair, Private Skluzacek crept forward enough to quietly snatch two of the kits. He took what he came for and reversed course. He had shouldered the kits without even thinking of potential booby traps. Later he would chastise himself, even though there were no surprises.

As quickly as he could, he retraced his steps and crept out of sight. The coupling thing he had witnessed would have to take care of itself, whatever it was. He hardly knew what to think. To begin with, he had thought Conner was dead. *What is with the Viet?* he wondered. *Unlikely she is a local villager who just happened to come along. Whoever she is, she decided to bang this half-dead Legionnaire lying on the ground?* None of it made sense to him, and he wasn't certain he could believe what he had just seen.

That was when his shoulder bumped a passing tree. It was his left shoulder, and it hurt like sin. He bent over, wincing, to keep from voicing discomfort. From there, Private Skluzacek was back on his normal worry path. This time it was finding his wounded comrades and somehow getting safely back into camp.

Their second night in the bush involved a typical, solid rainstorm. That probably saved the wounded bunch as they used large leaf fronds to channel rainwater into dry canteens. Dehydration was a serious problem in the tropical heat, temporarily remedied then by nature. The greater problem became a way to survive entry of the valley. The small troupe would look to Sergeant Phillips for direction, but not even he had a solution.

Phillips had been heartened when Skluzacek turned up with the two kits more or less in order. Both kits were loaded with medical supplies and bits of food. Even the dry socks were a boost of morale. Everyone but Phillips got a round of morphine. Phillips hurt plenty bad but felt the suffering kept him alert. He expressed no complaints.

Reaching the valley before another day ended was paramount for them. Infections had begun already, and a few crackers and some tinned meat wasn't enough to maintain strength and endurance in their condition. The night passed without additional trauma, but the next day was all-out gut check to keep moving. They had to reach journey's end before the supply of morphine did. It was literally sundown as the hobbling little group dragged itself to within sight of the valley. But what then? No one knew.

For better or worse, it was a dark night. There was consensus among them to attempt the main trail back into camp, the same they had gone out on. It would be the most direct and shortest route, and there was no reason for the enemy to expect anything coming in from outside the valley—not just yet, anyway. Phillips gave each of them the option. All chose to take the chance on reentry together, despite their condition. There was little choice, banged up as they were.

It was a simple and straightforward plan. If they were lucky, the air force would be making night drops. If that were so, a significant fire marker in the shape of an X would be lit in no-man's land between the Vietminh-filled hills and the camp. That would be the target for the Dakota and Packet pilots to drop their loads. If Sergeant Phillips could position his little group on the trail, where it was a straight run toward the fire marker, they might have a chance. Remaining on that line would be the shortest distance to safety, and there would likely be help from troops collecting the dropped supplies.

Three firearms among them, and plenty of ammunition had come from the retrieved kits. Only three of the troopers were in any condition to use a firearm, so nothing lost there. Those three, of course, were also the crutches and support of the other two.

There would be a Vietminh checkpoint close to the opening of the valley; they knew that. That would be the next problem. Assuming they could clear the checkpoint, it would then be a hustle on a long trek to safety. All wished for a radio. Headquarters could send out a tank, if need be, to bring them in. But, no smoke signals, no homing pigeon, and no radio—they were on their own.

They did have one thing, a *lampe de poche*—one flashlight. It would be a gamble to use it at all, but if the timing was right, it could be the difference. Using Morse Code, the short and longer bursts of light to mimic a brief message would have to do. Was there a message the enemy could not understand but the comrades in camp would accept as legitimate? "SOS" was out—that was the worldwide distress signal. Phillips suddenly smirked. He had an image, an idea that might work. Fact was, he had the answer.

They got themselves back on the trail, as close to the Vietminh checkpoint as they dared. Then it was the waiting for activity out of their control. Private Skluzacek had been tasked with putting the plan in action if a night drop materialized. That would take a little luck too. He had gone off trail to the right in order to flank the checkpoint. He carried the one grease gun they had. Then they waited.

Luck was with them. Within the hour, a fire marker was lit. Then more waiting. Fifteen or so minutes later, the drone of radial engines could be heard coming their way. The shooting began shortly after that. Green Soviet tracers filled the sky. Then they heard the sound of closer gunfire, the tinny, loud clacks of a grease gun issuing two bursts. There was no reply to them—a very good sign.

It was then or never. Phillips stepped out into the open and began flashing his signal: short-short-long-short / long / short-long. *Di-di-dah-dit; da; di-dah.*

"What did you flash, Sergeant?" one of the wounded asked, wincing.

"F-T-A," the Sergeant grunted.

It took two or three seconds. Then two of the others laughed out loud, which engaged all four despite their personal condition and present circumstance. It hurt to laugh, but, arguably, it was a good hurt. FTA was one of the more common Morse Code phrases among the communication types. When the chips were down, an idiotic order issued, or spirits low, there was nothing like that acronym to bring spirits up and the troops together. FTA was simply "Fuck The Army," something all privates could get behind. Any communications soldier would instantly recognize the authenticity of Phillip's signal. He had been a bonding private—twice.

Best as they could, the four sick, wounded, and beat-up Legionnaires headed toward safety. Phillips flashed his message again. They knew that, if identified by the enemy while still on their own, they did not stand a chance. If they didn't reach the fire marker on their own, they never would get there.

Private Skluzacek joined them on the run with a full thirty-round magazine in his greaser and more yet in cargo pants pockets. It would be extremely helpful if they could pass themselves off as Asian. And there was Skluzacek wearing straw headgear. He passed another to Phillips. In spite of any conical hats, they were too soon taking potshots from the near hills.

Two of the wounded began shouting in Vietnamese, as if to command the shooting to stop. It was strictly swearing, of course—the only thing they knew—but it was appropriate, and it allowed their emotions to rage. The fire may have hesitated briefly but then continued, and with more joining in. Light mortars started dropping. Still, they moved on, not stopping to protect themselves with low ground. Then, a strange and unexpected thing happened.

Mortar shots, heavier mortar rounds, began ranging farther out, into the hills now behind them.

"Those are friendly," Phillips shouted.

Looking toward the bonfire, they could see the silhouette of a jeep bounding directly at them. Besides the driver, it carried a gunner with a shouldered recoilless rifle, or was it mounted on the jeep? No matter. Looking back, they saw a trio of Vietminh, no doubt a fire team, coming after them. The driver and gunner saw them too. The jeep stopped. Seconds later, a flash, a whoosh, an explosion, and one less fire team for the People's Army.

"Get in! Get in!" the driver hissed again and again. Everybody knew it was impossible to fit seven guys plus a bazooka in one jeep, especially if most of them were wounded. Unless you had to. The loading process was less than delicate. They piled, some pulled, others pushed, but all got aboard very loudly as one American jeep paid for itself.

"How?" Sergeant Phillips wanted to know when they pulled up to Central Camp. "How the hell did you know we were coming in?"

"A little birdie told us," a captain smirked.

"Does this birdie have a name?"

The five survivors stopped their squirming and groaning. This was important.

"Oh, sure," the CO answered, "it was Private Conner."

They looked at each other. Nearly in unison, four mouths declared, "No! He's dead!"

Well, apparently he wasn't, and Private Skluzacek was then certain of what he had seen.

Chapter 12

Big Guns & Red Goo

Late December 1953, the linkup with the column from Southern Laos was complete. A Major Vaudrey had led his troops two hundred rugged kilometers through Laos to get there. Not only was the column harassed by Pathet Lao, the Laotian communist guerillas along the way, but they also had to battle Vietminh Regiment 148 to make the linkup.

The purpose of the whole thing? A photo op! It was a show, a public relations show. Prove to the enemy and the world that you can break what is already being called "the Siege of Dien Bien Phu," and link up with a relief column from Laos. So there! Strength. Posture. It was military, but more than that, a political ploy. From the privates' vernacular, it was bullshit. And it wasn't just the privates who thought so.

The fortress commander of Dien Bien Phu flew down to Sop Nao on the day of the linkup for a brief ceremony. Journalists and photographers came in from parts distant by helicopter. The requisite photographs were taken with commanders amicably shaking hands.

That was it.

One of the journalists later noted that Major Vaudrey's troops were haggard, many with fever and suffering dysentery, reminding her of Nazi labor camp survivors. The journalist knew where of she spoke. She was a labor camp survivor. After the ceremony, both columns turned on their heels and headed back from where they had come—into the hills, jungles, and swamps, knowing the enemy would be waiting for them. There was nothing more to it.

The three platoons from the 57th Regiment never did catch up to the French column. Moving lighter, the Vietminh would have caught and created havoc for the Legionnaires. Unfortunately for them, the mines and booby traps left in their path were a game changer. After the second explosion they moved off the trail. That was safer, but also slower—too slow.

Being in the third platoon, Private Pham had good odds against the mines. Moving off trail, however, his platoon rotated to the lead where they earned supper with machete work, clearing trail. But they were safe.

The French Force troops had played these games before—many times. It was a simple matter of choosing a different, although more difficult route, back to Dien Bien Phu. Traversing the hills' ridgelines was dangerous due to it being the territory of hostile indigents. Moving calmly and methodically, they were not attacked. The all-business nature and size of their column provided intimidation enough to get them through unchecked. Upon reaching Dien Bien Phu, their radio coordination with the fortress eased their valley reentry in a blazing night run.

As for Private Conner's reentry a few nights earlier, he had quietly evaded the Vietminh presence and slipped in unnoticed under a heavy drizzle. Two days after Conner's reentry, it was Master Sergeant Phillips's group of wounded at the gates, so to speak.

Already back inside, Conner reported the likelihood of a wounded group and its need for reentry support. What concerned Conner was that one of them had possibly witnessed his physical tête-à-tête with Thuy. He could only hope that was not the case, and if it were, that he could explain it all with overwhelming lies. He didn't like to lie, but if he had to, they should be profound lies.

Before leaving the mortar kill site, it was Thuy who realized two of the scattered French kits had disappeared since she had arrived. It was obvious that a group of wounded had moved off the trail from there, surely headed back to the valley. Because weapons were not taken and only two kits were, it seemed obvious to Conner that it was someone from the wounded group with limited capacity. *If someone came back to retrieve kit and I was unconscious, I was again assumed dead,* he reasoned. *If not, I should have gone back with whoever it was.* Then it occurred to him, *Thuy was with me since before I regained consciousness, so the kits went missing while she was here!*

"Oh no," he said out loud. "Somebody was here specifically to retrieve kits. You have been with me the whole time. If you and I were seen together, it would explain me being left behind. We must have been seen, right?" he cautiously asked.

"What do *you* think?" she tartly answered. It was a relief to her they both understood now their implausible circumstance. Neither denied gratification given or taken, but they did not speak of it. Enemies in tandem as they were, yet physically and emotionally intimate, was a preposterous reality.

What then could come from such tolerance was the question. There were no clear answers, especially after learning there was witness to the union. Strange, but the absurdity of the situation drew them even closer together, and it was a delicious illicitness brimming with danger. As enemies, it was somehow easier for them to trust each other. Being vulnerable and stripped of pretense, they were free to be themselves as far as honesty could take them.

On the hike back to the valley, side by side, each had similar unspoken thoughts. Shortly before reaching the Vietminh perimeter, they stopped, not yet ready for final goodbyes. Conner's hurt look resulted in Thuy taking him by the hand and moving them off-trail. They had no schedule or timeclock. Time was of their own making. But they could not relax, not with what was waiting for them, each contemplating the future. Silently, Thuy unrolled a dry poncho on the ground. Unspoken, they settled onto it, both on their sides, each staring into the other. This was the end for them.

Then it changed and turned physical. The tenderness from their first co-itus experience was contrasted by the brusque, gritty lovemaking that soon came from them both. Bodies taut and muscled invited hard kisses and flow-ing warm hands. There was, they knew, no way to contain the connection and make it forever; this would be sex to remember. They fiercely kissed and fondled, extending a sensation and then ending it while beginning another. Carnal entry was needy. Bone to bone, his pubic hair pressed against her scant wisps again and again until her muffled rumbles grew to final crescen-do. Only his concern of being discovered from their sharp sounds kept him distracted enough to last with her. Collapsed finally, each shielded a tear from the other.

They allowed a half hour to pass—to be certain, they told each oth-er, they had not been heard. Truthfully, those few moments were dances of dreams, dreams of what could have been. Then it was time—time to adopt reality. Dressed and loaded up with war-making gear, they left each other in peace, she returning into the hills, and he slowly and silently back into the dark valley fortress.

With their final look into each other's eyes, he pressed a smile. He meant to break the somberness with tease, if only for himself. "We'll always have Paris," he said in English. She couldn't—didn't—know, and she did not smile, but there were no questions. She knew what was meant.

French Force probes continued north and east of the valley, trying to reach the higher ground to locate gun emplacements and enemy positions. If unable to demolish them in real time, the probes would pinpoint them for consequential artillery salvos and airstrikes. Every French patrol was brutally contested and turned back.

As the fortress became established enough to send out battalion and multi-battalion missions, the Vietminh cordon was reinforced by full divisions answering every challenge. The Vietminh force defended from connected trenchworks and reinforced pillboxes. Superb camouflage added to the stout repertoire of defense, allowing for surprise and close-quarter ambush. One such mission resulted in the loss of ninety-six officers and men while gaining nothing for the French. For the French Force, there was no more leaving the fortress. It was a siege, and continuing losses were unsustainable.

It was to have happened on 25 January 1954. Intelligence shared the loose secret that the Vietminh major assault would be on that day. Everyone—both sides—expected it; wanted it. Just beyond French artillery range, the People's Army trained and rehearsed. Every unit was lectured using elaborate scale models, thanks to the 57th Regiment's intel teams. Some Vietminh units practiced on landscape similar to a fortress strongpoint. Over and over, thousands of Vietminh rehearsed imminent assaults.

The French Force defenders had turned a largely pastoral and agrarian valley into a denuded, dug-up, sandbag-filled, and weapon and explosives-wielding warehouse. The premier feature was the improved heavy-duty airstrip, sealed off from peril by tons of razor wire. Hundreds of self-assured infantrymen fairly itched to be challenged.

The food was good, the leadership generally better than good, and multi-national day visitors were plentiful, offering advice on what to do and how to improve the defenses. Small groups of Brits and Americans, be they politicians, military leaders, or journalists, were available to be entertained while offering opinions during daylight hours only. They were always careful to be out before dark. The Dien Bien Phu matter held the world's attention, and the visitors were a large part of that, and also an unintended sideshow and distraction for the defenders. Keeping a damper, so to speak, on communist aggression was worth a great deal to the free world at the time. America was picking up the tab for most everything at Dien Bien Phu and beyond.

"Bring it on!" was the general chorus. The Vietminh in the hills and the French Force in the valley agreed, "Let's get this over with!"

It was at the last virtual minute, a day before the scheduled 25 January kickoff, that General Giap pulled the plug. The Vietminh divisions, the coolies, the porters, and Chinese advisers all had more work to do before tempting the war gods. The experience at Na-San the year before convinced General Giap that preparation was more crucial than any timetable given him. Adjustments would have to be made and guns dug in and protected before assurances of victory could be extended to Ho Chi Minh. It was one of Giap's greatest and best decisions ever.

Until the jarring major assault was begun, the French Force artillery commander, a Colonel Piroth, seemed to delight in postulating the assumed poor disposition of artillery. He believed the Vietminh would not be able to physically maneuver 105s through the wilderness of the High Region, especially while the French Air Force roamed freely. If they did, however, and if the Viets were able to place them and fire, his forward observers in small planes would easily spot them. The result would be French batteries or the fighter-bombers now in shelter at Dien Bien Phu obliterating the harassing enemy guns before any significant damage could be done. Even if there were surviving guns among the enemy artillery at that point, the People's Army would not be able to provide an appreciable volume of ammunition to keep them firing. It all made sense.

As it turned out, none of it was true.

Despite the weather, the topography of the High Region and the French friendly skies, the big guns did make it to Dien Bien Phu. Their presence became known before the opening assault, but not their numbers and not their precision. The Vietminh hillside guns, large and small, pestered work parties in the valley day after day with ranging shots. Some days there were ongoing barrages, causing work disruption and much French return fire, some effective, most not. Limited to daytime artillery duels, there was little for the French batteries to shoot at since there were no gun flashes to be seen in the daylight.

Big gun artillery was new to the Vietminh; gunners hadn't much experience, and General Giap's initial gun placements at Dien Bien Phu were vulnerable. Giap's ultimate decision not to assault on 25 January was based on keeping the plan simple while protecting the guns. That meant starting over. Picks, shovels, and timber were the answer. It would be the order of the day for many days and for many thousands of blistered hands and aching backs.

For decades by then, artillery of all world powers had converted to indirect fire. A battery's guns are typically located beyond sight of the enemy, and, where possible, on the reverse slope of a hill, that hill offering protection. Firing was adjusted by a forward observer of the target far from the gun and battery but with a view of the target. Typically, that involved telephone or wireless radio communications back to the battery. Firing corrections given by the observer enabled the guns to make adjustments until it was "fire for effect," at which point the entire battery, four or five guns, could open up with accuracy.

In this instance, however, Giap placed his new guns on forward slopes to be used as direct fire, a see-it-and-shoot-at-it proposition, which hugely simplified their operation. With neither the tools, such as forward observers, nor the necessary training and experience, direct fire was much more effective for them.

What was yet needed was a solution to the vulnerability problem of being exposed on the slope facing the enemy. If the French Force could identify and locate an enemy gun, there was every chance they could destroy it with counterbattery missions or airstrikes.

The Vietminh guns had been well camouflaged in the hills, but after 25 January, they were reconfigured to be protected well beyond camouflage. Each gun was moved. Caves were dug into steep hillsides, providing yards of dense overhead protection. The caves became nests for the guns. A small opening for the barrel when shooting was the only view from the valley, and that quickly covered after shooting. Far from maneuverable within their nests, however, the guns had a limited shooting vector, but were well positioned toward one or two specific targets. Beyond that, faux gun sites were built to bait the French Force artillery into attacking them while the real Viet guns wreaked havoc.

Meanwhile, there were meaningful messages passing among the free world leaders. Early in January 1954, American Secretary of State John Foster Dulles received a telegram from the French High Commissioner regarding the French Force defenses of Dien Bien Phu, describing it as "many times stronger than Na-San."

By mid-January, Dulles received another telegram, this from an American perspective after a day visit to Dien Bien Phu. "Patrols have proved DBP to be surrounded on all sides by enemy forces lying just outside artillery range . . . it is certain that (enemy) divisions 308 and 316 are in vicinity of strongpoints . . . division 312 is likewise in area . . . there is no doubt that if three enemy divisions supported by artillery and anti-aircraft are thrown against DBP, strongpoint's position will be critical." In other words, things were, at best, dicey.

Besides the 105mm howitzers, the People's Army had gained an inventory of AA guns. They too were negotiated through the High Region. Giap began the major assault in March with 170 artillery pieces in "them thar hills." That would include heavy mortars and 75mm recoilless and mountain guns. That was more than twice the number of French Force artillery pieces.

Major Piroth was so devastated by the full-throated Vietminh artillery bombardment and the feebleness of his own artillery to counter that he went to his bunker, held a grenade to his chest, and released the spoon.

Overwhelming the outside ring of French strongpoints was the challenge for General Giap. Doing so would allow AA guns closer to Center Camp and the airstrip, plus potentially do great damage to aircraft, whether landing, taking off, or flying overhead for resupply.

Another interesting telegram came to the American Secretary on the twenty-first of January, this from his counterpart, the French Secretary of State: "Absolutely necessary for (General) Navarre to produce some (French) victories within next few months . . . best thing that would happen would be for VM (Vietminh) to attack DBP as they are expected to do and have French inflict a bloody defeat on them. That would greatly diminish French (political and public) opposition to war in Indochina."

Since well before 25 January, pickaxes and shovels manipulated by coolies and privates alike dug kilometer after kilometer of trenchworks, mostly in the dark of night. Winding zig-zag trenches crept toward the strongpoints. They became the approach and communication trenches—the avenues of attack when assault day came. Strongpoints Gabrielle to the north and Beatrice to the east received the greatest attention in the beginning. They were the furthest from Central Camp and, consequently, the most vulnerable, stoutly defended though they were.

Most of the digging was done in the dark, depriving the French mortars. Given a target, however, the French pounded the Vietminh trenches as best they could. Often the charges came close, occasionally scoring direct hits within the dirt walls. Bodies split open and splattered were summarily carried out. Replacement diggers often met and passed the afflicted within the same trench. Tools were retrieved or replaced, and the work continued. Night after night the scraping sounds of digging resonated in the strongpoints. Occasionally, small arms and flamethrowers highlighted a French Force assault on digging crews. More often than not, defenders spent their days backfilling trenches while sprinkling them with landmines. The diggers always returned, giving little regard to booby traps and the like. Life in Southeast Asia was cheap.

General Giap had other problems, in large part centering around transportation. One of the issues was clarified by an intercepted Vietminh message: fifty-five tons of rice was needed at Dien Bien Phu each and every day. That would feed seventy thousand troops, which gave the French a good idea of what Giap had available to use against them. Vietminh troops and their combat readiness suffered until the rations issue was resolved.

To end the deprivations and doubt, Soviet Molotova trucks began crossing the Chinese border in quantity, coming online with rice and matériel. They began rolling through the High Region on roadbeds primitive but improved enough to be passable. The trucks brought heavy artillery, 37mm AA guns, the necessary rations, medical supplies, and tons and tons of ammunition. There would be no backing down by either side. The French would have it their way: a set-piece battle; their opportunity to destroy a Vietminh army.

A great deal more than Dien Bien Phu was going on in Vietnam at that time. A People's Army division was headed again for the Laotian capital. Forces had to be found to defend Vientiane. General Giap put pressure on the relatively secure French Tonkin region by sending a division to infiltrate and create what chaos it could there. The military airfield at Cat-Bi near Haiphong in the Tonkin region was itself infiltrated by Vietminh commandos. Nearly a dozen aircraft were destroyed, including four B-26 bombers. That alone put a damper on the defense of Dien Bien Phu. Allowing such a strike to happen at Cat-Bi could be blamed on the French Force battalions siphoned off and redeployed to Dien Bien Phu.

An ambitious offensive by the name of Operation Atlanté was kicked off 20 January 1954, in the Central Highlands well south of Tonkin and the High Region. By May, the operation was meant to involve forty-five infantry battalions and eight artillery battalions, pushing enemy forces out of the Central Highlands. Doing so would lend control to the Vietnamese Nationalist government, a big step toward French victory. Atlanté was a much greater commitment than the defensive effort at Dien Bien Phu. It could not, however, live up to its billing. The crisis at Dien Bien Phu pulled from it both resources and attention.

Although flexible and adaptable, the French Forces were finite. They could stretch only so much for so long. Battalions and, often enough, multiple battalions were pulled from one hot spot directly into another. From a distance, it was an interesting chess game between two often desperate forces.

The French Air Force was taxed, trying to respond to all needs with limited and sometimes poorly trained personnel. Despite the potential to effectively limit the offensive power of the People's Army at Dien Bien Phu, the French bombing program on High Region trails was by and large a disaster. Transport pilots had been converted to B-26 bomber pilots, for example, to lead the charge. Transport pilots are not bomber pilots, not in training, not in experience, and not in shared temperament. Training and even elementary tactics had been sketchy at best since the World War. A waning command structure had not been replaced; rudimentary air tactics vacant. Trained transport pilots were often and understandably reluctant to suddenly face heavy machine guns and 37mm flak. The hills and jungles of the High Region seemed an endless canopy of undulating green, making isolation of targets nearly impossible when coupled with mediocre and unreliable maps. Needs for support, be they for munitions, bombs, or paratroopers, were far ranging across Vietnam. Multiple cries of wolf, while sincere, too often could not elicit the necessary support. When air support did arrive, too often it was less than effective.

Vietminh commandos infiltrated and blew holes in the runway PSP on 12 March 1954. The commandos were killed, but before they were, a Bearcat fighter was ignited. The resulting flame wall became the aiming stick the Vietminh gunners needed to direct their artillery fire onto the life-sustaining airstrip with its stable of French warplanes. The last flight in was a medevac C-47 Dakota. Managing somehow to land between artillery salvos, such good luck could not hold. It was destroyed as it rolled to a stop, crew and passengers incinerated.

Mechanics at the Central Camp revetments worked all that night to repair damaged fighter-bombers, the F8-F Bearcats. By morning, three of the nine were functional. Engines were started, warmed, and revved. They did not taxi but rather shot out of their holding pens at top RPMs and lifted off the ragged PSP into the sky in front of silent AA guns and their surprised crews. Fostering the instinct of revenge, Vietminh artillery soon opened up on the airstrip in joint harmony. The remaining six Bearcats were quickly smashed and wrecked along with every revetment.

That wasn't the end of it. The next night, the Vietminh artillery scored a direct hit on the French aviation fuel and napalm depot. The valley shook. There would be no more close air support. Even the spotter planes were extinguished. The loss of the airstrip and its accoutrements was a grave chink in the armor of Dien Bien Phu. Another one. The greatest one.

The grunts, the privates, the weeds, were not told this was the day, but it was clear enough. French officers and non-coms were tense and particularly critical on 13 March 1954. Every detail was questioned, checked, and checked again. The night before, the extent of enemy 105 batteries had been revealed. The French artillery commander had been wrong on all counts, and he had killed himself. Big guns were in the hills, and they were tearing the valley apart. There were French counterfires, but they were shooting at ghosts. There was little success in spotting single guns or even batteries, either from ground level or from the air. Gun flashes spotted and located in the hills were likely dummy guns. For a number of reasons, the big guns of the French, both the 105mm and the 155mm batteries, were positioned in open pits to allow for 360-degree traversing, a result of the hills all around the valley being hostile. There was little protection and no overhead shield for the guns. It was open season on French guns and crews.

At 17:00 hours it had hit, and it was the thunderbolt of many thunderbolts at once. Central Camp and the airstrip got their share of incoming, as did Strongpoint Isabelle, where much of the French artillery was located. Isabelle was south of the airstrip and Central Camp by some miles. Shells were landing everywhere in the bastion; nothing was given a pass.

Strongpoint Beatrice was on the receiving end more than all other targets. The Beatrice position was critical because it was tucked between the Nam Yum River and a formerly developed trail known as RP-41. It had been, and it remained, a natural avenue into the valley. Beatrice now both blocked and protected the passageway. Beatrice was critical too because it was well fortified and capable of supporting several other strongpoints. It also stood tall enough to view Central Camp and the life-sustaining airstrip. Beatrice was a natural forward observer. A Legionnaire battalion held the high ground with some confidence. Many considered Beatrice to be impregnable.

Disaster arrived early on in the barrage. A delay-fused 120mm mortar round penetrated the Beatrice headquarters bunker. The blast discomposed the entire defensive structure of the strongpoint. The battalion commander and two staff officers were killed outright, plus a company commander and two company staff officers. All communication devices, telephone and wireless, were demolished. Several company officers were wounded and put out of action. All battalion communication was dead, leadership vacant. One company was left without officers altogether.

There was a thirty-minute lapse before news of the damage reached Lieutenant Colonel Gaucher at Central Camp. He immediately called together a handful of field-grade officers to put in place a new chain of command for the foundering battalion. That meeting was stunted. A Vietminh shell penetrated the colonel's shelter, shearing off both his arms, opening wide his chest, and killing outright two of the officers present. Gaucher lived long enough to be taken to the field hospital. There he asked for water and quietly died.

During the barrage, Vietminh approach trenches were pitched open by adrenaline-jacked coolies and Vietminh. French Force troopers remained low as artillery shells searched out blockhouses, defensive trenches, and especially radio antennas. The ongoing cavalcade of explosions resulted in smoke and dust that sealed off any challenge to the opening of enemy trenches. A hoard of sappers and assault troops were able to mass at the foot of Beatrice. Hardly had the final Vietminh shell struck before the sappers were in the wire and opening assault lanes with bangalore torpedoes and satchel charges.

The hoard arrived to meet multiple machine gun and resounding rifle fire. In the face of the Legionnaires they fell, but with more assaulting comrades behind them. Again and again they charged as the wire became peppered with bodies. When a working radio was found, it was pressed into the service of directing mortar and artillery fire. The affect was soon felt. Holes were punched into the charging enemy, but the assaults could not be stopped. An overhead Dakota arrived to drop flares, and at 22:00 hours there came a quiet. A peculiar truce was called for each side to retrieve the dead and wounded. Later, the Vietminh would claim it never happened, but during the hour-and-a-half lull in the battle, reserve troops came online for both sides, and ammunition was resupplied and distributed. Oh, yes—and many of the dead and wounded were collected too.

At 23:30 hours, the incoming was renewed, closely followed by more human wave assaults. Master Sergeant Phillips's platoon was among the reserve Legion units brought up. Assessing the battered layout, he had just enough time to place a machine gun in an otherwise vacant avenue overlooking a Vietminh approach lane. When the enemy barrage halted, the next Vietminh assault wave sprang up and charged. Phillips' machinegun position proved invaluable, mitigating the charge and doing great damage.

Battle being what it was, a Vietminh recoilless rifle, probably a 57mm, was brought up into a flanking position on Phillips's gun. With one shot it eliminated the machine gun with crew. The blast came just as Phillips was advancing with two canisters of belted ammo. He wasn't close, but close enough. Hit by the blast, his helmet shielded a lowered head, but arms and chest were burned through a scorched fatigue shirt. Once again, he was hurt but had escaped death by a few steps. Nevertheless, he was out of the fight. A medic found him and hurriedly treated the burns with sulfa, then scampered away, overwhelmed by the needs for his duties.

All officers by then were dead or out of it. The remaining NCOs rallied the men, but after the key machine gun went down, it was man-to-man fighting as closely fired bazookas and recoilless rifles began collapsing blockhouses. On down the line, trenches were the target of Vietminh grenades.

Private Conner, true to plan, had remained close to Phillips and, fortunately, was behind him and untouched by the blast. The panoramic view of carnage left him wide-eyed and numb. It was not only the mayhem of noise and terror but the effects laying all about: the disfigured bodies, the putative disgust of vomit and torn intestines nicely spelled it out; the fearful stares of the wounded, their helplessness and cries, some calling for salvation and others for death. One cried for his mother. It was as cruel as it was real.

Both sides were having problems. Beyond the initial barrage, the Vietminh were expecting artillery support that did not come. They were bleeding and dying by the gobs, having to step over dead comrades to advance. Their radios too were out, therefore having no communication and receiving no direction. Still, looking at the big picture, they were doing well enough on their own.

The surviving Legionnaires were falling back when Strongpoint Dominique, which was between Beatrice and Central Camp, opened on the Viets with heavy mortars. The mortarmen witnessed their own effectiveness with the potential of turning the tide. However, another 120mm mortar shell then struck Dominique's ammunition cache, causing severe damage. Eleven were killed, three wounded, and much of the mortar shell stock destroyed. That ended support for Beatrice.

From his knees, Private Conner tried to maneuver his sergeant's groaning body for a fireman's carry. Falling back from Beatrice had become their only chance. Phillips declined assistance. He could not stand the sensation of touch on his burned torso. As the firing lessened, the sergeant looked up just in time to see the red Vietminh flag rising over the battalion shelter. Scant hours earlier it seemed an impossibility. Then, as Private Conner remained kneeling at his side, Phillips offered a small nod to the Vietminh rifles surrounding them.

As for the arithmetic, 194 Legionnaires of the entire battalion made it back to the relative safety of Strongpoint Dominique or Central Camp. Six hundred, probably more, began the battle that day. Five hundred Vietminh assault troops perished in and around Beatrice. How many more there may have been farther out was not known.

Morning daylight presented a gauzy wetness, the grounds unrecognizable from twenty-four hours before. Blockhouses, some yet standing, were battered and crumbling, while compromised shelters had caved into their own foundation spaces. The land itself was pocked with shell holes and drenched in obliterated sandbags. Litter swept the landscape with all things smashed: equipment, piles of spent shell casings, a variety and volume of armaments, and a demanding assortment of bodies and body parts. Lingering were the distinct aromas of death, medical dressings, both used and unused, burnt cordite, and yet dying bodies.

A number of compromised Legionnaires lay exposed, waiting their turn to die. Some begged to be shot. Some were. Some were not.

"Too late," the naysayers said later. Shortly before daylight, and supported by a Chaffee tank, a counterattack force pushed out from Central Camp to retake Beatrice. A blocking force of Vietminh was waiting for them with a significant volume of fire. It was more than enough to stall the French parade.

Unannounced, a bloodied and bandaged Legionnaire, assisted by another trooper, trudged delicately out of the woods. Behind the two of them came a group of walking wounded and a few badly wounded others on litters. A message came with them: the Vietminh 312th Division commander was offering a formal four-hour truce. French Force authorization had to come from Hanoi, leaving enemies staring at each other.

Granted, the exchange was made, sans fanfare. But why a truce? Speculation centered around dampening French Force aggressiveness. Perhaps give the French Force hope of an end to the killing? Witnesses in the form of wounded prisoners reporting the grit and determination of the enemy may have been hoped to diminish the fighting spirit of colonial troopers, and perhaps even the Legionnaire battalions now that they had been bettered at Beatrice.

There was something to that thought stream. The Moroccans, the Algerians, the Eastern Europeans, and others had been struggling with colonialism and its oppression for some time. The Vietminh were preaching brotherhood and the social justice of communism. While it may have been a good ploy, in this case it fell mostly on deaf ears. But not entirely. The point was made. Inroads of presumed justice under communism were enriched by the tactic. Until that day, the French Foreign Legion had been seen, especially by the indigent, as hard-core legend, an unalterable force.

The bandaged soldier leading the parade of humility out of the woods was Master Sergeant Phillips. He was assisted by Private Conner, who was saved from death or worse by witnessed loyalty to his sergeant. There was honor among combatants—at times, anyway. This was one of the few times during the French-Indochina War that wounded were returned, but such acts of humanity were neither satisfying nor understood. Did the Vietminh think the additional wounded would strain or overwhelm the scant French Force medical resources? Possibly. But more likely it had something to do with the woundeds' anticipated reports of robust Vietminh stockpiles and hearty personnel. Demoralizing the French Force was a strategy. In any case, Strongpoint Beatrice was lost for the duration.

On schedule, the battle renewed at noon with the dreaded artillery duels. It was a continuing one-sided affair, with the exposed French batteries having little in the way of specific targets, while still returning fire and taking casualties doing so.

The afternoon, however, brought good news for the French. Thirty C-47 Dakotas came through with a battalion of paratroopers, dropping them successfully inside the fortress perimeter. They were the 5th Bawouan, a Vietnamese battalion directed by French officers. While the drop was successful, the battalion was assigned to Strongpoint Eliane, which was on the other side of Central Camp. It was a ten-kilometer trudge to Eliane, and the troops were loaded down with gear. Once there, the order was to dig in for their own good. It would be a long day and an even longer night for the 5th Bawouan.

The word everywhere was that Strongpoint Gabrielle was the next to be hit. Except for Isabelle, a few miles to the south, Gabrielle was the farthest point from Central Camp and the airstrip. On a set of high hills due north of Central Camp, it was the obvious target for General Giap on 14 March 1954. The artillery prep commenced at 18:00 hours. Again, it was intense. First to go at Gabrielle was the mortar platoon—all tubes demolished, shells exploded. The Algerian battalion defending Gabrielle was no slouch. They were experienced and hard-core, knew what they had to face, and had done their homework with defenses.

As the artillery barrage continued, the Vietminh infantry descended the wooded hills opposite the strongpoint en masse, assembling for the wave assault. "It was as an anthill evacuation," one trooper noted later. At 20:00 hours, a shell penetrated the 4th Company's command post (CP). The result was another dead commander, two more officers killed, and two more wounded and out of the fight. Radios smashed; communication with battalion CP cut off.

Then came the first assault. Withering fire by the Algerians dropped rows of enemy rushing the perimeter, yet not all those following did falter. Wave after wave came at the forest of barbed wire, attacking; climbing; dying half climbed, embedded, and yet hanging in the barbs; others dead with unexploded satchels beside them. At the expense of all those before them, the Viet finally broke through. Still charging, they were mowed down but followed by others who were not. They challenged trenches and routed Algerians. Still they could not take the strongpoint, and the oncoming assaulters were stopped.

The Algerian reserves came to the fore, prompted to move forward and punish the intruders left within the perimeter. Grenades into overtaken bunkers were effective and, even more so, flamethrowers. Shot in head or heart was silent death, but the roasting by flame brought cries of misery and terror surpassing all other cries of wounded. The Vietminh left behind were viciously cut down, no chance to retreat. The respite continued, the enemy waiting for nothing more than a setting moon to fully depart. A greater darkness would bring back the perilous wave assaults.

But when the attack resumed, it was a more reasoned assault. The Viet infantry approached with some caution, using cover where they could and leveraging opportunity when and where presented. Still they came, and still they died, died by the proverbial fistful even as the defenders were pressed and weakened. Artillery continued during the assault, the remainder of the strongpoint's heavy weapons targeted and largely consumed by the blistering storm.

Again, at 02:00, the assault waned and then halted. Defenders hoped the attackers' immense losses had ended the battle. Surviving NCOs knew better. General Giap had lost well over a thousand infantry in the headlong assault and likely twice that many wounded. Solution? Replace the 312th Division with the 308th Division and continue the attack. Bodies were Giap's greater ammunition, greater even than the big guns. He could use up much of the living resource, but he could not afford to deplete the arsenal. The battle continued.

As defending Algerians tried to renew themselves for a continuing attack, the battalion commander called his staff together to plan the evolving defense of the enemy's next move. Much like what happened at Beatrice, a fuse-delayed shell penetrated the commander's shelter and wracked the battalion staff. The commander and others were badly wounded, and communication to the companies and Central Camp was cut. A surviving company commander was able, after some delay, to radio and notify Central Camp. Sight unseen after that, all arbitrary decisions for defense of the strongpoint would come from Central Camp.

That was a problem.

The Vietminh had made a feint in the night toward Strongpoint Dominique, close to Central Camp. That was reason enough to anticipate attack on Central Camp. Because of that, the two seasoned battalions ordered to counterattack at Gabrielle were instead held back for defense. In their place, the 5th Fifth Bawouan was ordered to Gabrielle. No plans had been drawn up for the Bawouan to counterattack. They did not know the terrain, and they weren't even aware the likelihood of being confronted at the crossing of the Nam Yum River necessary to reach Gabrielle. Starting from Strongpoint Eliane, they had the farthest to go. Their day had begun when loading onto the Dakotas nearly twenty-four hours ago. After their tension-filled jump into DBP came the ensuing long walk to Eliane. The remainder of the day was spent digging, leaving them short-fused and frustrated. In short, they were dog-tired and had no battle plan.

A compromise was worked out. Two companies of Legion would support the 5th Bawouan and act as guides getting them to Gabrielle. The Vietnamese paratroopers moved out from Eliane and headed to the north tip of Central Camp. There they expected to join up with the Legionnaires. However, the desperate calls from Gabrielle for reinforcements had prompted the Legion companies to move out before the 5th arrived. Not unexpected, the Legionnaires were hit by a strong enemy force at the river crossing. The first company across was badly chewed up, but the three supporting tanks with them made the difference and pushed the two companies through and off again toward Gabrielle. Despite their reduced numbers, the hundred or so Legionnaires prepared themselves to move in for the counterattack, even without the 5th Bawouan.

The 5th, disoriented as they were, managed to proceed and landed at Gabrielle about an hour behind them. They too had to contend with enemy and enemy artillery along the way. Some of them had refused orders to move forward, causing more delay. They expected a chaotic scene at Gabrielle, but their arrival proved an even sadder scenario. For one thing, the tanks were pulling out, and Algerian troops were literally rolling down the strongpoint's steep south slope. The tanks were loaded with dead and dying while the ground was yet littered with bodies. The Algerians were vacating the strongpoint even before the Legionnaires had joined forces with them inside. The Vietminh, on the other hand, were all too eager to replace the departing troops.

After all the fighting and dying, there would be no counterattack. The remnants of the Algerian battalion, the 5th Bawouan battalion, and the two Legion companies headed back toward Central Camp while still under fire. Vietminh artillery continued to pound, hitting one of the tanks and killing its commander. The greatest casualty was the Algerian battalion. It essentially ceased to exist after losing five hundred of its finest.

As per typical tragedy, there were many creators. Communication was poor. In fact, poor communication was the greater cause and reason Gabrielle was lost. Much of the radio traffic among Central Camp, the Algerian commander, the Legion, and the 5th Bawouan was garbled. The continuing artillery, machinegun, and small-arms battle sounds added to the fog, especially for the strongpoint commander. Central Camp had directed him to "retrieve" the Algerian companies and assume defense of Gabrielle. The only thing clearly heard was that the Algerian force was being "retrieved." The commander took that to mean Gabrielle was to be abandoned. That was logical, as the enemy was inside the wire and casualties made up the bulk of his battalion. Therefore, when the Legion companies arrived, the order was given to pull out.

The rest, as they say, is history.

After little more than two days of ground attack, the People's Army had rolled over the two most heavily defended and most critical strongpoints of Dien Bien Phu. Both Beatrice and Gabrielle overlooked the airstrip and Central Camp, making the entirety of the French Force more vulnerable. Advantage almost always went to the high ground. The loss of the two strongpoints allowed General Giap's recoilless guns, bazookas, and anti-aircraft to move in closer and forward observers to direct any and all artillery.

The drop zone was instantly reduced with the ground lost. From then on, the DZ would continue to shrink. Resupply drops became a nightmare for pilots and their crews. Leveling their runs at 18-hundred feet made for accurate drops, but not safe, with heavy machineguns and AA planted under them. The French drop-floor was raised to 6-thousand feet which still was not safe and only not-quite-as-deadly. The diminished DZ target was missed with regularity from then on. Pallets of artillery shells and other resupply often landed nearer the enemy than desperate French Force defenders. Soon, Vietminh guns were firing French shells into the French fortress. And, if that wasn't enough, then came the monsoon.

Chapter 13

Lost and Found

he so-called hospital at Dien Bien Phu was never intended to be used for much more than triage. Treatment would be cursory, critical patients flown out. One actual surgeon was it—at Central Camp; the battalions had aid stations. With scores and then hundreds of wounded, the landscape quickly became a dirty, stinking quagmire. After the first two days of assault, there were five hundred wounded vying for hospital space that wasn't there. From the beginning, the aid stations, which were damp dugouts, reeked of the various odors imagined, and within days, maggots multiplied many times over in the dank spaces. The shelling continued. Everyone who could remained under cover, which was in the deep dank spaces.

The morgue was worse. Nothing more than an outside pit. The bodies, sprinkled with lime, covered the red-clay floor. Then bodies on top of bodies became the norm, sprinkled with more lime. Daily rains made for slippery messes everywhere, but none more noticeable or more annoying than in the hospital shelters. The red-clay earth became slippery when wet and an oozing red goo when the monsoon emerged. By the end, conducting business in many of the shelters included pulling one boot after the other out of the sucking red mud in order to navigate, especially in some of the shelters. Litters filled with wounded covered many wet dirt floors while more wounded had to remain outside, even in the rain. Shelling barrages could make it worse, and they did. On the occasion of an enemy shell striking the morgue pit, there erupted an ill-advised soup that splattered a significant radius.

Master Sergeant Phillips was one of the wounded. He could walk, but doing so was painful. From his earlier mortar attack injuries there were still any number of iron fragments in his legs. The greater problem was the second-degree burns lacing his chest and arms. Dien Bien Phu was not the place for burn victims. It would be hard to imagine a more unsanitary environment providing a greater likelihood of infection. Although he fussed about it, he was slated for medical evacuation to Hanoi.

He was littered because of his leg wounds which meant he was a priority for evacuation, like it or not. He was one of the first on board a medevac C-47. For a few days after losing Beatrice and Gabrielle, the medevac flights came in and left with limited enemy resistance. Phillips was one of the lucky ones who made it out of the war in style. Off he flew, and into a sterilized environment for treatment of his burns, plus a surgical team to pick and carve shrapnel from his legs. He wasn't happy about leaving the platoon, but he hurt, and he was able to look back with satisfaction that this latest platoon had jelled in terms of teamwork and trust in each other. Too many were missing or otherwise gone, but they had been true Legionnaires.

The airstrip was in limited service only. Welding teams ventured out daily to doctor up the PSP that had been splintered from artillery hits during the night. Dakotas with large red crosses on their sides came in regularly. There was enough shelling by the Vietminh to make everyone nervous, but full loads went out, initially. Flight crews otherwise stranded were able to hitch a ride out, and matériel such as medical supplies and even ammunition came in on those flights.

That didn't last long. With the recently acquired line of sight to the airstrip, Vietminh intel teams could see the comings and goings of things that were other than medical and wounded. The result was artillery salvos as the Dakotas landed. It wasn't long before three Dakotas were hit, their crews incinerated—a taste of things to come.

After that, the medevac flights were a timed affair. A limit of five minutes on the PSP tarmac was decreed. Ambulances raced behind the Dakotas as they landed. Once the big bird turned and stopped, the gravest injuries loaded first. After that, as many others as there was time for would board. At the five-minute mark, engines already revving, a horn sounded, and the flight crews raced for blue sky. Those loads were never filled 100 percent. Many wounded were left on the PSP simply because there was not time enough to board.

As it was, the flight crews felt as birds in a turkey-shoot, and they surely were. With the loss of Beatrice and Gabrielle, more AA guns had come in closer to the airstrip and Central Camp, making them more deadly. As time went on, aircraft and crews were tasked with greater and greater risks. Pilots grew weary but could not be replaced. Plane maintenance became limited to critical issues only, and consequently, morale deteriorated. At that point, twenty-nine C-119 Packets from America were brought into the program. They were ideal for air drops of matériel, and most were piloted by American civilians. American mechanics came with them. At the same time, the drop ceiling over Dien Bien Phu was raised again to 8,000 feet, intending to lessen the AA danger.

The French Air Force was being bludgeoned on both ends: increased attacks on airfields, plus a buildup of AA over Dien Bien Phu. Because they were noncombatants, the American pilots voiced concerns over the danger of being in active combat situations. It was resolved that Americans would be involved in nominal risk transport only and airfields be given additional security. As it turned out, there were some pilots who volunteered to provide their services regardless.

The higher drop ceiling was not a good answer to anything. First of all, the 37mm projectile of the AA guns had an effective range of 13-thousand feet and their shells self-destructed at 16-thousand feet. Secondly, hitting a drop zone target at two-thousand feet or less was generally successful, although not guaranteed; but trying to hit a target from more than four times higher was nothing short of a crap shoot.

The biggest problem was air drift, although aim and release was too often imperfect as well. The latter was related to pilots who more than occasionally were distracted by exploding fireballs screaming past at whatever height the aircraft was. Air drift, on the other hand, spoke for itself. From eight-thousand feet, whether it was a pallet of medical supplies or heavy artillery shells, the pallets floated a good long time, all the while being pushed around by the vagaries of nature. Anything that ended up out of bounds not only *didn't* fuel the garrison's needs but went to the other guys to fuel theirs. And then, if you were a pilot who was shot down besides, it was a real bad day.

Sergeant Phillips's platoon was given half a dozen replacements—six men only. Three of them were Vietnamese, but none of the new guys was a rookie. Racial discrimination had become secondary; everyone in the valley was now a brother.

As for Private Conner, he was lost without Phillips . . . for about ten seconds. Comrade loss was a fact of life. He had been through plenty of loss by then. As a grunt, sentiment was a temptation but also a danger. To grieve was to weaken, and line troops could never weaken. Conner was by then a real soldier.

Speaking of loss, another was Corporal Mundt. Mundt had simply disappeared. No one had anything more to report about him than that. One more statistic.

Having shown himself a steady enough trooper, Conner was accepted in the platoon. The common enemy was in the hills, and what could be done about that beast was center stage in everyone's mind. There had yet been no assaults since Strongpoint Gabrielle fell, but enemy artillery continued to pound day and night. Everyone waited for the other shoe to drop, for the next assault. It was just a matter of who would be hit and when. The battle was no longer a great adventure. Virtually all strongpoint defenders were wearing thousand-yard stares by then, engaged only in the struggle to continue on.

Conner's thousand-yard stare was filled with the hurt from losing Phillips plus the end of his first and only intimate relationship. Soldier sentimentality was also a dangerous bogeyman. The likelihood of having been seen consorting with the enemy bothered him more than anything. He knew he would have to adjust to life in the platoon without a Sergeant Phillips, and surely without a Corporal Mundt and several others. He could only hope his association with Thuy would not come up, that whoever had come back for the kits on the trail had not seen him or was too troubled to make anything of it.

Private Skluzacek was in a lot of pain with his smashed arm. The prognosis of his condition had put him in the hospital and on the evacuation list. Priority littered patients were stowed in the ambulances next day, primed to chase an incoming medevac. The Vietminh artillery loosed a few rounds but didn't come particularly close as the C-47 landed. The loading of litters was done quickly with jitters all around, but the five-minute horn came too soon for the ambulatory to board. Engines revved and thick airplane tires began to turn.

Standing on the sideline and seeing there was no hope to board, Skluzacek took matters into his own hands, or more specifically, his legs. It was his shoulder and left arm in bad shape, not his legs. He took off running before the plane doors closed. He projected his intentions with yelps and motions. An orderly on board yelled back that it was too late. But Skluzacek gauged at full trot the angle of his run to meet the moving Dakota. At the last second he leaped at the open side door, his only chance. Had it not been for the orderly, he would have been splayed bare on the runway. He and the orderly clamped each other's wrist, and in one sweep Skluzacek was pulled aboard, scared but elated.

Never a dull day in the Legion. Word of the Skluzacek departure got around. The news entitled Conner to return to business at hand, to the war, to the prospect of being overrun again, only this time without his platoon sergeant.

Privates Pham Van Hieu and Le Thuy were in the 57th Regiment now, a part of the 304th Regular Army Division of the People's Army. Pham didn't notice much difference between the regional regiment he had come from and this regular unit. He hoped the leadership, at least his regimental commander, would prove to be better. *If it is not,* he then realized with a smile, *I will have something to report to The Party when the time comes.* He was still waiting to hear from The Party. He had made no reports about his commander; he had made no reports about anyone to The Party. He repeated to himself a humorless and self-deprecating joke: *The Party has made me so covert they cannot see me. But do they remember me?* he added.

That his regiment, the 141st, was annihilated, he blamed on the commander. *The Party must have had doubts regarding Colonel Dau. That was why I was sent there to be a covert commissar.* Doubts kept seeping in. *Maybe through some snafu I have been forgotten, my paperwork misfiled or something.* There was no avenue for him to pursue, no chain of command, only a willful trust that he really was a commissar. By all appearances he was just a private, a weed waiting to be scythed. Anonymity was repugnant to Pham, and he refused to make peace with it. Alone with hollow thoughts did not make him feel special. He began to ruminate routinely, isolating details of slights and rebuffs.

There was little time for Thuy in Pham's darker world, but he had come up with a loose game plan, provided she survived the war. *She isn't stupid, and she is attractive. Once taught what I expect of her, she will be an asset to my career,* he assured himself. Cream naturally rose in milk, and Pham expected he would rise naturally to the top as well. He was quite aware that he was gifted. *I simply need to be noticed to be advanced, and then I can be somebody. Why else would I have agreed to Comintern Academy?* he wanted to shout. *What I need,* he decided, *is a colleague—something along the lines of collaborator. Someone a part of dubious circles I cannot be a part of, someone who knows the opportunity of common deceit and can, perhaps, play the fool. Someone whose interactions may be limited but complement mine. Someone who would appreciate a silent champion and be willing to reach for enrichment. Yes, but where can I find such a comrade, such a wonderfully despicable rat?*

Like attracts like, and soon it was just such a despicable rat who presented himself to Private Pham.

He had been involved somehow in the death of Colonel Ky, but even that was seen in a positive light. It was commonly accepted that he had personally carried the body of his regimental commander from the valley floor through the hills and up to the colonel's regimental headquarters. And that the sniper had barely missed him, killing the NCO beside him.

Private Nguyen Dac Pho, introverted and plain though he was, had notoriety. Starting out as a laboring coolie, he began with nothing other than an aching back from the labor required. The quiet and humble boy became something of an engineer, a quasi-engineer, chiefly through sheer common sense and an open, quick mind. Over time, he had become the admired "genius" among his section of coolies and also the engineering wing of the Moving Forward Project initiated by leader Ho Chi Minh. Later, still a common coolie, he had sacrificed his body to keep a howitzer from sliding off a mountain. Inadvertently, Nguyen had showcased the kind of grit the Great Leader promoted. In order for his brand of communist independence to succeed, President Ho needed passionate dedication from everyone. Uncle Ho needed everyone to be a Nguyen Dac Pho.

The Party had provided surgeries and nursing for Nguyen's broken body after the howitzer incident. Through great effort and fit attitude, the young man was back to reasonably good health within a year. The Party had magnified his status by then as the "Private of the People." Among other things, that meant he would have to become a private. Nguyen became the living poster boy and salt-of-the-earth private of the People's Army—someone for everyone to look up to and wish to emulate.

Yet, true to his heritage and to his character, Nguyen Dac Pho remained plain and humble, understated but accomplished. He didn't understand that his actions were being heralded by the top levels of The Party or that he was being promoted as the epitome of the noble Vietminh soldier. Private Nguyen just *was*.

Everyone knew it was an insult to speak of him as celebrity. There are no communist celebrities since all are equal. It was the people, the masses, Uncle Ho announced, who simply brought Private Nguyen forward as a hero. Nguyen was an inspiration to the people, a communist version of Everyman. As a resolute man of the people, he was destined to go far. Obviously, someone had overlooked him as officer material. The Central Committee soon corrected the oversight. Welcome to the army, Lieutenant Nguyen.

Through artillery shells bursting onto the valley floor and anti-aircraft fireballs filling the skies, General Giap maintained pressure on the fortress while necessarily regrouping his infantry for more ground-floor, nose-to-nose battle against the remaining strongpoints and Central Camp. The duty of the many commissars at that point was to reinvigorate morale and boost confidence among the troops. The Vietminh grunts had overwhelmed two very stout strongpoints, but they had suffered greatly and lost hundreds and hundreds in doing so. Even the Vietminh could not sustain such loss over time. Still, the new plan called for insistent and continuing pressure. General Giap called for twenty-five thousand more privates.

After Beatrice and Gabrielle had been taken, the victorious attackers were given a breather. But idleness was not the answer to victory. The artillery of the People's Army kept hammering. As a bridge to further success, a routine was established that involved the digging of more assault trenches. Zigzagging here and there, nearly abutting the strongpoints, a hundred kilometers of trenchwork was no exaggeration.

For the many Vietminh privates, daily sleep was limited to a few hours. Still, it was more rest than the defenders could account for. Being alert and ready was an essential element of defense all hours of the days and nights. The attackers would pick and choose. They knew the when and the where and rested on that. After coming in from the trenches in the mornings, it was breakfast for the Vietminh privates, then a meeting to review the previous night's work. Into the hillsides they went after that to cut and bring in wood. After that, a social time before eating again and heading back to the trenches with pick and shovel. Each night's digging was a wager of life or death going forward or not. Digging to within ten meters of a strongpoint's perimeter was perilous and often unforgiving.

The open area west of the airstrip was the primary drop zone for the French Force. Vietminh flak guns and heavy machine guns were planted at the foot of the hills nearest the DZ. An infantry regiment was positioned there as security. The AA guns had been causing extensive damage to aircraft. Vital matériel drops were routinely lost or the airships turned away.

The fortress commander believed airstrikes were the resolution, certainly not ground attack, with his limited resources. He was less than overjoyed, then, when he received the order to immediately shut down the AA guns because the air force could not deliver under present circumstances.

The operation came about so quickly and was carried out so swiftly it had no name. Later, it was known simply as Operation Bigeard, named for the officer who was delegated the operation that evening and carried it out scant hours later. Major Bigeard accepted the challenge. He designated four of the best battalions at Dien Bien Phu and called in their commanders at 02:00 hours to work out actions and responsibilities. Never before had a combined multi-battalion operation with artillery, air support, and tanks been tasked to a major. The cherry on top was that the operation was expected to be completed within twenty-four hours. A skeptic might think it was an order with little expectation of success and therefore delegated downhill to avoid a higher-ranking failure. A solid bet.

The operation plan involved three infantry battalions and another in reserve, twelve 105mm howitzers, and two 155mm howitzers, although a dozen of the latter had been requisitioned. The addition of twelve 122mm heavy mortars allowed for the provision of a rolling artillery barrage. The nearer enemy positions were first targeted—whole batteries shooting together—and then the barrage extended farther out, a little at a time, constituting the rolling barrage. Tactical air support was on board but delayed an hour due to weather. The tank platoon rolled to the jumping-off point as quietly as they could under a moonless sky that early morning. To the enemy, any movement seen by them was intended to appear as normal night patrols.

Apparently, that rang true. It was a violent surprise to the Vietminh as the thundering artillery bit into them at 06:00 hours, right on time. The assaulting infantry, already within three hundred meters of their targets, began moving in as the artillery adjusted range and began their roll. Through thick clouds of dust and smoke, the Vietminh found themselves in defensive mode as the French Force moved forward as a solid line into the enemy trenches and positions. It didn't take long, however, for Vietminh resolve to kick in. Their artillery and mortars began pounding, but the French units waded in closer. The Vietminh fired back, on their heels, but not turning to the rear. The battle blazed back and forth. Every advance was a struggle for the French Force, yet they continued the advance. When the Vietminh got their feet under them, so to speak, the battle came to near standstill. It was a blistering slugfest.

If one thing could be credited for the difference, the tip of the hat would go to the visible prowess of the tanks. Rumbling up at top speed, their main guns fired directly into Vietminh bunkers. Seeing a secondary explosion come out of an enemy bunker was a king-size lift for attacking troops. Legionnaires cheered.

Not to be outdone, the late but anxious-to-make-up-for-it navy fighters, the chubby Bearcats and the steady Hellcats, tore the place up coming in low and hard. The Vietminh AA had its hands full against the ground assault, guns horizontal to face that rush. That meant the low-level, screaming fighters had almost free reign, wing guns rattling and rockets lambasting.

Major Bigeard was there, on his belly, directing the advance. Sergeant Phillips's platoon was there as well, but without the sergeant, of course. The sergeant had been flown out days before, but the troops were still adjusting. Following their French lieutenant now, they advanced, continuing to lay down a curtain of fire as they did. It was some time before they reached the second line of Vietminh defense. The first line of trenches had been cleared, finally, with grenades and automatic fire. The rate of enemy fire had not seemed to lessen, despite the losses.

Private Conner began to rise after a nearby mortar flash. The LT, standing tall, began waving the men forward. Rising from their knees, the entire platoon watched as the waving hand of the LT was simply blown away. It could have been by the wind, as it appeared. Conner and the LT realized the hand had been sheared at the wrist, leaving a contrast of white bone ends poking out from his forearm. Likely it was the work of a passing 20mm AA projectile. The LT dropped to ground, as did the entire platoon. The need for direction, for someone to step up and lead, was critical to the battle.

As the closest to him, Conner pulled open his med kit and applied a tourniquet, then covered the stub. Seeming to be stunned but still in the game, the LT nodded to the front, indicating their advance could not stop. It took two or three seconds for Conner to process. Then he realized he was the one in position to advance the platoon. He shook his head briefly, not to convey "no" to the lieutenant but to clear the cobwebs that had impulsively emerged. The LT yelled Conner's name, looked to his weapon on the ground, and nodded.

"You want me to take it?" Conner yelled.

Another nod. Then it was the three remaining magazines from the LT's web-belt pouch. It made sense. In the foreseeable future the LT would not, even if he survived the night, be putting out much effective fire from his M1A1 Thompson. And who wouldn't crawl over broken glass to snare a Thompson submachine gun? Not just Private Conner but the entire platoon was inspired by the gesture and act of leadership.

At Conner's urging, up they came, slowly firing at the rim of the next trench as they advanced. Mortars were dropping close by, but Conner hardly noticed. He was pumped. Fragmentation grenades were bouncing into the trench line of bunkers, and fewer and fewer stick grenades were coming out. The platoon continued on, and soon it was overwhelming a determined enemy.

The Thompson, or "the Annihilator" as some called it, was ideal for the *coup d'etat* in the trenches. There was little if any movement in those bodies as the platoon moved up. Private Conner swallowed hard and followed protocol. He stitched a line of .45-caliber slugs from one end of the trench to the other, not allowing himself to look back at the faces lying there. The platoon was flush with adrenaline, anxious to move forward as the AA guns, including the .50-caliber positions, were being torched by explosives, the mission essentially accomplished. But ahead was another trench line of bunkers.

At the same time, elements of the 57th Regular Regiment, 304th Vietminh Division, were moving forward from the hills. They were the reserves called up to combat the astonishing French Force assault. With others, the fire team of Privates Pham, Cho, and Thuy were closing fast on the front line of action. They could see that the trench line ahead of them was the last set of trenches holding. The trench line ahead of that was being overwhelmed by Legionnaires.

A shrill whistle called the 57th to a halt. They were hot and sweaty from running forward, yet from the ground now, and through the smoke and turmoil they could make out that any survivors in the not-so-distant trench line were being executed by a trooper with a submachine gun. The fire team gritted teeth, anxious to attack the murdering pigs.

French artillery was dropping closer and closer on a march soon to reach the reinforcements. Flat on the deck, their resolve naïvely strengthened. It was common sense and tactics that saved them. They did not get the signal to charge, despite the pooling confidence. They were angry and confident, but even more, they were well trained. A Vietminh bugle sounded behind them. At almost the same time, a siren directed the French Force behind their troops. Mission accomplished, the French units were to retreat immediately. No point in taking more casualties. The Vietminh strategy, their tactic, was to draw the French Force into the hills by moving back. This time it didn't work. Neither side advanced further.

Perhaps Conner and Thuy saw each other, and perhaps each could not recognize the other. In any case, both cursed their respective enemy. And both survived.

The final tally was sobering. Twenty of the French Force were killed outright and seventy more wounded. It was a sizeable bite out of the best battalions the French had to offer. But it was a successful operation, good for morale, and also a wake-up call for General Giap.

The Vietminh took a much bigger hit, based on numbers. The number of wounded would never be known but was typically about twice the number killed. Vietminh killed outright was 350, with ten more taken prisoner. As for the mission, five 20mm AA guns were demolished as were twelve heavy machineguns, two bazookas, and scores of light machineguns and personal weapons. The difference between the losses of the two belligerents was that the People's Army had every likelihood of replacing their losses, both personnel and equipment, while the French Force replacements were limited. The seasoned troops lost could not be replaced.

Operation Bigeard was the last, arguably the only, big hurrah for the French at Dien Bien Phu. While true that the strongpoints resisted Vietminh assaults again and again after that, the defenders were repeatedly forced to pull back into more defensible positions. Bigeard was the singular offensive French victory at Dien Bien Phu, a success designed and carried out by a major, not a colonel, not a general, nor a collection of any of them.

The fortress required eighty tons of resupply daily. The drop zone continued to narrow and the airstrip remained an enemy artillery magnet. As the air force heightened their drops to eight-thousand feet or more, shortages became glaring. Adding to the squeeze, when a flight of Dakotas or C-119 Packets came in with resupply, they didn't always release their loads. At times, it was worse when they did. If the AA was heavy, and the first airship shot up or downed, those behind would likely remain high and turn for the barn. Those that did drop loads after a shootdown were often giving General Giap a swell present.

Often it was 105mm artillery shells, dropped or drifted off target. Was it brag or was it a Vietminh joke that General Giap's artillery was kept busy returning French shells back to them? Near the end of the siege, there were accusations from the fortress that frightened pilots knew their drops would be off mark and released anyway, aiding the enemy. A perfect drop was less important to some aircrews than dumping their load and evacuating the DBP airspace filled with AA.

The rumor mill thrived in any army, and the garrison at Dien Bien Phu was no exception. Unofficial reports were kicked around about a relief column coming from Laos that would spawn a breakout for the garrison, and that a breakout from Strongpoint Isabelle was imminent, the plan already approved; that a US saturation flight of B29s would be carpet-bombing the hills around Dien Bien Phu, thereby turning the tables. Talk of tactical nuclear bombs raced through the valley and beyond as well. Truth be known, there was a kernel of truth in them all, but none came to fruition, and arguably with good reason. Another truth was that command hesitated to squelch the upbeat rumors. Morale was too great an implement of circumstance to be dimmed unnecessarily.

If only France could have resupplied successfully. If only French bombing could have isolated and thoroughly hosed the concentrated Vietminh force. If only the People's Army supply line had been cut. If any of those actions had been successful, General Giap would have been forced to melt into the background with a battered force. But France did not have the planes, the pilots, the crews, and the mechanics to make any of those happen.

The interesting and plausible plan that would likely have worked to save the fortress, as well as French face, was the prospect of American carpet-bombing. President Eisenhower considered such an operation. When asked to do so, he qualified a potential agreement: only if the Brits were involved. In other words, taking such a step unilaterally was too great a burden for the US administration, and probably history as well. Civilian casualties would have been horrific, and there would have been a political firestorm. In the end, Dien Bien Phu was allowed to go fallow within its own fetid mess.

On 6 December 1953, two weeks after the French Force took over the valley, Ho Chi Minh had issued his Order of General Mobilization. "Everything for the Front, Everything for Victory!" Thanks to Red China, the Soviet Union, and the functions of the general mobilization order, the People's Army had become a very competitive foe. Suddenly, the Vietminh were playing three-dimensional chess. Assaulting a fortified Dien Bien Phu was a dream for both aggressors, but only one could prevail. The slaughter ended when the defenders had nothing more with which to fight. Outnumbered five to one, the fortress troops could not outlast the relentless artillery and the never-ending human wave assaults. A Vietminh commander was quoted as saying, "They are thoroughly beaten, but they won't admit it." It was true. The French Force could bluff, but even that couldn't last.

As word circled the globe that Dien Bien Phu was on the verge of defeat, Legionnaires and former Legionnaires began making themselves available to preserve the honor of their brotherhood. By the hundreds, men asked to serve, to jump into Dien Bien Phu, to be there for and fight with their brothers. They came because "the Legion is Our Homeland."

In the end, a mixed battalion was activated and slated to be inserted on 6 May 1954. Perhaps most of those troopers believed they could turn the tide against the communist hoards, that with their Legionnaire brothers they could dominate the battlefield. Then again, perhaps not. On some level, all of them felt the crush of their Legionnaire brothers and themselves being diminished and humiliated. They could not stand idly by and allow it.

The flight of C-47 Dakotas was stacked that night. A particularly large delivery of matériel, much of it artillery shells, was dropped. The shells joined with the enemy, and only ninety-one of the men drifted down through amber skies that early morning hour. The advent of daylight and Vietminh anti-aircraft forced the remainder of the battalion's drop planes to turn back with their human cargo intact.

Ironically, the defense of Dien Bien Phu came to an end the next day. The free world shuddered.

The ninety-one who did jump were quickly caught up in the agony of Dien Bien Phu history. The free world may have been willing to see the defenders of Dien Bien Phu sacrificed, but these ninety-one resisted with the hope of action. Over the following decades, these brothers were asked many times why they gave themselves up to a hopeless circumstance. There were no proper words, so there could be no clear interpretation. The answer could be only that former Legionnaires were no longer suitable for civilian life. It was a pretense, always having to portray interest in immaterial matters and irrelevant things. "I volunteered because I craved sharing the pain of my Legion. By engaging the challenge of my brothers, we would both be renewed. I volunteered to save myself."

"Why, oh, why did you come back?" Private Conner piteously asked. "You are not fully healed, and unlike these others, you know the reality of this place. You, of all people, know better."

"Yes, I know this place and I know my status, my fine private friend. I have had my battles. Even won a few." Master Sergeant Phillips was being facetious. He was among the ninety-one.

"We could have won this one, you know," he added. "As for me, the fire is gone. I have no hate left in me, and I had none to begin with—not like many of these blokes. When I was hardly more than a boy, I wanted to be a soldier and help to save my country. After The War, when things didn't work out so well back home, I crossed the Channel again and joined up. I only wanted to be a good Legionnaire then, and perhaps be an example to you young scallywags. We all have reason enough, but depending on hate to get us through is not so easy and is of little comfort as time goes on. For me, it is not so easy to watch the pain and the endless sacrifice. I have seen plenty. Too much.

"This business is all I know, Conner. Can I survive on the outside—back in England as a butcher's apprentice, perhaps? For me it would be the same as living in a dungeon, people looking at me like a second or third-class citizen, an' it's true. I no longer fit in with regular folk, and sure as anything I fit only here. Too old to start over, Conner. Too much of me is weighed down. Normal people in the civilian world cannot understand we sorts live on a knife's edge—ready to fall one way or maybe t'other. You tell me, which is the real world?

"My soul is here, and my body needs to be here as well. Not in this spot, mind you, but with my people, the grunts, the weeds of war. Whenever I'm tempted to feel sorry for myself, what I do is think about my lads, the young men cut down because they gave of themselves to be a part of this something—this something we believe in."

He stopped there and met the eyes of Conner. Conner said nothing. The master sergeant continued. "That something is good enough reason for me to show up. It cannot matter from where we come and what language was our first. Not one whit does it matter, ya damn Irishman. But it is confusing, I will give you that. Here and there this . . . this thing seeps into our bones. We have a need to belong, and here in the Legion we feed on that. There is an understanding, Conner, you know that. We are the lot cursing each other to heaven on good days and bad. Next, then, you find us sharin' our last canteen in the bush without regret. It's what makes us strong, boy. Most of us long ago forgot how to cry, and some even before the start of our Legion duty. And it's not a cryin' towel that holds us together. We need each other for holdin' on."

He stopped for a moment, then chuckled. "After this business is over, then we can bellyache ourselves to tears and make the world proper again with our tongues and the good intentioned politicians."

Conner failed to suppress a smile.

"You should have seen me at hospital no more than a week ago," Phillips went on. "I was in greater distress there than I ever was here. I could not stand being gone from you wayward novices; the whole bunch of you. Here I can live as a man, swallow my medicine, and take my bows, but only where fitting. How many times do you suppose I could have—should have—been cut down in the field? Over these years, I done my best to pay back such oversights. I leaned hard on you saplings—givin' you a chance to grow strong and tall as a oak. Some made it; more, it seems, did not. Then, afterward, I feel it—the ones that was killed and bad hurt. But, Connor, it does not stop hurting, I swear. Little doubt I will soon be answering for those boys I lost. I pray they can forgive me, and I'm not much of a praying man. But I am a soldier, and I will be takin' up with my orders on the other side wherever I land and follow them best I can.

"I do not mean to be melodramatic; I know where and what I am. It is just that I intend to go out as a Legionnaire with my spine straight. Ho Chi Minh himself can blow my brains to kingdom come; Lord knows I tried to hurt him bad enough. However it comes, I intend to go down among my boys, my brothers, my family. That is reprieve enough. Those gone before me deserve such respect. I now feel them close. I want to see them, Conner; I want to be with them. I want to *be* them, and I am ready."

The sergeant went silent. He was at the juncture of his journey where there was no bother to portray the hard master sergeant. He was back in his element and at the same time accepting himself as he was. The down-home speak was good evidence. Both men's eyes bore into the ground in front of them. It was a strangely uncomfortable moment for Conner. He felt a compunction to respond yet pressured not to. He knew his mind would be processing the sergeant's words as long as he had breath.

Then Sergeant Phillips picked it up again. "You are a soldier, a good soldier, Private Conner. But this business isn't you. You are young and yet fresh enough. You have a chance to get free and have a life of your own. Settle down with a wife and brats. Get to know your mum again before 'tis too late. You are a sensitive and thoughtful young man. The life here eats us up. Engage with life at the River Foyle—a job, a business, something to pour your heart into. Some way, lower the temperature of this bloody business you know you never bargained for. You need to grow a place inside yourself, a place where you can stand to accommodate the neighbors and be a blessing; tell jokes and laugh; complain of the prime minister and your bloody MP. Be kind to yourself. To begin with, you don't need to believe it; you only need to accommodate the civilian world. You have already done what you come here to do: follow orders. That's all. You are not accountable to this fumble-fuck. Go home; go to the river with fishin' pole, a loaf of bread, and a beaker of wine. You could be lucky, and I know you to be the lucky sort. Now leave me alone. I have a good long walk ahead of me and I want to get started."

One final time, the Vietminh infantry advanced on the fortress. No white flags—that was the word. Firing faded, French Force troopers came out in the open, discharging rifles, barrels in mud. Others were busy detonating munition caches and destroying communications equipment.

Down at Strongpoint Isabelle in the twilight of the day, 7 May 1954,

Mohammed ben Salah could barely make out the approaching outlines. The enemy artillery barrage had finally lifted. Everything had been thrown at Dien Bien Phu the final twenty-four hours. More artillery, the whoosh of Katyusha rockets had come online—the screaming meemies known as "Stalin's Organ" by Wehrmacht troops ten years before. Mohammed remained distinctive as being the final senseless death at Dien Bien Phu. He was an ordinary gunner, if there ever was such a thing, of a 105mm howitzer. Of the six 105 guns still serviceable in the Isabelle artillery pits the day before, five had since taken direct hits. They and their crews were no more. The batteries of 155mm howitzers had been annihilated. Mohammed's 105 was the last operative piece of artillery on Strongpoint Isabelle. It was Isabelle alone that had not been breached by the human wave attacks of the People's Army.

The Moroccan gun crews had been distinguished in their service and devotion to duty. During the previous night, the hilltop strongpoint of Eliane depended on the support of Isabelle's artillery. The handful of Eliane defenders heroically fended off the enemy assaults again and again from three sides until the support of the Isabelle howitzers was finally smashed. Mohammad was well aware the bore of his surviving howitzer had burned out some time ago from unending overuse. It operated then as an imprecise, slug-firing shotgun rather than a precision indirect-firing instrument. Yet it remained as lethal as ever to what its shells struck.

Like all others in the valley by then, Mohammad was dehydrated, gaunt, gun-deaf, and emotionally dazed, his mind locked on performance of duty, the only relief available to him at the end of the fifty-seven-day siege. As long as his body performed by rote, his emotions needn't deal with the pandemonium. They did not shoot, but the enemy ensemble continued to advance on Mohammed ben Salah.

The enemy faces my howitzer with a pistol? he silently questioned. Mohammad blinked his eyes to refocus, but yes—the officer leading the advance gripped a .45-caliber pistol. The observation soured his mind. *My hands, the hands of the vanquished, hold the lanyard of a howitzer leveled against a victor who points at me a pistol? Endless days of righteous service, and our efforts are lost to a pistol? Allah works in mysterious ways.* It was Mohammed's one and only contemplation of acceptance. Still, the heart of Mohammed ben Salah was lightened by such a ploy of absurdity.

There was a degree of smugness in the officer's smile—he, a survivor, the victor and conqueror of the final strongpoint. Fifty meters before him, the duty-bound Moroccan came to attention and saluted with precision. Then, holding the lanyard close to his center with both hands, Mohammed primly and sharply rotated his body a quarter turn, advancing the lanyard. The final blast, a beehive round, instantly and literally splattered a pistol-holding conqueror into the mists. The final death went to the Moroccan. After a moment's hesitation, he was showered with the spray of many weapons. One last senseless death.

Chapter 14

Keep Moving

The march to the POW camps had begun two or three days earlier. Thousands of white parachutes still covered the landscape. Glum soldiers were still clearing bodies. General Giap decided to film onsite a re-creation of the Vietminh victory. Some of the French Force troops were detained to play their part. Giap, like all directors, turned up a couple of rough spots during the project. The Legionnaires flatly refused. Major Bigeard was asked to play himself in the film. "I'd rather die," was his only response. He was serious. A number of seemingly minor things, including unlikely background images and unfortunate dying performances, tagged the film as an amateur production.

Before French engineers and other technicians could leave the fortress, they were tasked with the recovery of landmines and maintenance and repair of electrical systems and generators. For the record, every last parachute was collected by the victors. It was unknown if the fetid conditions left cholera or other calling cards behind for the winners.

The long march was especially difficult for gaunt, emaciated men dazed to the marrow from continuous weeks of pounding artillery and the likelihood of sudden death. To insulate themselves against air strikes on the march, the Vietminh enlisted their own troops, the privates, to march in units between the blocks of walking prisoners. Vietminh officers and wounded Vietminh rode in the beds of Molotova trucks, also interspersed among the columns.

The several spaced-out convoys were indistinguishable from each other. It was friend and foe, then trucks and rolling armaments, and then the porters with booty-laden supply bicycles. All were in strict segregation but squeezed closely together. There were escape attempts, but attempts only. There were no wins against the Vietminh and the environment. Serious beatings were the result. A second attempt meant more drastic punishment. Daily, commissars lectured both Vietminh and French Force troops—the former to encourage and engage them in their glory, despite the obvious cost of victory, and the latter to encourage their salvation by admitting war crimes and expressing aspirations for communism. There was no protection against mosquitoes, day or night; malaria and dengue ran rampant. Friend and foe alike constantly dropped out to visit the bush and then had to catch back up. Prisoners who lagged behind or could not catch up were left behind to perish. The ants and rats would dispose of the carcass. It was a process. It was expected.

Even before the march began, Thuy had been considering her options. For Pham Van Hieu, she was a convenience. It had become clear that what Pham wanted was Thuy by his side, with her arresting good looks and panache as a kind of accoutrement or investment, even. She would be good for political positioning and, of course, baby-making—he needed her for that. That she was young and city-naïve was especially attractive to him. She would have to depend on him in certain ways.

As the march began, he busied himself looking for ways to be prominent. As a city boy gone to Comintern, he felt pretty wised up. That was one reason his status as private annoyed him so. He needed to get off that private train. Prominence would do it, but he no longer had illusions of being the heroic warrior. A bit of chicanery could be more effective and a whole lot less dangerous. As a private in a Vietminh infantry platoon, he was expendable. Equal parts nonsense and good looks could work wonders getting him to where he needed to be. Thuy's attraction to his good looks had faded considerably by then. He wasn't aware and never did notice.

It was the consistent makeup of the convoy, and because Thuy was a Vietminh soldier, that she could go up and down the line reviewing the blocks of prisoners as if it were her duty. She was looking for Private Aiden Conner. Truthfully, she didn't know if he was dead or alive. No luck; there were a lot of French Force privates, and *maybe he is in a different convoy,* she finally admitted to herself.

Just before sunset one evening, however, she heard English being spoken at a prisoner supper station. She heard the word "Kilroy," which jarred her somewhat. She couldn't see over the men, so she waded into the group. When they saw her scarf, the men stopped talking and stared at her. It was obvious something was up. It was Conner; he was there. The two made eye contact but neither said a word. Thuy pretended to be counting bodies, then turned and left.

She had remembered that, while on the Laotian trail with Conner, they had talked about the Kilroy icon seen on a Vietminh sandal. They had laughed and guessed it could be a number of things, including a spy or double agent thing.

They had to play it cool. Not long after, one evening, they were able to connect after the requisite brainwashing lectures. It had taken Thuy some time to work up a scenario where it would appear legitimate for her to talk to Conner.

"Stop!" she demanded of Conner's block. "No one to go." Her authority was unknown, but it was obvious she was Vietminh. They stopped. Then Thuy switched from French to English. "Raise hand if speak English." She punched it out strong and slow with authority. She raised her own hand in demonstration. The men mumbled among themselves but only looked back at her suspiciously.

Her English wasn't so good, but she was working on it and had been since Private Conner had accosted her on the trail outside Phu Doan. English-speaking commissars had been happy to help her. The pretense to learn English was that she could lecture to or interpret for the English-speaking POWs when Dien Bien Phu fell.

"Last chance. You know English? Please to raise hand."

Only Private Conner and one other, a light-skinned East Indian man, raised a hand. The latter was passing as English native. He appeared to be white, but his accent gave him away in a second. Thinking that was funny, Thuy almost gave herself away with a smile but quickly covered with a cough. Both hands waving, she shooed away the forty-eight others to their slight dash of supper.

As it turned out, the East Indian knew halting renditions of "hello, sir" and "goodbye, sir," "yes, sir" and "no, sir." There wasn't much more, and he hadn't yet acquired the word "ma'am." With the speaking of each small phrase, no matter which, the Indian accented with a sharp, well-practiced salute.

Thuy went on to portray herself as giving a stern lecture in English with plenty of hand and arm movement. Conner occasionally nodded while the East Indian nodded endlessly, obviously simple and lost as he was. Thuy and Conner were quite sure the latter understood nothing unless the word "sir" was included. Even then, it was doubtful.

Conner wanted to know where the column was going. "North and east," Thuy answered, "five hundred kilometer, maybe." The news was like a death sentence to Conner's ears. He could not see himself maintaining the pace for that long, walking that far.

"Sergeant Phillips will never make it," is what he told her. "His chest and arm burns will re-infect in this environment, and his legs are not good." Conner could do nothing about it other than what he was doing—sharing his concern with Thuy. It was proven every day, over and over, that the Vietnamese, at least the Vietminh, cared not at all about the individual life. Thuy seemed different, but he didn't know.

"I will see," she responded.

Conner held out little hope that she could or would do anything about it. He was wrong.

When she found the block that Sergeant Phillips was in, Thuy pulled the same ruse with the English speakers. She quickly learned that Phillips was struggling with walking, but his chest had not blistered open. Not yet. She would try to get him medicine if it did.

Another week passed and another visit. Conner told Thuy he did not expect to remain a private, but not because of promotion. "If I survive all this, I will leave the Legion," he told her. "My health is not good and likely will worsen with this lifestyle." In truth, he was sick of heart. He was sick, he was homesick, and he was disillusioned. As matters were, in his condition, the Legion could ask him to step aside. "After Ireland, it was the Legion what saved me," he admitted. "But after this, is it not time for me to move on and save myself?" He knew the next hot spot was Algeria, the French colony in North Africa. The Legion would next be thrown against resisting Algerians—it was happening already.

If they did cut him loose, he would lose the benefits of name and French citizenship, but at least he would be out of it standing on two feet. And he was proud of being a Legionnaire, of serving with honor. It had given him dignity like no other, and the Legion would always be his homeland in a gut-grimness way. Coming or going, he would never be far from that final talk with Sergeant Phillips. *I'm not a soldier at heart,* he silently grieved.

Out loud he said, "Better it happens now when I am young and can learn another trade." Thuy only nodded. She had her own future to consider. He continued, "I have gained *savoir-faire*—I can adapt and deal with matters. I simply have to survive this." Everyone was sick. A great many would not survive. Private Conner had learned that he identified more with peasants than the authority of this colonialism.

By the next week he was more run down. Passing that off, he learned that Sergeant Phillips's chest showed signs of infection, a deepening redness. When the East Indian had need of the bush for a few minutes, Conner expressed to Thuy a fantasy, but a fantasy with clear tones of confession. His deepest wish was for a partner, and that partner being her.

"If I survive, and after I am free of both Vietminh and French authority, I wish to be with you." He didn't exactly ask for her hand in marriage, but it was pretty obvious in what direction he was headed.

Thuy felt a sudden thrill but had to play it cool. She too was a soldier, embedded in a strictly controlled environment. Arms fluttering, her mind flush with incredulity, Thuy seemed to threaten Conner. The East Indian returned and interpreted what he saw, which was piercing. Quickly squatting, he covered his head with both arms, head ducked between knees. Out of breath, Thuy finally calmed. Quiet but for loud, short breaths, the excitement for all three of them circulated—each for a different reason.

"News!" Thuy announced the next week. "Vietnam to split at middle—north communist, south not communist. US send ships for people to go south. Live in south." Then she seemed angry, or was it a stern smugness? "Maybe, Private Conner, I go to ship. Also, Private Conner . . . I be late," she sneered. Abruptly, she jumped out of her animated squat, turned, and was gone.

To be sure she was really gone, the East Indian peeked between fingers covering his face. He then relaxed and offered Private Conner a smile. The two men nodded to each other and moved across the trail for their day's handful of rice, no salt.

The next week involved a good deal of brutality. The water made them sick. The food made them sick. Their wounds made them sick, and their circumstance made them sicker still. Most of those carrying one end of a litter by then no longer could. Soldiers were left behind. Men were falling out. Those who had weakness of one kind or another either dropped out or pushed hard to maintain presence. The eight-hundred-calorie diet and the march had depleted even the most able.

Conner spent the week confused about Thuy, although thinking of her helped him maintain the pace. It was a persistent pain watching strong lives falter and fade day after day, then left to perish alongside the trail. He imagined open talks with Thuy and continued on.

When she next returned, her expression was more composed. The East Indian did not acknowledge her. His normally comfortable squat included squinting closed eyes and an anxious rocking motion, neither a good sign for longevity. Paying no attention to the other, Conner immediately expressed his confusion regarding her behavior the week before.

Her supplication to him was a modestly terse apology. "I sorry to confuse you. I also sorry to tell you . . . Sergeant Phillip pass away two day ago." At least the phrasing meant to Conner that it had not been a brutal death.

"I'm not surprised. It is what he wanted." A calm silence left them looking at each other. The East Indian continued rocking.

Finally, she began again, also in English. "He last say you need strong female. Strong female! Me!" she emphasized, touching her chest. "That what he tell before he pass on."

Conner remained silent, but he was not surprised by that either. He was pleased it was over for his master sergeant and that his final thoughts had involved the future. There was hope in that. The surprise and the hurt were that the belabored sergeant had lasted so long.

Thuy was insistent. "You say," she firmly stated.

"If you are asking whether I agree with Sergeant Phillips . . . ," he ventured and then stopped. To be certain she understood what he was about to say, Conner looked to see who was near them, and then spoke softly in French. "Tell me how we can remain alive and be together. That, with all my heart, is what I want." Then he added, "Does the tender and loving Thuy remain in you, or has she too passed away?"

Thuy said nothing. Her lips remained silent, but a large tear rolled down her cheek. It landed on the soft dust of the flat space between them, announcing its own arrival. The world stopped.

The eyes of the East Indian blinked open. Thuy and Conner looked at him, toward the presence he held. Several seconds he studied the large drop, for now resting whole. The spell was deepened when he looked back at them. "God bless you both," he said in perfect English. "May your baby be healthy, loved, and live long." His eyes closed; he began rocking again. He would not be with them the next week, his karma lightened.

Astonished he was, but Conner suddenly understood. His posture strengthened and his face questioned the truth of it. Thuy paused. Her head lowered, she humbly nodded. When she looked up seconds later, the private's eyes were welled with tears. Seeing his reaction to her answer, Thuy felt her heart lift and beat with purpose. Truthfully, there was little hope in their situation, but for the moment that was not a factor. They now shared a joy, a distinct joy, despite its presence in a strongbox of misery and death. But it was joy, a joy that endures, and endures quietly.

Conner was wearing a bush hat when Thuy came next. As she settled, he politely placed it on the ground between them. The East Indian had bequeathed the hat to him. It was no small gesture, a sharp arrow in the quiver of survival on the march. This time, he and Thuy spoke "Frenglish," one could say—English with French words and phrases helping along the way. The ratio of French to English depended on who was nearby.

"Saigon," she stated. "People's Army say I no soldier. They say I go home when prison camp come. No. I go Saigon." That she was being cut out made a certain amount of sense. It was Captain Ngai, at Private Pham's insistence, who had accepted her into his company. There would be no record of her belonging anywhere, even among the coolies. Coolies disappeared during wartime for a myriad of reasons.

"Keo-woi," she struggled saying. No response from Conner. A little louder, "Keo-woi!" Conner shook his head. "You look. Paper say keo-woi. You see!" It wasn't helping.

"Soldier," a strong Vietnamese voice interrupted, "what you do with him—Legionnaire!"

Thuy jumped up, then explained succinctly in native tongue to the senior commissar. She was lecturing the private on the benefits of working with the Vietminh—that he would receive favors, a banana perhaps, from Uncle Ho if he reported subversive activity to her. That is why she speaks to this private alone.

"Another soldier normally here died this week, to the benefit of all," she added.

The political officer watched her face of concern change to proud and productive comrade. She was good. The Legionnaire's face was one of confused anxiety. The commissar's look remained impassive.

"Carry on," he uttered; turned, and was gone.

Together, Thuy and Conner expelled breaths of relief. Did he detect the lies? They couldn't be certain he did not. For Conner, it brought to mind stories of Vietminh commanders leaving 9mm holes in the backs of deceitful recruits' heads. Thuy knew those stories to be true.

"Must go now. You know—Saigon. Keo-woi. You see on paper."

Before he could ask again, she leaned forward in her squatting position and seemed to slip something under the rim of the bush hat. "Ciao, Legionnaire," and she was gone.

Carefully picking up his hat by the brim, Conner later unrolled from a leaf a handful of peanuts and several small chunks of mango. He then promptly collected his handful of rice, no salt, and immediately stepped into the bush. There was a party about to be going on, with bounty.

Whatever Thuy was talking about, he was pleased to know her heart, but there was so much more. She did not return the next week. No more peanuts. No more mango. No more English and no more Thuy. He would have time to consider her words, and he then thought of her final words to him. *What did she mean by "Ciao, Legionnaire?"* he asked himself. Italian was the one language he hadn't yet heard on the march. Now that was covered. He smiled so it wouldn't haunt him. Ciao indeed.

Private Pham needed a breakout, or he would be a private for the rest of eternity, it seemed to him. No longer did he assume commissar status would miraculously one day be his, with all due honor and respect. Consequently, he spent much of his time on the march looking for the shill—that phobic personality whose fear and greed surpassed personal dignity.

Then he spotted Corporal Mundt. Mundt spent downtime alone. *Perhaps he is different from the others.* It didn't take long to find out. Mundt was a Nam Yum rat. There had been an unquantified number of French Force troopers who had abandoned their units well before the battle ended. They chose the relative safety of riverbank dugouts to the pain of continuing courage. Private Pham saw opportunity and, perhaps even, his man.

"Legionnaires are not humble in defeat, I think," Pham suggested to the corporal who sat alone at the end of the day's march. Pham effortlessly squatted in front of the corporal. "They see themselves as iron men, even as they founder. And truly dismissive they are to those who justifiably wish to survive and live an honest life." It was beautifully judgmental, and the pandering of it depended upon the listening ear.

Mundt only grunted. Intentionally not making eye contact, the corporal muttered something about the actions of others not bothering him. Pham quickly responded that he could see that, and Mundt probably deserved extra rations because of his demonstrated strength of character. That resolved the eye contact issue.

"What about rations?" he wanted to know.

The bait was loaded with hook, and the mouth was already open. Pham was pretty sure he couldn't miss. "Perhaps someone such as yourself would like the opportunity to set the record straight on those *dummkopfs.*"

"I don't know what you mean," Mundt coyly begged off, nevertheless impressed with the use of an appropriate German word. He knew the bargaining would continue.

"There are so many things," Pham leisured back. "There could be contraband hidden about, or some may speak of escape—who knows? Some may even think badly of the commissars and call them names behind their backs. Everyone knows the commissars are only trying to help the lost souls, but these Legionnaires fight against it so. Someone like you in the NCO block would know of these things. We could be such good friends, Corporal." With that, he slid a small tin of sardines under a green frond between them.

"The bastards are not as perfect or clever as they think. I could tell you the names they call the commissar and who does so. Two are planning for escape, I know of. As for contraband . . ."

And the fisherman reeled in a prize lunker. They would both be noticed, and they would be in the news in days to come.

The sun seldom set on the mind-workings of Private Nguyen. His humorless nature would be a liability for most, but to the People's Army he remained a hero under Uncle Ho's continuing prompts. Nguyen Dac Pho was both humble and loyal, and General Giap was well aware of him and his serious nature. As the war wound down, the general wanted to continue using the private's example, to extend the myth surrounding him. The ranks of the People's Army would be thinning a great deal after the French departure, but there was still much to be done, particularly in the south. Perhaps Nguyen Dac Pho could be of assistance there too.

A far-flung idea being bandied about was to design and build a network of hidden trails through Laos and Cambodia from North Vietnam to the middle of South Vietnam. It would be used to safely convoy troops and war matériel to the intended new war zone. Fortunately, labor was cheap, and the adjacent states of Laos and Cambodia were weak and well positioned to host such a network. As for South Vietnam, it was anticommunist, but it was also quite plainly corrupt. The royal and ruling prince of the Republic of Vietnam found the Western world appealing; he enjoyed life as a playboy in Paris. With covert cells in the South, a communist takeover would be relatively quick and easy against the unstable new republic.

The question for Uncle Ho was how much the United States would interfere with his intentions in the South. The US was already providing support to South Vietnam via greenbacks, training, munitions, and advice, but all with little effect. American combat interference seemed a longshot to the communist world, since the Korean Conflict had never officially ended, and it was clear America wanted no more wars. The certainty of Chinese and Soviet Russia's backing of renewed war, however, was the green light to ramp up the heat on the South. Whatever it would take, the tools were available to prosecute more war.

What did that have to do with Private Nguyen? General Giap discussed with his chiefs of staff the potential upside of using Nguyen in the proposed project. In a matter of hours, there was consensus to continue promoting Nguyen to the people, both military and civilian. It was believed his skills—but particularly his reputation—could continue being useful.

At the time, he was a lieutenant in the 57th Regiment, a storied unit that was early to the cause as guerilla fighters and had fought admirably throughout the war, particularly at Dien Bien Phu. Nguyen could remain with the

57th until the politics settled—until Ho's plan for subjugation of the South could move forward.

Of course, to fully benefit from the Nguyen Dac Pho name, he must attain some recognition of authority. Perhaps the greater benefit would be to name him director and chief architect of the proposed Ho Chi Minh Trail. The only remaining question was whether he should be a lieutenant colonel or a full colonel. It was quickly determined that, technically, he would be directing other colonels, so full colonel would be the proper rank. It was understood his rank would be respected but lacking in authority. The battlefield commission to second lieutenant had nicely normalized his status as competent officer and leader. For the time being, he would serve as engineer with the 57th Regiment of the 304thth Vietminh Infantry Division.

Meanwhile, Corporal Mundt chose to remain in North Vietnam after the French left. The newly promoted Corporal Pham had been good to Mundt, and both had been promised greater opportunity. Pham was showing continuing signs of stress, however. Officers and Vietminh NCOs had become guarded in his presence. His recent claims to be a covert commissar were perplexing, not even funny. Even Mundt believed that wasn't possible. Fortunately, the new corporal was doing good work and perhaps could continue being useful in a covert capacity.

She was in excellent physical condition and did not yet show much when the column arrived at the prison camp. Like most of life, if you knew what you were looking for, you could likely find it. The first prison camp they reached was 350 kilometers from Dien Bien Phu, and roughly half the POWs were placed there. The remainder, including Private Conner, would have to hike 150 kilometers more to the final prison camp.

Le Thuy did not wait for the camp dust to settle on her ultimate decision. After a day's rest at the first camp, she headed for the nearby Red River, where she could catch a sampan family with produce or charcoal, maybe, going to Hanoi, Haiphong, or anywhere in the Tonkin region. From there, she would move south along the coast to reach the US ships picking up refugees transitioning to the South. Thuy didn't miss out on any payroll by leaving so quickly; the People's Army was a "volunteer" army. Vietminh troops were not paid. Captain Ngai, now a company commander with the 57th Regiment, was happy to see her gone, since he was not comfortable answering questions about her, her status, or how she came to be a private in his company.

Despite the absence of cash, life on the beautiful Vietnam coast was good. There was no need to hide her growing baby bump there. In fact, it was to her advantage to highlight it, although with a degree of subtleness. Families, and especially the women, were willing to share their meager essentials with the pregnant widow of a deceased soldier. Seafood was plentiful all down the coast, and life there bustled.

It was nearly two weeks before the first ship arrived. The people who had left their homes and situations to go south were almost all Catholic, fearful of communism. Traveling emptyhanded, Thuy was first in line when she surmised when and where people would be boarding. Most of the others were collecting bags and parcels, organizing kids, and even livestock. As she boarded, a sailor asked why she didn't display a cross. She understood.

"Must I have a cross to prove I am Christian?"

It was days later that she realized the sailor had picked out a pretty girl traveling alone who might want to earn a few piasters—or just be nice to him.

"Of course not," he answered. "But here." He pulled from around his neck a cross on a chain, one of three or four. "We had a little accident on our last run," he explained. "Life will be easier in the South with this."

Thuy smiled and thanked him, wondering if she understood correctly where the crosses had come from. It looked very nice on her, he offered.

Saigon was the big city times four. Families willing to share were not so easy to find there. Street corners were dotted with beggars, many with missing limbs, others with disfigured faces, while the blind sat against corner walls with a sign and a cup. Their pain left a mark, and the overall scene did not leave a favorable impression on Thuy.

Fortunately, the sailor also distributed boxes of food that would help the people. She could read some of the English words on the boxes: "C-ration" was the major print on them. The food was canned—and different, she soon learned. Opening the cans was a challenge, but she was nothing if not adaptable, and she could trade the cigarettes and other sundries inside the boxes for things useful. Thuy's needs were minimal.

Right away, she had some concern she would have to pay the sailor for his caretaking. Thuy knew what she had that the sailor wanted. She wasn't interested. Still, he was a nice young man. Her concerns vanished with the crush of people boarding. Their bustle and business quickly negated any requirement from her. She and the sailor were soon separated, which bothered the sailor more than Thuy.

Having been a coolie and then a soldier, Thuy had no trade or much in the way of practiced market skills, but she had worked at a small village bakery for a few months before joining the coolie crew. Although accustomed to deprivation, Thuy knew that eating regularly would be important for her unborn baby, and perhaps a job would feed them both. She crisscrossed parts of the city looking for a bakery family who would take her on. All of them, it seemed, had many relatives trying to eke out a living within.

Then she entered a French-owned bakery, bigger than most of the others she had been referred to. It turned out that an attractive and well-spoken young lady with good French and some experience could be used in the shop's front, pandering to the clientele. Of course the French customers would be dismissive toward her, but kowtowing without going too far was universally practiced and always done well by Thuy. The Vietnamese customers appreciated her light touch, meaning she did not cheat them, and she earned a nominal wage as well as day-old bread when there were leftovers. It was a win-win. Her conduct earned the proprietor's trust, which provided Thuy the honor of sleeping on a straw mat just inside the back door. There would be no break-ins while Thuy was employed there.

He remembered the crowds and the coolness of Parisians from three years before. Suspicion was in the air and on peoples' minds then, so soon after The War. In the newspapers, the ever-popular President De Gaulle was busy declaring himself a great leader, while overt complaints and general unrest continued. French politicians were throwing thunderbolts while they themselves proved fragile. De Gaulle had resigned his presidential post over some authority issue. When he had retired altogether from politics in 1953, there was a sense of national letdown. That happened just as Dien Bien Phu was becoming an earnest topic within the military as well as Parliament.

French attitude had been altered by The War—so many families broken and people missing. Paris, the city itself, had been spared despite Hitler's fond wish, but there was still an anger or resentment among doubting citizens. The one safe subject of conversation seemed to be religion, but even that was seldom exercised. Overwhelmed at first, he was certain he could never adapt to such a world, and besides, his French was lousy. Patrick Cavanaugh was thoroughly intimidated, but there was an energy in Paris that inspired the boy Irishman. And another thing—he was hungry.

Aimlessly wandering the streets, he had noticed an office of the "Gendarmerie nationale," which he took to be something of a police station. Once inside, and in his halting French, he had announced himself as new there, looking for work, and could he be a gendarme?

Whether it was his innocent naïveté and quiet desperation, or something else, his admitted dilemma had drawn attention. It could have been the timing. Stress of the times found little to bring cheer in Paris. The office was brightened a bit just by his freckled appearance. Two of the men, and then three and four, joined in asking the boy about himself and his situation. No malice intended, but the men began stringing the Irish boy along as far as he would take them seriously and answer their frivolous questions.

Patrick had already known the French were different, but he had never before doubted their sincerity. Therefore, the game eventually played itself out, the Irish accent and all. One by one, the men broke away with one or two not feeling so proud of themselves.

The three women of the office were born of a different heart than their counterparts. Rising from their desks, they excused themselves. Before leaving the room, the older of the ladies asked the boy if he would join them for an early lunch. Patrick blushed, quickly saying he wasn't hungry. By the looks of him, the claim did not ring true, and the three ladies shepherded him through swinging doors to a back room. The men, meanwhile, only shook heads and fiddled with tobacco and pipes.

In little more than a half hour, the young man was released by the ladies—still lean, of course, but stomach sated after cheese, bread, and half an apple. The boy was smiling and cheerful. His spirit could not be denied, and the men could not help but be cheered by him once again.

The uniformed officer at the head desk motioned him over. "Boy, your obvious Irish roots will keep you from being a gendarme," he carefully spoke. Then in English, "Still, if your bones will not rest without adventure, you might try asking at the Foreign Legion office of recruitment." The officer wrote the address on a slip of paper, folded it precisely, and stuffed it into the shirt bag the boy carried everywhere with him. He then shooed the boy toward the door.

Not knowing the proper thing to say, Patrick had turned before going out and, with open hand, threw a generous kiss to the room. "*Au revoir,*" and he was gone. Once outside, he couldn't help but hear the sound of guffawing and laughing inside, but he didn't take it personally. He had been recommended for the French Foreign Legion. And he had their address.

Three years had passed. He was still listless and again alone, but now in Saigon. Some of the strangeness had to do with not shouldering a rifle. He felt defenseless, and he was—not even a knife, although that wasn't exactly true. The veteran did have a switchblade in his pocket. One of his chums had given him that before he left the platoon, saying that Saigon hoodlums trafficked in sailors and all others with jewelry on their bodies or money in their pockets. "Stay out of alleys," was the advice; even gangs of youngsters would surround and rob a plump goose like him. Patrick wasn't anywhere near plump, but he was a Westerner, and that was close enough.

He stood looking at scores of sampans on the Saigon River, or the *Rivière de Saigon* in the local French vernacular. He was where the Arroyo Chinois, a tributary, intersected the big river. In his pensive mood, it seemed ironic in the moment. Saigon, Vietnam: home of millions, but neither Patrick Cavanaugh nor Aiden Conner belonged. Home was so many miles away, and those miles seemed like millions. There was no going back, and there wasn't much looking forward. The confused, still-young man was defeated and suddenly feeling quite sorry for himself. *Being captured with Sergeant Phillips on Strongpoint Beatrice was not more lonely than this.*

Meanwhile, vendors had filled the streets with stacks of baskets, ducks, chickens, and all manner of bundles somehow connected to bicycles and scooters for the trip back home, wherever that might be. Sounds of people were everywhere, even this late in the afternoon. There was the constant bickering, the bartering, and the sweet aroma of marijuana cloaking the occasional wisps of sewage and river rot. Crowds of kids screeched as they played their alley wars—the littlest ones naked from the waist.

Out of uniform, he was rudderless and alone in Saigon with who-knows-how-many people around him. What he had were memories. Also, some money. Since he had spent virtually none as a Legionnaire, he had collected a fair sum at final pay call. He was gone from his mates, and he missed them, especially the Limey he had wanted to hate. Patrick was so lonely he nearly missed Corporal Mundt.

Speaking of Mundt, what Patrick didn't miss was the harshness and downright depravity he had witnessed as a Legionnaire. Both friend and foe on the long march to the prison camps had gone off the rails emotionally. There were certain types who had become nasty and paranoid. Conner kept his distance, hoping it wasn't a foretaste of days to come for him.

Sergeant Phillips may have been correct in his advice for Private Conner to leave the Legion, but that didn't mean being a civilian wasn't wrong. After all, weren't character calluses developed both inside and outside the military? For a fact, Patrick knew that was true. Tough transition it was, learning to be civilian.

No longer a Legionnaire, there was no chance for French citizenship. He would have to get used to being Patrick Cavanaugh again and a hunted man. It seemed like a million years since he had been Patrick. Thuy didn't know about any of that. He had a good deal of trouble taking on faith alone that Le Thuy would be in Saigon waiting for him. So many things were likely to have gone wrong. Besides, how could he expect to find her in the hot, smelly mass of confusion known as Saigon? *A man takes his life in his hands just trying to cross the street here.* But people did. They weaved between multiple lanes of traveling motorbikes, rickshaws, cars, and trucks, all with apparent ease. That's not the way it worked in Strabane or even Lifford on the Republic side of the River Foyle. *Surely it would do folks good to take notice of what is reckless and what is not in Saigon.*

He had made certain he had a room before dark. Then he went back down along the river looking for a dinner place. No problem. It was his first time eating on a floating restaurant. The ambiance and gentle rocking helped him relax, as did a bottle of Ba Muoi Ba. The food was excellent, as was the service.

Survived, he had healed nicely, at least physically, once in the hands of French health services and good food. The conditions of the Dien Bien Phu siege had resulted in misery for all. The long march with little food had left him gaunt and ill. A residual effect was a chronic appetite, an ongoing hunger, at least in his mind. Released from the Legion, he was relegated to local food, which was fine, but it wasn't Mum's home cooking.

As much as food, Thuy was on his mind. With his chair back against the far wall of the dining room, Patrick's neurosis mellowed with his second Ba Muoi Ba. The warm beer had good taste and a good affect, all things considered.

A kid came through hawking newspapers. Patrick recalled what Thuy had said about newspapers or reading something. He never understood quite what she meant. There were no English language papers. A copy of *Saigon Eco* would have to do. He went through it all, understanding much of the French.

Then he saw it.

Like the proverbial ton of bricks, it hit him. Patrick had to put the paper down for a minute, then go back and look again. It was still there; it hadn't changed. In the middle of the classified section, an eerily stark ad stared back at him: "Most Distinguished Bakery" was all it said. Below it was the renowned icon that silently stated, "Kilroy Was Here."

Yes, the ideographic Kilroy was what he had seen soon after jumping into Dien Bien Phu. It was on the sandal of the Vietminh he had failed to kill. It was etched into the edge of the thick rubber sole. At the time, he had simply thought it odd. Everyone knew it was an icon during The War, but it was still common enough around and about. It wasn't that big a deal. But it was funny and unilingual.

Still, he wondered, *how does that fit in with a bakery in Saigon?* Then he realized, *There is no address on the ad, if it even is an ad. What a city! What a country! What a people!*

Patrick stood up in a bit of disgust and left, leaving the paper on the table. He went directly to his hotel and to bed, hoping not to dream. When he remembered his dreams, they were always bizarre. He had had enough for one day. It was a deep sleep, but not a long sleep.

Somewhere around 4:00 a.m. Patrick awoke, tired but fully awake. Knowing from experience there was no chance of more sleep, he went down to the lobby and annoyed the on-duty desk clerk who behaved professionally nevertheless. Buying yesterday's French paper and getting a street map from the clerk, Patrick went to work back in his room, familiarizing himself with the Saigon streets and points of interest. At first daylight, he headed out for a walk. The spirit of challenge was returning to Patrick, and he now felt a degree of inspiration. The air was fresh. Saigon was hopeful today.

Two hours of brisk walking slowed him somewhat, but already Patrick had seen sights. The Presidential Palace was the most impressive, but he hadn't yet come across what he was hoping to find. Resorting to inquiry, Patrick approached a Saigon municipal policeman, a *Sûreté* officer on the next street corner. It was an odd question, and Patrick could not phrase it well in French despite his obviously serious intent. The officer frowned as he listened, waiting for the point of concern. When Patrick pointed to the icon in the newspaper, the *Sûreté* officer positively cackled.

"The freckled Irishman wants a croissant," the officer seemed to be saying. He could hardly stop laughing. He then pointed across the street, holding up three fingers indicating the bakery was three blocks over.

Patrick had not wanted to ask directions, and that was why. Whether it was the language issue or the freckles, it didn't matter. Patrick was not a good fit for Saigon, even as someone who nearly gave his life for her, or something like that. He only smiled, thanked the officer, and turned to the street. Then the combat veteran had to work up the courage to cross the street.

The "Kilroy" bakery was indeed three blocks over. A croissant would have been perfect, but Patrick wasn't thinking food despite the heavenly scent of the fresh breads and pastries wafting down the street. He could see it was a French bakery, not Vietnamese, which was not necessarily assuring to him.

Before going in, he stopped at a streetlight pole and tried to reason out what was going on and how he had arrived to where he was. Thuy's adamant instructions were Saigon and reading. OK, that had gotten him here. *What else is there?* He forced himself to concentrate. *Why would Thuy be connected with a French bakery? What was the enigmatic message she had added?* His eager brain cells worked over their conversation until her words slowly took shape. He was pretty sure it was something close to "Kio-Woi," or was it "Keo-Way"? At the time, he had had no idea what she was saying, but maybe . . . *was she trying to say 'Kilroy'?* Oh man! Kilroy was their first sharing, their joke. It was personal. The thought pushed his backside against the streetlight post. Saigon—newspaper—Kilroy; it all made sense.

Am I to ask about her there? It could be nothing but subversive Vietnamese. If so, are they Vietminh and connected to Thuy? It could be anything. It could even be a French bakery!

The possibilities tired him. Feeling defenseless again, Patrick steadied himself and swallowed hard. He walked through the door with vague intention. The shop was smaller than he had expected. A Frenchman just this side of middle-aged was at the register. A somewhat younger European woman, likely his wife, was gingerly stocking warm baguettes. He could tell they were fresh from the oven by the way she handled them. Seeing her like that felt like home, and he relaxed somewhat. Pleasantries were exchanged with the man. Patrick fumbled with his French. He had found the language more difficult to use with civilians than with his Legionnaire mates or Thuy.

He went basic and slow. "I am looking for a friend. Perhaps you know her or have heard of her," Patrick fibbed.

"And does this friend have a name, *monsieur*?" the Frenchman responded. "As you can see, we are quite busy." People were coming and going, the pretty woman helping them.

"*Oui*, she told me some time ago that she intended to be in this neighborhood when I arrived in Saigon."

"Her name, *monsieur*. Does she have a name?" The man was becoming annoyed.

Patrick was reluctant to identify her as a young Vietnamese woman, though he knew he must. "Of course. I beg your pardon. She is of the Le family. Thuy is her given name. Can you help? She is about this tall, long black hair, and she may be pregnant." Now he had done it all.

"If she is of the Le family, sir, I would *expect* her to be about this tall, have long black hair, and what business is it of yours, might I ask, that she be pregnant?"

Patrick didn't know what to say. Instantly he was defensive as well as defenseless. "I knew her from the north when I was there," he stumbled.

"She—" and he could go no farther. His eyes welled, perhaps with frustration, perhaps not.

"Were you by any chance a Legionnaire in the north?"

Patrick hesitated but nodded.

"And taken prisoner by the Vietminh?"

He nodded again.

"You look surprisingly well recovered after such a long march when so many died." The Frenchman seemed to know.

Patrick could feel energy lifting his spirits, then realized this knowledge he had given the man could be as bad as it seemed good if he were connected with a certain element. The perplexed look on Patrick's face begged for release of what was happening.

Entering the shop just then, a couple abruptly interrupted them, cheerily greeting the proprietor. The Frenchman returned their greeting and moved to attend them.

The young woman from the baguette shelf cleared her throat. "*Monsieur.*" Her right index finger beckoned to him.

Caution immediately came to Patrick, but he followed her anyway. They passed through the curtain behind the register. It reminded him of the family shop in Strabane. They continued to a set of stairs, squeaky stairs as it turned out. The young woman was pleasant and gentle. She introduced herself as Brigitte. Patrick did not reciprocate. By then he had resigned himself to whatever awaited him on the second floor. The landing was dark, which renewed Patrick's apprehension of a subversive undertaking. The young lady looked up at him and smiled as she reached for and pulled the cord hanging from a bare-bulb fixture. In that moment, the world opened and embraced Patrick Cavanaugh.

In a well-worn rattan chair, a startled Le Thuy was patting the back of a sleeping baby lying on her chest. She squinted, her eyes adjusting to the light, then realized the young woman, Brigitte, was relieving her of the baby. It was then Thuy noticed the man in the doorway. She blinked. "Private Conner?" she barely whispered.

He stepped forward. "No, Thuy. I am Patrick Cavanaugh. In another life I was Private Conner." He held out his arms to her. She did not respond. "Are you not well? Can you stand?" He did not understand it was his startling appearance that caused her numbness.

"*Non*, my dear soldier, or whoever you are." She rose and slowly reached out.

He too could hardly take it all in. Stepping forward, Patrick reached for her hands and held them to his chest, kissing them over and over. Released, his hands moved to her shoulders and effortlessly pulled her into him. She was warm and soft. He was gentle and tender as he had nearly always been with her. The tears rolling down his cheeks were quickly kissed away. Patrick parted her silky black hair, his lips enjoying again the bronze skin of neck and shoulder. She smiled, remembering. They were together again— this time, a family.

Chapter 15

Sunset – Sunrise

To Patrick, family meant Papa and Mum—and himself, of course. Papa was gone—dead, like so many other familiar and unfamiliar faces now pooling in Patrick's head. Thinking about Papa's death still dished out anguish, but then again, it was a fact—it happened—so there was nothing to be done. *I'm being realistic now,* he insisted to himself.

As for Mum, he knew nothing of her since the day he walked to the docks from Strabane. Patrick had written her a short note after reaching the continent. He assured her he was in France, he was well, and that he hoped to be accepted and trained as a gendarme or constable and be like Nolan. That was three years ago, and not another communication between them. Of course not; he had offered no address to her.

Aideen had written letters. She continued to write a letter to Patrick each Sunday evening, storing them in a special box under the front counter. They were filed by date, address left open. When people asked about her son, she always told them she expected to hear from him any time now. For three years, she had not. It was after a year or so those close to her politely stopped asking.

Day after day, as he had cleaned and pressed stacks of woolens in his youth, Patrick's mind drifted to fantasy, a time where he was out and about, feeling the sunshine on his face and being a part of world events, although it was state or Strabane events almost always. He had been a bit of a dreamer; he would have his pick of pretty girls when he was just a little older, he was certain. But he wasn't certain at all. Settling down as a grownup had never occurred to him, probably because, in those formative years, he couldn't imagine reaching adulthood; it seemed so far away. A life of his own beyond the family shop was a stretch of the mind. He would be stuck in the shop forever and a day, he was certain, especially after Papa had passed.

Thuy had been a dreamer too, when she had time. It was assumed in her village that she would be matched up with an eligible village boy and

223

have babies, all the while working in the paddies. As a youngster, she had displayed resources of vibrant energy along with a competitive spirit. In Western culture, she would have been seen as a nervy tomboy. In the rice paddies, she was a good worker when it was time to work, otherwise respect your elders. Those days began before her first double-digit birthday. Thuy had a mind of her own, asked lots of questions, and was game for most anything dynamic. That pretty much explained why she had volunteered as a coolie and wasn't offended when her breast was gauged as "adequate" by Private Pham.

She didn't know what it was about her lover, *this Irishman who changed his name from one thing to another and then back again.* From the beginning they just clicked—more than lovers. It was like she could see inside him, understand his thinking, and know his heart. She sensed that his heart was the kind she needed, even if he was the enemy, or had been.

He, on the other hand, had been instantly smitten by her spontaneous kiss on his cheek that day at Phu Doan. She was so delicate yet strong, so full of assurance and yet tender and kind to him. As she had walked away that day, it came to him that she was the second Vietminh he had failed to kill. After what they had gone through since, he was ashamed of himself. He was ashamed he had had thoughts of killing her, but there was yet the view that maybe he should have. *Thank God I am out of the war and away from all that,* he thought.

"You found me," she breathed. "We can be together?" It was as a dream. Thuy needed to be told this was real, that he wanted her. "No more?"

"No more war, and I will not miss it. The French are done here. What will happen to Vietnam now, I do not know. What I do know, Thuy, is that I need you to be part of me. More than half of me if you can," he tried to joke. The irony was that she wasn't much more than half his size. He looked into her eyes. Neither of them laughed. He tried to smile but failed. She dared not smile. Emotion filled every space between them as he held her. Le Thuy felt safe for the first time in her life.

When consciousness returned to Thuy she turned to the young woman with the baby—who was no longer there. They were downstairs, the baby still sleeping in a back wrap.

"The baby?" Patrick began to ask, stepping back. There was a quick glance down at Thuy's midsection. He wasn't about to assume something so important.

"If you had looked you would have seen the baby's green eyes and fat cheeks. Do you think that could be the offspring of Brigitte and André?"

"Do you say I have fat cheeks?" he responded with an instant twinkle.

"Of course not. It is only the babies of the Irish that have fat cheeks and green eyes. Do you not agree?"

That was his answer. The baby was his. And hers. He picked up Thuy and whirled her around until she giggled, unusual behavior for a responsible mother such as she. No longer was Thuy a single mother.

When he finally set her down, she ventured to inform him, not without trepidation, "Monsieur Patrick, I have named her Gisèle." She said it in her strong, assured voice, anxious he may not approve.

"Green eyes, chubby little cheeks, and a French name? I think, here in Indochine, Vietnam, it is perfect." He lifted her again, but this time not from under her arms. This time, his strong hands lifted her derrière up and tight to him, molding the rest of her into him. Her legs wrapped around his waist. He moaned and they shared goosebumps.

"Please," she said. "We must not soil my white *ao dai*."

Brigitte kept the baby for the hour Patrick and Thuy went out for lunch and catchup talk. The couple had much to catch up on—and plans to make. Over bowls of pho, Patrick learned that Thuy had worked at the bakery almost since arriving in Saigon. She had begun work at another shop until she discovered the Kilroy Bakery.

Kilroy was the mystery that needed unwinding for Patrick. Under her breath, Thuy quickly told him they would talk about it later. Later was in Patrick's hotel room that night. For now, Thuy and the baby would be staying with him there. She promised André at the bakery that she would continue to work, and it was agreed Patrick could join her in learning the business if he wished.

Bakery mornings begin early. Brigitte suggested Thuy and Patrick get settled and "sleep in tomorrow," she added with a wink. Thuy agreed to be at the shop by midmorning.

None of the three could sleep in the next morning, so the little family lazed and played in their room. It was quite the adjustment for Patrick to see himself as part of a family. After they had reached the hotel room the night before, he introduced himself to his very own six-week-old. In the early morning, he studied her every feature, her nose, chin, and especially her eyes—windows to the soul. Yes, she was his, and he was willing to give his life for her, for his family. He could only hope his little family would never be in such jeopardy.

Thuy was busy. She now carried the responsibilities of motherhood, work, and family. War and the 57th Regiment were gone from her mind most days. But being busy didn't eliminate the concern of someone from the north recognizing her. That would likely be a very big issue for her, and now for her family as well.

Having a Caucasian baby was reprehensible to most of her countrymen. Being with a European made it only more dangerous. She had been fortunate to be employed and accepted at Kilroy with the more open-minded French proprietors. Life was funny and fast changing. Not that long ago, she had some notoriety for saving a fire team and personally killing Legionnaires. In Saigon now, the mixed-race family would be socially taboo, or considered in poor taste at the very least. Human nature being what it is, rumors would run rampant. Coming from the north was enough to not be trusted.

Gisèle was nursed and changed as soon as the sun contributed daylight. A little later, Gisèle splashed her way through a sink bath. Patrick helped despite the giddy handicap of a smile that could not be wiped from his face. Gisèle was not a difficult baby. She seemed to take to Patrick, but not until he learned how babies are securely held. The energy among the three of them was appreciated by all of them. They were safe, they were clean, and they had each other. Since their parting on the trail leading to the Viet Bac Prison Camp, Thuy's English had improved. At the bakery, she had opportunity to practice with a surprising number of customers. Her French and Vietnamese were taken for granted at the shop, as was patriotism.

As time had gone on, she was taken into the confidence of André and Brigitte. The shop was a better fit for her than she had imagined. It began to seem like she had been handpicked to join the little team there. She was a good worker, never complained, and was excellent with customers regardless of race or nationality. Pregnant as she was at the time, they had taken her in, given her room and board upstairs, and supported her when she delivered. Was it too good to be true?

Before Gisèle was born, Thuy knew she could pass as a soldier's widow only so long. Almost assuredly her baby would have Caucasian features, and then would come the consequences. She could still, however, claim to have come south, to Saigon, as a Catholic fearful of the dreaded communists, which was essentially true. OK, partly true. Not the part about being Catholic, but she was now fearful of communism.

Early morning in the hotel involved baby activities and lots of talk beyond even babytalk. Gisèle nursed a bit more and then Thuy patted her into an empty dresser drawer for a morning nap. That left Thuy and Patrick free to play with each other, quietly, and on practically clean sheets. The lazy ceiling fan droned on, giving them white noise for assurance of privacy. Already, Thuy knew how to please Patrick. His smiling continued.

Afterwards, alongside her, he lifted himself up on both elbows and reviewed her taut body, end to end. "Love is not the same as appreciation," Patrick tried to explain, "but for me, you are both in one. I do not love you more than I appreciate you, and I think I do not appreciate you more than I love you. It is all one, but it is two." His words were pleasing and a needed light moment for Thuy.

Reacting to the micro-attention, Thuy pantomimed a draw on the proverbial post-sex cigarette. Patrick gladly "oohed and aahed" her sultry depiction of life on the erotic side.

"Monsieur Patrick—and I like saying that so much more than Private Conner, thank you—we do not know each other. You know nothing of me, and I know nothing of you other than the obvious and our little experiments together. You see?" she flirted while sweeping a gesture over them both. "But love is love," her serious side continued. "You and I have it, is all. It is what will keep us bound together if we choose. I cannot help that, here in Saigon, I am a romantic. Perhaps in another life I was French or Italian; perhaps both. In this life, I have learned well what love is not, and I am fortunate in that. With you and Gisèle, I believe I now know why love is so well spoken of."

Patrick's smile changed as Thuy spoke. Still a smile, it had somehow evolved and become more of a serious upturn. He felt Thuy's words as calming assurance, topped off, perhaps, with a good dollop of affection and understanding. Lying now on his side, watching her, he reached over and pulled the petite one atop him. He softly laughed as each felt the contrast of the other's skin once again. She nuzzled into the deep crevice under his chin, feeling warm and protected. They simply lay naked against each other.

Minutes later, he felt something quite unfamiliar. Breastmilk was running down and dribbling off his chest. He chuckled before she even smiled, neither of them remotely self-conscious. So relaxed, their lips dreamily touched—just as Gisèle began to fuss.

In an instant their free time vanished, and the work world filtered to responsible minds. It would be an adjustment for all considered but especially for Patrick. Going to a new job reminded him of the first day of school. That reminded him of his first paratroop jump and the dressing down Sergeant Phillips had given him. *With my new family now, this will be my best first day ever.*

Half a block from the bakery, the whole world blew up. There were two explosions: one at the rear of the shop, but shortly after the bomb in front had ruptured violently. The volatility of confined flour dust generated an instant firestorm. The second floor burst into a furious blaze in less than a minute. Any thoughts of survivors inside were pointless. Gisèle screeched. Thuy appeared impassive. People on the street shrieked and ran. Patrick Cavanaugh's family did not run.

This kind of thing happened in Saigon from time to time. The insurgents, the communist agents, were good with terrorist tactics. Typically, it was a crowded bus or a busy restaurant that was targeted. Almost always it was just one bomb. This was different, and it was also curious. Surprised but not shocked, Patrick instantly reviewed surroundings. He was no longer a Legionnaire but he would always behave as one in certain ways.

Something stood out. Across the street at the far corner, within a small, aroused crowd, he saw a familiar face—someone he knew. Or had known. Almost involuntarily, Patrick stepped behind a lamppost, concealing himself. Thuy was shaken but first looked to Patrick, then occupied herself trying to calm Gisèle. Patrick looked again from behind the post to be sure.

Europeans generally stood out in a crowd of Vietnamese. This was no exception. Putting his arm around Thuy's shoulder, he moved them to the shadows under a shop awning. At a somewhat normal pace, they returned to the hotel. The street was crowded, frightened people rushing away from the explosions, and the curious rushing toward them. Reaching the hotel, they did not enter through the front doors. Passing them, they turned into the alley and went in through a service entrance.

Thuy did not resist Patrick's direction in the least, trusting him while tending to Gisèle. Once inside she asked, "What did you see?" Patrick said nothing. Then she demanded, "Who did you see?" Again, Patrick did not answer. Thuy understood. They moved down the hall to a back staircase that would take them to their floor. On the street, Patrick had picked up the day's French language newspaper.

Once inside their room, Thuy turned on the ceiling fan and Patrick put out the Do Not Disturb sign. They worked well together. Gisèle had calmed as Thuy continued rocking and patting her.

Without speaking, Patrick's intense gaze said plenty. "I saw someone I know from the north—a Legionnaire who does not belong here." He opened the paper and headed straight for the classified section. "There it is!" He punched his finger on it—the Kilroy icon. "What is this, Thuy?" He was intense and seemed afraid. "On the trail to prison camp you told me to look for this in Saigon. True?"

Thuy was often intense, but now more calm than he. Surprising Patrick, she spoke in English, considerate of thin walls. "You know this figure, this icon," she began. "Not so unusual. You remember we talk on trail; maybe is secret spy message we say?"

"Yes, I remember, Thuy. It was our secret that maybe Kilroy was a spy—our joke."

"That is why you look in paper. I was to put secret notice in paper for you to find me."

"So that is the connection! Then what about the bakery?"

"I know nothing of the Kio-woi Bakery then. After I here and working for little time in different shop, I meet Brigitte in busy café. She learn I from north and we meet again, and then again. She ask if I like to work in bakery with husband and her. I would have upstairs room and her for friend. More good than sleeping on floor, so I go with her. As time go on, they very good to me, but I begin to see passing of documents and private talk with customers. Then I am asked to pass documents to others in Saigon. I suspicious so ask why all this. They know about me, but I see this secret happening, and I not know. It is the *Kil-roy* Bakery, I am told. You see? I say Kio-woi much better now."

He didn't smile. "What does it mean?" Patrick insisted. "We could have been killed, and don't think Brigitte and André were not! Any number of customers as well!"

"We must understand as one. Please to listen. There is undercover in bakery."

"The bakery is a front!" It was a statement more than a question.

"*Oui!* I mean yes, of course. It is French peoples and Vietnam peoples working together to crush the tyranny of communism. We do not need Russia and China here. Kio-woi is growing and gaining strength. The people coming from north, like me, are investigated to determine if we are pro- or anti-communist. Most, like me, are not communist. We see how that communism work—and not like."

"But the icon? How does it fit? There are yet Kilroys here that people draw for *beaucoup* years."

"That is true, but listen. This Kio-woi is different. What in paper here is different."

"No, it's not. Kilroy is Kilroy—they are all the same. I know that much."

"No, you do not, Inspector Poirot. There is the icon from the past, and there is—how you say it?—acranom? Acra-something."

"Acronym?"

"*Oui.*" She put her finger on the paper: "Kill the Revolutionary Order Together as One."

"What are you talking about? Kilroy really is a covert organization?"

"That is what must be done. Do you not see, inspector?" she intentionally mocked him. "Vietnam peoples do not want those French who disgrace the people, but we not want to be as China, ruled with iron fist. All new Kio-woi icons fight against communist in secret. Soon it be that France to release the colonies. We can be a Vietnam state with people who make laws for the people, not laws to oppress the people."

"I am pleased to hear that," Patrick answered. He was impressed on some level, but he needed more. "This is the icon I knew in Northern Ireland, and it is exactly the same as any other," he finished with an air of finality. "How do you know about this anyway?"

Becoming a bit huffy herself, Thuy let it rip. "Great Britain does not own all books in the world. For my English learning, Brigitte helped me to read *The Mysterious Affair at Styles*. I think you like. You maybe try it. Hercule Poirot is most clever."

"And Jesus wept," Patrick muttered. "The icon is what we're talking about. What is different about the old icon and this one? I say they are the same."

"I am happy to hear so," she calmly said with feigned annoyance. "Then maybe the communist no brighter than you—and we all be safe. But I do not think so. You look. All the old Kio-woi have four finger. This Kio-woi have three. Very simple but most clear. You see?"

"Damn," was all he had to say. "Wait a minute. The *Y* in your acronym doesn't work."

"Patrick, you to lighten up and listen. Kio-woi is sign of opposition to communist and Ho Chi Minh. It is 'K-I-L the Revolutionary-Order: Together as One.' Listen now—this tricky. Together-As-One come from the two upper branches of *Y*. Branches go down into one strong stem. It will take all people, Asian and others, to do this, and there are many who will. That is what Kio-woi Bakery is—connect with many people to stand out communist cells."

"Stamp out, you mean," Patrick corrected her. "The bakery is gone. I'm afraid Kilroy was found out, and André and Brigitte were silenced." The obvious then occurred to him. "Or maybe they didn't figure it out. Maybe they were after us—you and me. We were the targets!"

"I do not understand. Why do you say that?" Thuy quietly asked, suddenly unbalanced.

"Because what I saw on the street out there was a Corporal Mundt from my platoon at Dien Bien Phu. At least, he was in my platoon until he disappeared. At the end he came out of the riverbank caves—a Nam Yum rat. He protected his own ass by abandoning his brothers and the Legion. He was a traitor then, and he is a traitor now. He followed me here, and this bombing is his malice after seeing me with you and Gisèle. He and I despised each other from the start."

Along with all else, Thuy could have cried with the news. "It is so much more than that," she sighed. "I do not know your corporal, but I too think I see him. He was standing near someone I know, a Vietminh private by the name of Pham Van Hieu. At Phu Doan, he claimed me for his wife after the war. He is arrogant and demeaning. On march to prisoner camps, he befriended a Legionnaire who I think is your corporal. As I grew cold to Private Pham, he wished to influence me by speaking of some great authority making him important and greatly respected. He had only to contact The Party for it to happen. I say nothing, but I think he is spy, here to report traitors. The Vietminh proclaim covert commissars to be everywhere, and—"

Patrick interrupted her. "And, for preferred treatment, Corporal Mundt would gladly be the stooge to report Legionnaire or other French Force actions meant to hinder the Vietminh."

"What we know is that these two have something to do with the Kilroy Bakery and maybe us." That she said in French, just to get it out less painfully.

Patrick disagreed. "They meant to kill us—and Gisèle. Maybe it is even more than that, but right now, we are targets."

"*Non!* They must think we are dead from the bakery."

"And if we remain here, we will be dead. Sooner, not later, we will be discovered. Our remains will not be found in the ashes of Kilroy Bakery. There must be others here, like those two, or soon will be. One of them may have seen us on the street just now. They may know!"

Thuy cut him off. "We will leave. We must leave now!"

"I agree," Patrick whispered. Then he spit it out, "But where? Where can we disappear to? Where can we be together and be safe? As a family we are obvious, you know."

Thuy was not deterred. In her typically confident tone, she gracefully responded, "We will go to Ireland. No, to Northern Ireland. That is what we will do."

Surprised but not tone-deaf, Patrick quickly responded, "I have money for tickets." Then he added, "I left there because I attacked two men, men who killed my father. They will come after me there."

"You speak of family, your mother. She longs for you, I know. What were you when you left—a boy? You are no longer a boy. You are now a man, a Legionnaire. There will be more battles in life. Do you wish to battle there against two injured men or in Vietnam against communism and armies?"

It all swirled around in his head. This had come out of nowhere, but she was right. He then realized only two things kept him from going home: old fears and himself. Not only was he a Legionnaire, but his better half was a bad-ass Vietminh veteran with notches on her belt. He had never asked about that, and she had never asked about a Legionnaire with a submachine gun silencing a trenchful of defeated Vietminh. That wasn't for now. Now was for acting sensibly and with dispatch.

They had no bags other than for the baby. They would make do. That sort of thing was in their nature—both their natures. Leaving the ceiling fan on, they locked the door, left the Do Not Disturb sign out, and headed downstairs. From there, it was down the hall to the kitchen and out a different service door. Keeping mainly to the alleys, they walked past many reasons to leave Vietnam. As they headed south toward the docks, a rugged-looking man approached. The out-of-place Irishman challenged with his eyes and reached into his pocket. The man backed off—only a beggar.

Appearing casual, Patrick and Thuy both maintained awareness of their surroundings. Tickets purchased, they could board. Their timing was good. The SS Andrea Doria would pull out of port early the next day for Liverpool, England, a busy port any time of year. Life wasn't perfect, future unknown, but they could make do and find home from there.

Together, with love and grit, they walked off the gangplank and into a new world—new for them. Thuy and Patrick knew their differences would be seen by all and assessed by most. They also knew the future was what they made of it, and so far, they had beaten the averages. They could hardly wait for the next better-than-average sunrise.

The End

Epilogue

As the Dien Bien Phu victors came forward at the end, vanquished airborne troops could be seen incinerating cherished berets to prevent them from being desecrated by the enemy. Others of the airborne wore them in defiance. In lockstep, however, no Legionnaires raised a hand in capitulation.

POW Corporal Claude Sibille: "I thought I was going to be shot. We hadn't eaten much for eight days, no cigarettes, and we were out of rations. As we were herded away, I heard a bird singing. That was my best day at Dien Bien Phu."

Being herded out of the rancid fortress, one POW recalled filing past hundreds of bodies covering the grounds of an abandoned strongpoint. In a pastoral valley beyond were seen thousands of clean and fresh Vietminh soldiers; wide-eyed youngsters just arrived, it seemed. They would have been part of the 25,000 reinforcements General Giap had called for and needed—had the French not been forced to capitulate.

Estimates of the Vietminh supporting cast for the Dien Bien Phu effort numbered to 300,000. The number of those killed: coolies, porters, and other support people, substantial but unknown. From the initial assault wave forward, about 8,000 Vietminh troops were killed. As the battle ended, the wounds of an estimated 15,000 Vietminh were being treated. The number of them surviving is unknown. Of the hundreds or more seriously injured French Force troops surviving to reach prison camps, the total *is* known: Zero.

Gaining full control of the north of Vietnam, Ho no longer needed the support of the wealthy and the bourgeois or middle-class peoples. Although a communist North Vietnam could not have emerged without the general support of those people, the full communist system was applied. The people had been promised opportunity, equality, and redistribution of land.

Cadre teams were sent out across North Vietnam to make right those promises. The program was effective but harsh. Illiterate thugs willing and capable of dispensing cruelty were used to make up the teams. Citizens were rated on a scale ranging from true patriot to enemy of the people. The rich and the relatively rich were rated as enemies of the people, which included landowning farmers, large and small. At the other end of the spectrum were the property-less laborers who were classified as true patriots.

Those who reported 'unpatriotic' neighbors or relatives were routinely declared true patriots. True patriots were awarded property of the accused. That perk alone produced an industry of treachery, whether for greed or revenge, and whether or not the wrong-doing was factual.

Another step forward in civic regression was a quota of enemies prescribed for each community. The Party dictated a minimum number of public enemies to be found in each hamlet, village, and town. Guilty and innocents alike were put out of their homes, beaten, tortured, and often executed. The consequence of land-owning farmers banished or killed was starvation. Dormant land and poor farming resulted in tens of thousands, as many as 100,000 persons starved to death.

The fall of North Vietnam to communism cast an amplified defensive pall on the Free World. President Eisenhower dictated a barely coherent message to Secretary of State Dulles. In part, "... the great idea of setting up an organism is so as to defeat the domino result. When each, standing alone, one falls, it has the effect on the next, and finally the whole row is down. You are trying, through a unifying influence, to build that row of dominoes so they can stand the fall of one, if necessary."

The Iliad, some three millennia ago, recorded Homer as saying, "After the event, even a fool is wise."

Acknowledgements

Beaucoup credit goes to former wife, Sherry Kluge, the first to support and promote my writing, especially that of a military bent. Daughter of a WW II G.I. stitched by a German machinegun, her patriotism and military support is second nature to her and truly appreciated by me. She is now well placed as social worker in a Wisconsin Veterans' Home.

Megan Basinger of Fine Fuse Editorial Services performed timely and detailed service in proofreading *Weeds of War*. Her quick-study of things military and her research of all things questionable was impressive. Megan introduced me to The Chicago Manual of Style, an opportunity for me to accept progress. I accepted much of it.

Having read every word of this novel—multiple times—a great debt is owed to my friend, Clare Mather, French Language and Literature professor, now retired from St. Olaf College. Dr. Mather's assistance and suggestions have been nothing less than paramount in the achievement of this project. Her critical eye has always been spot-on while her empathic support some-how warms and heartens the joy of creativity.

Thanks and blessings to Jill Loree who has authored and published many of her own works. She has been the mainstay to corral these pages between covers. Her experience and sharing has led as well as pushed me through the steps necessary to offer a robust product that hints at the complete story. This telling is for the historical fiction reader, the curious, and for the service member of all generations, but especially the Vietnam War veteran and fam-ily—those few who know the truth.

Profound thanks to my brothers-and-sisters-at-arms. You brought to me a world of immense scale with generous and brilliant diversity, a world of joys and endless tears I can't imagine living without. I think of you and '68 Tet daily. I would do it all again, if only for the opportunity to make honest the story of Vietnam. This is the first rendering.

About the Author

Growing up on a Wisconsin dairy farm in the 1950s was hard work, but it also fostered a close connection with country church, 4-H, and rambunctious cousins on backyard ball fields, along with the birthing of Holstein calves on cold winter nights. Needing, however, to learn more about himself and the world around him, Paul reached for whatever was beyond the farm and maybe more. *More* became a four-year Army enlistment after high school. *More* included nearly two years with an infantry brigade that deployed to Vietnam in late 1966. He left that war in June '68, although the Tet Offensive remains inside him.

Adjustment to civilian life was a challenge. Supporting his family was a challenge. Menial jobs were followed by warehouse management. By then divorce meant starting over. Eventually came merchandise buyer, and finally human resource work within a large and diverse workforce. There he was able to contribute to many needs of the generally underserved. Paul flourished in such work and continued in it until retirement.

Having already done some community theatre acting, by the turn of the century Paul was writing theatre. His full-length plays include *Local Rules Apply, Final Intrusion, Lam Moui Hai*, and *Can of Worms*, three of which have been produced locally.

On several occasions Paul has been invited to speak at Veterans Day and Memorial Day gatherings. His message has always addressed some aspect of veterans and the Vietnam War. In his retirement, Paul has continued to write on the war, to research history, and to speak to the story of Vietnam, all of which has become the eye-opener *Weeds of War*.

Paul currently resides in quintessential Northfield, Minnesota, the town that routed the Jesse James Gang in 1876, and later welcomed Mary Tyler Moore's friend Sue Ann Nivens, aka Betty White, at memorable St. Olaf College.

Made in the USA
Columbia, SC
18 February 2021

33177554R00133